NEITHER DESPISE NOR FEAR

—·—

V M KNOX

For
A.W.B.L.

PREFACE

Tallinn

Soviet Controlled Estonia

6th September 1965

Dieter Stecker switched off his desk lamp. He'd worked late and now he was alone in the Design Office. He looked out through the glass partition of his private office, his gaze settling on the door to the corridor. Beyond it, he knew the guard, Boris, would be waiting to escort him out of the building. Dieter stared at the long, blueprint filing cabinet in the centre of the outer office then licked his dry lips. The silent office seemed to surround and envelop him, creeping over his clammy skin and making his pulse rate rise. It was now or never. He got up, reached for his coat and hat on the stand behind his desk, and put them on. From the corner of his eye he saw Boris's broad face peering through the small glass panel in the door to the outer hall. Dieter swallowed hard. Grasping his briefcase, he closed his office door. He knew Boris would be waiting for him in the corridor. Flicking a glance at the door, he went straight to the middle drawer and withdrew the top blueprint. Folding it quickly, he dropped it into his briefcase, locked the filing cabinet, and turned to leave.

'Good evening, Boris.'

'You're working late tonight, Herr Stecker.'

Dieter smiled. Boris was the only man who referred to him by the German title. Dieter hadn't been in his native land since the end of the war. With the expansion of the Soviet Union and the descent of the Iron Curtain, he and thousands of others in the Eastern and Baltic States were cut off from the rest of Europe.

They walked together along the grey linoleum hall and down a flight of stairs. Boris opened the door to the outside. A cool wind blew in and Dieter buttoned his overcoat. 'Have a good night, Herr Stecker. See you tomorrow.'

Dieter lifted his hand in acknowledgment but didn't turn around. He strode towards his small car. In the Soviet Union, it was a privilege to have a car; a mark of respect for his twenty years of service with the Soviet run Electronic Equipment Factory.

Sitting behind the wheel of his new Moskvich 403 car, he closed the door and placed the key into the ignition. 'Just one night,' he muttered, his hands gripping the steering wheel. He drove in silence. Half an hour later he parked outside his unit block in the Russian quarter of Tallinn and took the stairs to his home on the second floor; a one bedroom apartment. As he climbed the stairs, the handle of his briefcase in his grasp felt like a death sentence.

Since the recent loss of his wife, his elderly neighbours had made it their business to keep an eye on him. They were quiet and polite people, but of late they had taken to cooking meals for him and insisted on bringing whatever they'd cooked into his kitchen. While he was grateful for the gesture, he knew they had a telephone and people with telephones were informants for the KGB. As he reached the second floor, he heard their front door click open. 'Good evening,' he said, lifting his hat. The woman nodded to him then closed her front door. Dieter fumbled for his entry key. Unlocking his door, he switched on the lights then closed the door to the stairwell. Leaning against the door, he held his breath and waited to see if his neighbour would knock. Two minutes passed, then three. Not tonight. Removing his hat, he walked into his sitting room and drew the curtains, then slumped into his chair. Too late now for doubts, he thought, his eye on the briefcase beside the hatstand in the hall.

He sat in the stillness for some time, trying to quell the rising nausea. 'Everything the same and it will be alright,' he whispered. With his mind on the enormity of what he'd done, he went into the kitchen, switched on his radio and prepared his dinner. 'Everything the same,' he repeated, slicing some cabbage, although he wasn't hungry. It hadn't been exactly how he'd foreseen it but with his neighbour's increasing inquisitiveness and the arrival of the new KGB officer, Major Vlatkov, to the factory, he knew the time had come. Vlatkov was younger than the previous security officer and with a new broom had come tougher measures.

While the sausage sizzled in the pan, he laid the blueprint out on his kitchen table, then went to the tea caddy and, lifting the lid, retrieved the miniature camera hidden beneath the loose black leaves. Frank Quinn had given it to him months previously, but until this night, Dieter hadn't used it. Ten minutes later, he'd taken four photographs of the blueprint for a new, portable microwave device that could jam all electronic equipment. Returning the camera to the tea caddy, he folded the blueprint and replaced it in his satchel. Half an hour later, he ate his dinner, the briefcase in his field of vision. 'Just one night. No one will know,' he told himself. But despite a scheduled visit to Finland in two days, it would be another month before his bi-monthly rendezvous in Finland with his British contact, Frank Quinn of British Intelligence. And until then, he needed a safe place to secrete the film.

At precisely eight o'clock, Dieter walked into his office. Yuri, his deputy manager, was already at his drawing board.

'Good morning, Yuri,' Dieter said. 'Could you go down to supplies and get me two extra rolls of adhesive tape? I see we are nearly out.'

'Of course, Gospodin Stecker.'

Dieter smiled, reached for the cabinet key, and bent to unlock the filing cabinet. Although he couldn't see Yuri, he sensed the young man was watching him. Straightening, he smiled at him then walked towards his private office. As soon as Yuri had left, Dieter replaced the blueprints.

The day was long and tedious. Dieter had felt the nervous tension of his actions all day. He'd also been careful to follow his daily routine. But nothing had been said and, it appeared, no one had noticed anything unusual. Despite this, he worried about Yuri. The young man was a fervent and devoted member of the communist party but even he hadn't shown any sign of suspicion. In fact, Yuri was always happy the day before Dieter's regular trips into Finland to inspect the electronic monitoring and surveillance equipment at the dams that lay on the border between Finland and the Soviet Union. Yuri would be in charge for the day. It was a routine they had followed for some time, and Dieter's loyalty to the USSR had never been in question. Even the KGB men who always accompanied him on the ferry from Tallinn to Helsinki chatted to him like a friend.

But since the death of his wife, Gisela, Dieter knew his regular trips to Finland would be questioned. Especially in view of his work. The Soviet authorities had permitted him to travel to the West while ever Gisela was alive. Now, with no family to remain in the East during his absences, they would consider him a defection risk, and, he surmised, his ease of travel out of the Soviet Union would soon be terminated. 'Good night, Yuri. Don't stay too late,' Dieter said. He had one last task before he left; he wanted the young man to see him lock the filing cabinet. That accomplished, he handed the key to Yuri.

'Thank you, Gospodin Stecker. I won't.'

Dieter left the office to join Boris in the corridor.

'Off to Helsinki tomorrow?' Boris asked.

'Yes. Always plenty to do,' Dieter answered. 'Good night, Boris.'

The day dawned cool but fine and the half hour passage across the Baltic to Helsinki was calm. The sun came and went behind clouds that knew nothing of borders. Dieter usually enjoyed the crossing, no matter the weather, but today, every time someone moved or sat closer to him, his muscles tensed. He was relieved when the ferry finally berthed. He walked down the gangway with his two guards. While he could enter Finland, his guards could not. They would remain at the terminal until his return in the evening. Dieter didn't know how they spent their day and he didn't care. Striding away, he walked into town, taking the paths that led through the park between Helsinki's two major thoroughfares. Crossing the Pohjoisesplandi, he entered the café attached to the Kämp Hotel and ordered a hot chocolate drink and a cloudberry cake; a treat not available to him in Soviet controlled Estonia.

It was a routine he'd been careful to follow on every visit in preparation for this day, in case unknown Soviet eyes were watching. He sat in a booth at the rear of the café, his gaze scanning the people present, his eye on the door to the street. He withdrew the envelope containing the film from his briefcase and addressed it. Careful not to overstay his time there, he finished the hot chocolate and placed the cake in his briefcase. He grasped his coat and hat, then took the rear connecting door into the hotel foyer to hand the envelope to the concierge for posting. Returning to the café, he left by the front door.

Twenty minutes later, he entered the railway station and bought a ticket for the ten o'clock train to the border town of Ivantra. He leaned his head back on the seat as the train pulled away from the platform. Closing his eyes, he thought back on the man to whom he'd sent the envelope; a man in Norway he hadn't seen in over twenty years and a man who owed Dieter his life.

CHAPTER ONE

London

7th September 1965

Alistair Quinn stood on the overpass bridge at Whittington Hill Railway Station, the early September sun pleasantly warm. He watched his friends as they trudged along the road towards the waiting school bus, their shoulders drooped under contemplation of the winter term ahead. Some struggled with trunks, while others, like himself, had their trunks sent on ahead to the school. His gaze lingered on their hunched posture. He thought it had more to do with the weight of family expectation than luggage; their futures as predictable and inflexible as concrete. He smiled. Maybe it was a smirk. 'Sheep! Bloody sheep!' he swore aloud to them. They hadn't heard him. He watched them, each one coalescing into a smudge of dark grey. Not one of them had said they'd run away with him. With their every step, they faded from his life. His eye settled on Delprado, his friend and co-conspirator in their clandestine enterprise, operated under the noses of the school authorities. His smirk returned as he thought about his friends from Whittington Hill School. The last conversation, held only ten minutes previously, repeated in his head.

'What!' they'd said, almost in unison. 'You can't, Quinn!'

'Actually, I can,' he'd replied, adjusting his new sunglasses and tossing back his thick, dark hair.

'You can't!' Delprado had said between gritted teeth, his voice a harsh whisper.

'Leave him, Delprado. He's always been a cocky little bastard!' The oldest boy among them had turned to face Alistair. 'I always thought you'd amount to nothing, Quinn. This just confirms it!' And with that, they'd turned and walked away. All but one.

Delprado had leaned into him, his voice husky with emotion. 'What about the business? What about Misty? What am I to tell her?'

Alistair held his friend's incredulous gaze. 'Why don't you come too?'

'Are you mad!'

Alistair had stared at his friend as though seeing him for the first time. In that moment, he understood the difference between them; that distinct and irreversible line between a schoolboy's foray into deception and a life-changing leap into the unknown. For Delprado, the excitement lay in the clandestine nature of their underground business, but his future was sacrosanct. Alistair beamed. He didn't care about his future; he wanted out and not just from school. 'You'll think of something, Delprado. You're good at that. And thanks. It's been fun.'

Delprado's expression had been one of total confusion. He'd left Alistair after that, his short, rotund body hurrying after the others. From where Alistair stood on the railway overpass, he could see the growing dark-grey mass of boys who were now boarding the waiting bus. He watched until the last boy boarded. Delprado had waved to him, but he didn't respond. 'Sheep,' he muttered again as the bus drew away. He picked up the suitcase and, without looking back, he crossed the overhead bridge and descended the stairs to the platform on the opposite side of the station. He waited only minutes for the London train, his mind on the future.

While his snap decision to run away had amazed even himself, where he intended to go wasn't any surprise. There was never any doubt about that. Soho. The thought of it made him grin. He wanted it; the excitement, the buzz of humanity and the storm of life that crammed into those few streets in the biggest city in the world. While he acknowledged there would be ramifications for his decision, he simply didn't care. Nothing his parents or teachers could say would dissuade him. His pulse raced; not with regret, but with the sheer audacity of it and the anticipation of adventure. With his decision not to return to school, there was no going back. Ignominy lay there and the dread of it spurred him on. He stepped into the train as the guard closed the door behind him. He felt excited; no, more than that. He felt exhilarated. He felt free for the first time in his life and he wanted to laugh.

Settling into the first compartment with an unoccupied seat, his mind went back to Delprado and their illicit business conducted in secret in an abandoned cellar situated directly beneath the senior boys' study. He considered it a foretaste of life for him, as if it had all been pre-ordained as a preparation for his future. But for the boys at school, all they had to look forward to was the quiet, predictable life of a public school education, then reading classics at Oxford, followed by either Sandhurst or a career in the Civil Service. A few brief years of illicit adolescent fun was all they would know of an adventurous life. In his mind's eye Alistair could see them years hence, telling stories of the underground room where stolen mat-tresses lined the walls and ceiling and where he and Delprado had sold for sixpence a cigarette, a tot of whisky and a kiss from the divine Misty, a girl from the local village who came with her mother on occasions to clean the boarding houses. He smiled, thinking about Misty. For an extra sixpence, a boy could touch Misty's breast; that exquisite forbidden land of feminine flesh. He liked Misty. A part of him would miss her. They understood each other. There was no guilt or hint of exploitation on her part; she had been a willing par-ticipant and had made good money from the adolescent desires of the nation's future leaders. The smile faded as he recalled Delprado and his final wave before boarding the bus. Perhaps Delprado had thought he'd change his mind and come back, cap in hand. And maybe that was why Delprado had been one of the last to board the school bus. Alistair thought Delprado's actions naïve; cowardly even. But while his co-conspirator wouldn't join him in running away, at least they'd had fun together outwitting the teachers and senior boys and had pocketed a tidy sum, enough for them to take a holiday to the Channel Isles last summer. If their underground business had ever been discovered, it would have been six of the best and instant expulsion for them both. No Civil Service honours list for them in their old age.

Despite the business never being discovered, it didn't stop the seemingly never-ending beatings for spurious misdemeanours; from teachers, the headmaster, even the older boys, but most frequently from his father. Alistair felt the sneer curl his upper lip. In his mind, he pictured the detached house in Richmond where his family existed. Family wasn't the correct word for them. He felt the heavy, cold pall descend whenever he thought about his home. It was a loveless place where no one talked to one another and where he was an outsider. Perhaps it was because they had sent him off to boarding school at the age of six that made him feel a stranger to his parents; Mr and Mrs Frank Quinn. Or perhaps it was because he'd never spent much time there. Even during the school holidays, he'd been packed off to various uncles' properties around the country. Unwanted and forgotten. He closed his eyes, remembering. He had little to do with his mother, whose daily routine was caring for his fragile sister, Angela. His mother's name was Grace, but he saw little evidence of it. It was said she was a strong woman. He didn't know her, and she'd never given him warmth or comfort. Not that he despised her. She seemed always occupied with his sister, who suffered from nightmares that made her scream in the night. Alistair thought about the people who'd conceived him. They so rarely talked to him. He had no memory of ever seeing his mother laugh. His father was another matter. The sneer returned as Alistair contemplated the man who claimed that title. There was a man who was a complete blank to Alistair. Ignored from a young age, he'd

11

attempted to win his father's approval by achieving good results at school, but when that didn't work, he just became rebellious. That always lead to beatings. His enduring memory of his father was seeing him asleep in the large, frayed chair in his study, a cigarette permanently attached to his lower lip. In fact, Alistair now realised, not only did his parents not speak to him, they rarely spoke to each other. They didn't even share a bedroom. His father was often away. Something to do with his work. Alistair didn't know where he went, and now he didn't care. All he knew was that his father held some low-ranking, back-room job with the Security Services, but it was never discussed. He visualised the man sitting in his chair, a wave of revulsion welling up. But it wasn't hate. Hatred required emotion he just didn't feel. The truth was, he felt nothing; not even contempt. Frank Quinn was a pathetic creature: nervous, introspective, yet, it was said, clever. Some said an academic. He spoke ten languages but had no interest in his son.

Alistair cast his eye around the train compartment, surveying every passenger as the northern suburbs of London slid past the windows. The people looked ordinary, tired, with little enthusiasm for life. Three women and two men. There was nothing exceptional about any of them. They'd stared briefly at him when he got onto the train, the public school uniform distinctive. He removed his hat, then ran his hand through his hair. He knew his life differed from these bored people who, to his mind, wanted so little from life. His life would be adventurous and he intended to make it so.

When the train pulled into Piccadilly, he went straight to the men's lavatory and changed his clothes. He stuffed his uniform into his suitcase and dressed in the least noticeable clothing he had with him; a pair of jeans and a cream jumper. His summer hat, which he'd worn on the first day of the winter term to annoy the schoolmasters, he tossed nonchalantly towards the rubbish bin in the corner; the hard brimmed boater flying majestically through the air and landing perfectly in the middle of the bin. Pushing his hand into his pocket, he checked the wad of cash his parents had given him for the term's expenses. Fifteen pounds; surely enough for him to find a room somewhere. Checking his hair in the washroom mirror, he slipped the comb into his pocket, grasped his bag, and left.

Bright sunshine greeted him as he climbed the steps up from the tube. He sniffed the exhaust-filled air as buses and cars sped past him. Waiting only a few seconds, he crossed Piccadilly Circus, heading north. He didn't need a map. He knew the name of every street. People, mostly young, stood in doorways or hurried along the narrow paths, several pushing past him, hurrying to get somewhere. The men wore tight-fitting, slim trousers with leather jackets and long, pointed shoes. Many were smoking and several carried a guitar case. Their hair was slicked back. The girls looked amazing, their skirts short and their hair teased high and into a French roll at the back. No one took any notice of him. No one cared about him. It felt wonderful!

Half an hour later, Alistair stood in Old Compton Street, a mass of humanity flowing through the labyrinthine streets around him. Narrow-fronted shops clung together, selling everything from flesh to shoe polish. He made his way through the crowds, his heart beating with excitement, and found the famous 2i's Coffee Shop he'd read about in magazines. It was where Rock'n Roll singers came to be discovered. Several big names had started their careers in the basement there. Stepping inside, he ordered a coffee from the bar then slouched in a vinyl covered armchair by a small chrome and glass side table. He felt free, liberated from all the expectations placed on him by the adults in his life. Every time someone came into the café, he stared, hopeful of seeing a famous pop star.

An hour later, he left the café, crossing the road into Frith Street and found a bar. While he was still only sixteen, he was tall, and he hoped with his slicked hair and dark sunglasses, he looked older. He stepped inside.

The bar had only just opened, and he seemed to be the first customer. The barman's eyes looked him up and down as Alistair sat on a stool. 'What are you havin', Gov?'

'Scotch and dry,' Alistair said, trying hard to disguise his public school accent. Reaching into his pocket, he put a ten shilling note on the counter. The barman placed the drink in front of him, picked up the note and flicked it, then moved towards the cash register. Alistair took a quick gulp before looking around the room. Behind him, some booths ran along the wall where a vast array of pictures and mirrors hung. Some photographs were of London's famous landmarks, but most were of celebrities laughing and enjoying themselves in the smoke-filled bar there. Turning around, he took another sip from his drink and checked his watch as the barman put the change on the counter in front of him. Alistair looked up and caught the barman's eye. 'Know where I can rent a room?'

'Could do,' the barman said, then turned to a new customer.

Alistair felt her presence before he saw her. The fragrance of her perfume seemed to envelop him. It wafted over him; a spellbinding and alluring miasma of sophistication. He half turned towards her, not wanting her to think he was staring. She was older than him, but astonishingly attractive. The barman placed a drink in front of her. It was a dark shade of pink. Alistair hadn't heard her order, so he guessed she was a regular. He watched her gracefully lift the drink to her lips; her fingers caressing the glass. She stared forward, her eyes steady. It was then he realised she was watching the room in the mirror on the wall behind the bar.

'What's your name?' she asked without looking at him.

'Alistair,' he said. He saw no reason to lie.

'You a runaway?' she asked.

'No!'

'You're a bloody liar!' She turned to face him, her all-knowing gaze flowing over him. She paused just long enough for him to feel uncomfortable, and he felt his face flush.

She grinned. 'Drink up, Alistair. I know a better bar than this one. And one where the barman won't call the police and have you sent home to mummy before dark.' She stood up, her blue eyes fixed on him. 'Too pretty to leave here anyway.'

He reached for his suitcase and followed her. He didn't really know why. She was mesmerising, hypnotic even as she glided towards the door. He hadn't planned to go with a woman, but he wasn't saying no if it were offered. He thought of Misty and her beautiful, pearly skin. 'What's your name, then?'

She turned to face him. 'Valerie. And a gentleman always walks on the outside of a lady.'

'Sorry. Of course, I knew that. Valerie what?'

'Just Valerie.'

'Where are we going?'

'Not far.'

Valerie led him further along Frith Street before turning briefly into Bateman Street, then into Greek Street. About halfway along, she paused beside a four-storey building with a black door and a brass plaque on the wall. It read *The Club*. A doorman stood to one side, holding the door wide as she approached. 'Good afternoon, Miss Valerie.'

'Thanks, Fred. This is Alistair. He'll be staying a while.'

Fred nodded, but didn't speak to him. Alistair stepped inside, the door closing behind him.

Inside was a short corridor and just beyond it, a staircase on the left side rose to the upper floor. To the right was a wide arched doorway leading into a lounge. It had two long windows overlooking the street and heavy, elegant curtains with festooning folds held back by thick tassels. The room was painted brick-red with a navy blue ceiling. A bar was to one side. There were six girls seated in the room, all wearing stunningly glamorous clothes, like the models he'd seen in expensive magazines. They sat with their legs crossed and wore high stiletto heels. They were magnificently coiffured and not a hair was out-of-place. As he and Valerie entered the room, they all looked up, but none of them spoke to him.

'Pour yourself a drink, Alistair,' Valerie said.

Alistair put his suitcase down and went behind the bar. Finding the whisky, he poured a large glass, then sat on the stool.

'Can I pour one for you too, Valerie?'

'No, darling. You can stay here for a few days; until the police give up looking for you. After your drink, go downstairs and make yourself comfortable. If you decide to stay with me, there'll be a few rules. You'll remain indoors for at least four days. That should be long enough for the police to lose interest in you. After that, you can only go out if I say so. You can live here rent free and do some odd jobs when I ask. And under no circumstances do you sleep with the girls. And,' she paused, leaning towards him, 'do not get drunk! Do not get drunk,' she repeated, emphasising each word.

'Of course, Valerie.' He didn't understand why he shouldn't, but he wasn't going to ask. His heart was thumping in his chest. He'd never before been called darling by any woman and he felt ten feet tall. He knew he was in a brothel; a high-class brothel but a brothel none-the-less. He visualised Delprado and the others doing their algebra homework. A sly grin spread across his face.

'And Alistair, whatever you see or hear, you don't get involved. Understand?'

Alistair nodded.

'Do you smoke?'

'Yes,' he said.

Valerie smiled, then tossed a packet of Sobranie's towards him. 'Light one for me, would you, darling?'

Alistair fumbled with the packet and lit the cigarette, then passed it to her. His heart was racing. Deftly, she fitted it to a cigarette holder and inhaled. As she blew the smoke into the air, she inclined her head towards the staircase. Alistair picked up his suitcase and, taking the narrow stairs, descended to the lower floor. The first room was a bathroom, the next a bedroom.

It was nice; even homely. Painted light pink with Victorian furniture. A large double bed with numerous pillows dominated the room. Beside it was a bedside table with a telephone and on the opposite wall was a long chaise.

It was early evening now and for the first time, he thought of his mother. He wondered if he should call. Delprado and the others would surely have informed the school and they would have contacted her. His father, if he was even there, Alistair felt sure, wouldn't care. He considered it amazing providence that he'd met Valerie. Had he not, he believed he would surely have been picked up by the police by now. He beamed at his good fortune. His former dreary life was in the past.

CHAPTER TWO

Soho

London

15th September 1965

Alistair leaned back on the chaise and blew smoke into the air. He stared at Valerie; at the curve of her thighs and back, the way her hair fell over her shoulders. His mind lingered over the memory of the warmth of their passion. They'd made love all morning.

'I want you to do something for me,' Valerie said, reaching for her negligée.

'Of course. Anything.'

She got up, her naked body to him like a Michelangelo sculpture, and pulled her negligée around her. Opening a drawer in the bedside table, she took out a long envelope. 'Take this to the newsagent on the corner, would you, darling?'

'What's in it?'

'Never you mind. A man wearing a blue raincoat will ask you if you're a friend of mine. Give it to him. Then straight back here. Ok?'

He nodded.

She propped the envelope against a lamp on the bedside table, then left him. He felt as though he'd been dismissed, but he would do as she asked. Heading for the bathroom, he showered and dressed, then, returning to Valerie's bedroom, reached for the envelope and felt the slight bulge inside. He guessed it was money, but he didn't really know. Shoving it into his coat pocket, he closed the door behind him and went upstairs.

Fred opened the door and Alistair stepped outside. It was the first time he'd been out in just over a week. He stood on the step, watching the busy street for a minute, then lit a cigarette. People were everywhere, jostling and hurrying or just standing on the narrow footpaths talking to one another. He'd missed the Soho chaos, but he couldn't deny he'd enjoyed his days in Valerie's bedroom.

Alistair sauntered down the steps and wandered along Greek Street, heading for the newsagent on the corner. The early autumnal sky was a cloudless blue, the sun shone and even the London air seemed like heavenly nectar to him. He adjusted his sunglasses as he reminisced about the past week. He'd been picked up by a goddess and in eight glorious days had been transformed from a gawky teenager into a man-about-town. He felt mature and worldly, almost invincible. He thought of Delprado and his former school friends. 'Boneheads!' he muttered to himself as he swaggered along Greek Street, flicking back his hair to emulate James Dean.

He didn't even see them coming.

Two men were beside him. He couldn't see their faces. Their arms were under his, their bodies hard against him, propelling him forward and onto the street. One ripped the envelope from his hand, then a black car pulled up beside them.

'Keep ya' mouth shut and get in!' one snarled into his ear.

In the space of a few seconds, he was pushed into the rear of the car; the men sitting on either side of him. A hood was over his head in an instant. The car sped away.

'What do you want? Who are you? Where are you taking me?' Alistair shouted.

'I said, keep ya' mouth shut!'

There was no noise except the sound of the car's engine. His mind spun. Then the realisation. Of course! he told himself, his tongue running around his dry lips. He allowed his head to drop forward. He should have known. His father, or Uncle Laurence, his father's great friend, who also worked in the Security Service at MI5, had orchestrated this. When the police had failed to locate him, his father and uncle would have intervened and had him traced. That was what MI5 did. He sat quietly, feeling powerless and overwhelmed. His life in Soho, along with all his dreams, had vanished in a split second and freedom would be denied. His future, like that of all the others at Whittington Hill, was ordained. He pursed his lips at the thought and felt the rising anger. Then within the space of a few minutes followed frustration, resignation, sadness and defeat. He clenched his jaw, feeling the ignominy of it all. But while his heart brooded, he planned what he would say to them when finally the hood was removed and he could stare at his father and uncle; see their faces and tell them he wouldn't go back. He'd tell them they couldn't order him around like the sheep that worked for MI5.

The car came to an abrupt halt.

The journey was short. He surmised he was still in Soho. Although, if it were his father or uncle behind his capture, it was more likely to be Mayfair.

'Out!'

Alistair wriggled his way from the centre of the rear seat to the car door and swung his feet out onto the pavement. He felt both men beside him again. They whisked the hood from his head. He looked around. He was on a street he didn't recognise and in front of a building that looked as though it had been hastily constructed in the years after the war. He looked up. There were six floors and all the windows facing the street had a mesh covering. Both men escorted him to the front door; a large, mirrored, glass-panel that slid open on their approach. One man pushed him inside.

In front of him was a security guard dressed in a grey uniform. The place felt cold with little light. He looked back over his shoulder at the street. The sliding front door had closed, but he could see the cars passing and knew it was one-way glass.

Climbing the stairs to the first floor, they propelled him along a corridor, through some doors, then down several flights of stairs to a basement. Behind him, a door slammed shut. In front of him was a long, unlit corridor with numerous closed doors on either side. His captors pushed him along the hall to a door on the right. He stepped inside. It was small with grey, concrete walls and it smelt stale and damp. The door closed behind him. In front of him was a table and three chairs. He saw they were all bolted to the floor, and he felt the adrenaline surge. His gaze darted around the room. But there was no escape. Everything was grey and hard and easy to hose out. He stared at his captors. He had never seen either before. Both were, he guessed, in their forties, clean shaven and even featured. Nothing remarkable about either of them.

'Sit!' one said.

Alistair stared at the table. On it was an unappealing cheese sandwich on a thick, porcelain plate that looked as though someone had stolen it from British Rail. He frowned. Given the menacing room, the sandwich was a confusing addition. The corners of the bread had turned up in the stale air. Beside it was a cup of tea. Alistair walked towards the table and stared into the matching British Rail cup. From the milk film on the surface, the tea had been poured some time ago. One man switched on a light, the searing beam making him squint.

'Sit, I said!

Alistair sat at the table facing the window, as instructed. Both men then sat, one beside him, the other facing him.

'Eat!'

Alistair leaned forward and prodded the bread. It was dry and hard. He wondered if the gesture was an attempt at civility or if the tea had been laced. Either way, he wasn't touching it. He sat back in the chair, watching them. No one spoke.

Five minutes later, the door opened. He turned around and saw another man enter the room. He was older than either of his guards; men he'd nick-named Bill and Ben, like the children's television programme. This man looked middle-aged, was well-dressed in a three-piece suit, with short, light brown hair. There was a commanding air about him. Bill and Ben stood.

'Any trouble?' Three Piece Suit asked.

'None.'

Three Piece Suit stared at Alistair. 'Well, young Quinn. You've had quite an adventure. From now on, you'll be doing as I say. Got it!'

'Who are you?'

The man laughed. 'Don't be naïve. You can be of use to us. You'd like to serve your country, wouldn't you?' Alistair was about to ask which country that was, but Three Piece evidently considered the question rhetorical. 'You'll continue to live in Soho at that club. Anything you hear or see there, you'll inform us about. Understood?'

He thought of Valerie and what she'd said about not getting involved. 'Why should I?'

The man leaned forward, his clenched fists on the table supporting his weight. 'You can always go back to school!'

'You want me to be an informant?'

'I was told you were smart!' Three Piece wandered over to the covered window and leaned against it. In the stark light, Alistair couldn't see him. He guessed it was intentional.

'We want you to keep your eyes open, Quinn. And your ears. We want you to tell us who comes and who goes from that club in Greek Street. And anything else you hear or see.'

Alistair would've liked to ask why MI5 was so interested in The Club, but he thought better of it. 'How do I contact you?'

Three Piece reached into his pocket and threw a slip of paper onto the table. 'Memorize it. Only call it when you have something. No tittle-tattle. You'll be told to call another number. That line will be secure. Got it!'

Alistair glanced at the note and read the number to himself a few times. 'There are a lot of people in the club sometimes and only two telephones. What if I can't use either without being overheard?'

'You know that newsagency; the one on the corner? Get the newsagent to put a card in the advertisement window. It should read *Set of fine bone china for sale.* Got it!'

'Set of fine bone china for sale,' Alistair repeated.

'Check that window the following day. There'll be a card in it for a flat to rent in Frith Street. It'll have the street number and time displayed. Just make sure you keep the rendezvous. No excuses. Got it?'

'Got it!'

'That's enough cheek from you. Just do as we say and everything'll be fine.'

'I probably should contact my mother.'

'No need. We'll do that.'

'I'll write down her name and address.'

The man smirked. 'We know everything there is to know about you, Quinn. Everything! Including that little business of yours at school.'

'What?'

'Your friend, Delprado, by the way, was expelled. And we'll look after your mother.' The man looked up at the two men who stood waiting. 'Take him back.'

Alistair sat in the car, the hood over his head, but his mind was on Delprado. Stupid arse! he thought. He knew his short friend would have been severely punished by the sadistic headmaster, Dr Petit. Small by name and petty by nature. The car stopped, and the door opened. Bill pulled the hood from his head and told him to get out. Alistair found himself back on Old Compton Street, the parcel of money back in his hand. The car sped away.

He wasn't really sure what he felt. Amazed. Dumbfounded, more like. Certainly confused. A week ago, he'd run away from school and now he was informing for MI5. At least, he thought they had to be MI5. As he stood on the narrow footpath, people rushed past. He needed time to think. Turning, he wandered towards the 2i's coffee shop. Ordering a coffee, he sat in the seat near the window and stared at the people outside, this time with a keener eye. He was sixteen years old, had been with a goddess for eight days, and was now working for MI5. He leaned back in the chair, a slow broad smile settling on his face. Did life get any better than that? He sipped his coffee. For the first time in his life, he felt part of something, like he belonged.

Now, everything had changed. He didn't stare at the passing world anymore; he watched it. They weren't just people in the crowd. He wondered if MI5 was still watching him. He lifted his gaze to the buildings opposite and scanned doorways for people lingering. But he didn't see anyone. That he hadn't seen his father or uncle no longer worried him. His father was probably away, and Uncle Laurence was far too high at MI5 to bother with him.

Alistair drank his coffee, then grasping the package, threw a three-pence onto the table and left. He'd been gone too long and Valerie would ask questions. Crossing the road, he hurried towards Greek Street and the newsagency. A man wearing a blue raincoat approached him. 'You're a friend of Valerie, I believe?'

Alistair nodded.

'Inside,' the man whispered.

Alistair followed him into the shop, and they stood beside a stack of newspapers like two strangers. He waited for the man to take the envelope from him, but the man turned his back, pretending to read the newspaper he'd picked up. Alistair placed the envelope on a stack of magazines in front of him. A second later, the man reached down, folded the top magazine around the packet and walked away. Alistair saw him pay the newsagent behind the counter for the periodical. Two seconds later, he left. He hadn't looked back.

Alistair checked his watch. He had been away for almost three hours and knew he'd need an excuse. Running along Greek Street, he planned to tell her that the man in the blue raincoat had been late. When he entered The Club, Valerie was sitting at the bar.

'Looks like you could use a stiff drink, darling!'

CHAPTER THREE

Soho

5th October 1965

A mist of exotic cigar smoke and noisy chatter filled the front room at The Club. Alistair kept himself busy behind the bar, watching who came and went. In the month he'd been there, he thought he'd recognised a lord and possibly a member or two of parliament who'd been in the newspapers lately, but he wasn't sure. Valerie was mingling with the guests, handling out expensive Havana cigars from a silver box as several of the girls went upstairs with their clients.

Alistair watched Valerie. She was mesmeric. He knew he was in love with her. Perhaps it was infatuation, but regardless, he was utterly devoted to her and, if he were honest with himself, he envied her. She knew how to charm: her laugh, her smile, her manner; she understood people and what they wanted. And, from what he'd witnessed, they wanted to please her. Gertie had told him that Valerie had been born and raised in a brothel. Dealing with people, especially men, was all second nature to her.

She caught him watching her and she winked as Fred quietly approached, grasping her elbow.

'Sorry, Miss Valerie,' Fred said, then whispered something in her ear. Valerie glanced towards the front hall. Alistair followed her gaze.

Two men wearing tailored suits had come in. They stood like statues in the hall, staring into the front room, their eyes roving around those present. They had slicked back dark hair and were not unattractive. Alistair realised he was staring at twins. He found them hypnotic; lean and taut and built like athletes. But there was a presence about them; both arresting and decidedly sinister. One looked directly at him, the dark eyes piercing into him.

Valerie stepped forward. As she passed him, she whispered, 'Go downstairs and stay there. Don't come up again before I come for you.'

He heard the edge in her voice. She walked slowly towards the twins and engaged them in conversation. He also noted the deep frown on Fred's face. Alistair grabbed a crate of empty champagne bottles and hurried out of the room. He wanted to get downstairs as fast as he could. There was something about these men and that gloating sneer that actually frightened him. He'd held the gaze of one twin for just a moment, but the intensity of that glare was one he would never forget. It had made his skin creep and his heart thumped in his chest. He knew what it was; fear. Not even Bill and Ben had had such an effect on him. Leaving the main floor, he hurried downstairs and closed the door to Valerie's bedroom, his hand fumbling with the lock. Sitting on the chaise, he lit a cigarette and drew in a long breath. He had never felt fear like it, and he could taste the sweat on his upper lip. Ten minutes later, he heard her voice at the door.

'Let me in, darling.'

'You ok?' he asked her, opening the door a crack.

'Of course. He's not interested in me! He's a homosexual, darling,' she said. 'And a violent one at that. Not a nice man. Neither of them are.'

'Who are they?'

Her eyebrows rose almost involuntarily. 'Reggie and Ronnie Kray. You've never heard of them?'

His eyes widened. Of course, he'd heard of the Kray twins; the murderous heads of organised crime who called the East End of London their own.

'Why are they here?'

'Rumour is they want richer turf. They're just flexing their muscles at present, darling, but you stay away from them, especially Ronnie. Make yourself scarce when they come in.'

'I will. Have they gone?'

'Soon. They won't be long. Reggie's upstairs at present,' she said.

Above them, they heard shouting, two or three men's voices, then Fred's attempts to stem the rising tirade. Valerie's lips tightened in disapproval. She went back upstairs. Alistair followed, but hung back waiting on the stairs. Above him, he could see a reflection of one of the Kray twins in the front hall mirror. Another man had joined him, as well as Fred.

'I tried to stop him, Miss Valerie,' Fred was saying.

Alistair edged a step higher. He could see them now, through the balustrades. A man stood in front of Ronnie Kray, his shoulders squared, both like boxers in a ring.

'You ever come here again, you're dead!' Ronnie said, his face only inches from the man's head.

The man looked behind him, as though seeking support. Alistair thought he seemed to be on his own. Then another voice joined in. Within seconds, Alistair saw a reflection of the second Kray join his twin. Reggie and Ronnie's fists were already clenched. The unknown man backed away and made towards the front door. 'Don't think you own the Blind Beggar! It'll be ours within the week.'

One of the Kray brothers rushed forward, his massive fist ready for the fight. 'Get out! And tell Richardson if I ever see him or any of his thugs on our turf again, they're dead! Dead!'

'Boys! Boys! You're being too loud for our clients,' Valerie said, her soft conciliatory tone diffusing the tension. 'You'll get me a bad name. Come and have a cigar, Havana's best.'

Alistair heard the front door close. He retreated downstairs and locked the bedroom door again. Sitting on the chaise, he lit another cigarette, trying to remember all he'd heard. Who was the blind beggar? He glanced at the telephone on the bedside table wondering if he should contact Three Piece Suit. Was the information important enough? No tittle-tattle Three Piece had said. He decided to wait a few days. Then he'd place the card in the newsagency window.

CHAPTER FOUR

Helsinki

Finland

6th October 1965

Frank Quinn crossed the street, then climbed the steps to the massive Lutheran Cathedral in the centre of Helsinki. Entering the vast, quiet and light-filled space, he sat in a pew on the western side. Two minutes later, a man dressed in a dark suit and carrying a heavy overcoat sat in the pew in front of him and about ten feet to Frank's left. The man knelt down, as though praying.

Frank's bi-monthly visits to Helsinki were always timed to coincide with Dieter Stecker's routine inspections of the Finnish-Soviet border dams on the first Wednesday of every month. That Frank met with Stecker in Helsinki was ignored by the Finns primarily because the Finns trod a fine line between assisting the West while being seen to honour an arrangement with the Soviets that required them to denounce Soviet spies. Frank and Stecker would both enter the massive Lutheran Cathedral but did not make contact there. If Stecker had nothing for Frank, he waited there twenty minutes, then left the Cathedral by the eastern door. If he did, he left by the southern door. Thirty minutes later, Frank and Stecker would make contact in the busy ferry terminal where numerous Baltic ferry services came and went.

Although they rarely spoke, for Frank Quinn, there was history with Dieter Stecker. Frank had recruited him in Berlin in late '45 while assisting with the processing of surrendering German troops. He'd seen Dieter standing in a line of defeated soldiers and recognised him immediately. He'd been in the German Wehrmacht and stationed in Norway. It was there in '42 that Stecker had saved Frank's life and the lives of his Special Operations Executive team when a Gestapo officer had found them transmitting from a fishing hut. Frank had never fully understood why Stecker had risked his life to assist them, but he'd never forgotten the gesture. He'd taken Stecker out of the line and processed him personally, recruiting him to British Intelligence. Finding Dieter a place to live in the war destroyed city, they met frequently. During those early meetings in Berlin, Frank had learned that Dieter had an ability with all things electrical, even to constructing his own radio transmitter from scavenged metal and wood he collected from shattered building sites around the city. Frank had supplied the valves and code books. Then, when the Soviets overran eastern Germany, Stecker found himself in Soviet territory and not long after, transferred to Tallinn where he was employed in the Soviet-run, Electronic Equipment Factory. For Frank, Dieter Stecker had become a highly valuable asset.

Frank saw Stecker stand, then exit by the southern door. It was just after three. Gathering his hat and overcoat from the pew beside him, Frank slowly made his way out of the southern door and stood at the top of the enormous flight of steps to the Cathedral. Waiting there, he placed his hat on his head, then lit a cigarette. He could see Stecker crossing the vast Senate Square below him. It was a cloudless afternoon, but already an icy wind was making the air feel frosty and the night would be bitter. It promised a bleak winter ahead. A light dusting of snow had fallen and the wet streets had patches of slush and ice lying in drains and gutters. Frank drew his coat around him, then tucked his scarf tighter around his neck and slowly descended the steps, his eye on the man ahead. Dieter Stecker's dark-coloured, Soviet-supplied overcoat, fur hat and scarf stood out against the pastel painted buildings that surrounded the square.

Dieter took the road to the ferry terminals on the opposite side of the wide intersection. Frank hung back, waiting for Stecker to go inside the building. A few minutes later, Frank opened the door to the terminal. Inside was warm. In front of him was a waiting area with glass partitions in the shape of a hexagon. To his left were the lavatories. Ahead was the entrance to the platforms and, to his right, a cafeteria. Frank stood in front of the departure board as though studying the timetables. In that time, he'd counted the number of people present and checked all the exits. An older woman sat on benches near the door to the platforms. She'd looked up at Frank when he entered the terminal with the haunted, wide-eyed expression of the oppressed. Outside, a ferry was berthed but, as yet, it wasn't boarding. He knew it was the return ferry to Tallinn that Dieter would take. Frank checked his watch. The ferry was due to leave in twenty minutes. Adjacent to the door were two Finnish border guards who sat at a table, ready to check passports. Beyond the glass door to the platform sat two more men; thick-set with heavy clothing. Frank knew they were KGB men there to make sure Stecker returned to Tallinn. Frank walked towards the cafeteria.

Collecting a tray, he bought coffee, a pastry and a newspaper, then went to sit at a table at the back near the window from where he could watch the terminal complex. A minute later, he saw Dieter exit the men's toilets and enter the cafeteria. From Frank's observation, neither he nor Dieter had been followed. One of the KGB men waiting outside stood, his gaze on Stecker.

Dieter stood in line and purchased some food. Carrying the tray towards the table next to Frank, he put the tray on the table and bending, fussed with his overcoat and scarf, wrapping it around the chair and dropping his newspaper. 'I cannot say much. I'm being watched. There's a letter and note in the envelope as well as a film. Leave Finland as soon as possible, Frank,' Dieter muttered in German.

'Be careful, Dieter. Lie low for a while and thank you,' Frank responded in German without lifting his gaze. He continued to spread some butter on the pastry he'd purchased, but a tight knot was developing in his stomach.

Dieter opened his briefcase and pulled out a magazine. Placing it on the table beside the tray, he shifted in his seat, as though adjusting his position and drawing the chair closer to the table. He placed an envelope under him on the seat of his chair. Dieter drank his coffee and ate the food. But Frank could almost smell the man's fear and it worried him. Five minutes later, the bell for boarding the Tallinn ferry sounded. Stecker stood up, drained his coffee, then took his tray back to the counter and left the cafeteria. Dieter hadn't made eye-contact with him once.

Frank ate the pastry, then stirred some sugar into his coffee. He could see the envelope on the chair. Allowing his teaspoon to fall to the floor, he bent to retrieve it, grasping the envelope on the chair as he did so and slipping it into his pocket. Outside, the two KGB men were talking with Dieter. Frank glanced around the room: two teenagers kissing and totally engrossed in each other; a woman with two young children and an elderly man who appeared to be asleep, plus the woman who still sat outside the cafeteria. In Frank's opinion, whatever the cause of Dieter's agitation, it wasn't emanating from Finns sitting in cafeterias. He looked through the glass partition to the KGB men, who were now on either side of Dieter Stecker, going through the contents of his pockets and looking in his briefcase. Frank lowered his head, a feeling of doom engulfing him. He ate the pastry. For one second, he wondered if he should have told Stecker to stay in Finland and claim asylum. There was nothing he could do now for Dieter. Stecker had risked his life many times just by meeting with him, but Frank thought there was something different this time. Dieter would know it was only a matter of time. Perhaps that time had come.

Frank kept a watch on what was happening outside in his peripheral vision. The Finnish officials were talking to the young mother, checking her papers and stamping documents. Dieter made his way up the gangway, a KGB man on either side of him.

A minute later, Frank heard the sounds of another ferry pulling into the wharf.

He rose, put on his overcoat, folded the newspaper and left the cafeteria, melding into the crowd of disembarking passengers leaving the terminal. Walking away, he quickened his stride, the temperature now below freezing. What had happened in the ferry terminal disturbed him. Fifteen minutes later, he stood beside the Havis Amanda statue, and checked that no one had followed him. It was nearly five and a bitter night was descending. He walked north, taking side streets and crossing many times through the deserted park that runs down the middle of the main thoroughfare in Helsinki until he was certain he wasn't being followed. Fifteen minutes later, he crossed the road, returning to his room at the Hotel Kämp on Pohjoisesplanadi.

Inside his fourth-floor room, Frank drew the curtains, switched on the light, and opened the envelope. With the film, there was a hand-written letter, and a hastily scribbled note. Lifting the film to the light, he could see it contained four negatives of a blueprint. Pocketing it, he opened the letter.

It was carefully written and on thin Soviet stationery Dieter had evidently brought with him for the purpose and dated this day, October 6th. Frank read how Dieter had taken the photos of a Soviet microwave device four weeks previously, as the Electronic Equipment factory where he worked had tightened security and a new KGB officer named Major Vasali Vlatkov had recently taken over. Dieter had then taken the film with him to Helsinki and posted it from Finland to Per Sangolt in Norway with instructions to bring the film to the Ivantra Hotel on the 6th of October. He lowered the letter and thought back. Per Sangolt was a man he hadn't seen in over twenty years. He'd been part of Frank's Special Operations Executive team and another man who owed his life to Dieter Stecker.

Frank laid the two-page letter on the bedside table and reached for his camera. He glanced at the note. It had the Ivantra Hotel crest at the top. Frank skimmed through it, a deep frown forming. The note said that Dieter had seen Finnish soldiers carrying out some sort of exercise near the river while he was in the observation tower on the Ivantrankovski Dam. He'd also learned from the Soviet border guards when he'd gone to the Russian border town of Svetlovorsk to report in with them, that they had crossed onto Finnish soil to investigate the area and found a sizeable underground bunker. Frank stared at the note. He felt sick. Dieter had taken an enormous risk in even carrying the note. Other than the very obvious and illegal trespass of Soviet guards on Finnish soil, the Soviet discovery of the Finnish military group on the border and the bunker could have huge ramifications in the West. At least Dieter hadn't mentioned the Soviet guards saying anything about any weapons found there. Frank turned the note over in his hand. Its discovery, by either side, would have seen Dieter arrested. Frank crushed the note into his top pocket. While it had been dangerous enough for Dieter to photograph the blueprint and get it into Finland along with a handwritten letter, the note was another matter entirely. Hastily written and a last-minute inclusion, Frank worried about the man's future. Just because he'd got away with it didn't mean the KGB wasn't suspicious of him. If a good man had taken a substantial risk in getting the information to him, Frank needed to get back to London without delay. He photographed the letter, then took it to the bathroom. Turning on the shower, which set off the exhaust fan, he held the letter over the basin, lit a match and allowed the thin paper to burn. Blackened fragments of paper fell onto the porcelain and he washed the ash down the drain. Making sure none remained, he turned off the water, then the shower. The fan gradually slowed, then stopped. Returning to the bedroom, he put the tiny camera in the lining of his hat. Changing his clothes, Frank packed his suitcase. Attaching a false beard, he donned a pair of tortoise-shell framed glasses, left enough money to pay for his room on the bedside table, closed the door behind him and took the stairs to the foyer.

The hotel lobby was busy with evening guests. Skirting the excited groups assembling there, he left the hotel and crossed Pohjoisesplanadi. Halfway through the park, he checked the area, his senses on high alert. Securing his hat firmly on his head, he crossed the park, picking up his pace once clear of the open spaces. Striding across Eteläesplanade, he headed south, weaving his way along the streets and into parks, stopping near people waiting for buses to check on anyone tailing him. Fifty minutes later, he walked into the British Embassy. That night, Frank Quinn sat in the jump seat of a BOAC jet heading for Heathrow.

* * *

Major Vasali Vlatkov stood in the Design Office of the Electronic Equipment Factory in Tallinn. 'What are these plans for?'

'A microwave device, Comrade Major.'

'Explain!'

'It is an electronic device, one that uses high-powered microwave technology, Comrade Major. Directed at a specific target, the device can be plugged into any easily accessible power supply, then focused on a target. Its function is to disable electronic equipment and can be operated from a mobile source, making it entirely portable. The technology uses directed energy microwaves that convert energy from the power source into radiated electromagnetic energy. While the beam damages equipment, it is noiseless, uses readily available power, small to transport and completely harmless to humans, making the device entirely secret and undetectable. Such a device would ensure even encrypted secrecy was unworkable and make communication between our enemies or even within the one organisation impossible. And we could do this anywhere in the world, Comrade Major.'

'You are?'

'Yuri Maskovski, Comrade Major.'

'Your role here?' Vlatkov asked.

'Deputy Manager, Comrade Major.'

'Why do you think someone has tampered with these plans?' Vlatkov asked.

'The fold lines, Comrade Major,' Yuri answered. 'They have been hastily folded. The actions of a guilty person.'

'And you suspect Comrade Stecker?'

'I do, Comrade Major.'

'What evidence do you have?'

'Only he and I worked on the microwave project. Even so, he didn't include me in every design alteration. But only he has the key to the filing cabinets. He worked late one night about a month ago, then the next day ordered me to requisition more adhesive tape when we had plenty. I believe it was for me to leave the room so he could replace the blueprints, Comrade Major.'

'Where is Comrade Stecker?'

'In Finland inspecting the Ivantrankovski Dam electronic equipment, Comrade Major.'

Vlatkov's eyes flared. 'Why have you left it till now to inform me?'

'Comrade Major, only Gospodin Stecker has the key. I only ever have it when he is away.'

Vlatkov paused, but all eyes were on him. 'How well did you know Gospodin Stecker?'

The young man shook his head. 'Hardly at all. He kept to himself. He's German.'

Vlatkov looked around the room at the anxious faces. 'How long has he been working here?'

'Almost twenty years, Major Vlatkov.' Boris answered.

Vlatkov's needle-like gaze darted to the guard.

'I'm sure there's some mistake, Major. Herr, I mean, Gospodin Stecker is a loyal member of the party. He is today in Finland but will be back at work tomorrow. He goes every month to the dams and always returns. He has guards to go with him. He cannot have done this. He wouldn't.'

Vlatkov stared at the guard. 'Don't be naïve. Perhaps you took them?'

41

'Me? Not me, Comrade Major. I'm a very loyal member of the party, Comrade Major.'

Vlatkov's fixed stare remained on the man until his eyes were a narrow squint. Sweat was building up under Boris's moustache and his hands were shaking. The room was silent. Vlatkov relaxed his stare. He turned to Yuri. 'Would this man know how to read these blueprints?'

'Boris, Comrade Major?' Yuri responded. 'Impossible. Only someone with superior knowledge would understand it. This imbecile wouldn't know what he was looking at.'

'I'm sure you're right, Comrade.' Vlatkov continued to stare at Boris. 'But if this German doesn't return tomorrow, you will be replaced. A guard who allows employees to take secret information out of the building is stupid, corrupt or a traitor. So which one is it?'

Boris stood, his hands trembling. 'I don't know, Major Vlatkov. I'm sure he will come back.'

'You'd better hope he does!'

Vlatkov looked around the room, then left the factory, going straight to his office in the old city. The name Dieter Stecker was familiar to him. He'd read it in this morning's KGB report on a list of people who travelled regularly into Finland. Vlatkov stared at the name, his fingers drumming the page. It wasn't so much the regular nature of Stecker's visits to Finland that concerned him. This German, who held a senior position in a tightly restricted company, had access to secret information, did frequent trips to the West and, so Vlatkov had learned, the man had recently become a widower. The combination set off alarms bells for Vlatkov and he wasn't waiting for further instructions from his superiors, which he knew would take hours he didn't have. He telephoned one of his most trusted junior officers. 'Take the last ferry to Helsinki, but do not get off. There are two KGB officers waiting there to escort a man named Dieter Stecker back to Tallinn this evening. They will identify him. Travel back on the same ferry and see that this Dieter Stecker has an accident. A permanent one. Then bring his guards to me. If Stecker fails to return to the ferry, shoot the guards.'

CHAPTER FIVE

London

7th October 1965

Frank left his club and went straight to the underground facility at Leconfield House in Curzon Street, where a technician would develop the film from his miniature camera. He'd decided not to take it to the MI6 laboratory in Broadway for three reasons: Leconfield House was closer, the content of the note had major implications for the internal security of Britain and he didn't wish to sound an international alarm with only circumstantial evidence.

His stomach churned with anxiety about Stecker and the content of his note. Frank had been meeting with Dieter in Helsinki for years and although, in that time, the man had passed some interesting information to him, Frank had never seen the man so nervous. He also didn't believe Dieter had fully comprehended what he'd seen and heard. How could he? It was possible the Soviet border guards hadn't fully understood it either. Regardless, as soon as they reported what they'd seen, their KGB handlers would investigate it. Whatever the blueprints contained, Frank believed it would be significant and that it had been potentially deadly for Stecker. But the content of the note was dynamite.

'How long?' he asked the technician.

'I can do it now, sir, if it's urgent. Will you be upstairs?'

'Yes. I can wait there. I need to see The Director General, anyway.' Frank climbed the stairs to the upper floors and went straight to the Director General's office. Opening the door, he saw the Head of MI5 was alone.

'Come in, Frank,' The Director General said. Frank placed his briefcase on the floor beside a chair and sat down.

'I'll have Laurence join us.' The Director General pressed the button on the desk.

A minute later, the connecting door opened and Laurence Dalrymple walked in. 'Frank. How's Helsinki?'

'Cold. A film is being developed. We'll know what it's about soon.'

Laurence took his usual seat. He stared at both Frank and his immediate superior, neither of whom spoke, then reached for his handkerchief and rubbed his glasses. A knock at the door broke the silence.

'Miss McKillick, come in!'

The secretary handed Frank an envelope.

'I'd like you both to have a look at these and tell me what you think?' Frank spread the developed photographs on the desk.

Laurence picked one up and studied it. 'Seems to be some sort of portable interception or jamming device. I'll have our scientists take a look.'

The Director General gathered the photographs together and returned them to the envelope. 'Whatever these blueprints are, Stecker took considerable risk in getting them to us. Although, I'm not thrilled about him sending them to Norway in the interim.' The Director General paused, the thin lips pursing. 'You should know, Frank, that I received some disturbing information from C an hour ago. It appears that you were seen!'

'What! Not possible. I know when I'm being followed, and I wasn't.'

'I'm reliably informed that Dieter Stecker is missing, presumed dead.'

'Is someone going to tell me what's going on?' Laurence asked.

'It's a miracle you're alive, Frank!' The Director General said, ignoring Laurence's question.

Frank sat in a chair and cradled his head. 'That's terrible news. I saw him get on the ferry in Helsinki yesterday. I also told him to lie low. He was worried about tightening security at the factory. A new KGB officer, apparently. Is it possible he's been transferred somewhere else?'

'Like a labour camp?' Laurence said.

'I hope not.'

'Either way, he's of no further use to us,' the Director General snapped. 'Pity! He was a good asset. Not easy to replace one of such long standing.' The Director General's intense gaze shifted to Laurence. 'Tell the scientists top priority on those blueprints. I want to know exactly what Stecker gave his life for us to know.'

'This device, if it is for jamming, would have us and the Americans running around in circles,' Laurence said.

'And the letter?' Frank asked.

'Interesting that he sent them to one of your old SOE team, Frank,' Laurence said. 'Why not post them directly to you from Helsinki?'

'Added precaution, perhaps. A letter to Norway would be less likely to receive attention than one to London, but who knows? He saved our lives in Norway during the war. I suppose he knew Per would honour the debt.'

'No!' The Director General leaned forward on the desk. 'They killed him! They didn't interrogate him! What does that tell you, Laurence?'

'They knew he'd passed on the information about the microwave device, surely,' Laurence said.

'No!' The Director shouted, hitting the desk blotter. 'If the KGB had suspected him, they would've stopped him from leaving Tallinn. No. They were tipped off. He was a doomed man the second he stepped foot back onto that ferry. They will have suspected he secreted the film in Finland. Or sent it to someone. They'd have checked every flight into Helsinki from London, looking for a person with a past connection to Dieter Stecker. That's why Stecker didn't send them to Frank here. So he sent them to someone from his past who doesn't live in England. Someone real who has no current connection to Frank or us.' The Director General leaned back in the chair. 'We must also consider that if the KGB suspected Stecker, the blueprints could be fakes.'

'So what now?' Laurence asked.

'We wait. I'll inform C. But for now, I'm going to suggest we handle this, not SIS. Alright with you, Frank?'

'Could be best,' Frank said.

The Director General stood and peered out the window behind the desk. 'We need to know if these blueprints are genuine.' A long and awkward silence ensured. 'If only we had someone on the inside at the Soviet Embassy.'

CHAPTER SIX

Moscow

The Soviet Union

8th October 1965

Vlatkov took the night train from Tallinn to Moscow. He wanted to inform his ultimate superior personally about Stecker. He'd already arranged for the guard at the factory, Boris, to be arrested. His junior officers would attend to the interrogation. Thereafter, he would be sent to Siberia. The indolent officers entrusted with escorting Stecker into Finland were now on a train and heading for the labour camps in the north. Vlatkov was proud of his decisions. His juniors respected him, although he acknowledged it was probably more fear than respect. Either way, he had made his presence felt in Tallinn and he intended things would be different now he was in charge. He stared at his briefcase. Now he had the proof of the German's treachery. He wanted to be the first to break the news to his ultimate superior. He wore his best uniform for the meeting.

Vlatkov strode through the intercity station and took the stairs to the underground. Twenty minutes later, he stepped from the train at the Lubyanka Station and took the escalator to the ground floor. Outside, a cold wind tore at his coat as he strode across the square. He liked Moscow, even on a grey day. He liked its size, its air of importance and superiority. He especially liked the Stalinskie Vysotki, the tall buildings known as the Seven Sisters; massive Russian baroque skyscrapers built after the war that dotted Moscow's skyline. He also liked that his uniform had a palpable effect on people. They stood out of his way. Whenever he went to Moscow, which wasn't often, he always stayed overnight at a hotel near Red Square. For him, Red Square was the beating heart of the most important city in the world; the solid Kremlin walls, the tomb of Lenin and the brightly coloured St Basil's made him feel important and connected to the halls of power.

Ten minutes later, he entered the headquarters of the KGB in Moscow and went directly to the third floor for his appointment at eleven.

'Major Vlatkov to see General Moshenko,' he said to a long-faced, mature-aged woman sitting at a typewriter outside the General's impressive office.

The woman lifted a telephone receiver. 'Major Vlatkov to see you, General.' A minute later, she hung up. 'You can go in.'

Vlatkov straightened his jacket, then knocked on the highly polished door.

'Enter!'

Vlatkov opened the door and stepped inside. Closing the door behind him, he walked towards his superior's desk, then stood to attention and waited for General Moshenko to look up.

The General lifted his head. 'Well?'

Vlatkov showed Moshenko the mishandled blueprints. He told him he believed the German, Stecker, had photographed them and taken the film with him to Finland. He'd received information that the German had met briefly with a Norwegian in Ivantra on the day he'd inspected the dam.

'Is this Stecker in custody?'

'No, General. He's dead. He had an accident on the return ferry.'

The General stared at Vlatkov. 'You're sure he was the traitor?'

'Yes, General. Gospodin Stecker was the only person to have the key to the blueprint filing cabinets and the only person working on the device other than his deputy, Yuri Maskovski. If Stecker was away for the day, then Maskovski was entrusted with the key. It was the deputy who reported the incident to me.'

'What do we know about this Stecker?'

'He was in the German Wehrmacht stationed in Norway during the war. He surrendered to the British in '45 in Berlin, where he lived for six months, then moved to Tallinn, where he worked for the Electronic Equipment Factory working his way up to department head of the design office. He goes every month to Finland to inspect the dams on the border between Finland and the Soviet Union. He has held this position for about ten years.'

'Finland, you say?'

'Yes, General.'

Moshenko paused. 'Does he have family?'

'Not anymore, Comrade General. His wife died recently.'

'Was she German too?'

'No, General. Estonian.'

'And no children?'

'None, General.'

'You're sure he is dead?'

'Yes, General.'

'Good. Traitors should die. It is the least they can do for the country that has supported them. Who arranged for him to travel through Finland?'

'My predecessor, General. He died last year. I understand the arrangement has been in place for some years.'

'Has this German shown us any cause for concern previously?'

'None recorded, General.'

'There is only one reason a loyal man suddenly becomes a traitor, and this is because he always was one!' The General slammed his fists on his desk then stood. 'So, the West now knows of our microwave devices!' Moshenko wandered over to a large window, his gaze on the grey skies, his back to Vlatkov. 'Perhaps we can use this situation to our advantage.' Moshenko returned to his seat and sat down. 'I would like to know more about your informant, who witnessed the meeting between Stecker and the Norwegian. But we must be careful not to show our hand before we have further details.' Moshenko paused, his thick lips moving in and out as his eyes focused on some papers on his desk. 'You can be of service to me, Major. How would you like to work in our London Embassy?'

CHAPTER SEVEN

Soho

14th October 1965

'I want some cigarettes, Valerie,' Alistair said.

She lay back on the pillows and watched him. 'Five minutes. No longer.'

He nodded. Leaving her lying on the bed, he climbed the stairs two at a time. No one was in the front room and the curtains were still drawn. It was early, around ten o'clock, too early for clients. Fred let him out. Stepping outside, Alistair stood on the steps and drew his coat around him. Although not yet raining, it was an overcast day, and a wind was rushing through the streets, sending discarded newspapers in all directions. People clutched their coats and umbrellas. Such weather always made for a busy day for the girls. It had been just over a week since the Krays had visited The Club, but they hadn't returned and there'd been no further mention of any blind beggars. Alistair walked to the newsagency and placed the card in the advertising window. Buying the cigarettes, he returned to The Club.

As he entered, a man was descending the stairs from the upper floors. Clients rarely stayed overnight. Alistair looked at Fred, who just raised his eyebrows but made no comment. Behind this man was a girl he didn't recognise. She had long blonde hair and wore a simple green paisley mini-length dress with matching headband and sunglasses. Valerie joined them from the front room.

'Thanks, Val,' the girl said.

'Please don't make a habit of it, Caro.'

'Any press outside, darling?' Valerie asked Alistair.

'Not that I saw,' he said.

'Look again, would you? Use the front windows, no one can see in.'

Alistair went into the front room and, drawing back the curtain, looked outside. A man was standing in a doorway opposite The Club. 'There is a man there. Do you want me to ask him what he's doing?'

'Nothing so obvious, darling. Engage him in conversation. Get him to turn his back so my friends here can get away.'

Alistair flicked a glance at the man with Valerie's friend, the one she called Caro, then went outside. Actually, he was pleased Valerie had asked him to do this. He wanted to test his skills, try himself out by talking to strangers and seeing what he could find out from them. Crossing Greek Street, he paused on the footpath near the man and lit a cigarette.

The man approached him. 'Don't suppose I could bot a cigarette, mate?'

'Sure.' Alistair pulled the packet from his pocket.

'You go there often?' the man asked, drawing a cigarette from the packet and putting it between his lips.

'Sometimes.'

'How'd you like to earn a few extra quid?' the man said, pulling a box of matches from his pocket and cupping his hands around the cigarette, lit it. He flicked out the match and dropped it into the gutter.

'Maybe.'

The man drew back on the cigarette. 'Tell me who comes and goes and I'll make it worth your while.'

'Really?' Alistair said. He shifted his feet, then nodded towards a recessed doorway further down the street. He strode away, the man's footsteps hurrying after him. Stopping, Alistair paused outside a music shop, and the man joined him in an alcove there. Alistair inhaled, then blew the smoke from the side of his mouth. 'Who wants to know?'

'Daily Mirror.'

'You know the 2i's café in Old Compton Road?'

'Of course.'

'Be there Saturday at four.'

The man nodded.

'Now hop it. If you're seen anywhere around here again, the deal's off.'

The man left.

Alistair watched him hurry away, his head down, his shoulders hunched under an old and fraying trench coat. Without looking back, Alistair disappeared into Bateman Street and walked the block, returning to The Club about ten minutes later.

'Who was he?' Valerie asked as soon as Alistair returned.

'Press. Did your friends leave?'

Valerie nodded. 'They said I was to thank you.'

'Who did I endanger myself for?'

Valerie smiled. 'You know better than to ask, darling. Now get me a drink.'

The next morning, Alistair made an excuse about leaving The Club to buy the morning news. He ambled to the corner and checked the newsagent's window. A one-bedroom flat was advertised for rent; Flat 2 at 6 Frith Street. The card said it would be open to view the next day between noon and two o'clock.

Inside, he bought a paper, then wandered back to The Club. On the front page was a picture of the parliamentarian, John Greenslade, with his girlfriend, Caroline Channon. Alistair recognised the girl immediately.

That night he and Valerie had made love again several times during the dark hours, but Alistair felt something was wrong and he hoped she hadn't tired of him already. He woke before her. He kissed her check and slid from the bed. Dressing quietly, he left her room and tip-toed upstairs. He could hear Gertie in the kitchen, but no one was in the front room. He let himself out and walked to the corner, the rendezvous with Three Piece Suit still two hours away. He wandered towards Soho Square and sat on a bench there people-watching for a while, then walked to 2i's for coffee. He hadn't seen the Daily Mirror journalist again, but the morning papers were filled with pictures of Caroline Channon and the parliamentarian.

A few minutes before midday, he left the café and walked to the address in Frith Street, his eyes constantly searching for any black cars. At exactly noon, he opened a frosted glass-panelled door to a staircase. Inside was gloomy. The walls looked like they hadn't been painted since the war and there was a smell of male cat or dead rodent. The carpet on the stairs was faded and brown. Upstairs, he found Flat Two and pushed open the door. Standing in the middle of an otherwise empty, dilapidated room was Three Piece Suit.

'What have you got?' Three Piece asked.

Alistair told him about the altercation between one of the Richardson's gang and the Kray twins and about the woman he believed to be Caroline Channon he'd helped to leave The Club unnoticed.

'But the man she was with wasn't John Greenslade?' Three Piece asked.

'No. I don't know who he was.'

'You're sure about all this?'

'Which bit?'

'Let's deal with the Krays first.'

'Richardson's man definitely said they'd own the Blind Beggar by the end of the week. Who is he?'

'It's not a person; it's a pub in the East End. Now the other matter.'

'Like I said. I recognised that woman, Caroline Channon. Her picture is in this morning's paper with that parliamentarian, John something, so I know she stayed in The Club Wednesday night.'

'And the man?'

'He was older than her but not old.'

'But it wasn't Greenslade?'

'No.'

'And you've never seen him before?'

'He may have been in the club once or twice before, but I don't know who he is. I've never seen her before. I don't know anything else about them.'

'And this journalist?'

'I told him I'd meet him at 2i's at four today, but I had no intention of keeping the meeting.'

'We'll look after him.'

'Can I go now?'

'No. You're to come back with me. You'll be leaving here, Quinn.'

'What do you mean?'

'I mean, you're leaving. Not coming back. We have other things for you to do now.'

'Can I at least say goodbye?'

'Not a chance,' Three Piece said, his hand on Alistair's shoulder.

Alistair stared into Three Piece's impassive glare. The gesture wasn't a reassuring arm from a more experienced colleague. Alistair sniffed loudly and shrugged Three Piece's hand from his shoulder. While he was considerably younger than Three Piece, he was taller. In his mind, he saw the older boys at school who'd tried many times to intimidate him. Such volatile school-boy confrontations never ended well; for him, almost always a visit to the Headmaster for insubordination and six of the best; for the senior, a term of bitter remorse in being denied Misty's charms.

Alistair stood on the narrow footpath in Frith Street with Three Piece for what he guessed was only three seconds before the black car pulled up beside them. Three Piece opened the rear door and Alistair got in. Bill and Ben weren't there. Only a driver occupied the front seat, and Alistair couldn't see his face clearly. He looked through the car window as Three Piece jumped in beside him. It was Saturday and lunchtime. Despite the cool weather, people were clogging the streets. Others hung out of pub windows talking to people standing on the pavements. Ahead, a delivery van jammed the narrow thoroughfare. He studied the faces of the people passing, wondering if anyone had witnessed him getting into the car. But no one in the bustling crowd appeared to have paid him even a sideways glance. Three Piece reached into a seat pocket and pulled out the hood.

'Is that really necessary?'

'Just a precaution,' Three Piece said.

'I haven't told anyone about any of this.'

'I know. You passed our test.'

'What test?'

'Money's the great tempter, Quinn,' Three Piece said as the car crawled past the delivery lorry. The hood was replaced over Alistair's head. 'They say power corrupts and absolute power corrupts absolutely. I say money corrupts and shit loads of the stuff corrupts like nothing else.'

Alistair felt the car turn left, his mind on the envelope of money Valerie had asked him to take to the newsagency.

'Does Valerie work for you?'

'Not for you to know. It doesn't matter now, anyway. You'll never see her again.'

Alistair leaned back, the hood like a shroud around his memories. He no longer cared about where he was going. He felt as though he'd been punched. What Three Piece had said about Valerie saddened him more than he cared to admit. He closed his eyes; all he had now were the memories. He recalled the night before. She'd been distant with him, and now he believed he knew why. In his mind, he saw her naked body, the curve of her back and thighs. In the seclusion the hood offered, he smiled, the memory of her fragrance lingering, the smell of her in the morning. How she'd looked at him. What she'd taught him about people, about life and sex. He'd always known it couldn't last forever, but he hadn't considered it would end like this. No fond farewell. No we-must-catch-up speech. Despite his melancholy, his smile lingered. Whether or not she worked for MI5, for him, she'd always be a goddess. He'd love her forever. Neither would he forget her.

The car pulled up suddenly.

Alistair guessed from the time he'd been in the car that he was at the same mesh-windowed building. Three Piece opened the car door and Alistair wriggled out. He stood waiting for the hood to be removed. Before him was the sliding entry door with its one-way glass.

Three Piece pushed Alistair towards the door and they went inside. To his right was the same security guard sitting behind his large desk in the grey-green marble entry foyer. He nodded to Three Piece but didn't speak. Despite the ugly post-war building being in Mayfair, it was decidedly austere. To the uninitiated, or any random members of the public who tried to enter there, it appeared to be a routine office building full of secretaries and office workers. The whole place exuded institutional impassivity with its indifferent, cold, green-grey stone and black metal railings.

Three Piece took him upstairs, and they walked some way along a corridor to a door, then downstairs again to the room on a lower floor at the back of the building. Three Piece pushed open a door. Alistair saw it was the same room with its bolted furniture that he'd been taken to before. Or one exactly like it. A dry cheese sandwich sat on the thick porcelain plate on the table, and Alistair wondered if it was the same one. Beside it was a cup of tea, the stream rising. In addition to the hot tea and sandwich, there was a shortbread biscuit on the saucer. On the opposite side of the table was a cream folder with a thin red stripe in the corner. Three Piece sat down and indicated for Alistair to do likewise, then reached for the file and opened it. Passing the document across the table, he looked into Alistair's eyes. 'Help yourself to the sandwich and tea. Then read this. And sign it!'

Alistair sat, his right hand reaching for the tea. He took a long sip before opening the folder. It held one document. In bold type across the top of the front page were the words, "Official Secrets Act". He sipped the tea, his gaze on the document. Taking his time, he read through the pages. Three Piece stood and paced the room, his shoes squeaking on the hard floor. Alistair's heart was pounding. Not from fear, nor even from apprehension; it was pure adrenaline. He felt the excitement of what he was being asked to do. It was what he'd always longed for; to be included, to be part of something important. And it wasn't just any job; it was MI5! This was about as big as it got. No longer an informant, but a card-carrying member of Britain's Security Service. He felt the enormity of being involved in such an organisation. And with the signing of the Official Secrets Act, it was just that; official. Replacing the cup on the saucer, he bit into the biscuit, then brushed the crumbs from the page. The room was silent. Even Three Piece had stopped pacing the room and was staring at him. Alistair felt the eyes watching, waiting. By the time he'd read the last page, he put the empty cup on the saucer and reached for the pen. Three Piece leaned over the table and placed his hand over Alistair's.

'Just so you know, Quinn,' Three Piece said. 'No divorce!'

'Sorry?'

'Hopefully, you won't be. I mean, Quinn, you never leave. Never! This is for life. When we call, you answer. Understand!'

'Understood,' Alistair said, steadily holding the man's gaze.

The frown on Three Piece's forehead deepened. He leaned forward, his knuckles pressing into the table so that his face was only inches from Alistair's head. 'I'm serious. This is serious. Try to leave us. Try to fuck us over. You'll be dead. And no one will find your body. Here today, gone tomorrow. Got the picture?'

Alistair nodded. His heart was pounding as he gripped the pen. He signed his name.

For one second, he thought of his father and Uncle Laurence. Strange, he thought, following in daddy's footsteps after all. But for him, it would be different. For Alistair Quinn, that was the end of any similarity with his father. No back-room job for him. 'What now?' he asked, putting the pen back on the desk.

'You'll be taken to a safe house. Then tomorrow you'll be given your instructions.' Three Piece reached for the signed document, checked it then returned it to the folder. 'Cushy life's over, Quinn. It's time you were toughened up.'

CHAPTER EIGHT

Mayfair

London

16th October 1965

Alistair finished his tea and biscuit, but left the sandwich for the next unsuspecting recruit. Three Piece led him back to the stairwell, then to a lower floor and through a fire-exit door into a car park.

'Where are we?' Alistair asked.

'Near Marble Arch.'

'That's a bit vague, isn't it?'

'Maybe. But it's all you're getting.'

Alistair waited, but they didn't walk towards any of the parked cars. 'What are we waiting for?'

'You ask a lot of questions.' Three Piece turned to look at him. 'There's a time for questions. When you're on safe ground. And there's a time to shut up. Remember, you have two eyes and two ears. But only one mouth. It'll get you into more trouble than your eyes and ears.'

'Aren't we on safe ground here? I mean, this is still England, isn't it?'

'You don't get it, do you? We don't exist! And we sure as hell don't exist in the world of other people; the innocent, naïve stuff of most people's lives. That life is gone, Quinn. Everyone you meet from now on is a potential threat. Everyone is capable of treachery. Some will sell their soul for a quid. And some will be capable of killing you when you least expect it.'

'A quid?'

'One or thousands. If you're on the take, you're expendable. Even if you're not, you'll still be a target. There was a thousand pounds in that package, Quinn. Yet you didn't open it. Or if you did, you resealed it without taking any of the money. So I ask myself; is he stupid or a patriot? What makes a person work for Security? For some it's ideology, for others it's their ego and for some it's always and only ever about money. So what is it for you, Quinn, if not for money?'

'To be part of something important.'

Three Piece laughed. 'Shit! I hope I was never so naïve,' Three Piece paused, then added. 'Everything we do is important! And none of it matters in the end.'

'What does that mean?'

'That's the riddle you have to work out,' Three Piece leaned in close. 'How far will you go, Quinn? Will you turn to jelly when the shit hits the fan? Would you shoot your own mother for your country? Well? How far are you prepared to go to show your loyalty to queen and country?'

Alistair held Three Piece's glare for three seconds. 'You're a bull-shit artist.'

'Cocky little bastard, aren't you?' Three Piece laughed. 'You'll do alright. But remember, the nation may be grateful for what you do, not that they'll ever know about it or say as much, but you'll still die alone.'

'Why did you join?'

'None of your business.'

Alistair heard an approaching vehicle. A minute later a blue Cit-roën pulled up beside them and Three Piece opened the rear car door. 'Get in!'

Alistair sat in the rear seat.

Three Piece reached for the handle and began to close the door.

'You not coming?'

'Not this time.'

'See you then,' Alistair said through the window.

'Hopefully not.'

Alistair was alone in the car with the driver. He didn't know where he was going, but he guessed the driver did. He also guessed Three Piece knew. Three Piece's speech had rattled him, but Alistair hoped he hadn't shown it. He also hoped Three Piece had been right when he'd said it was unlikely they'd meet again. Alistair gazed out the window as they drove up several identical floors of concrete carpark. So much had happened this day, he almost couldn't take it in. He heard his stomach rumble. He was hungry and a whisky wouldn't go astray. He thought of Valerie. There, he felt sadness. He wondered if she was missing him. Perhaps she'd send Fred out to look for him. He visualised The Club. 'Got a smoke?' he called to the driver, but the man didn't respond. Minutes later they drove out of the carpark and into the London streets. It was late afternoon now and October's shortening twilight had almost passed. The roads were dark, and the streetlights were on. Evening traffic was filling the streets with impatient drivers wanting to get to their Saturday night entertainments. He wasn't entirely sure where he was. He knew he was no longer in Soho where the neon signs would be turned on, flashing out their enticing temptations. At night, the spectacle was like nothing he'd ever seen, so bright and exotic; its brilliance intoxicating.

He stared through the car window as the car drove on. To his right was a vast park and on his left were four-storey buildings, painted white and all the same. He guessed they were in Park Lane. Then the car negotiated a busy round-about in the centre of which was the Wellington Arch and statue, before heading west towards Knightsbridge.

The road veered to the left, passing one of the world's most famous department stores, then left into a side street. At a building half concealed by scaffolding, they entered a ramp that led into another underground carpark. Without stopping, the Citroën drove to the lowest floor and stopped beside a fire exit.

'Knock on that door, *sir*,' the driver said.

Alistair got out, and the Citroën drove away. He'd never been called sir before and he rather liked it. He knocked at the solid steel door as instructed. Within a few seconds, it opened, and he stepped inside.

An enormously muscular man of average height, dressed in a British Army sergeant's uniform, stood before him. He had a terse face, bulging upper arm muscles, and a very large machine gun. Alistair guessed him to be in his forties, or maybe fifties. His finger was poised on the trigger. 'Name?'

The man had a thick Glaswegian accent.

'Alistair Quinn.'

'This way.'

Alistair followed the Glaswegian along the corridor to a room at the end. It was almost completely empty except for a utilitarian table and chair; neither of which was bolted to the floor, and a telephone that hung on the wall by the door. The sergeant then told him to turn out the contents of his pockets and place them on a table. There wasn't much: a few coins, a packet of cigarettes, a box of matches and a lace handkerchief, one of Valerie's she'd used to remove some of her lipstick from his face.

'Spread your legs,' the sergeant bellowed, then ran his gigantic hands down Alistair's legs, groin, and under his arms. 'Sit there.' He pointed to a metal chair in the corner and reached for the telephone. Alistair heard his name mentioned, then the Scott replaced the receiver. 'This way.'

Alistair grabbed the contents of his pockets from the table, sniffing the handkerchief as he did so.

'Leave those there!' the sergeant ordered.

Alistair threw the cigarettes, matches, and coins onto the table.

'And the handkerchief! No mementos. No keepsakes.'

Alistair placed the handkerchief on the table, his fingers lingering over the lacy white linen. He stared at it, his heart sinking. It felt like a goodbye, a final one. Leaving it lying on the table, he followed the burly man out of the room, wondering if another stark room with bolted furniture and a crusty cheese sandwich awaited him. At the end of the corridor, they climbed three flights of stairs before the man pushed open another door.

What Alistair saw almost took his breath away. He was inside what looked like a gentleman's club, complete with gleaming marble floor, plush carpets and rugs, busts of famous faces and miles of wood panelling. The smell of cigars and brandy hung in the air. In that instant, he was immediately in the past and about nine years old. As a boy, he and his mother had been invited to tea with Sir Laurence Dalrymple to his club in Pall Mall. Uncle Laurence, as Alistair called him, held a high position at MI5 and had been in America, where he'd brought back a cowboy outfit for him. Alistair remembered not liking it much, but his uncle wanted to see him in it and so, dutifully and under some duress from his mother, Alistair had complied. He pictured his uncle, a short man who waddled slightly and always smelt of cigarettes. Uncle Laurence was a close friend to both his parents, but he wasn't really an uncle. Why did adults force their children to call their friends aunt or uncle when they weren't? What was so socially unacceptable with just using their name? Alistair could hear her voice now. *That would be disrespectful*, his mother had told him when he'd asked the same question years ago. He had three real aunts on his mother's side, only one of whom had married and his father had been an only child. Despite Uncle Laurence being one of his father's oldest friends and colleagues, Alistair didn't recall his father being present that day.

'In here,' the Scott said. Alistair was shown into a plain, but pleasant room. It was lined with shelves and cupboards and looked like a gentleman's outfitters in Saville Row. Some fitting rooms were off to one side. The sergeant then went about assembling some khaki trousers, leggings, shirt, and jacket, along with some thick socks and black boots. 'Put these on. From now on, while you're here, you'll wear this uniform.' Alistair went into the fitting room and dressed in the scratchy apparel. Half an hour later, he was wearing the uniform of a British Army Corporal. The sergeant then took him to the foot of a grand staircase in the entry foyer. 'Go upstairs now. The Duty Officer for the day is expecting you.'

Alistair climbed the stairs to the upper floor, his eyes taking in the sumptuous surroundings. It couldn't have been more different to MI5's other property near Marble Arch. This was luxurious in every respect; tall marble columns with intricate pediments highlighted in gold leaf stood in the entry hall, chandeliers hung over the carved, wide staircase and thick plush carpet cushioned his feet despite the heavy boots. At the top of the stairs sat a lieutenant like a maître d'. Alistair wondered if he should order luncheon or salute. He decided against both alternatives. Besides which, as far as he knew, he wasn't in the army.

'Evening, Quinn.' The lieutenant stood. 'This is your Security Identity Card. Keep it on you at all times, unless, of course, possession puts your life in danger. Happily, that isn't the case here. Now come this way and I'll show you to your room. You've been allocated No. 39 on this floor. You can use it every time you're here.

'How often will that be?'

The lieutenant laughed. 'When you're in London. You have your own private bathroom and a maid. She'll look after your needs here, and by that I don't mean sexual. You are free to move around and use the downstairs library and lounges. The dining room is also downstairs, opposite the library. You'll soon know your way about. Supper is at seven, breakfast is served in your room at whatever time suits you. Luncheon is at one in the dining room. Conversation with others must be limited to small talk; weather, publicly available news, that sort of thing. You don't discuss your past or anything you've done or are about to do and you don't question others you meet here, either.'

'How long am I here for?'

'Unknown at this stage. But it's never long; a week at most.'

Alistair took the key from the smiling lieutenant.

'Dorothy, your maid, will be along to meet you soon. Any questions, ask me.'

'Is there anything I'm supposed to be doing now?'

The lieutenant shook his head.

'I'm starving. Can I get something to eat?'

'Of course. Anything you want. The waiter in the library will look after you.'

Alistair unlocked the door to No. 39. While it wasn't as sumptuous as the foyer, it had a single bed with a blue damask bedhead, a bedside table with a telephone, a mahogany chest of drawers, a small wardrobe, navy blue carpet with a fleur-de-lis motif, and an understated yet distinctly British aura of permanence.

'Good evening, sir,' a female voice behind him said.

He turned around.

'I'm Dorothy, your maid.'

He smiled. Dorothy was a middle-aged woman; softly spoken and, he sensed, kindly, something he'd experienced only a few times in his life. She seemed warm, almost affectionate and motherly in a way his mother never had been.

'Nice to meet you, Dorothy.'

'Likewise, sir. Anything you want, just call,' she said, indicating the telephone on the bedside table.

Thanking Dorothy, he left No. 39 to have a look about. Locking the door behind him, he flipped the key into his pocket and went downstairs.

On the ground floor was a large library. Exactly like a gentleman's club, the room had many leather armchairs and sofas, a fireplace that was lit, and several low tables with recent periodicals and newspapers displayed. Around the walls were shelves of books. The curtains were drawn. He glanced at his watch. It was already after six. He wondered if Valerie was missing him as much as he was missing her.

Alistair approached a circling waiter. 'Could I have something to eat?'

'Of course, sir. Dinner is at seven, so perhaps a sandwich?'

'Thank you and a whisky, please.'

'The bar is there, sir. Just help yourself.' The waiter pointed to a long bar at the far end of the room, then left.

Sauntering over to the bar, Alistair poured himself a whisky, then sat in a deep leather armchair by a window, his right hand lifting the edge of the curtain. He had expected to see a dark evening, the London traffic scurrying past, heading for the theatres, restaurants or nightclubs. What he found was a solid wall. The windows were entirely fake; the whole place was completely cut off from the outside world. He glanced at an older man sitting opposite him, wearing the uniform of a major. He appeared to be engrossed in the evening newspaper. Alistair looked around the room. All the other occupants were men, and all were dressed in varying ranks of military attire. He didn't know if any of the ranks were genuine. Some men were sitting together near the fireplace. He stood up and wandered towards them.

'Mind if I join you?'

'Please do,' one said.

'I'm...' Alistair began.

'I'm guessing you're new. We don't use real names here. We call each other John, if a name is required.'

'I see.'

The waiter brought him the sandwich.

'Cheers, John,' the man said.

'Cheers,' he responded. Alistair smiled, then drank his whisky. Over half an hour passed in stilted conversation. He ate his sandwich, then poured himself a second whisky and took a cigar from a box on the bar. 'Does one dress for dinner here?' he asked the man opposite, wondering what he should wear if the answer was yes.

'Not usually. We wear the uniforms given to us while here. Anonymity is what it's about.'

A gong sounded in the hall.

'Ah! Supper. Good English fare here, John,' the man said to Alistair.

Alistair nodded and, finishing his whisky, followed the others across the hall to the dining room. He rather enjoyed being called John. He had been baptized with four names, none of which was John, but it reminded him of his Uncle John. In fact, he had two bachelor uncles named John. Neither was actually related, but he loved them as much as any nephew could. Years spent with them during the school holidays had cemented his affection for them. One was a farmer and lived near Oban in Scotland. Alistair had learned a great deal about farming from him. And drinking whisky. But his other Uncle John was his favourite. A great bear of a man, Uncle John McPherson owned a large estate also in Scotland, in Perthshire. Alistair remembered travelling as an unaccompanied minor to Scotland to spend the summer holidays there, and cherished fond memories of riding horses and playing with the dogs. Uncle John had taught him to stalk deer, fish for trout, and how to shoot a rifle.

Alistair sat at a table with the men he'd met in the library, but there was little conversation of any importance. During the meal of lamb chops, boiled vegetables and steamed pudding, people, always men, came and went constantly. It was like a revolving door. He finished a glass of wine, then left to have coffee in the library. No one was there. Even the men with whom he'd sat at supper had disappeared. Sitting alone, he was served coffee, but no one joined him there. He glanced at the clock on the mantelpiece. Nine o'clock. He thought of Greek Street. There, the night was just starting. He left the library and wandered back to his room just as his maid, Dorothy, was closing his door.

'Just turning your bed down, sir,' she said.

Alistair smiled. The woman walked away, disappearing into her own domain somewhere further along the corridor.

Closing the door to his room, he saw Dorothy had left some neatly ironed pyjamas on his bed. A silk gown hung on the stand in the corner of the room and some slippers were under the chair. She reminded him a little of the cook at Uncle John's estate in Perthshire. Bertha was a warm and caring woman, as he recalled, with a lilting Scottish accent and a large bosom. He had wonderful memories there of the kindly and nurturing woman who'd cuddle and kiss him and let him lick the cake batter from the bowl. She'd shown him genuine fondness and affection. Something he'd received nowhere else.

There was a loud knock at his door, breaking into his sleep. Alistair jumped out of bed and opened the door. The Duty Officer stood before him, an envelope in his hand.

'This came for you, sir.'

'Thank you,' Alistair said.

The man turned and left. Closing the door, Alistair placed the envelope on his bedside table. He hadn't slept well; he'd dreamt of Valerie. He reached for his watch and found it was just after ten o'clock. It amazed him that a room without windows could distort time so completely. Lifting the telephone receiver in his room, he ordered breakfast. Thirty minutes later, he was sitting in his silk robe and slippers, eating scrambled eggs and bacon. Finishing the meal, he reached for the envelope and tore it open. The letter told him he'd be leaving for Scotland the next day and that someone would come to escort him there. He beamed; he loved Scotland. He thought running away from school had been the best decision of his short life.

CHAPTER NINE

London

18th October 1965

Sir Laurence Dalrymple knocked on the door that connected his office with the Director General's.

'Ah, Laurence! Is it eleven already! Do sit down. Tea?' The Director General said, returning a document to a file on the desk.

'No, thank you. So, where is he?' Laurence said, sitting in the comfortable brown leather armchair he claimed as his own.

The Head of MI5 laid the pen down on a stack of files and stared at Dalrymple. 'By that, I'm assuming you mean Alistair. He's in Knightsbridge. I'm sending him to Commando Training at Achnacarry.'

Laurence Dalrymple raised his eyebrows, then removed his spectacles, took a handkerchief from his trouser pocket and began to polish the lenses vigorously. 'You think he'll stay the course?'

'He needs to be toughened up, and he needs weapons training, Laurence. And some discipline wouldn't go astray.'

'Good luck with that,' Laurence said, the handkerchief going back into the trouser pocket. Replacing his spectacles on his nose, Laurence sat back in the chair and crossed his short, chubby legs, then lit a cigarette. He enjoyed a close working relationship with his immediate superior, so he knew he didn't need to ask permission to smoke in The Director General's office. 'He could be useful to us. It would also give him something to do.'

'Quite! If he isn't controlled, he'll end up back in Soho and on the wrong side of the law, which would be embarrassing for us all.'

'His information was useful though.'

'We'll see. We've put a woman in the Blind Beggar. Barmaid. She'll let us know if something happens.'

'What are you expecting?'

'If the information is correct, Richardson et al. will make a move on the Kray brothers, and when they do, she'll inform us. As long as they're in the Blind Beggar long enough, we'll finally have the Krays where we want them.'

'And the other matter; this new KGB man at the Soviet Embassy, what's his name, Vlatkov? And the Honourable John Greenslade?'

The Director General stood abruptly and paced the room. 'Complicated.'

Laurence shifted in his chair, his nicotine-stained fingers still grasping the cigarette. 'Bloody fool! When will they learn to keep their,' Laurence paused, 'manhood in their trousers? I blame that photographer. Too many...' Laurence paused again, he'd wanted to say orgies, 'parties. Led John astray.'

'Can't excuse him totally, Laurence. But I expect we'll find a way.'

'Didn't the war teach them anything! You'd think it would be heads down and work hard. Instead, it's drink, party and as much sex as can be fitted into twenty-four hours. I don't know what we fought for, with such behaviour.'

'Times have changed, Laurence. Our enemies no longer wear a uniform. Besides, why shouldn't the world party after such a nightmare?'

'You don't condone it, surely?'

'I don't judge them for it. Unless they are public figures or prominent politicians.'

Laurence stubbed out his cigarette in the ashtray on a table by his chair, then lit another. 'Alistair's done well for his first time, wouldn't you say? His information about the Krays could net results. And what he told us about Caroline Channon could well have short-circuited a very embarrassing situation.'

'Greenslade's involvement with the Channon girl has complicated things. From all accounts, Vlatkov is proving difficult. His initial indication of wanting to turn has gone cold either because he's got cold feet or because it's a double bluff.' The Director General walked around the desk and gazed through the window at the grey-white clouds. Autumn was turning to winter, and the days were becoming colder and shorter. Christmas would soon be upon them and everyone would be thinking about festivities, not Soviet KGB operatives. 'But, it may be possible to bring about the same result another way. Regardless, it's weeks of careful work now rendered useless. And it could be months of equally careful work to make it happen.'

'You think it still can be done?'

The Director General turned to face Laurence. 'Yes. Provided we can keep the press out of it and Greenslade gives up this obsession with Miss Channon. We cannot afford to have anything else compromised, if this is to work.'

'I'll grant you it's become a tad messy with her screwing both Vlatkov and Greenslade. How will you manage it?'

'With luck and a lot of money.'

'How much, K?

'Acting K. And I wish you would not use that title. K hasn't been used since the war. Besides, I'm only a stop-gap. As soon as an official replacement is found for our former Head, I'll retire. And to answer your question; several hundred thousand, I should think.'

'There'll be questions about such a large amount, so it better be worth it.'

The Director General glared at Laurence. 'Well, that's for me to worry about, not you!'

There was an awkward pause. 'When does Alistair go?'

'Tonight. He'll be there three months minimum, maybe longer. I'd like him to learn a language, too. Russian could be useful.'

'I thought you intended to keep him in MI5?'

'Yes, well. If he has a talent for languages, the SIS may find him useful at Century House.'

'Following in father's footsteps?'

'To have to deal with people like you, Laurence? Over my dead body! Leave him alone. Understand me? Jenkins can handle him.'

'Well, perhaps just an avuncular guiding hand now and then.'

Laurence Dalrymple returned to his office and stood by his window, his mind on Alistair Quinn. He'd known the boy for years, since he'd been born, in fact. Laurence cast his mind back to when he'd first met Alistair's father, Frank Quinn, at St John's College, Oxford. They'd both studied classics and graduated at the same time, then entered the Civil Service together. They'd even started their careers on the same day; Frank to the Secret Intelligence Service or MI6 and him to the Security Service known as MI5, or *Box* to those on the inside. Laurence had been Frank's best man at his wedding to Grace. His friendship with Frank had endured over the years, however, Frank's son, Alistair, was a completely different personality. Not like either of his parents, Laurence considered Alistair was an accident waiting to happen. Many families Laurence knew had their black sheep, but he thought Alistair was not so much a black sheep as a throw-back. Possibly like his paternal grandfather, who had been an Intelligence Officer in the British Legation in the Belgian Congo before the Great War. Alistair, just like the stories Laurence had read about Frank's father, old J. W. Quinn, was completely without fear. J.W. had preferred to act alone and without any form of direction. That was sometimes a requirement when based so far from London. But men who operated without fear, in Laurence's opinion, were frequently reckless.

He lit another cigarette, inhaled, then blew a smoke-ring. 'You could be useful,' he said, sotto voce. 'But we shall see!' He stared out his window, as memories of the infant Alistair resurfaced. Laurence grinned at the memory of Grace's reaction when they'd discovered the three-year-old Alistair riding his tricycle a few inches from the edge on the roof of the block of flats in Clapham, where she and Frank had once lived. Alistair Quinn may have been described by Ian Petit, the Headmaster at Whittington Hill School as dishonourable, hedonistic and arrogant but the lad had guts, and from what Laurence had witnessed over the years, the boy didn't care a jot for authority or rules. With the privileges of a public school education, Alistair had become egotistical and pleasure-seeking but above all, he was a risk-taker and just about perfect for a job on the front line of the Security Services or possibly even the Secret Intelligence Service. Laurence sniggered as he thought about Alistair's most recent escapade; running away from school. 'Cheeky boy,' he said to the window, and the huddled passing crowds four storeys below. While Laurence had always had Alistair in mind for either Five or Six, it should have been via Oxford or Cambridge, but now it no longer mattered. Returning to his desk, he reached for the training programme that had been devised for the young Alistair Quinn.

CHAPTER TEN

London

18th October 1965

Alistair woke to the loud thump on the door to Room 39. Rising, he reached for his watch. Six o'clock. His initial thought was that Dorothy had mistaken the time for his breakfast tray. Opening his door, he saw the gargantuan Scott standing there.

'Get yourself showered, dressed and downstairs in fifteen minutes. We're leaving.'

'What now? At this hour?'

The Scott didn't wait for further conversation. Leaving Alistair standing in his bedroom doorway wearing his silk robe, the sergeant turned around and thundered down the hall, his head back, laughing loudly.

On the stroke of his allotted fifteen minutes, Alistair descended the stairs to the front vestibule. He could hear voices coming from the library, but the dining room was closed and the Duty Officer was nowhere to be seen.

'Do we leave by the front?'

The Scott emitted a sound halfway between a derisive sneer and contemptuous gurgle. 'Same way you came in. There is no front door to this building.'

The blue Citroën was waiting for them in the carpark.

'What do I call you?' Alistair asked, his hand on the car door handle.

'Sergeant-Major.'

'Sergeant-Major what?'

'Just Sergeant-Major.'

'Where precisely are we going?' Alistair asked, but the Sergeant-Major didn't respond. With the prodigious man beside him in the rear seat, the Citroën sped up three levels of the car park, then pulled out into the street. It was a dull day and rain was falling. Despite the weather, crowds still hurried along the streets, their umbrellas turned to the inclement conditions. The car turned left, then merged with traffic heading right. Skirting Hyde Park, they drove towards Marble Arch. Alistair glanced through the window. He guessed they were heading for either King's Cross or Euston Stations. After that was anyone's guess.

At Euston, Alistair bought several magazines for the trip north. 'Will you tell me now where we are going, specifically?'

The Sergeant-Major stopped walking and spun around, his large face pressed into Alistair's. 'You're headed for the Highlands of Scotland, laddie. A place that's cold and dark and wet! A place that'll kill you, if it can.' With every word, the Scot's face had clouded until it looked almost maniacal.

Alistair turned to walk away.

'And where do you think you're going?'

'Mind if I go to the men's?' Alistair said. 'You can come and watch me, if you like.'

The Sergeant-Major squinted, his nostrils flaring. 'That'll be enough of that! But I'll be standing outside.'

Alistair pushed open the door into the men's lavatory. He checked over his shoulder to see if the Sergeant-Major would follow. The man stood to one side of the doorway, his pack at his feet, his size eleven boot propping open the swing door.

From inside a cubicle, Alistair heard an educated voice say, 'Well, I never thought to see you here, Jock? It's been a long time. Have you left the camp?'

Alistair buttoned his fly. From what he could hear above the rattling of the lavatory fan, the Sergeant-Major had bumped into someone he knew. Alistair silently unlocked the cubicle door and waited.

'No. I'm baby-sitting a snotty little runaway who I have to train. Not my idea of fun, John. But that's our masters for you.'

'Have you time for a drink?'

'No, sorry. Trains to catch.'

'Heading to the old camp?'

'Aye.'

'Well, it was good to see you. Sorry we couldn't chat longer about old times.'

'Aye. Next time.'

Alistair flushed the toilet. When he stepped outside the cubicle, whoever had been talking to the Sergeant-Major had gone.

'Meet a pal?' Alistair asked, washing his hands.

'Never you mind.'

'Meeting men in toilets isn't a good idea, Sergeant-Major.'

A man pushed past the Sergeant-Major. Alistair endeavoured to suppress a smirk. He felt certain that had the man not entered the men's lavatory when he did, the Sergeant-Major's massive boot would have connected with his shin.

'Get outside. We're late and I don't want to miss that train,' the Scot snarled.

Alistair waited while his companion purchased the tickets. Standing behind the Sergeant-Major, he heard the Scot ask for two tickets to Edinburgh, then Inverness.

His eye searched for the distinctive Flying Scotsman, but the Sergeant-Major pushed him towards a run-down train on a different platform still painted black from its wartime service. They settled into a compartment. It was obviously not a sleeper.

Alistair closed his eyes as the train pulled out of Euston. While he liked Scotland, he was under no illusion that where he was going would be anything like his uncle's estate. An army training camp in the Scottish highlands in winter promised neither heat nor welcome.

Alistair stood on the platform. A grey dawn mist enveloped him and snow was falling. The journey had been long and monotonous, with no conversation. He'd read every word in the magazines he'd bought in Euston, even the advertisements. They'd changed trains in Edinburgh and again in Inverness, the cold waiting rooms adding to the tedium. Food had been purchased from kiosks in the stations and eaten either on the train or in a waiting room and while he had managed to doze, sleep was, at best, intermittent.

Alistair stared around him at the bone-chilling, desolate scene. No one, other than himself and the Sergeant-Major had alighted at the station and no one had boarded the train there. He turned a full three hundred and sixty degrees. He couldn't see a single house. According to the sign on the platform, he was at a place called Spean Bridge. It was bleak, isolated and freezing cold and to him, it seemed like another planet. A dour, grey day wrapped around him and an icy wind tore through the mist-filled valley, making the snow-covered, high cliffs beyond the station and the surrounding country bleak, treacherous and unwelcoming.

Alistair checked his watch; just after seven. He gazed up at the high mountains that surrounded the lonely Spean Bridge. Everything looked wet and uninviting, and he knew it was intended to be. The Sergeant-Major, who Alistair believed was enjoying himself, clutched his pack and walked across the platform. Alistair followed. From the other side of the station building, he could see a parked lorry. The Sergeant-Major strode towards it, Alistair following at a discrete distance.

'Get in!' the Sergeant-Major ordered.

Alistair walked towards the passenger door.

'Not there! You fuckin' little snot-rag. And another thing; lose that fuckin' posh accent. And don't speak unless spoken to,' the Sergeant-Major growled, then suddenly roared with laughter and turned swiftly so that again his face was inches from Alistair's nose. 'The lads training up here,' the Sergeant-Major snarled, his eyes wide, 'they're from the roughest areas of London, Cardiff and Glasgow. They'll eat you for fuckin' breakfast. Get one thing straight, Andrew. You have no privileges here. You are a snotty little toe-rag who rides in the back. Now get in!'

'My name isn't Andrew...' Alistair began.

The loudest scream Alistair had ever heard came from the Sergeant-Major. It seemed to reverberate around the surrounding cliffs. 'Get the fuck in!'

Alistair climbed into the rear of the lorry. It smelt of urine and blood. He hoped it was the entrails of an animal and not some poor sod like himself. He knew the Sergeant-Major despised him. Not because of anything he knew about him, but because of what Alistair represented and because the Sergeant-Major had had to come all the way to Knightsbridge and personally escort a snot-rag to Scotland. And probably because of his public school accent and his habit for answering back. Perhaps he'd asked one or two more questions than the Sergeant-Major was in the habit of answering. Alistair believed the enormous man had managed to keep his anger under control while ever they'd been in public. But now, on his turf, his anger and frustrations were boiling over. And Alistair knew who would bear the brunt of it. His mind went back to the Official Secrets Act he'd signed and Three Piece Suit. Three Piece had wanted to know why Alistair had joined the Security Service. Actually, Alistair didn't really know why. It seemed like a good idea at the time and he'd wanted to be included. He'd spent so much of his life on the outside looking in that it seemed like a heaven-sent opportunity. He sighed rather deeply as the lorry's engine roared into life. 'Well, Quinn, you wanted it,' he said aloud. 'So you'd better act like a man and get on with it!'

Less than half an hour later, the lorry stopped.

'Get out, Andrew!' the Sergeant-Major bellowed.

Alistair jumped the five feet from the rear of the lorry. Losing his balance, he landed face down in a pool of mud. 'My name isn't Andrew!' Alistair blurted, spitting the mud from his mouth.

'It is now, you little prick!' And with that, the size eleven boot hit him just below his ribs. Alistair doubled over, rolling further into the mud.

'Get up you horrible little twerp!' the Sergeant-Major shouted again. But before he could, the man's massive hand had him by the collar and was dragging him through the mud towards the door of a nearby Nissen hut. As he released his grip, Alistair fell once more onto the wet ground. He stood, his clothes, face and hands now thick with mud and a sharp pain in his side. The Sergeant-Major threw open the door, and they went in. Everything was utilitarian; stark, bleak, and very cold. Twelve metal-framed beds filled the hut and Alistair could see a bathroom at the end. One bed had a large quantity of equipment laid out on it, including a toothbrush. The inclusion of the toothbrush seemed odd to Alistair. It clearly didn't worry the Sergeant-Major that his latest recruit may have a cracked rib, but his teeth couldn't be allowed to develop gum disease. Alistair ran his gaze along the equipment lined up on the bed. He noted there was no gun. He thought that was probably wise, for by now he believed he could have used it.

'Welcome to Achnacarry,' the Sergeant-Major said, a sneering grin spreading across his face.

CHAPTER ELEVEN

Achnacarry

Scotland

19th October 1965

The Sergeant-Major stood in the doorway, his muscular frame blocking the light. 'Shower and change into the uniform on the bed. Be outside in seven minutes. Not eight. Seven.'

'Then what?' Alistair asked, knowing it would irritate the Sergeant-Major.

The Sergeant-Major moved forward with surprising speed. A swift knee-jerk landed in Alistair's groin, and he sank to the ground.

'I told you. You don't speak unless spoken to. Six minutes now! And counting,' the Sergeant-Major said, striding through the Nissen hut and slamming the hut door shut behind him.

Alistair stood slowly and walked towards the showers and toilets at the rear of the hut. If the hut was cold, the bathroom was colder. There were no doors on either the lavatories or the showers. In fact, the showers comprised six shower heads protruding from the wall and one tap marked 'cold'. A communal trench set alongside the wall drained the water away. There were no tiles on either the walls or the floor. Everything was hard, cold and Spartan. Throwing off his clothes, he launched himself under the freezing water, then hurried back to the bed. Shivering, his gaze scanned the items on the bed. No towel. He shook his head, wondering why the army thought it necessary to make life so difficult. Using the vest he'd worn from Knightsbridge, he towelled himself as best he could then, starting with the vest on the bed, dressed as quickly as his freezing, damp skin would allow, then went outside. The Sergeant-Major was standing, waiting, his legs astride, his hand on his watch. He ambled towards the Sergeant-Major knowing it would annoy him.

Studying the surrounding buildings, he saw Achnacarry was essentially a large stone house of some age surrounded by an equally ancient barn and some other farm buildings. Numerous hastily constructed Nissen huts, most likely erected during the last war, were off to one side. The place had all the hallmarks of a Sir Walter Scott novel, that curious mix that only the Scots can produce; romantic mystique and medieval barbarity. So remote, however, was Achnacarry, that Alistair wondered if anyone had told them the war with the Nazis was over.

He toyed with the idea of asking the man's name again, then thought better of it. His ribs and groin had suffered enough for one day. Despite overhearing the unknown man in Euston Station call the Sergeant-Major, Jock, it was almost certainly not his real name. All Scots were referred to as Jock. Alistair settled on the nick-name Dick.

'Take ya' hands from ya' pockets and get moving!' Dick shouted.

'Where would you like me to go?'

'Move!'

Alistair set off across the compound towards a wooden hut, the sergeant-major at his heels like a snapping dog. The sign outside the door said, 'Commanding Officer'. Alistair hoped the C. O. would be a kindly man; the sort of officer who frequented his club and had civilized manners. Dick knocked twice. Without waiting for a response, he thrust open the door, and they stepped inside. Dick stood in the corner. Alistair waited in front of the Commanding Officer's desk.

'Stand to attention!' the C.O. said.

'I don't know how to...' Alistair began.

'Shut up!' the C.O. screamed, spittle spraying over the papers on his desk.

Alistair stifled a smile, then reaching forward, grasped the back of a chair in front of the C.O.'s desk, intending to sit down. The officer's eyes bulged. 'This isn't a holiday camp! You horrible excuse for a human being! Sergeant-Major!'

'Sir!'

'You will be responsible for Andrew here. For his training, his life, his very existence. Understood?'

'Sir!'

Alistair watched as the CO's face turned from red to puce. 'Manoeuvres start in one hour. Go and get your gear on. You'll be sleeping with the deer tonight.' The C.O. leaned forward on his desk, a slow leer curling his upper lip. 'Now get the fuck out of my office!'

While marching back across the compound, Alistair realised he had a choice. Life at Achnacarry could be one of constantly baiting Dick and the C.O. as he would have done at school, or he could actually take it, shut up and learn something. For whatever reason, Three Piece and his superiors had deemed his sojourn at Achnacarry a necessity. Although he doubted he'd learn anything of importance. His gaze fell on a group of rough looking lads wearing full kit and standing at attention. He didn't know how long they'd been there, but none moved. Dick barked an order from behind them and the patrol turned left in unison, then began to run, leaving the compound.

'Get going, Andrew. Collect your pack and follow them.'

Alistair ran towards the Nissen hut. Assembling his pack from the kit on the bed, he ran outside, his eye searching for the patrol. He couldn't see them anymore, but he guessed they'd gone in the direction he'd seen them leave; towards a steep hill behind the camp. Alistair looked back at Dick. The man was laughing. It occurred to Alistair that Dick could have stood the patrol down while he was in the hut, making him go alone into the freezing hills to lose his way and die in the frozen night. Or the Sergeant-Major would have chosen the most difficult terrain for his initiation. As Alistair quickened his pace, he muttered to himself, 'Who knows, Quinn, all this may one day save your life!'

Alistair's muscles ached from running. When he saw the patrol ahead, he slowed his pace and breathed in the chill air. As long as he could see them, he didn't need to catch up with them. By night fall, he and the group of nine others, whose names Alistair didn't know, had covered eleven miles on a non-stop route march. As they descended to a lock, the men removed their packs and clothes and bathed in the icy waters. Alistair flopped down onto the hard ground; despite the sweat from the march, he felt wet, cold and exhausted.

'Bathe, you'll be warmer that way,' one lad with a strong Welch accent said to him. Alistair allowed his pack to fall, removed his clothes and rushed into the freezing loch. He emerged with pink skin from the bitter cold but he felt better. He smiled at the Welshman, but there was no conversation. He lay back on the hard ground and, using his pack as a pillow, thought on what he'd traded; the divine naked body of Valerie for hell on earth.

CHAPTER TWELVE

London

9th November 1965

'We'd love to,' Grace Quinn said into the telephone. 'Angela will be delighted. Thank you so much.'

'And Frank too,' John McPherson said.

'He's not here at present, John.'

'That's a shame. I'm sorry it's such short notice. I'm in London this week to see my solicitor about my Will. With no dependents of my own, I thought I should leave Glenrothie to someone I hold dear. I was hopeful of catching up with a few of the old faces and perhaps go to the cenotaph in Whitehall on Thursday.'

'Of course, Remembrance Day. What time tomorrow?'

'Say three. Does that leave you enough time to get home?'

'I'm sure that will be fine. And I don't mind catching a crowded bus if it means Angela and I can have tea at Fortnum and Mason's. They may even have their Christmas displays out. It will look wonderful and Angela will love that. It'll be so good to see you. We haven't seen you in ages.'

'Tomorrow then.'

Grace and Angela stepped off the bus and crossed Piccadilly just as the clock above Fortnum and Mason's chimed three. Angela stopped, her eyes wide and focused on the delightful display. Grace grabbed her arm and led her across the busy street. Angela wore her newest dress and a matching coat Grace had bought for her from Mary Quant's shop in the King's Road. Grace glanced at her daughter. Angela didn't come into London all that often, and Grace hoped she wouldn't become unruly. While simple things entertained Angela, crowds flustered the immature fourteen-year-old and made her behaviour unpredictable. Outbursts of loud and, on occasions, somewhat violent behaviour had been exhibited, and Grace had needed to remove her daughter from the public gaze. It was a worrying trend and lately Grace had seen several sides to her daughter's volatile personality. She hoped it was just puberty, but Angela's increasingly different mood swings were causing her concern.

She led her to the side entrance of the famous establishment, and they made their way through the piled high display tables, groaning with attractively packed seasonal delectables, down a few stairs to the charming café at the far end of the shop. Delightful Christmas decorations were everywhere. Grace could see that Angela was entranced. She considered it a blessing; enchantment kept Angela quiet.

John McPherson was already seated at a table by the Jermyn Street window. He stood as Grace and Angela approached, then kissed Grace on both cheeks. 'Grace. How wonderful to see you. You're looking well. And Angela, what a beautiful young woman you're becoming.'

'John, you'll turn her head, I'm sure, with all your flattery. How are you?' Grace nodded to Angela to take the seat by the window so she could see the passers-by.

'I can't complain, Gracie. Although, I have to remind myself that I'm not a young man anymore. What's that old adage? The spirit is willing, but the flesh is weak? I try to keep up my fitness levels with long walks around the hills when I can, but old age is catching up with me. And old wounds don't help!' John laughed.

'It gets to us all, John,' Grace said, smiling.

'Well, enough of my ills. How are you? How's Frank? I haven't seen him in so long.'

'I don't see that much of him now, John.' She paused, glancing at Angela. 'There's been a bit going on. We always were different people. I suppose with hindsight, we shouldn't have married.'

'I'm sorry to hear that. But I don't think I'm surprised. Are you still living in Richmond?'

'No. I've bought a house in Reading, actually.'

'Reading?'

'Further out of London means I can afford a larger place, now that it's just me and Angela.'

'And Frank? Where's he living now?'

Grace frowned, her gaze looking through the window to the sky beyond. 'I don't know. At his club, I suppose.'

'Something wrong?'

'Oh, it's nothing, really. More annoying than anything else. We were burgled two days ago. I just wondered if, perhaps...'

'Did they take anything valuable?'

Grace smiled. 'I don't have anything valuable, John. But I suppose anything's possible.'

'Did you inform the police?'

'No. Nothing appears to have been taken.' Grace drew in a long breath. 'Ransacked the house, though. All the boxes that came out of Frank's old study had been upended. So perhaps they were looking for something specific. He's always been a mystery. Just another reason why I shouldn't have married him.'

'Think of it this way, Gracie,' John said, patting her hand. 'You wouldn't have Angela or Alistair if you hadn't married Frank.'

Grace withdrew her hand.

'Will Alistair be coming up to Scotland next holidays? I'm looking forward to seeing him again,' John said.

'He isn't at school anymore, John.'

'What?'

'He ran away. He has a job now, so I don't see that much of him either. That's boys for you; they have their own lives, don't they? And the last person they'd tell anything to would be their mother.'

The waitress arrived. 'Which tea would you prefer, sir?'

'Lapsang Souchong, please. Alright with you, Gracie?' John asked.

'Perfectly.'

'And we'll have a selection of sandwiches and some cakes. I expect you call them gateau?' John said, winking at Angela.

The waitress smiled, noting the order, then walked away.

'You do surprise me, Gracie. About Alistair, that is. I'd never have thought he'd do such a rash thing. Your father must be very upset. From what you've told me, he was very proud of his grandson being at such an excellent school. What does Frank think of it?'

'I don't know, John.'

John paused. 'Come to Scotland, Gracie. Bring Angela. Glenrothie is too big for one man. And Alistair too, when he can spare the time.'

'I'm sure you're much too busy for guests, John.'

'I miss the old days, Gracie. The war, SOE, me and Frank and the others outwitting the enemy. I should've stayed and joined MI5 with the others. Too restless after the war, I suppose. And you? You did your bit in Berlin after the war. Are you sorry to have left?

'I don't miss those days at all, John.'

'I suppose Frank is still working for MI5. Or is it Six?'

The waitress placed a plate of perfectly cut sandwiches and one of small cakes on the table together with a silver teapot. Grace reached for the handle. 'I don't know what he does. It was all a long time ago. Shall I be mother?'

CHAPTER THIRTEEN

Achnacarry

14th January 1966

Days of the week had no names. Neither did months. Nor people. Except Sergeant-Major or sir. Christmas came and went. He wasn't sure exactly when because the daily routine didn't change. All he knew was weather: cold, wet, rain, snow, wind. Night. Day. Someone told him it was now 1966. He'd be seventeen in March. He'd been at Achnacarry three months during a winter that hadn't stopped snowing, neither had the wind eased. Snow drifts, feet thick, and icy freezing water were his life and his world. Despite the severity, he felt fit and strong. He could navigate by the stars and catch and skin a rabbit. He could track and stalk a man and ford a torrent of water using nothing more than a rope. And he could strangle a man using nothing but his hands or cut his throat with a blade. He could also hold his tongue when he had to.

By mid-January, he and his patrol were engaged in daily exercises in the mountains. Today it was sighting and capturing a small amphibious invasion force and interrogating the landing party. Alistair stood on a narrow ledge overlooking the confluence of the River Loy and River Lochy. Below, he could see a landing craft coming across the icy river. He trained the binoculars on it, then panned the instrument down to a narrow unsealed track adjacent to the river and about fifty feet below him, where he expected the small assault force to land. A vehicle was parked there. He waited for the anticipated patrol of men to alight from the lorry. Within a minute, the driver's door opened, and a man stepped out. Alistair adjusted the binocular's focus again. He thought there was something familiar about the man. He was large, with grey hair, and he wasn't wearing an army uniform. This man wore the tweed clothes of a ghillie and carried a shooting stick. Alistair frowned. There was no mistake. Slowly, Alistair replaced the binoculars into his side pocket. He didn't understand it.

Retracing his footsteps, he re-joined his patrol, the small group of men who waited higher up the hill.

'Sergeant-Major,' Alistair whispered. 'There is a lorry parked on the road below. It isn't an army vehicle. There's a driver and possibly a passenger.'

Dick squinted at Alistair. 'Well, Andrew, take two men and take him.'

'But he's a civilian, Sergeant-Major. I know him.'

'Do you now! So what's he doing here?'

'I have no idea.'

'Who?'

'Uncle John.'

Dick made a high-pitched sound like a moaning wind. 'Ooooh! Uncle John, is it? Give me those binoculars.' Alistair pulled the instrument from his leg pouch. Dick snatched them and disappeared further down the track. He was back within minutes.

'Pack up everything. Leave nothing behind. And you, Andrew. Stay here.'

'Sergeant-Major?'

'You heard me.'

'How long should I stay?'

'Be back at dawn tomorrow.'

The patrol left quietly. Alistair could see them snaking their way down the steep incline towards the river. Achnacarry was only a few miles to the east, over Beinn Bhan. While the mountain pass would be covered in snow, it was passable and he didn't need a compass for the return trip to camp. But he had no idea why Dick had wanted him to remain.

As soon as the patrol left, Alistair returned to the ledge where he'd seen Uncle John and the lorry. Dick had taken the binoculars with him, but Alistair could still see his uncle. He was in conversation with the C.O. Captain Mug-Face, as Alistair called him. Alistair bit into his lip. He didn't understand why his uncle was there. The conversation lasted about ten minutes before his uncle returned to the lorry and it drove away. Mug-Face walked away towards the river where a boat was tied up.

As evening became night, Alistair cooked a meal of dried slush in a small mess-tin, then settled himself for another damp, cold night under the stars. At least it wasn't snowing, but what he'd seen perplexed him. And without Dick constantly barking orders, he had the time to think about it. Despite the cold and the uncomfortable terrain, any time spent without the Sergeant-Major breathing down his neck was almost as good as a holiday. His thoughts returned to his Uncle John. He knew the man was a friend of his father's, but why was he here? Alistair remembered the men at the building in Knightsbridge, who all called themselves John. If Uncle John, who wasn't really an uncle, was his father's friend, was it possible he also worked for MI5? Was that why he was here? Mug-Face appeared to know him. Alistair wondered if Uncle John had known he was at Achnacarry. Perhaps his father had asked his uncle to check up on him. That made more sense. But why? His father took so little interest in him that Alistair thought it unlikely his father even knew he was in Scotland.

With the first rays of dawn, Alistair packed up his kit and headed down the ravine. He was bone cold. He stood on the narrow track where the lorry had been parked. Only the depression of its tyre tracks remained in the snow and they were all now filled with icy slush. He glanced up to where he and his patrol had been. He felt sure Uncle John would not have known of his presence there. He walked towards the loch. The boat Mug-face had used to cross the river had also gone. Walking further upstream to where the river narrowed, and using ropes, he forded the partly frozen waters and headed up into the hills heading east.

He arrived back at Achnacarry just on breakfast. He was wet through but he needed food. Joining his group, he ate the hot meal, feeling the porridge radiate through his chilled body. No one, it appeared, had even noticed his absence. Nothing was said, and no explanation was given for the hasty retreat or the abandoned exercise.

An hour later, they had assembled outside the huts.

'You'll be handling weapons today and we'll start with the Browning L9A1,' Dick said, but Alistair's mind was on his uncle. During the previous long night in the mountains on his own, he'd questioned whether he'd imagined it. But seeing Mug-Face with his uncle and Dick's reaction to his uncle's presence on the lonely road convinced Alistair otherwise.

Dick handed out the Brownings and began prattling on about the weapon's attributes. Alistair felt the cool metal in his hand. He knew he should be listening, but the feel of the weapon in his hand felt amazingly natural to him. He'd shot rifles before on Uncle John's estate, but not handguns.

Dick was shouting. 'This is a compact weapon. The magazine can hold ten rounds. It has a disconnect device here and has an external hammer.' Dick's thick fingers moved over the pistol like he was petting a cat. 'It's quick to assemble and disassemble and can kill a man at fifty yards.' Dick swiftly assembled it, then disassembled it. 'Until you can do this in two seconds, you won't be firing it.'

Alistair held the pistol and practiced the action. Much to Dick's amazement, or possibly annoyance, Alistair was the first to master it. Which also meant he was the first to fire it. He could see this annoyed the Sergeant-Major. But he surprised himself by not passing any comment. No wise-crack, no provocative banter. He didn't even smirk. Perhaps, he thought, he was learning not to be such a pain in the backside. Perhaps all this discipline and harsh army training was helping him to grow up after all. He remembered Three Piece telling him he had two eyes and two ears, but only one mouth. Alistair hadn't understood the comment at the time, but he felt he did now. But if Dick thought him a good shot with a pistol, Alistair couldn't wait for the rifle shooting. Uncle John had taught him to shoot deer. He knew he was an excellent shot. With his feet spread, he held the Browning up, his arms straight, his eye lining up the sights and squeezed the trigger, letting off two short blasts. Both bullets hit the bull's eye.

A week later he stood on parade, wearing full kit and ready for the morning's long march in the rain.

'Andrew. Report to the C.O. Now!' Dick yelled.

Alistair stepped back, turned smartly and marched towards the C.O's hut. Over his shoulder, he saw the troupe of men remain at attention, waiting for Dick's instructions about the day's route march. He saw Dick break away and follow him towards the C.O.'s door. 'What have I done now?' Alistair muttered. He knocked at the door and waited. Dick stayed on the porch.

'Enter!'

Alistair marched into the C.O's office and stood to attention.

'It appears you are leaving us. And from your assessment results, it appears you've done well, Alistair.'

'Thank you, sir,' Alistair said. He eyed the C.O. who clearly had always known his name. Alistair recalled the first time he'd stood in front of the C.O's desk, and despite his own rebelliousness, which he believed he still had, he didn't answer back this time.

'I would even go so far as to say that the Sergeant-Major is proud of you. Quite a transformation.'

Alistair allowed a tiny smile. 'Thank you, sir. Sir. May I ask a question?'

'Quinn?'

'John McPherson.'

The C.O. stared at him as several seconds passed. Any semblance of a smile on the man's face vanished. Alistair watched his eyes closely.

'I know no one of that name.'

Alistair could see he was lying. The C.O. reached for Alistair's assessment papers. 'You have considerable ability with knife and firearms, as well as stalking both deer and people. How long have you been with us?'

'Just over three months, sir.'

'Sergeant-Major?' the C.O. bellowed.

Dick came in and took up his customary position in the corner.

'Alistair is leaving us,' Mug-Face paused, then reached for an envelope on his desk. 'Your instructions are inside. Change into the uniform you wore when you came here and leave everything else behind. You can take a pack, but nothing else.'

'Sir.' Alistair waited, but there were no words of a job well done or a celebratory drink in the officer's mess, if there was one at Achnacarry. Alistair turned and left the C.O.'s office. He stood on the veranda, the envelope in his hand.

The rain was heavier now. Behind him, Alistair heard the C.O.'s door open. The Sergeant-Major walked past him but there were no words of congratulations. Instead, the brusque Scot marched towards the men of Alistair's group who had remained at attention while he and the Sergeant-Major had been in the C.O.'s office. Alistair watched them standing in the pouring rain, waiting for Dick's orders. He tore open the envelope. He was instructed to get himself to Edinburgh where he was to meet a professor at the University there. He had no idea why.

Alistair went to the Nissen hut and changed his clothes. As he walked away from Achnacarry, a lorry of fresh-faced recruits was arriving. The Sergeant-Major stood ready to receive them. Alistair grinned. Sergeant-Major Dick had glanced at him, but it was the briefest of acknowledgements. Alistair thought he perceived the slightest of nods from the stern man. Behind him, Alistair heard the C.O's voice. The Captain was addressing the group of men he had trained with. He stood listening for a moment, then smiled to himself; their futures lay with commando units in the British Army. Regardless, there was a sense of déjà vu for him about the parting but even though the paths of these men were unlikely to cross again with his, he felt a sense of pride in having survived Achnacarry with them; that sort of camaraderie that comes from shared hardship. Alistair had to admit that, even though he'd never learned their names, he'd never felt anything like it before. Endless days of exertion and forced marches with full packs, of gruelling assault courses, of running up steep inclines and scaling high cliffs, of wading through waist-high freezing waters and being shot at with live ammunition had had the combined effect of building team morale yet also developing individual courage and the ability to improvise no matter the obstacle.

He'd been a part of something at Achnacarry, but now, although proud of his own achievements, he was on his own again. 'I did it, you bastards,' he said aloud to the air as he walked away, his boots crushing the snow with every stride.

CHAPTER FOURTEEN

Edinburgh

2nd March 1966

Alistair sat by the tiny mullion window in the Professor's rooms high up in the oldest part of Edinburgh University. He gazed out on the stone city. As much as he loved Scotland, he had now been here for the entire winter and he was looking forward to some warm weather. He shivered, then went to poke the coals burning in the smallest Victorian fireplace. Even at Achnacarry, he'd never felt so cold as he did in Edinburgh. He almost longed for the physical exertion on the wild, open hills and the cold wetness of the Scottish Highlands. Six weeks had passed and now the winter was gone. Every morning, sun, rain or snow, to keep himself fit, he ran to the castle, then through the back lanes and steps around the old city, then down to Waverley Railway station and back before lessons began.

'We'll speak only Russian from now on. And you'll move in here for your last few weeks with me so that you are not tempted to speak English,' the elderly professor said.

Alistair felt his whole body groan. He liked the old man, but he was a hard taskmaster and the language had not come easily. He reminded himself that his father spoke ten languages; surely, he could master just one foreign tongue. He had a reasonable amount of French, learned from school, and some Spanish he'd picked up from Delprado, but Russian had proved a wholly different experience. Hours spent in learning long lists of vocabulary, of conjugating verbs, and impossible reflexive pronouns had made the six weeks there seem like eternity and now, for the next four weeks of his time in Edinburgh, his professor wanted them only to converse in Russian. He almost longed to hear Dick's harsh growl.

By the end of March, he talked in Russian, ate in Russian, thought in Russian, dreamt in Russian, and even washed in Russian. So much so that he wondered if he could still speak English.

'I'll miss you. You've been a good student.' The old man smiled. 'Best of luck to you.'

Shaking the professor's hand, Alistair walked away from the university and headed to Waverley Station. Waiting on the platform for the London train, he wondered if London had changed in the time he'd been in Scotland. If London hadn't, he knew he had. The insolent schoolboy had gone. His birthday, only a few days previously, had come and gone with no acknowledgement from anyone. He knew he looked older than his age, but he also now felt it. He was seventeen and fitter than he'd ever been. He wondered if Dorothy would recognise him. So much had happened. His mind went to his school friends: Delprado and the others. They were still schoolboys, their future ahead. He thought about Valerie. He'd like to see her again.

Once on the train, he opened again the letter he'd received from Uncle Laurence telling him to report to Leconfield House in Curzon Street. He wondered if another dry cheese sandwich awaited. Closing his eyes, he dozed as the train rattled south.

Reaching for his pack, he alighted from the train at Euston Station and walked along the platform towards the ticket collector. Standing by the gate was Three Piece.

'You better not have that hood with you this time.'

'Not this time.'

'That's good, because now I could kill you. If you tried.'

Three Piece laughed. 'You're not the only one who's been to Scotland. Jenkins is the name, by the way,' Three Piece said, holding out his hand.

Alistair shook it. 'Forgive me for not saying it's a pleasure to meet you.'

'I've a car outside.'

'Where to this time?'

'Knightsbridge for tonight then Reading. You're going home to mother for a rest.'

'She lives in Reading now? Since when?'

'How would I know? I don't keep tabs on mothers. But you have to stay fit. Lots of running.'

'How long?'

'Not looking forward to time with mummy?'

Alistair pulled up abruptly and turned to face Jenkins square on. 'For your information, I adore my mother. And she's off-limits to you.'

'Understood. To answer your earlier question; anywhere between a week and two months. But you are required to come in every week to the pistol range and language lab. Just to keep your skills honed.'

'Right. Is Leconfield House the building near Marble Arch?'

'Yes. But first you're to go to Knightsbridge. Inform the Duty Officer before you leave tomorrow the day that you'll be in London each week for your practice shoot, then you'll be collected in the underground carpark. It's best this way, just in case anyone's watching you.'

'How do I reach you, Jenkins, if I need you?'

'We can meet each week, if you like, when you come in.'

'Can't wait!'

Jenkins pulled the car up beside the V&A. He handed Alistair an envelope. 'There's some money inside.'

'I thought I'd passed your test.'

'Not a test this time. It's just in case you need something. Your salary will be deposited into your bank account automatically every fortnight.'

Alistair put the envelope into his pack.

'Can you walk from here?' Jenkins asked.

Alistair laughed, then got out of the car.

Jenkins lowered the passenger window and called to Alistair. 'You look well, by the way. Cold climes obviously suit you.'

'No comment.'

Jenkins laughed, then raised the car window and drove away, disappearing into the throng of cars heading back into the West End. Alistair walked past the museum and crossed the road. The streets were crowded and people hurried past. He breathed in the warm air. London in spring! Even though the Londoners around him were still wearing their coats and scarves, he thought it was like a warm summer's day. Colourful flowering plants were beginning to bloom and daffodils filled the parks. Tulips were poking their heads out of the window boxes and railing planters. And best of all, the early afternoon sun felt warm on his skin. It had an instant effect on him, and he smiled. Finding a restaurant, he ate a delicious lunch then browsed the locals shops where he bought a pair of jeans, some shirts and a black leather jacket. Across the road, he saw a fruit shop. He stared at the exotic produce for sale. Buying two oranges, he returned to the street and ten minutes later found the side street, the scaffolding and netting still in place around the entrance to the underground car park. It was just on six.

'Welcome back, Sir. You look exceedingly well, if I may say so, sir,' Dorothy said. She glanced at the oranges. 'We can get those for you, you know, sir.'

'I don't doubt it, Dorothy. I just wanted to do something normal.'

'I understand, sir. How long will you be with us this time?'

'Just tonight,' he said, smiling. He didn't imagine she did understand, but she was a kind woman and he enjoyed seeing her again.

Dorothy smiled and left. He sauntered down to the library and poured himself a whisky.

The taxi pulled up and Alistair alighted at the Reading address he'd given the cab driver; 34 Beechworth Road. It was a newly built, semi-detached house constructed of timber and pebble-dash with a pitched roof and in a mock-Victorian architectural style with a garage, even though, as far as he knew, they didn't own a car. It was exactly the same as every other house in the street. He wondered if his parents had gone completely mad? It was so unlike them. He allowed himself a cynical laugh, then opened the garden gate, walked along the short path and knocked at the door.

Angela opened it. 'Ali!' she shouted, and flung her arms around him. 'Mummy! Come quickly! It's Ali!'

His mother walked into the front hall, a tea-towel in her hands, her grey eyes fixed on him. Alistair looked at his mother. Nothing about her looked different; the same short cropped greying hair, the same expressionless eyes and pale skin.

'Mother,' Alistair said, entering. He kissed her cheek. It felt cold.

'Tea?' she asked.

'That would be nice.'

He had been expecting his mother to berate him for his desertion from school, not to mention his disappearance for more than six months without so much as a telephone call or explanatory letter. But she busied herself with filling the kettle and putting cups on a tray. 'Are you expecting to live here, Alistair?'

He looked at her. 'Father here too?'

'No!' Her answer came quickly and with a degree of finality about it. 'Well? Are you planning on staying? I haven't got a lot of room here for guests.'

'I'll stay a few days, Mother, if that's alright. Just until I can find a flat somewhere.'

'That's as best. Finnish making the tea and pour yourself a cup. I've got to see where Angela is.'

Alistair made the tea and pulled a cosy over the pot. While he'd never expected a warm embrace from his mother, he hadn't expected to feel so unwelcome. Or was it unwanted? She hadn't even asked him where he'd been for the last six months. And she'd even referred to him as a guest. He wasn't sure why it had pierced him so deeply. He knew Angela's needs were all-encompassing and perhaps his mother had nothing left for her other child. He sat at the kitchen table and reached for a magazine. John Greenslade and Caroline Channon were on the front cover.

Angela came running in. She seemed agitated and was wearing a different dress than the one she had been wearing when he first arrived. He didn't comment.

'Who are you?' she said, her eyes flaring.

'Brenda, will you pour the tea?' his mother said as she entered the kitchen, her question directed towards Angela.

Alistair looked at his mother, but didn't speak. He frowned, then stared at his sister. She hadn't only adopted a different dress; it appeared she was a different person.

His sister stared at him, her eyes intently focused on his face. 'You must be Alistair. I have a job. She doesn't.'

'Brenda's referring to Angela, Alistair. It's with a distribution company, folding newsletters and such,' his mother said. 'If you're staying, you'd better find yourself a job, too. I have enough to do.'

Alistair couldn't take his eyes from his sister. He'd always known she was fragile, but schizophrenia was another matter. 'That's alright, Mother. I have things to do as well. Is there a local bus service into Reading?'

'Of course. There's a stop at the corner. Don't be long, if you're going out. Supper is at seven.'

He finished his tea and stood to leave. He wanted to ask her if she'd ever wondered where he'd gone or what he'd been doing. He held her gaze for a second, but she turned away, putting the washed cups and saucers back on the kitchen dresser. Perhaps it was better she didn't know. And with his sister so ill, he knew his mother had enough on her plate. 'I won't be long,' he said. He contemplated whether to kiss her goodbye, but something about her countenance made him decide against it. He walked along the hall. Reaching for his leather jacket, he closed the door, then sauntered down the street.

It was just before seven when he arrived back at the house. They ate together, his mother, his sister, who was Angela again, and himself. There was no mention of either Brenda or his father.

'I've found a room I can rent in Reading, Mother. It's immediately available. I'll move there tomorrow. And I've applied for a job as a salesman selling furniture.'

'That's nice. Your school trunk's in the garage, if you want it.'

That night in bed in his mother's new house, he thought about his family or what was left of it. He felt sadness about his sister and whatever future she had. But he was also angry. Angry about the situation his mother had to deal with alone; anger for his sister's mental state and anger at his father. Where was he while his family was disintegrating? Tomorrow, Alistair intended to find out, and he knew exactly who to ask.

He took the train into London and a taxi to Knightsbridge, then walked to the windowless building accessed from the carpark. He went straight to his room, No. 39, and placed a telephone call to Jenkins.

'Need to see you.'

'What's wrong?'

'Not over the phone.'

'Where are you?'

'Knightsbridge.'

'It's a secure line from there.'

'I'll be at Marble Arch within the hour. You'd better be there.'

Alistair took a cab to Marble Arch. Jenkins was waiting for him on the corner. They walked together along South Audley Street to the corner with Curzon Street, then entered the grey building with the mesh-covered windows and the sliding glass door.

Alistair nodded to the security guard on duty on the ground floor as Jenkins led the way up the familiar stairs.

'I want to speak with my uncle. I'm assuming you know who that is?'

'Of course, but I'm your contact. Everything goes through me.'

'Not this. It's personal.'

'Very well. Come into my office. We can phone Joan McKillick, Sir Laurence's secretary, from there to see if he's in.' Jenkins pressed the button to summon the lift.

Jenkins's office was just as Alistair envisaged it: stark, utilitarian, and neat. Jenkins lifted the telephone receiver on his desk and dialled the extension number. 'Miss McKillick? Is he in?'

Alistair waited.

'Could you please tell him his nephew would like a chat?'

Ten seconds later, Jenkins hung up. 'Can't see you. He's busy.'

'No, he isn't.' Alistair stood. 'He's here somewhere and I will shout until he pops his head out of his plush, wood-panelled office.'

Jenkins lifted the receiver again and spoke to Joan McKillick. 'Can he make an appointment?'

'Tell him I want to see him, NOW!' Alistair bellowed so that his uncle's secretary would hear him.

'Third floor. At the back,' Jenkins said, replacing the receiver.

Alistair decided against the lift. He climbed the stairs two at a time. He didn't knock. A neatly dressed woman sat at a desk. He guessed she was Joan McKillick.

'You can go straight in,' she said, smiling.

'I intend to,' Alistair replied, and headed straight for the door. Without knocking, he pushed it open.

Laurence Dalrymple sat at his desk, a pile of papers stacked to one side. He stood as Alistair entered. 'How are you, dear boy?'

'Cut the crap. I want to see Father.'

'You can't. He's away.'

'He's always fucking away.'

'Calm down, Alistair.'

'Just tell me where he is!'

'I can't!' Laurence sat again at his desk.

119

Alistair stared through the window to the grey skies beyond. He made a mental note that the offices on the third floor didn't have the same mesh coverings on the windows. 'Is he here?'

'No.'

'Where?'

'I can't tell you.'

'My sister is schizophrenic and my mother's at her wit's end. He is needed! It's his responsibility. So where is he?'

Laurance sat down. 'You've signed the Official Secrets Act, haven't you?'

'You know I have.'

'Perhaps it's time you knew.' Dalrymple leaned back in his chair, his expression stern and completely focused on Alistair. 'Your father does a secret job, Alistair. And by that, I don't just mean paperwork. Surely you've realised this! He's away a great deal and speaks multiple languages. You can't be so naïve as to think him a back room clerk.'

Alistair stared at his uncle. What his uncle had just told him hit like a hammer blow. It had never occurred to him that his father was anything more than what he'd always purported to be. 'So where is he?'

'Away.'

Alistair sat dumbfounded.

'He's due back soon. I'll let him know you'd like to see him. I think he'll be pleased to hear it. Where are you staying?'

'Knightsbridge.'

'He'll meet you there.'

'When? A week? Two?' Alistair persisted.

'Not so long. He'll telephone you there once he's back.'

CHAPTER FIFTEEN

London

1st April 1966

Laurence opened the door to the Director General's office and walked in. He took his usual seat, then reached into his coat pocket for his cigarette case and lighter. In one action, he put the cigarette to his lips and cupped his nicotine stained hands around it and lit it. 'Frank joining us?' he said without removing the cigarette from his mouth.

'Yes.'

The Director General glanced at the clock on the wall. A moment later, they heard the door to the outer office open and Frank Quinn walked in.

'Morning, Frank,' Laurence said, his cigarette dangling from his lips.

'Sit down, Frank. Any success in recruiting a replacement for Dieter Stecker?' the Director General asked.

'Morning, Laurence,' Frank said, then turned his face to the Director General. 'Slow on the recruitment front. I've been in Helsinki twice since Stecker's disappearance, but no one's talking. The KGB have those ferries covered. And no one from Estonia even wants to walk beside a stranger, much less talk to them.'

'What progress are we making with turning Vlatkov, then? I don't need to remind you both how much money this is costing us,' The Director General said.

'Not good there either,' Laurence said, drawing on the cigarette. 'The Americans have tried, but according to Max Guzmann, it's slow progress. Every time they think they're making headway, Vlatkov goes cold. It's exactly the same for us.'

'We need someone!' The Director General barked. 'What's been tried so far?'

'Thorne has had a chat with him at several embassy functions. Said Vlatkov seems receptive. Then when he suggests a meeting, Vlatkov either doesn't turn up or has some excuse. Doesn't know if he's just winding us up or terrified to put his foot forward.'

'And the Americans?'

'Who knows! Since Philby and the Cambridge lot, the Americans are keeping their cards close to their chest. They don't trust us. And can you blame them! What we need is a fresh face.' Laurence paused. 'What about Alistair? Vlatkov won't know him. Surely worth a try.' Laurence paused again. 'By the way, Frank; I think I should tell you that Alistair knows you're not a back-room johnny.'

'And who told him that, I wonder?' The Director General snapped, glaring at Laurence. 'You had no right!'

'He had to know. Besides, he would have found out in time. And may I respectfully remind you, it wasn't my idea to bring him in so early.'

The Director General stood. 'The circumstances were right. And don't be too quick to absolve yourself, Laurence. You wanted him here just as much as he wants to be here.'

'Does he know I work for MI6 not *Box*?' Frank asked Laurence.

'No. In fact, I told him you were still away. He asked where, of course, but I didn't say.'

'I suppose we should be thankful for small mercies then, Laurence,' The Director General said.

'Perhaps I could see him,' Frank said. 'You're right; he's not a child anymore. Couldn't conceal it forever.'

'What about Vlatkov? Fresh face, that sort of thing?' Laurence said.

'I feel guilty enough about Stecker's death. I don't want to be responsible for my son's as well. And besides, he's too young and far too inexperienced for something like this.'

The Director General paced about the room. 'Frank's right. He's young and untried. And too fond of an indolent life. The Soviets would have him on the payroll in a day.'

'He didn't touch the money,' Laurence said.

'Regardless. He's inexperienced; and Frank too valuable. If Alistair ever let slip that he knows his father is more than what he's always believed, it could be dangerous for us all, especially Frank.' The Director General paused. Frank and Laurence waited. Laurence reached into his pocket and pulled out a clean, neatly folded handkerchief, then rubbed the lenses of his spectacles. The Director General went on. 'But he could be useful; especially with Vlatkov. From all reports, Vlatkov's a smooth customer. What do we know about him? What are his foibles?'

Laurence put his handkerchief back in his pocket. 'Rank of Major. Has been in the KGB for ten years. Speaks English fluently. Has a taste for the seamier side of London's night life, or so I hear. Has been seen at theatres and restaurants. A bit of a new broom, apparently. While he has been to their embassy in London before now, one assumes on KGB business, he wasn't posted here till recently. In fact, until now, he held a senior KGB post in the Soviet Union's Baltic States sector. Responsible for security there.'

Frank looked up. 'What! So, it could have been this Vlatkov who had Stecker killed. Alistair wouldn't stand a chance against someone of Vlatkov's experience.'

'If Stecker taking those blueprints and photographing them happened on Vlatkov's watch, why would his bosses in Moscow reward him with a plum post in London?' Laurence said.

'Unless it was a reward for unmasking Stecker?' Frank said.

Silence settled in the room for a few minutes. The Director General was the first to speak. 'Vlatkov would know he'd have the upper hand in the relationship. It may appeal to his ego. As I see it, we have two choices: we can keep Alistair on the sidelines at Follow and Report level until we're sure of his abilities and loyalties, or, we take the risk and use his talents at a higher level of involvement.' The Director General glanced at Frank and Laurence. 'Thoughts?'

'I'm all for it,' Laurence said, lighting another cigarette.

'I'm not. He's too young,' Frank responded.

'Why not, Frank?' Laurence said. 'He speaks Russian now, and he's learned how to look after himself. He's your son, after all.'

'I know whose son he is, thank you, Laurence. My life has been one of living on the edge. Always being alert. Always watching shadows. Waiting for the bullet fired from the dark. I don't want that for him. Besides, as you've said, he's hedonistic. The Soviets would only have to dangle enough money and he'd be hooked for life. Or until caught by either us or them.'

'Have you seen him since he got back from Scotland?' Laurence said, stubbing out the butt of his cigarette and lighting another.

Frank shook his head. The Director General scowled at Laurence, but neither spoke.

'I think you'd be surprised. He's really grown up. And not just physically.'

'He's seventeen!' Frank shouted.

The Director General hit the back of the desk chair. 'Only old men become sentimental, Frank. If the boy has talents, we should use them. And may I remind you, he signed the Official Secrets Act. He did so willingly. He wants this as much as anybody.'

'So what now? A father and son team?' Laurence asked.

'Not yet! We'll try him out on his own first. On home soil,' the Director General said. 'Let's test out Vlatkov and see if he's willing to talk to a fresh face. I want to know if Vlatkov's pillow-talk with Miss Channon, and Thorne's fireside chats are just fishing or if there's any truth to him wanting to turn double agent. Either way, that club in Soho is compromised now, what with Greenslade's continued involvement. And who knows? Now that Greenslade has compromised the Channon–Vlatkov connection, perhaps Alistair will have greater luck with him. Give Alistair an alias. Better the Russians don't know Alistair is Frank's son. Get him in the circle. Nothing dangerous! Just low level. Let him attend some parties, especially the ones at embassies. And preferably the ones the Russians attend. We'll see if Alistair can sweet-talk Vlatkov.'

'It can't hurt!' Laurence said. 'There's a party at the Soviet Embassy tomorrow night, actually. We can set him up with an invitation, say he's joining the British Council and could they please add him to the guest list?'

'Good.'

'And what about Alistair seeing Frank?'

'No. Frank's focus must be on the Soviets, and he can't do that if his mind is on Alistair. You go instead, Laurence, and tell Alistair he's to attend the Soviet Embassy party tomorrow night. Jenkins can arrange it. And get Jenkins to show him some pictures of who's who. Make sure he sees a photograph of Vlatkov. And Frank, get some rest, you look exhausted!'

* * *

Alistair sat in his room in Knightsbridge by the phone. He'd waited all morning. His nerves were on edge. He felt like a schoolboy again, the way he used to the night before returning to school for another term of beatings and the leering attentions from older boys and teachers. He sighed heavily. Waiting. He'd never been good at it. He'd rehearsed what he'd say to his father so many times, but now it was really about to happen, he wasn't sure what he'd say when they finally spoke. He stared at the telephone, willing it to ring, annoyed with himself that it meant so much to him. Just before noon, the telephone in his room rang. Even though he expected the call, the shrill ring tone made him jump. He reached for the receiver. 'Hello, father.'

'It's Laurence, Alistair. Your father can't make it.'

Alistair clenched his teeth, then let out a scoffing laugh. 'I should've guessed!'

There was a pause before Laurence spoke again. 'I'd like to take you to lunch. At my club.'

'Ok. When?'

'Why not come now? I can see you there in half an hour. We'll have a drink first.'

Alistair hung up. For several minutes, he stared at the telephone. He felt empty. And bitter. He wondered why his father's not calling should have annoyed him as much as it did. Perhaps his father was still away? Alistair chastised himself. 'Still making excuses for him, you idiot!' he said aloud to his silk dressing gown where it hung on the stand in the corner. His father was a constant disappointment to him, as doubtless he was to his father. 'Ironic, really,' he said aloud. 'Well, fuck him!'

Dressed in a suit and tie, he grasped his overcoat and scarf and left his room. Leaving via the car park, he took the stairs to the street, walked along Brompton Road, and hailed the first unoccupied cab he saw.

'*Boodles,* please,' he said, closing the door.

'Right you are, Gov,' the cabbie responded. Alistair settled himself in the rear seat. Gov! In his mind, he heard the barman in the pub in Soho where he'd first met Valerie. As the car drove along Brompton Road, he contemplated going there. He pictured her smiling, calling him darling. She would see how much he'd matured and they could be together again. Perhaps he would go. Why not! He was his own master now. He could take a cab to Greek Street after lunch. Who'd know?

Paying the taxi driver, he walked up to the door and was admitted to the private and prestigious club in Pall Mall. It was just on one o'clock.

'I rather hoped he might have been with you,' Alistair said as he and Laurence met in the foyer.

'As I said, he's away at present,' Laurence said.

Alistair grinned. 'Right!' He didn't believe it.

'We have a job for you,' Laurence said, escorting Alistair by the shoulder through the club's quiet luxury to the dining room. 'It's an important one, as it happens. We want you to attend some parties. You know the sort; the ones held in important embassies where you rub shoulders with diplomats and chat with their wives.'

'Who's the target?' he asked. He knew Laurence had diverted the subject away from his father, but it no longer mattered to him now.

Laurence raised his eyebrows. 'So cynical for one so young.' There was a brief pause. 'Let's go in. The beef wellington here is marvellous.'

Just after four, Alistair left *Boodle's*. He'd consumed a good deal of alcohol in the three hours he'd been with Uncle Laurence. Standing on the pavement in Pall Mall, he thought of Greek Street. He cupped his hand and smelt his breath. In his head, he heard Valerie's voice; *do not get drunk!* Perhaps not, he thought.

He went instead to the tailor in St James's Street that Uncle Laurence had instructed him to visit and was measured for two handmade outfits for formal and not-so-formal occasions; one black tie, the other white, along with the appropriate waistcoats, shirts, shoes, and accessories. He hadn't paid a penny for what he guessed amounted to well over a thousand pounds, but he guessed Uncle Laurence had telephoned the tailor in advance. Checking his watch, Alistair saw it was nearly six o'clock. He'd enjoyed his time in Piccadilly; just being there and doing little on a beautiful mid-spring day was, he considered, like walking down one of Heaven's streets. London, a city filled with life, brimming with excitement and well-heeled people frequenting the Piccadilly shops and arcades where almost anything could be purchased from militaria to diamonds the size of golf balls and every size in between. It was about as different as could be imagined to the bitterly cold and desolate Scottish Highlands. Hailing a cab in Jermyn Street, he returned to Knightsbridge in time for supper.

Sitting in the library in Knightsbridge, Alistair poured himself a whisky and thought about his Uncle Laurence. In the three hours he'd sat with him at *Boodle's*, his father hadn't been mentioned once. While the revelation that he was more than a back room hack had surprised Alistair, the man who was his father remained a complete blank. All Alistair knew was that Frank Quinn, if he cared about his family, was nowhere to be seen. It was as though he didn't even exist.

It was already after nine when Alistair heard the knock on his door. Opening it, he saw Jenkins standing in the corridor.

'It's late for the Civil Service to still be at work, isn't it?'

'Ha! Ha! I have some photographs to show you.'

'Really! I wouldn't have said you were the type, Jenkins.'

Jenkins pulled a contemptuous face.

'Library, I think,' Alistair said, and reaching for his jacket, he closed the door to No 39. They walked downstairs. Two men sat further away, both intent on the evening newspapers. Drawing up two chairs, Alistair waited while Jenkins pulled a folder from his briefcase and laid some photographs out on the coffee table for him to study.

'This is the man you need to talk to,' Jenkins said, pointing to one photograph.

Alistair picked it up and stared at it. 'Name?'

'Vasali Vlatkov.'

'What's his position at the Soviet Embassy?'

'Cultural Attaché.'

'And really?'

'KGB officer. Rank of Major.'

'Has he been approached before?'

'Good question. Yes. By both us and the Americans. Their attempt was unsuccessful, and it looks like ours is too.'

He held Jenkins's gaze. 'Why?'

'The Soviets use an acronym for approaching a potential asset that we pretty much follow, too. M.I.C.E. Money, Ideology, Compromising material, and Ego. The first and the last usually go together.

If that doesn't work and you're uncertain about their ideological affiliation, then it's compromising material or behaviour. Quicker and almost always works.' Jenkins leaned back in the comfortable chair and reached for his whisky glass. 'But, as I said, it's been compromised.'

'What went wrong?'

'The escort who was passing information to us about Vlatkov has been seen with a prominent member of parliament.'

'John Greenslade?'

'You know about that?' Jenkins asked.

'I've been in Scotland, Jenkins not Siberia.' Alistair paused, his gaze on the photograph of Vlatkov. 'I've met her; Caroline Channon, that is. She was at The Club in Greek Street with this man,' Alistair said, flicking the edge of the photograph.

'What! You've met him?'

Alistair nodded. 'Not officially. And no names, of course. Does it make it easier or more difficult?'

'Good question,' Jenkins said. 'Let me think.'

Alistair waited.

'If your information about the Krays hadn't been spot-on, I may not have believed you. Would he recognise you?'

'Unlikely. He only saw me for a few seconds. Besides, I didn't have a British Army hair cut then and, who would expect to see a gawky teenager from a brothel in Greek Street at a Soviet Embassy cocktail party dressed in formal attire from St James's?'

Jenkins raised his eyebrows. 'Well, put that way.'

'Worth a shot, at least.'

'As long as it isn't directed at you.' Jenkins glanced at the photos. 'I'll come too, but don't approach me or even talk to me.'

'Got it!'

Jenkins rolled his eyes.

'And what's my cover?'

Jenkins placed the whisky glass on the table in front of him and reached into his briefcase. He placed a file on the table and took out a single sheet of paper. 'Your name is Bruce Spencer. You work with the Foreign Office. Your role is administrative. You assist our embassy people to move from one location to another; arrange the removalists, book the darling children into good schools and make sure the wives are happy.'

'I can do that,' Alistair said with a wink.

'Yes, I imagine you can. The dress is white tie. Do you have one?'

'Yes, well, I will have. I was in St James's earlier.'

'I'll call him and get him to make it top priority. You'll be able to collect it late tomorrow.'

'Really? When is this party?'

'Tomorrow night.' Jenkins stood. 'Here's the invitation and remember, don't acknowledge me in any way. I'll be watching.'

'Got it!'

Alistair rose late. He spent the day in Knightsbridge studying the photographs and learning the names. Just after five, he took a cab to St. James's. By his appearance, Alistair thought the tailor must have been awake all night with his white chalk and measuring tapes. A team of seamstresses had evidently spent hours creating the suit in so short a time. Thanking the obliging man for being so prompt, he collected both his new evening outfits, then returned to Knightsbridge to dress. Dorothy tied the white bowtie for him. 'You look very distinguished, sir.'

'Thank you, Dorothy,' he replied, smiling.

Dorothy closed the door behind her as she left.

Making sure he had the invitation in his pocket, he took another look at himself in the long mirror. Tall and fit and wearing formal attire, he thought he looked handsome and the patent shoes he considered rather stylish. If someone had told him a year ago he'd look like the person in the mirror, he would have thought them mad. His mind flashed to Delprado and his last memory of the rotund little body hurrying away to catch up with the others heading back to school on the bus. Alistair felt bad about his short co-conspirator and wondered what had happened to him. 'You should've come with me,' he whispered to the mirror. Delprado was probably attending another equally repressive school by now, he thought. 'And certainly not wearing white tie and going to Soviet Embassy cocktail parties.' He tapped his top pocket, checking he had his cigarette case and lighter, as well as the invitation.

Leaving Knightsbridge, he took a cab to the Soviet Embassy. The taxi drew up in the Bayswater Road. From the cab window, Alistair saw Jenkins hand his invitation to the security guards at the gate. Alistair waited a few minutes, pretending to fumble with his fare, while Jenkins moved inside. A minute later, he got out and closed the taxi door, then passed the fare to the cabbie through the window. Turning, his gaze searched for Jenkins. Alistair saw he had progressed in the queue to get in and was walking along the path towards the front door. Alistair joined the short queue. Immediately in front of him was a large man Alistair recognised from the photographs Jenkins had shown to him. Max Guzman was the Cultural Attaché at the American Embassy in Grosvenor Square and also head of the C.I.A. there.

Alistair stepped inside the elegant Georgian building, where everything glittered with more gold and chandeliers than he'd ever seen. Exotic flowers were everywhere and the double-headed eagle stood at the base of a staircase under a portrait of Lenin. Alistair moved along the hall and into a ballroom. He'd never seen so much luxury. He thought it odd, given that the communist ideology dictated that wealth should be shared. He moved into the ballroom and stood near a table holding trays of Beluga caviar. Solemn-faced men with ill-fitting coats and wires in their ears stood around the periphery of the gradually filling room, their arms crossed in front of their bodies, their eyes missing little. Alistair made his way towards a waiter holding a tray of champagne glasses. Taking one, he turned, his eye falling on an astonishingly beautiful woman wearing a low cut, bejewelled evening gown who stood beside the dullest looking man Alistair had ever seen and who he recognised from the photographs as the Soviet Ambassador. He had a thick head of hair, a serious, almost solemn face with wrinkles the depth of crevasses. On the other side of the Ambassador's wife was the man he recognised as Vasali Vlatkov. Alistair made his way towards them slowly, sipping his drink as he went, pretending to be looking at the paintings on the walls of Communist agricultural workers dressed in rags.

'Good evening, madam. Sir. May I offer my thanks for inviting me this evening?' The Ambassador smiled insincerely, the crevasses barely moving, then focused his attention on the next person to approach him. Alistair caught the eye of his stunningly beautiful wife. 'You live in a delightful part of London, madam. Do you enjoy living here?'

The woman smiled. 'It's delightful. Always something going on in the park.' She smiled again, but there was no joy in it. Her eyes shifted to the next person. Moving to his left, Alistair sipped his drink. Vlatkov was beside him now.

'Do I know you?' Vlatkov asked, his eyes boring into Alistair's.

Alistair's heart skipped a beat. 'Bruce Spencer,' he said confidently, returning the penetrative stare. 'I'm with the Foreign Office. Administrative duties. Not a very glamorous job.'

'But considered important enough for your office to see you attend our embassy?' Vlatkov added.

'I arrange the removalists for our embassy staff when they're transferred. Nothing at all exciting, but I suppose my superiors think it desirable for me to know a few people of importance in other countries. It helps get their children places in good schools. Ah! Those school waiting lists! I have to find some way around them.'

'You seem very young to me to have such an important job?'

'Really! I suppose I've always looked younger than I am. But thank you for the compliment.'

'Perhaps you should meet our removalist, Mr Spencer?'

'I'd be most grateful,' Alistair added, hoping Vlatkov was talking about furniture and not one-way trips to the seabed.

'Do you have a card?' Vlatkov asked him.

'I don't. Remiss of me to forget some. Not used to all this,' Alistair said truthfully and gesturing around the room.

'Then take mine.' Vlatkov held Alistair's eye a second or two too long.

Alistair took the card and pocketed it, trying to hide his nervousness. 'Thank you.'

Vlatkov walked away.

From the opposite side of the room, Alistair saw Jenkins engaged in conversation with an Italian-looking man. He reached for another glass of champagne as the waiter passed him. From the brief conversation with Vlatkov, Alistair couldn't tell if the Russian had recognised him or not. He drained the glass, wondering if he should leave.

'I don't think we've met, have we?'

Alistair turned around. It was the American.

'Max Guzmann,' the man said.

'Bruce Spencer.'

'Sure. If you say so.' Guzman leaned in. 'I don't know who you are, buddy, but know this. It's been tried before. And by better than you. You're wasting your time.' Guzman shook his head slowly. 'When will you Brits learn? Vlatkov won't turn!'

Alistair took a cab back to Knightsbridge. He felt defeated. But above all, he felt like an amateur. He alighted at the V&A and walked towards his building. It was just after eleven, but he was much too wired to sleep now. He needed a drink. He thought of Valerie. He needed that, too. Perhaps he could go out again. The Club would only just be coming alive. He was about to hail another taxi when he saw Jenkins across the road. His handler appeared to be waiting for him. 'Just what I need, a debrief at this hour!' Alistair mumbled and crossed the busy road, joining Jenkins on the footpath.

'Don't chastise yourself too much. You did alright for a first time.'

'How did you know?'

'Guzmann said he'd spoken to you. The important thing is whether Vlatkov recognised you.'

'Not sure.'

'What do you mean, not sure?'

'He gave me his card. Said he could introduce me to their removalists. Wasn't sure he was genuine or warning me off.'

'Only one way to find out. Call him Monday morning. But then you should have a weapon. Come to Curzon Street tomorrow.'

CHAPTER SIXTEEN

London

4th April 1966

Alistair dialled the number on Vlatkov's card. He heard the clicking and crackling of telephone lines being intercepted, traced, and monitored. 'Hello? Vasali?'

'Who is this?' a deep-voiced official said.

'Can I speak to Vasali Vlatkov? It's Bruce Spencer here.'

'Wait.'

Alistair smiled at Jenkins, who was listening to the conversation.

A minute later, Alistair heard the receiver being picked up. 'Mr Spencer. What can I do for you?'

Vlatkov's voice.

'We met last Saturday evening. At the embassy. You said to call. I'd very much like to speak to your removalist. As well as yourself, of course.'

'Of course. Why not come here. You know where we are.'

Jenkins was shaking his head vigorously.

'Great. When?'

'Why not this evening?'

'Excellent. Should I dress in white tie again?'

'That won't be necessary, Mr Spencer.'

'Bruce, please.'

'Shall we say eight o'clock?'

'Eight it is.' Alistair hung up.

Jenkins stared at him, his eyes wide. 'Are you mad! You can't go! If Guzmann spotted you, and Guzmann's not that bright, count on it, so did Vlatkov. It's a trap, Alistair.'

'What do you suggest, then?'

'At five to eight ring back and say you can't make it.'

'Ok. Ok! I've no wish to end up in some Siberian gulag. Don't worry, Jenkins. It's not good for the complexion, you know.'

'Bloody hell.'

'Go home. I told you, I won't meet him.'

Alistair walked with Jenkins to the tube station at Marble Arch. He watched his handler descend the steps into the underground. Waiting a few minutes, he crossed Oxford Street, then caught a bus that took him along Bayswater, alighting just beyond the Soviet Embassy at Notting Hill Gate. He crossed Bayswater road and walked back towards Kensington Palace Gardens. From his position on the opposite side of Bayswater Road, he could see the Soviet Embassy, a curious mix of Gothic and Georgian yet an elegant building surrounded by hedges and black iron railings. The thick shrubs and tall trees made it difficult to see into the grounds and what windows could be seen from the street were covered with curtains or blinds. The illuminated red flag was flying on a pole outside the residence. The whole place exuded a feeling of separation, almost exclusion, certainly intimidation. He watched the embassy for a few minutes, wondering if he should keep the appointment and just present himself to the guards at the gate. A minute later, the gate opened. Alistair stood and waited. He lit a cigarette and saw a black car drive out of the embassy compound, turning left into Bayswater Road. He watched the car as it waited to merge into the traffic. Then something unexpected happened. The rear passenger window opened and a cigarette butt was tossed from the window onto the road. In that split second, Alistair saw the face of Vasali Vlatkov. The man had held his gaze for no more than a second longer before the window closed. The car continued on, turning left again into Palace Gardens Terrace.

Alistair watched the burning cigarette roll over the bitumen, the lit end still glowing. 'Russian cigarettes!' he muttered, remembering the heady aroma. Filled with dichromate, doubtless to keep them lit during bitter Russian winters, the taste was delicious. Stronger than the Virginian tobacco of Western cigarettes, they were more like a bold French tobacco. The only Russian cigarette he'd ever smoked had been at The Club. He frowned, wondering if it had been Vlatkov who'd left a packet there. Alistair checked the road. In both directions, traffic lights had halted the evening congestion and cars and buses were stationery. Seizing the opportunity, he ran across the road towards the tossed cigarette, picking it up as he ran. He wondered if the Soviet KGB officers inside the embassy were watching. He thought they must be having a good laugh watching a desperate Londoner run after a Russian cigarette. Holding it between his fingers, he pinched out the burning end and hurried on towards Kensington Palace Gardens. Putting the cigarette to his lips, he lit it and drew back, his lungs ready for the heavenly taste.

He spat the butt from his mouth. Small wonder Vlatkov had thrown it out, he thought. He stared at the cigarette, the image of Vlatkov sitting in the rear of the vehicle replaying in his head. It had been only a fraction of a second, but he was sure they had seen each other. Squeezing the end quickly, he extinguished it. The remaining dichromate and the smallest amount of tobacco fell onto the pavement. He frowned. Turning the cigarette over in his palm, he saw it contained neither a filter nor more than a few flakes of tobacco. Carefully, he unrolled the fragile paper. Standing under a streetlight, he read the note rolled up within the cigarette paper. He looked around him to see if anyone was watching him. In the darkness, he saw no one. He re-rolled it quickly and placed it carefully into his pocket. Backing away from the glare of the overhead light, he hurriedly returned to the Bayswater Road and hailed a taxi.

Alistair ate his supper alone in the dining room at Knightsbridge. He felt exhilarated that Vlatkov wanted to make contact; the note had requested a rendezvous in a week's time at some dam near the Finnish-Soviet border. Where Guzmann and others had failed, he'd succeeded. He wondered if he should contact Jenkins immediately. He checked his watch, already well after nine. There was nothing to be done now. If Vlatkov was returning to Mother Russia on a late flight, any attempt to stop him would alert the Soviet officials to Vlatkov's intentions as well as MI5's. And the rendezvous in a week's time would not take place. Doing anything at this stage could be catastrophic for Vlatkov and possibly also for himself. He'd see Jenkins in the morning, anyway.

Alistair sauntered into Jenkins's office and sat in the chair opposite his desk. It was just after ten.

'Afternoon,' Jenkins said, looking up from a stack of files on his desk.

Alistair ignored the slur. 'Vlatkov's gone.'

Jenkins stared at him. 'What! I told you; you were not to make contact.'

'I didn't. Well, not really.'

'What does that mean?'

'I was standing in Bayswater Road last night. Just before eight o'clock, a car pulled out of the Soviet Embassy. Vlatkov was in the rear.'

'I'm not even going to ask why you were there. Did he see you?'

'I think so. Possibly.'

'Bloody hell, Alistair! You've just compromised everything. Sir Laurence will not be happy.'

'Oh, I think he will be.'

'What do you mean, he'll be happy? He's going to be apoplectic! It's taken months of careful grooming to get Vlatkov to this point.'

'Apoplectic! I think I'd quite like to see that.' Alistair reached into his pocket. 'This might put a smile on his face.' He handed the partially unrolled cigarette to Jenkins.

'What on earth...'

'Unroll it! Carefully!'

Jenkins blenched as he read the note. He looked up at Alistair. 'He wants to make contact. A rendezvous at 10pm, on April 11th, at the Ivantrankovski Dam on the Finnish-Soviet border. That's in six days. How did you get this?'

Alistair told him what had happened. 'And my guess is that he was on a flight to Berlin last night.'

'Bloody hell!' Jenkins said, his voice almost like praying. He reached for the telephone. 'Miss McKillick, I need to see Sir Laurence. It's urgent with a capital U.'

CHAPTER SEVENTEEN

London

5th April 1966

Laurence closed his office door. Jenkins had been in his office only ten minutes, but what he'd said was beyond extraordinary. Alistair's rather unorthodox approach made Laurence smile. He'd always known the lad had guts, but this went beyond bravado. He checked his smile. It had also been extremely dangerous. Laurence's mind processed what Vlatkov's unusual approach meant. He found it confusing, to say the least. How had Vlatkov known Alistair was there? Coincidence? Playing a hunch that Alistair could keep the eight o'clock rendezvous? Vlatkov would know the Soviet Embassy would be routinely under surveillance by the Security Services, so perhaps the message was not specifically directed at Alistair. Either way, it had been Alistair who'd picked up the cigarette. 'But what game are you playing?' Laurence muttered. Did the Russian really want to defect or work both sides, or was it a trap? Had Vlatkov's KGB bosses become so suspicious of his frequent trips to London's nightclubs and theatres that they'd recalled him? Could it be as simple as that? Going straight to his desk, Laurence telephoned Frank. 'Can you be here in half an hour?'

'Of course,'

'The Director General's office, I think.'

Laurence rang off. Finishing some correspondence, he lit another cigarette. Twenty-five minutes later, he heard Frank's voice in the outer office talking with Joan McKillick. Stubbing out his cigarette, he went to the Director General's door and knocked.

'Come in, Laurence.'

Laurence opened the door and went in. Frank was already sitting there. He nodded to Frank and sat down.

'Alistair has been contacted by Vlatkov,' Laurence said.

'What?' The Director General said.

'He was watching the Soviet Embassy last night apparently and Vlatkov made contact with him.'

'How?' Frank asked.

Laurence told them what he knew.

'There's no way he's keeping that rendezvous. They're on to him. He'd be dead before he even left the hotel on Pohjoisesplanadi.' Frank's mind was racing. Vlatkov had requested that Bruce Spencer meet him in Finland. Did they know the name, Bruce Spencer, was an alias? Was it possible they wanted to compromise Alistair, or worse? There was another possibility. 'Is it conceivable the Soviets orchestrated for Dieter to pass on those plans then killed him to make it look genuine?'

'Why would they do that?' Laurence asked.

'The only reason I can think of would be to either plant misinformation or to compromise someone.'

Laurence stared at his boss. 'Could they have learned of Frank's true position with SIS?'

'Unlikely,' Frank said.

Laurence frowned. 'If they wanted to compromise Frank, who would tell them about him when even his own son didn't know?'

'They'd have to have a description and photograph of me.'

'So what now?' Laurence said.

The Director General paced the room. 'Alistair keeps the rendezvous. But we send a back-up support team with him. Jenkins can arrange it.'

Frank glared at the head of MI5. 'What! He's too inexperienced! And look at what he's just done. Without back-up. He's unpredictable. No one here knew where he was. If the Soviets had seen him, he'd be dead by now.'

'Not on our soil!' Laurence said.

'Don't be naïve, Laurence,' Frank said.

'It must go ahead!' The Director General said. 'It's the first and only time Vlatkov has taken the bait. We cannot lose this opportunity. Besides, it's just a rendezvous. Jenkins will be there if anything goes wrong.'

Frank stood. 'I don't like! But, I concede it is an opportunity too good to miss. So, I'll go too. But I have one stipulation.'

The Director General looked at Frank, the frown deep. 'What?'

'Only you two know I'm there. No one else! Especially Alistair.'

* * *

Vlatkov stepped into the General Moshenko's office and closed the door quietly. Standing to attention, he waited for General Moshenko to look up. His nerves were on edge. The late night flight from London to Berlin, then another to Moscow, meant he'd hardly slept before his ten o'clock appointment with his superior.

When Moshenko did look up, his face was stern, his jaw set firm. 'I hear you have a liking for the nightlife of London, Major Vlatkov. You disappoint me! And I had such high hopes. Convince me why I shouldn't send you to Irkutsk?'

'I did it for a reason, General.'

Moshenko stood, his eyes glowering. 'And that is?'

'I can get one of MI6's best operatives, General.'

'Who?'

'Frank Quinn.'

Moshenko paused, his eyes widened, then reduced to a mere squint before fixing on Vlatkov. 'And how would you do that?'

'His son, Alistair, works for MI5. I have asked him to meet me next week on the Ivantrankovski Dam wall, General.'

Moshenko leaned back in the chair. 'Why would he come?'

'He is young. Wants to make a good impression. He thinks he can turn me to work for them.'

'And can he?'

'Of course not, General.'

'Why should I believe you?'

'If you allow me to keep this rendezvous, I will bring you Alistair Quinn. Then, I will bring his father.'

Vlatkov waited. General Moshenko stood and paced his office, his large hands clenched behind his back, a thick finger drumming an unheard beat as he walked. 'You think it can be done?'

'Yes, general.'

'Fail me again, Major, and you will regret it!'

'I won't, General.'

Vlatkov left the General's office. His heart was racing. As he descended the stairs to the street, he took several long, deep breaths. His gamble had paid off. At least for now. But if he couldn't get Alistair Quinn to take the bait, Vlatkov wanted insurance. Something that would not only guarantee he was never sent to Siberia, but something so important that he'd be promoted to a plumb job in Moscow. And he believed his Scandinavian contact could provide him with just what he needed.

* * *

Alistair sat in Uncle Laurence's large office on the third floor of Leconfield House. Through the window, he could see the pale blue sky and a gentle spring sun was casting its afternoon glow across the carpet. With him, and grouped around Laurence Dalrymple's desk for the hastily convened meeting, were Jenkins, Bill and Ben, a young woman with a disarming smile, and, of all people, Sergeant-Major Dick.

'Sit down, Alistair. You know Jenkins, of course. These men are Thorne and Harper. This is Miss Ingrid Larsen from our Scandinavian desk who will act as interpreter and, of course, you know Sergeant-Major Cox.'

Alistair clenched his jaw, trying hard to suppress the rising laughter. While he wasn't happy to see the sadistic Sergeant-Major from Achnacarry, who had tormented his life, he was more than delighted to know the man's name. He played with the idea of calling him cock then slowly adding the 's'. But while Dick was at least one generation older than himself, Alistair was in no doubt that Sergeant-Major Cox could kill him in a heartbeat, if he felt so inclined. The memory of Cox's size eleven boot was all too painful. Alistair reconsidered. He decided it was a joke not worth risking one's life over. But he did wonder if, perhaps, the Sergeant-Major's name had dictated his career path.

Laurence leaned forward, his elbows resting on his desk. 'Needless to say, security for this mission is Most Secret. And there's no guarantee that it will net any positive result. Vlatkov, as we know from Alistair, has left England and we presume returned to Moscow. It has been confirmed that he was on the late flight to Berlin last night. His contact with Alistair was, to some extent, pre-arranged, but, again, there was no guarantee it would be acted upon. Vlatkov took a chance that Alistair would arrive for the eight o'clock meeting and notice the cigarette. Therefore, we must assume that he is being watched and monitored closely and he wishes to defect, or his intention could be to work both sides. There is a third alternative, which is a genuine possibility. It could be a KGB attempt to identify and / or remove one or more of our officers. Which is why we are sending you all as a team. Jenkins, make sure you have night vision weapons so that you, along with Thorne and Harper, can be mobile should there be problems with Soviet snipers in the surrounding area. But it will be Alistair who's exposed. He'll be the one standing on Ivantrankovski Dam wall. Sergeant-Major Cox will accompany Alistair to the rendezvous on the dam but remain at a distance with a weapon trained on Vlatkov should anything go wrong.'

Alistair stared at Dick. 'Sergeant-Major Cox. Did you volunteer for this? Or lucky coincidence that you were in London to escort another unfortunate north?'

Cox smiled, but there was no bonhomie behind the yellow teeth. 'Something like this; you, on your own? You'd be mince-meat. Cold, wet places, laddie. Ma' specialty!'

'Still responsible for me then, Sergeant-Major,' Alistair said, but while he knew Cox hadn't answered his question, now it no longer mattered.

'Aye. Something like that.'

Laurence stood, signalling the meeting was over. 'Right! Jenkins will co-ordinate the whole thing. Sergeant-Major, you are to make sure Alistair is covered at all times; his safety is your priority. Thorne and Harper are to act as runners and snipers, if necessary. Miss Larsen is only available for interpreter duties and must not be exposed to any danger whatsoever. Is that understood?'

'Sir Laurence, am I to go to Ivantra as well?' Ingrid asked.

'You can go to the hotel there but under no circumstances do you attend the rendezvous. Jenkins will look after the details.'

Leaving the third floor, Alistair went with his team to Jenkins's plain office on the fifth floor.

Jenkins sat behind his tidy desk and reached for a file. 'Our cover for this operation will be that we are from a British Engineering company hoping to sell turbines for hydroelectricity to the Finnish Government. Joan McKillick will book the flights to Helsinki and arrange the passports. We'll go on separate days. I'll need one day to co-ordinate weapons and accommodation. Miss Larsen and I will go first so I can arrange for some local currency and, with Miss Larsen's help, book the train from Helsinki to Ivantra. Jenkins looked at his desk calendar. We'll leave on April 7th. Then Harper and Thorne on the 8th and, finally, Sergeant-Major Cox with Alistair on the 9th. Once we're all there, we'll meet in Alistair's room at the Hotel Kämp on Helsinki's Pohjoisesplanadi. I'll make sure all the rooms are booked on the third floor. What handgun do you prefer to use, Alistair?' Jenkins said.

'Browning. L9A1.'

'Cox will have the rifle. G3K A4, isn't it, Cox?'

The Sergeant-Major nodded. 'One magazine and a spare will suffice.'

'I should have them all by tomorrow afternoon at the latest. Thorne and Harper and I will arrange our own weapons. Miss Larsen, you'd like to have tomorrow off to prepare, I'm sure.'

'Thank you, Mr Jenkins,' Ingrid said, smiling.

'And remember, everyone, pack warm clothes. It was twenty-five degrees there last night. That's almost minus four if you prefer centigrade.'

CHAPTER EIGHTEEN

London

5th April 1966

Frank sat on the bench in Hyde Park, some sandwiches Joan McKillick had purchased for him in his lap. A warm early-spring sun had brought Londoners out-of-doors. They sprawled on deck chairs or simply lay on the grass, their fair legs in the sunshine, their faces lifted to the celestial radiance. His gaze settled on the nearby beds of budding plants. In the next few weeks, their brightly coloured flowers would fill the garden beds. They always made for a brilliant spectacle. But he didn't feel any joy from either the warm day or the prospect of vibrant blooms. What he felt was tension and profound uncertainty. He reached into his pocket for a packet of cigarettes and lit one, his mind trying to understand how Vlatkov had contrived a rendezvous with Alistair at the Ivantrankovski Dam. It could not have been arranged by someone who the Soviet Union suspected of turning double agent. While Frank knew the dam straddled the border between Finland and The Soviet Union, it was a fragile alliance. The two countries shared a border and a heated past. The Winter War of '39, and the continuing hostilities in the conflicts that followed, had created an enduring and mutual distrust. It was why the Ivantrankovski Dam had two observation towers; one at the western end, controlled by the Finns, the other by the Soviets. Frank pondered the logistics involved in arranging such a rendezvous at short notice. It would surely require co-operation on both sides. Something only the highest level of Soviet intervention could achieve, even if the Finns were willing. And why the Ivantrankovski Dam? The choice of location worried Frank. He thought of Dieter Stecker and the envelope Dieter had died for. Its content, if the Soviets ever learned of it, had the potential to cause a war, one that the West would most likely lose. Britain and Europe simply weren't ready for another conflict. And given the strained relationship with the Americans since the Philby disaster, would the Special Relationship between the two countries continue?

He bit into his sandwich, wondering why Vlatkov had been re-called so suddenly? Could the Soviets have learned that Vlatkov had been approached by not only Britain's Security Services but also by the C.I.A.? Or perhaps Vlatkov had become too enamoured with life in the West? Was it just a straightforward decision by the Soviet government to remove their new boy before he was tempted? While Frank considered nothing the Soviets did was straightforward, why had Vlatkov chosen such a desperate and clumsy method to make contact? Frank closed his eyes. Vlatkov had taken a risk that some-one from Security would be watching the embassy. But why the Ivantrankovski Dam? That was the burning question for which Frank had no answer.

But while his conjecturing was still nothing more than a hunch, he was reluctant to share his thoughts with anyone. He needed information. What if Vlatkov was, and always had been, a loyal KGB agent and his approach to Alistair was an elaborate plan to compromise SIS? Or was it a person? Or persons? Could the Soviets know Alistair was his son? Frank allowed his gaze to settle on some children playing a game of chasing around their parents' deck chairs. He thought of the few people who knew Alistair's real significance. His mind went to the Cambridge five who'd caused such havoc in the Secret Intelligence Service in particular and Britain's security services in general. But none of them had known about Alistair, who would have been just a young boy at school when they defected. Could another as yet unidentified traitor exist? Was there another Soviet mole in the SIS? Or perhaps someone undiscovered in MI5? Frank flicked his cigarette butt away and took another bite of his ham sandwich. He thought of John Greenslade, whose career was on the line because of his infatuation with the escort Caroline Channon. That relationship had destroyed any chance either The Security Service or SIS had of turning Vlatkov last year. Frank stared at the daffodils as their bright heads bobbed in the light breeze. He didn't understand why clever men exposed themselves to such risks. Intelligent men who couldn't control their urges often lost everything they'd worked their entire lives for, for nothing more than a few brief encounters of illicit sex. Frank folded the brown paper bag that had held his sandwich, his mind again on Dieter Stecker, and the blueprints he'd photographed. If the KGB had wanted Dieter to pass on fakes, Dieter would have known they were and told him in the letter. Valuable time had been wasted confirming what Frank had always believed; the blueprints were genuine. Dieter, who guessed he was being watched while in Finland, had sent the envelope to Per Sangolt for safekeeping. Then they'd been brought back into Finland by Per. If the Soviets had known the blueprints had been photographed and where the film had been secreted, Per Sangolt would also have been killed. Frank stood and, tossing the paper bag into the nearest bin, returned to Curzon Street.

'Got a minute?' Frank said, poking his head around Laurence's door. He'd timed his visit to coincide with Miss McKillick's lunch break.

'Frank! Of course, come in.'

Frank sat down. 'Could you find someone for me?'

'Of course. Who?'

'Per Sangolt.'

'Per Sangolt! Now there's a name I haven't heard in a while. Why?'

'Per had the envelope containing the blueprint film in his posses-sion for about a month. If the Soviets knew Dieter had smuggled the film out when he did, did they know he had posted something to Per? If they did, surely they would have killed Per and retrieved the film. Does that mean they didn't know where Dieter sent it? I want to know if Per is alive.'

'We'll find him. But I may not have an answer for you till after your return from Finland. What troubles you about this, Frank?'

'I cannot get out of my head the feeling that Dieter's death, Per Sangolt, the blueprint photographs, and Vlatkov's sudden recall to the Soviet Union are connected. And why does Vlatkov ask for the rendezvous to be on Ivantrankovski Dam? A place where Dieter Stecker visited regularly? In fact, the last dam Dieter inspected.' Frank leaned forward in his chair. 'What worries me, Laurence, is what Vlatkov wants? Is he really wanting to defect? Or is it a ruse? Is it a trap for Alistair?'

Joan McKillick had arranged Frank's flight at short notice for him under the name of Patrick Scully, an accountant from Manchester. Frank sat in the first-class seat on board the early morning Scandinavian Air Service flight for Helsinki. He hadn't slept well these past nights. Something nagged him about Vlatkov's return to Russia. Something wasn't right about it. He leaned his head back on the headrest. It was all too contrived, too coincidental, and much too clever. As the aeroplane taxied out onto the tarmac, he closed his eyes and permitted himself to doze for a few hours.

As Alistair and his team were staying at Hotel Kämp, Laurence had thought it prudent for Frank to stay overnight in Helsinki at the British Embassy, an elegant pink building on Itäinen Puistotie, only a twenty-minute walk from the centre of town.

Frank knew Alistair was due to arrive in Helsinki around three, but he wanted to make sure for himself. At half-past two, Frank left the British Embassy by a rear door heading for the park opposite the Hotel Kämp entrance. He wrapped his coat around him. In England the spring weather had brought warmer temperatures, but in Helsinki, it was still cold and the trees were only just coming into leaf. From time to time, he did a circuit around the park, checking to see if anyone was taking an interest in either him or the entrance to the hotel. He sat on a different bench each time he returned to the Pohjoisesplanadi, always checking to see if the other members of Alistair's team, who'd already arrived in Finland, were anywhere nearby.

A few minutes before three, a bus drew up outside the hotel. Frank stood and crossed the road. Standing by a shop window about a hundred yards to the east of the hotel entrance, he pretended to window shop, staring at the intricately designed Nordic jumpers displayed there. From the corner of his eye, he saw Alistair and Cox alight from the bus, collect their luggage, then go inside the hotel. Frank crossed back into the park, found a suitable bench, sat and waited. He watched the hotel entrance for about half an hour. Satisfied Alistair had not been followed, he left the park.

Now that Frank knew Alistair and his team were all safely in Helsinki, he intended to take the train to Ivantra and wait there. He hastened away, heading towards the Kappeli restaurant at the eastern end of the park to buy a warm drink and something to eat out of the cold and before returning to the British Embassy. Four hours later, he was on the train for Ivantra.

Frank took a room at the top of the four storey Ivantra Hotel at the front, just above the entrance, with a view of the road in. In the twilight, the building, constructed in the early years of the century for tourists, had elegant windows and picturesque turrets and sat close to the river. With its snow covered roof, it resembled a fairy-tale castle. It was only a short walk to the Ivantrankovski Rapids Dam, a large grey concrete structure that Frank considered had all the architectural ambiguity of a joint project; one that was austere in appearance and utilitarian in construction.

He spread the map of the Ivantra district out on the bed. Approximately one mile to the east of the dam lay the Soviet Border town of Svetlovorsk. Frank knew it would be well guarded and patrolled by men and possibly dogs. Meetings in such a place between anyone, let alone foreign agents, would not go unobserved. How had it been arranged? Alistair aside, Vlatkov himself would need Soviet backing to get to the remote border outpost, then approach and walk onto the dam. Many things about this mission worried Frank; there were just too many threads, none of which had certain outcomes. He wondered if Vlatkov would entice Alistair across the dam to Svetlovorsk. There, Alistair would be completely vulnerable. Frank decided to reconnoitre the area. He needed to be as familiar as possible with both the Ivantrankovski Dam and the country to the east.

He sat by the small window in his room, waiting for darkness to descend, his binoculars already on the windowsill. He thought about his son. Alistair was too young. Just seventeen. Not even old enough to vote. Yet old enough for both MI5 and MI6 to ask him to do this insane thing. Was that why Vlatkov had requested Alistair? Because he was young, he would unwittingly fall into their trap? But why take him? He knew nothing useful. Unless they knew his true identity. Frank shivered. If they did and Alistair survived months in the Lubyanka, he would be used as a trade.

CHAPTER NINETEEN

Helsinki

Finland

9th April 1966

Alistair walked into the elegant Hotel Kämp. Its luxurious interiors, marble columns and graceful staircases were an instant reminder to him of the building in Knightsbridge, but this was on a grander scale. And a far cry from Achnacarry. He collected his key from reception and left Jenkins in the foyer, talking to Cox. Looking up, he saw Ingrid walk into the hotel carrying several shopping bags. 'Can I help you with those?'

She smiled, and they went to the lifts. He noted his room was only a few doors away from hers. Carrying the bags, they walked in silence towards her room. Smiling, he opened her door, took the bags in and placed them on the bed, then turned to leave.

'Thank you,' Ingrid said, smiling.

'My pleasure,' he replied, watching her. He left her to find his own room.

Alistair heard the knock at his door. Opening it, Jenkins and the others filed in. Jenkins, as the senior man present, took the chair by the window. A minute later, Ingrid joined them, sitting with Alistair on the bed while Cox, Thorne and Harper stood.

Alistair felt the proximity of Ingrid's body. Even though they weren't touching, warmth seemed to flow from her, and he thought of Valerie. Jenkins began to talk, but Alistair's mind was elsewhere.

'I've booked the train to Ivantra,' Jenkins said, handing out the tickets. 'We'll take the 8.45am tomorrow morning, but we'll travel in three groups. Alistair, you and Ingrid will go together. Cox with me, then Harper and Thorne. We'll all be on the same train, but no mingling between groups.

'And no mingling within the groups,' Cox said, his penetrative gaze squarely on Alistair. 'I'll be right behind you, laddie.'

'Once in the hotel,' Jenkins continued, 'we don't meet up till I contact you. Then we meet in Alistair's room. Tonight you are free to move around but, don't leave the hotel and don't drink too much. We have an early start tomorrow and I don't want anyone missing.'

Alistair held the door as the team filed out of his room, making sure Ingrid was the last to leave.

'Drink in the bar before dinner?' he whispered into her ear.

'I don't think we should. Mr Jenkins may not like it.'

'If we are to be travelling together tomorrow, it's best I know something about you.'

'I suppose so.'

'See you downstairs then, in an hour?'

She nodded.

The bar was bustling when Alistair entered. Checking any mirrors didn't reflect his image to the ever-watchful Cox, he selected a booth to the left of the door. In his mind, he saw Valerie, when they'd first met; the way she watched the room from the mirror in front of her. He believed what he'd learned from her had made him a man in more ways than one.

Ingrid walked into the bar. To say she was stunning was an understatement. She looked glamorous and sophisticated, her lightly tanned skin making her long blonde hair almost gleam. She turned. Standing, he smiled at her then gestured towards the table, his smile broadening.

'I've ordered champagne. I hope that's acceptable?'

She nodded and slid into the seat beside him. 'May I ask you a personal question?'

'Of course. I may, however, choose not to answer it.'

She grinned. 'How old are you?'

'Don't worry. It won't be carnal knowledge.'

Her eyebrows rose. 'You're very self-assured, aren't you?'

'I had an excellent teacher.'

They sipped champagne. Forty minutes later, Alistair was in her room on the third floor. It was nicer than his, but he expected it to be. Jenkins, who'd booked the rooms, was old school. Alistair wondered if his handler had desires of his own with Ingrid. But old school didn't cut it now. This was the sixties! Girls didn't wait for marriage proposals anymore. Alistair moved towards her, their eyes locked onto each other. Holding her in his arms, he unzipped her dress.

At seven, Alistair and Ingrid took a table in the dining room near the long arched window. He could see the street. People were out of doors and already the evening crowds were gathering. The Kämp hotel, it appeared, was a favourite meeting place for the well-heeled.

'Where were you this afternoon, or need I ask?' Cox said, his eyes shifting to Ingrid. 'No more disappearing or this mission is off. Jenkins is furious.'

Jenkins, with Thorne and Harper, entered the dining room and took a table one away from Alistair. As Jenkins passed Alistair, he dropped an envelope onto the table.

'Well, it's been great seeing you again, laddie,' Cox said loudly and slapped Alistair on the shoulder with a little too much force. He went to sit at a separate table for one by the door to the kitchens, where his Gaelic eye could watch everyone.

Alistair opened the envelope. 'Our room numbers in Ivantra. Consecutive!' Alistair said, a smile crossing his lips.

'If I didn't know better, I'd say you arranged it perfectly.'

He poured the champagne.

Alistair walked with Ingrid to her room. Sergeant-Major Cox stood about three feet away from them. Alistair rolled his eyes. 'See you in the morning.'

Ingrid winked, tightened her lips and blew an air kiss to him.

Cox moved forward. 'We'll say good night, Miss Larsen.'

Cox lead Alistair under the arm to his room further along the corridor. When Alistair opened his bedroom door, Jenkins was inside.

'What the hell are you playing at?' Jenkins said as Alistair entered, Cox right behind him.

'Getting acquainted.'

'Box isn't picking up the bill for French champagne.'

'Oh, I think they will. Besides, who's going to tell them?'

'And no fraternising with Miss Larsen.'

'You booked us to travel together. We were just getting acquainted.'

'Well, that's enough of that. As I once told you; what we do is serious and you are too flippant. You'll end up in trouble and we're the ones who'll have to get you out of it.'

'Keep your shirt on, Jenkins. I'll behave. For now.'

'Get some sleep. You must need it after such a busy afternoon.'

'And I'm next door. No escaping!' Cox said.

Alistair woke, then checked his watch. He'd slept well. Dressing, he went downstairs, hoping to see Ingrid. Cox was the only other member of the group in the breakfast room. Alistair avoided him, taking a seat at the table for two by the window. From there, he could see the park. While technically spring, Helsinki had had a dusting of snow overnight and the park looked amazing. Conifer trees were festooned with snow and sparkling icicles glittered in the pristine morning sunshine. Jenkins was the next to enter. He made straight for Alistair's table and sat down.

'Come to my room in twenty minutes.'

'I had no idea..?'

'Shut up! I've got the Browning for you.' Jenkins left to get breakfast from the buffet. Alistair smirked as he watched Jenkins fill his plate. What was it about Jenkins? At times his tongue could be acerbic while at other times the man was almost fatherly towards him, fussing like an old hen. Alistair glanced around at the other guests in the dining room. Mostly middle-aged couples. And, he believed, all Finnish. Perhaps Jenkins behaviour was an act, designed to make onlookers believe he was a true British gentleman abroad.

Alistair ate his toast, hopeful that Ingrid would soon join him. He finished his scrambled eggs and ham, then wiped his mouth on the napkin. Ingrid still hadn't shown. He left the dining room, returning to his room to pack his few possessions, then went, as instructed, to Jenkins's room.

'You know how to use this?' Jenkins asked, handing him the pistol.

'Of course.'

'Just don't get scared at the last second.'

'I won't. I'll visualise you holding that hood as I pull the trigger.'

'Not funny.' Jenkins stood.

Alistair took it as his cue to leave. Returning to his room, he checked the weapon, then secreted the pistol into his coat pocket, collected his suitcase and left.

Downstairs, Alistair sat in the foyer and waited for Ingrid to appear. A few minutes later, he saw Jenkins standing at the reception desk, attending to the bill. Thorne and Harper were the next to emerge from the lift. Alistair stared at them. Bill and Ben. He could see the slight bulge of weapons under their coats. But no one else would have noticed. He studied them as they joined Jenkins at the reception desk. He knew nothing about them. They were perhaps in their forties, clean shaven, short hair. Neither wore glasses. They were about as nondescript as two men could be. He didn't even know where they came from or anything about their personal lives. As far as he was concerned, they'd been born old and came from some science fiction world or Madame Tussauds wax museum. The lift opened and Cox stepped out. Alistair knew little about his tor-mentor either, and he didn't care to. Cox was one of those career military types who never leave the army. Most likely thrown out of his own family for being a bully; Alistair believed men like Cox saw it as their mission in life to make other people's lives miserable.

Ingrid stepped into the foyer from the lift. The sight of her almost took his breath away. She wore a long black leather coat with a wide fur collar and fur hat. Alistair thought she looked like a model from a fashion magazine. He stood, grabbed his luggage, walked towards her and, taking her elbow, swept her outside, where he hailed a cab.

It was a quick ride. Alistair held Ingrid's hand as she alighted from the taxi. He wanted everyone to see him with such a goddess. Smiling, they walked as a couple into the railway terminal. For one second, he felt as he had when Valerie had found him in the bar in Soho, only this time he was doing the leading. Making their way to the platform, Alistair saw the train for Ivantra was already there, and people were boarding. He handed their tickets to the guard at the gate, then ushered Ingrid along the platform, weaving his way through the piles of luggage. From the corner of his eye, he saw Cox and Jenkins arrive. They were about twenty feet from him, with Harper and Thorne a further ten feet behind them. Jenkins had a newspaper under his arm.

'He's pretending to read Finnish. As if,' Alistair whispered to Ingrid.

The train rattled along, crossing low country and so many lakes Alistair lost count. He decided Finland was either an ocean with hundreds of islands or a country with more lakes than could be counted. But it was tantalisingly beautiful, the colours vibrant like something from an artist's paint box. By early-afternoon, they arrived at Ivantra and made their separate ways to the hotel and took their rooms on the second floor.

Alistair's gaze scanned the foyer for surveillance cameras or Soviet informants. People were everywhere. Some, like them, were checking in; others, most likely tourists, were there to see the fairy-tale castle-like building, and for some it was just a respite from the cold and a warm drink. While he didn't see anyone suspicious, he didn't really know who he was looking for. Perhaps a Soviet version of Bill and Ben. He decided that as Jenkins was there, fussing again like a boy scout leader, he didn't need to worry about it. Alistair collected their keys, then went to the lifts. Ingrid was at his elbow.

Stepping from the lift, he cast his eye around the corridor, again checking for any surveillance cameras, but he saw none. He thought that as the hotel was so close to the Soviet border, the absence of surveillance cameras in the public areas would make it more likely that some form of electronic surveillance may be installed in the rooms.

He opened Ingrid's door for her. 'I'll leave you to settle in. Just knock on the wall if you need anything.'

Once inside his own room, he put his luggage on the stand, then checked the light fittings and lamps for any listening devices, then inside the radio and clock. There was no television in the room.

Satisfied that it was clean, he stared through the window. Jenkins had arranged for them all to be on the second floor, but each of the men had a room on a different side. Alistair's looked towards the front. He could see the river. He stared at it for some minutes. A knock at his door made him turn. He beamed, hoping it was Ingrid. Jenkins stood in the corridor, Cox behind him. Alistair held the door wide, but neither came in.

'Maps of the area. Study them! And if you're not too busy, check the Browning and ammunition in your pack. See you at dinner.'

Alistair left Ingrid's room and went downstairs. It was already mid-afternoon. Checking the foyer and reception area, he located the bar, then the dining room. Somewhere within the hotel, he could hear an amplified voice. An entertainer was speaking rapidly in Finnish, his audience laughing heartily. Alistair cast his eye through the glass panel into the dining room. It was empty except for one waiter, who was setting up the tables to prepare for the evening meal. Alistair watched him come and go between the restaurant and the service area. Leaving there, he crossed the foyer and stepped outside. A cold wind blew over him and he pulled up the collar of his coat around his neck. Above him, the sky was a clear soft blue, but the temperature was falling to somewhere around zero. It promised a clear night. And a cold one. He shivered into his coat, then shoved his hands into his pockets. Descending the front steps, he walked along the road, away from the hotel. Five minutes later, he turned to see if anyone had followed him. He lifted his gaze. A man stood at one of the upper floor windows, binoculars covering his face. From the angle of the instrument, Alistair believed the man was looking out over the snow-tipped trees of the nearby forest and thawing river. It was a pretty sight. Alistair turned, his gaze taking in his surroundings, then walked back towards the hotel, turning again just as he passed the rear of the building. He did a complete circuit of the hotel, returning to the service and staff entrance. It was the only external entrance or exit unavailable to the public and paying guests. Directly behind this area was a car park where a few cars waited for their owners; behind that, a forest of trees extended to the rear and western side of the hotel. Returning to the front of the building, he walked towards the river and stared into the partly frozen expanse. The riverbanks were steep and snow clung to the edges. In the still air, and beneath the melting ice, he could hear the quick, high-pitched trickle of thawing water. He looked back at the hotel. He wanted to see the dam before nightfall. Hurrying, he set off along the road, increasing his stride as he went. The road was wet and ice and snow sat in drifts beside the jagged-edged bitumen. Twenty minutes later, he saw the Ivantrankovski Dam.

It was impressive and profoundly intimidating. On the wall were two observation towers. Both looked formidable structures and were each easily large enough to secrete a patrol of men. Two large spillways swept away from the dam's edge to the river below. Large patches of snow and ice still clung to the grey concrete, making the frozen water on the spillway resemble two rolls of white carpet. A path, or possibly a narrow road, ran along the top of the dam wall. He pulled the map from his pocket and located the Soviet border town about a mile to the east. His gaze fell on the riverbed below the spillway. It was rocky, with large boulders protruding above the remnants of partly frozen water. It would be easily forded. When the water was gushing through, firing the turbines and creating electricity, it would be a raging torrent of white water.

He returned to the hotel. Opening the door into the welcoming warmth, he saw Cox sitting in the foyer. Alistair scanned the foyer area; Jenkins et al. were nowhere to be seen. He looked towards the bar. The mirror revealed Ingrid sitting at one of the tables. He walked in and sat beside her.

She smiled at him. He liked Ingrid. He liked being with her. She reminded him of both Misty and Valerie. Although he'd never had sex with Misty. He decided he loved women; their softness, their smell, the way their hair felt on his skin. They ate their supper together. That evening he didn't open the maps Jenkins had left for him to study.

Just before midnight, Alistair crept out of Ingrid's room and returned to his own. He changed into his winter leggings, trousers, parka, and balaclava. Secreting his knife into his boot, he strapped the pouch containing his Browning on his right leg, then checked he had his night-vision binoculars, tools and compass. He then wound a length of rope around his waist and put on his overcoat. Quietly opening his door, he stepped into the corridor. Finding the fire escape stairs, he crept to the lowest floor and pushed open the door. It was a basement corridor that led to the kitchens and other areas rarely, if ever, frequented by hotel guests. Creeping along a corridor lined with stacked dining chairs, he leaned on the door to the kitchens, opening it only one inch. He could hear some of the kitchen staff chatting and calling out their farewells to other members of staff. He waited a few minutes, then entered the now deserted kitchen. As he passed the ovens, he took a large-handled knife from a block on the bench and went to the rear door. He leaned on the handle and pushed the door ajar. A chill air blew into his face. Through the crack, he could see a beam of light over the parked cars. A few of the remaining kitchen staff were getting into a small bus that, moments later, drove away. Alistair stepped outside, then wedged the knife handle under the door, propping it open by less than half an inch. Huddling into his coat, he ran past the cars parked at the rear of the hotel and into the line of trees.

Keeping to the forest edge, he followed the course of the river back upstream towards the dam. It was dark, and the light from the waxing quarter moon barely penetrated the forest floor. He slowed his pace and moved closer to the path that led up to the dam. At the edge of the path, he stopped. In the half blue light of the moon, he could see the opposite bank. It was steep and the tree cover was thick.

Ten minutes later, he stood near the dam. The sight was astounding! Unlike earlier in the day, floodlights now lit up the upper walkway, the observation towers and spillways like a stage. No one could meet on the dam after dark and remain unseen. Eight stanchions supporting huge lights flooded their intense glow over the whole dam wall, their arcing circles of light criss-crossing the entire scene. Two lights, one in each of the observation towers, told him at least one guard would be on duty in each tower. Returning to the tree line, Alistair retraced his steps and chose a site beyond the lights, where the path veered to the right and about a hundred yards below the frozen spillways. He tied the length of rope to a tree on the western side and the other end to his waist and carefully lowered himself down the western bank. Scaling the large boulders that criss-crossed the area below the spillways, he crossed the river to the eastern side, navigating the patches of ice, and clambered up the slippery eastern bank. He crouched in the undergrowth, his breath condensing, his eye scanning the dam, but no one had come out on the wall. He untied the rope and looped it around another tree, then pulled his compass out of the pouch. Checking his position, he disappeared into the tree line. He was in the Soviet Union.

CHAPTER TWENTY

Finnish-Soviet Border

10th April 1966

As Alistair ran through the trees, the overhead branches swayed in the wind, the dappled moonlight flicking ghostly shapes across the forest floor. He hurried on, his footsteps sinking into the fresh snow. Slowing, he checked his compass again. The moving shadows heightened the nerves, making him see shapes that weren't there. His heart was thumping. Heading due east and staying within the forest, he ran for about a mile before he saw the Soviet border town of Svetlovorsk.

He crouched at the edge of the tree line. He could see the lights of the village across a wide, snow-covered field, about three hundred yards away. Svetlovorsk was small, he thought, most likely a farming village, with about a dozen run-down timber buildings, none of them large. A huge watch tower stood about two hundred yards from him, and a little distance from the village. It had large lights illuminating the surrounding area. Beside it was a high, razor-wired gate. From where Alistair crouched, he could see the fences, approximately twelve feet high and topped with more barbed wire. They extended in both directions. The wide open field before him made for a sort of no-man's-land.

Alistair pulled his binoculars from his pocket and trained them on the tower. Two guards kept look out there, their sub-machine guns slung over their shoulders. Crouching on the cold, snow-covered ground, he reached for his watch and waited. Fifteen minutes later, a guard descended the tower and walked about fifty yards along the perimeter fence. Alistair could see the torchlight flashing over the snow then the guard returned and checked the gate, his torch pushed through the wire, the beam of light panning across the area and over the snow-covered road, beyond the reach of the tower lights. Alistair couldn't see any footprints or recent tyre tracks on the road, and he guessed no one had approached the Soviet outpost from the Finnish side since the last thick coating of snow had fallen. The flashlight flicked over the ground, then the guard turned and walked along the fence line, the torch beam constantly arcing over the snow. The guard was beyond the tower light now. He walked on until he was about twenty yards from where Alistair crouched. He held his breath. If he tried to retreat deeper into the forest now, the guard would see him. Alistair lowered himself onto the ground so that his body lay flat, his head down and half concealed behind the trunk of a large tree. Drawing in some cold air, he held his breath, not wanting his warm exhaled air to float away in the cold night. He lay motionless as the torch beam flowed over his head. Then it moved away. Alistair exhaled. He lifted his head. He could hear the guard a little further away now. Silently standing, he crept further into the trees and waited for the man to return to the tower. If the guard had dogs, Alistair believed he would surely have been found. He checked his watch, each time returning to where he could clearly see the guards and time their routine. Four times in the hour, one of the two guards came down the ladder and patrolled the gate and immediate area, always following the same route.

He waited, the temperature reminding him of nights spent on the hills around Achnacarry. Time passed slowly, but he kept his eye on the guards in the tower. Then at one o'clock, both guards descended. Steadying the binoculars, he watched them walk towards a hut about twenty yards away from the tower. They went inside. Pocketing the binoculars, Alistair ran east through the trees beyond the point on the fence line, where he'd seen the guard stop. He checked in both directions. No guards either on the fence line or in the tower. Now or never, he thought. Hunching low, he crossed the open space. He knew he couldn't conceal his footprints in the snow, but if the guards continued to follow the same routine, where he'd crossed the open field wouldn't be seen until daylight. Retrieving the pouch of tools he'd attached to his belt, he cut into the wire, then folded a section of it back and crawled through. His heart was racing. He had little time. Even though he'd been on Soviet soil for several hours, if he were seen now, he'd be shot. Hunching low, he ran towards the village, keeping the road to the border gate on his left. Once beyond the guard's hut and staying on the village side of it, he crossed over, then ran back towards the hut. Covering his mouth with his glove, he drew in several deep breaths and squatted on the ground beside the hut, just below a window. Inside, he could hear several men's voices. They were laughing. He listened. Their Russian was quick and, in parts colloquial, which he didn't fully understand. He heard them complaining about the cold snap so late in spring. He stood slowly, his ears straining, a frown on his forehead. He stared at the snow, his mind concentrating on their conversation. Then he heard them discussing some soldiers they'd seen on a reconnaissance mission they'd done into Finland. Alistair frowned. Why had Soviet guards gone into Finland? Surely that was illegal? From what he could make out, they'd seen some soldiers wearing a plain uniform coming and going from an underground bunker on the western side of the river. But was that unusual? Surely, Finnish soldiers would be stationed on the border between a democratic country and the Soviet Union. So why were these guards so surprised by what they'd seen?

Two minutes later, he heard the hut door open. The relief guard was coming on duty. Remaining where he was, he held his breath and waited several minutes for them to walk the twenty yards towards the tower. Creeping to the end of the hut, he edged his head around the corner. He could see the men walking towards the ladder to the tower. He crept back to the window and listened. He heard the crackle of radio hash, then the voice of one guard reporting in. From what Alistair could overhear, someone, whoever this guard was talking to over the radio, must have asked about any sightings of Finnish soldiers. The guard had said they hadn't seen any more soldiers during their time in the tower. Alistair checked his watch. He needed to get back if he was to time his return to fit the guard's routine.

Leaving the hut the way he'd come, Alistair returned to the forest and found the hole he'd cut in the wire fence. Crawling through, he folded the wire back into place and threaded some wire along the cut, then, again checking his watch, ran the short distance over no-man's-land into the trees. Half an hour later, he retrieved the rope from the tree on the eastern side of the river and crossed the exposed boulders back into Finland. Whilst he felt exhilarated at having been in The Soviet Union undetected, he was relieved to be back on friendly soil.

He'd been gone around five hours and his body yearned for warmth. Entering the hotel around five, he made his way through the kitchens, silently closing the door and replacing the knife before making his way to the second floor. Changing his clothes, he left them over the radiator and slipped into bed.

'When is sunset?' Alistair asked Jenkins, while filling his plate with French toast and ham.

'Does it matter? We'll be on that dam wall tonight at ten, regardless,' Jenkins whispered. Jenkins followed him to a table for two, away from the other guests.

'You might like to know, Jenkins, that it's lit up like a Christmas tree after dark, that's all.'

'What?'

Alistair nodded.

'You went out?'

Alistair leaned in to speak in a low voice. 'That's the marvellous thing about having a reputation for insouciance. No one expects you to do anything energetic or dangerous.'

'So it is a trap.'

'Maybe. But I don't think so.'

'Too dangerous. I'm calling it off.'

'No. It goes ahead.'

'You can't be serious?'

'I want to know what Vlatkov wants.' Alistair studied Jenkins's blank expression, deciding it was incredulity, not sudden deafness. He leaned back in his chair and sipped his coffee, for once enjoying having the edge over Three Piece. 'So, I repeat; when's sunset? It's much later than in the UK, isn't it?'

'About nine.'

'And how long does the twilight last?'

'Around forty minutes.'

'So dark by ten. Let me tell you a few things I've learned about Ivantrankovski Dam and the Soviet border.'

Jenkins listened, his face blenching. 'Meeting. My room. Twenty minutes.'

Jenkins left to find the others just as Ingrid wandered into the breakfast room. Alistair poured himself another coffee and went to sit with her. They chatted small talk for a fifteen minutes. 'If you'll excuse me, our master wishes to speak with me further,' Alistair said, throwing his napkin onto the table. As he left the room, he turned to see her. He beamed his most provocative smile. She winked back.

Alistair pressed the button to summon the lift and rode it to the second floor. Sauntering along the corridor towards Jenkins's room, Alistair pondered whether to tell Jenkins what he'd learned from overhearing the Soviet border guards. But the purpose of the mission was to learn what Vlatkov wanted. Besides, it was hardly earth-shattering intelligence; it would be routine for Finnish guards to be patrolling and surveying their own border on their own land, especially when they had the Soviet Union as their neighbour. Alistair dismissed the guards' chatter as unimportant babble, probably designed to fill a radio schedule or to keep their KGB masters off their backs. His mind returned to Vlatkov and the forthcoming rendezvous. This was his big chance to impress, and he didn't want to make a mess of it. But he knew it was risky. Especially for him. If the dam lights were turned on at sunset, then by ten o'clock the entire area would be brighter than day and the surrounding areas could conceal any number of snipers in the darkness. But the lights also meant that the night vision weapons they'd brought would be overloaded and turned off. It applied as much to them as it did to the Soviets. Neither side would be aware of concealed snipers on the dam. It had to be assumed there would be some. Alistair recalled the observation towers. There was no protection on the dam wall if a sniper fired from there. He wondered if Vlatkov had made the rendezvous to be on the dam wall at ten o'clock because he knew the place would be lit up like a stage, rendering night-vision weapons useless. Regardless, it was a very big gamble, and totally crazy. He shrugged. He'd always taken chances. Why stop now? Besides, something, gut maybe, told him Vlatkov wanted to make contact with him specifically. Alistair frowned. Despite the very real possibility of being killed and what he'd overheard, he realised he hadn't seen any Finnish border guards. Despite the light being on in the western observation tower, it didn't mean someone was actually there. That reasoning, although he considered it unlikely, applied to the Soviets as well. With no Finnish border guards, how would the Finns even know if anyone crossed into their territory? Was that also why Vlatkov had chosen this site? There was another possibility. What if Vlatkov had told his handlers he could convince Bruce Spencer to turn a Soviet double agent? To inform them which British diplomats were moving and to which city. Would that information be highly prized by the Soviets?

He knocked on Jenkins's door.

'So glad you could join us!' Jenkins said when Alistair walked in. He saw the cool, disgruntled stares. But he couldn't decide if it was judgemental indignation or envy.

Jenkins began. 'Now that we are all present. This may come as a shock to some here, but last night, Alistair did a preliminary re-connoitre of the dam. He says the lights there make the place like day and that no one could meet there unobserved. It's my belief that the mission should be cancelled, but Alistair is adamant that it goes ahead.'

All eyes were on Alistair.

'Didn't think you had it in ya', laddie,' Cox said.

'With me, Sergeant-Major?' Alistair stared into the big Scot's face.

'Aye. I'm with you.'

'This is crazy!' Jenkins said.

'Forgive me for saying it, Jenkins... What is your first name?'

'Bloody hell, Alistair, but you're a cool customer. And never you mind.'

'As I thought... something poncey!'

Cox's left eyebrow rose and Alistair thought he glimpsed a slight grin on the austere man's face.

'It's Andrew, if you must know.'

Alistair covered his smirk with his hand. He could see Cox was suppressing a chuckle.

Jenkins looked up at Alistair. 'You were saying?'

'It isn't your life on the line, is it, Andrew? It's Sergeant-Major Cox and me in the firing line. And I say we go. Cox?'

Cox stood. 'Fine by me.'

'Bloody hell! Two idiots. This isn't SOE, you know, Cox. It's the Cold War, not the last one.' Jenkins looked at Alistair and Cox. 'Ok. Ok. It's your skin, not mine. But I'll have to explain it and most likely I'll be the scapegoat for letting you do it, if it all goes arse-up.'

Alistair watched Cox. What was it about the man? Was he attempting to be friendly now? He hadn't known Cox was a former Special Operations Executive, but he should have guessed. Was the man really there to watch his back or to stab him in it? Only one way to find out, Alistair thought.

Jenkins stood up. 'Personally, I think it's madness. But if you're both determined to go then, Alistair, you and Cox will walk onto the dam wall at five minutes to ten tonight and wait for Vlatkov to arrive. Thorne and Harper will be on the western end of the dam with their weapons trained at the centre of the wall. As soon as Alistair steps into the light, Thorne and Harper will advance closer to the dam at the western end, weapons trained on Vlatkov and the eastern end of the dam wall. Alistair, remain there until Vlatkov approaches you.

On no account, approach him until he meets you halfway. And no going beyond the halfway point of the dam.'

'And where will you be?'

'I'll be mobile. Checking for snipers on the dam or in any of the trees around the area. Any sign of entrapment, any hint of a double-cross, it's shoot to kill. Got it?'

Heads were nodding.

'Check everything. Make sure your clothing is dry. No drinking from now until after the rendezvous and no other activities, either. And that's an order.'

Alistair had never been much good at taking orders. They returned to their rooms. Five minutes later, there was a soft knock at his door. Hurrying, he opened it, hoping to see Ingrid. Cox stood there, but he didn't enter.

'I just want to say this, Alistair. I'm not your enemy. I'm not your friend either, but I'm certainly not your enemy. I'm here to watch your back and I'll do everything in my power to make sure you survive tonight.' The Scot marched away.

Alistair closed his door. He wondered what had prompted the outburst. First an attempt at friendship with a shared joke and now this! Had the Scot meant it as encouragement? Cox evidently believed he may die tonight. If it was meant to be comforting, Alistair didn't find it so. He sat in the chair by the window, then laughed aloud. 'If only Captain Mug-Face had heard that!'

CHAPTER TWENTY-ONE

Ivantra

Finland

11th April 1966

From his window, Alistair saw Jenkins leave the hotel with Thorne and Harper at the allotted time. He didn't know their intended precise locations, and perhaps that was for the best. He wondered if the Soviets were doing the same thing. Perhaps they should've just met in 2i's coffee shop rather than all the cloak and dagger stuff. Certainly would've been warmer, he thought.

He let the curtain fall as a loud, single knock on his door told him Cox had arrived. The Scotsman came in and settled himself in the chair.

'So, you were in SOE, Sergeant-Major. With anyone I know?'

'Irrelevant now. Do you have leggings on underneath those trousers?'

'Of course.'

'Where's the Browning?'

'Don't worry, mother, I have everything, even a clean handkerchief.'

Cox drew in his upper lip, his eyes boring into Alistair. The man appeared to be chewing on his lip for a few seconds and Alistair wondered if the Sergeant-Major would take a swing at him. While he knew it would irritate the man, Alistair grinned at him.

Cox stood. 'Well, if ya're ready, ya cocky little toe-rag, we'll go!' Cox strode towards the door and flung it open.

Alistair couldn't resist a smile. Grabbing his coat, he pulled it on, making sure the weapons were covered, then pushed past Cox and descended the fire escape stairs. Carefully, he opened the door to the foyer. It was full of evening guests chattering loudly. Slipping out of the stairwell, he and Cox crossed the foyer, weapons concealed beneath their heavy coats. A porter opened the door for them and they left. Neither spoke.

The cold night air caught his breath and Alistair covered his mouth with his gloved hand and drew in some warmed air. England was cold in winter, Scotland colder, but on the Finnish-Soviet border, heightened nerves and near-freezing temperatures meant cold took on a whole new meaning. Not that he was worried about the rendezvous itself. Vlatkov wanted to make contact. That fact should have given him comfort, but it didn't. Standing in a pool of light waiting to meet a Soviet KGB man while unknown others with machine guns were trained on him wasn't his idea of a pleasant evening's entertainment.

They broke into a slow run. Five minutes later, they saw the Ivantrankovski Dam. The lights were already bright. Alistair turned to see Cox's expression. He'd expected astonishment, but what he saw was an array of emotions: memories and war-time experiences were being relived in the Scotsman's eyes. 'We're not here to blow it up, Sar-Major. Just meet a man. And maybe get killed.'

'Shut ya mouth and concentrate. Or I'll shoot ya for them.'

Twenty feet from the dam wall, Alistair slowed his pace until he stood completely still. The narrow pathway was in front of him now. He could feel his heart thumping. The arc of brilliant light was a few feet away. He cast his eye over the observations towers. He wasn't worried about the one closest to him, the one controlled by the Finns, and even though he didn't need to go as far as the eastern tower, it was easily within range of the mid-point of the dam for a sniper. He looked at the windows that overlooked the dam walkway. He couldn't see any machine gun barrels poking out of windows. A light was on in both towers, but he didn't expect to see anyone before Vlatkov actually appeared.

Stepping onto the wall, he stood in the darkness at the edge of the searing beam, Cox behind him. He knew Jenkins with Bill and Ben, were out there somewhere in the darkness. The dam walls were only metres away from him on both sides; the cold black waters with their thawing covering of ice to his left, the spillways and rocky riverbed on his right. To add to his heightened nerves, from time to time the ice cracked violently as it slowly thawed. He told himself to breathe. His eyes were wide and his mouth dry. He hoped the three men from MI5 were good shots.

He stared up at the starry night sky then checked his watch; 21. 58, almost ten o'clock.

'Now or never, Cox,' he whispered.

Alistair swallowed hard. With his pulse beating fast, he took a step forward into the circles of light.

He heard Cox squat, then lay flat on the gravel path at the edge of the strong beam cast from the last stanchion on the dam wall. Alistair knew Cox's machine gun would be focused on the mid-point.

'I've got ya' back,' Cox whispered from the darkness.

'It's not my back I'm worried about,' Alistair said and took another step forward, into a brighter arc of light where two beams bisected. With his heart pounding, he walked slowly, one foot in front of the other. He passed the first observation tower, his eyes searching the end of the wall; that void of darkness beyond the intense brightness.

Alistair stopped in the middle of the wall and waited, feeling exposed and vulnerable, waiting for the sudden impact of death, each second grindingly slow. Running his tongue around his dry mouth, he took in a long breath and breathed out slowly, his warm air floating away into the emptiness. He saw the human shape appear out of the gloom. It was the weirdest thing he'd ever seen; like a human form materialising molecule by molecule out of empty blackness. A man in a dark coat wearing a hat was walking towards him. It could have been anyone. The man walked into the light.

'You came, Mr Spencer.'

'Mr Vlatkov.'

Alistair took a step forward. The two men stood together. Alistair kept his back to Cox, his gaze over Vlatkov's shoulder.

'You are concerned you will be shot?' Vlatkov said.

'The thought never crossed my mind, Vasali.'

Vlatkov laughed.

'I'm curious to know how you arranged this at such short notice and how your masters permitted this meeting.'

'That is not important now.'

'So what is it you want to tell me, Vasali?'

'You are either very brave or very stupid. I cannot decide which.'

'I could say the same of you. But I've come a long way to keep this rendezvous you requested and I'm freezing, so can we get on with this?'

'Your father took something that belongs to us. We are not happy about this.'

'What are you talking about?'

'Please don't be naïve, Mr Spencer. Or should I call you Mr Quinn? That is your name, isn't it? Meet me here again in eight days. Tell your father he is to come here also or we will release some compromising pictures of Sir Laurence Dalrymple. See you next Tuesday, Alistair Quinn.'

Alistair watched Vlatkov turn and disappear into the dark void at the end of the dam wall. The man had turned his back on him. It was a brave but defiant gesture. Alistair waited a few seconds before retracing his steps. His mind was reeling. The reference to his father was puzzling. What could he have taken? And he knew nothing about compromising pictures. Alistair needed to think quickly. Jenkins would want a debrief, and he wasn't sure what to tell him. Vlatkov's words were ringing in his ears.

Alistair heard footsteps running and knew Bill and Ben had broken cover and were heading back to the hotel. No one spoke. He re-joined Cox. The air was freezing and snow was beginning to fall. He needed a drink.

They met back in Jenkins's room. Alistair swallowed the whisky whole. He was suddenly hungry. He cast his eye around the men seated.

'Where's Miss Larsen?' Alistair asked.

'I sent her home. Left on the evening train for Helsinki. We don't need her anymore,' Jenkins said.

By you maybe, Alistair thought. He was sorry not to have seen her again before she left. He liked her. He enjoyed seeing her. But it was probably for the best.

Jenkins refilled Alistair's glass. 'I think I speak for all here, Alistair, when I say that what we witnessed tonight may be the stupidest and bravest thing I've ever seen. So, does Vlatkov want to defect?'

'I can't decide.'

'What does that mean?'

'He wants another meeting next Tuesday.'

Jenkins's face was a study in confusion. 'Why? What exactly did he say?'

'He said my father took something which they want returned and that I was to meet him again in eight days and bring father along. Do you know what he's talking about?'

'Did you agree to it?'

'Didn't get the chance. So he's pretty sure I'll be there.'

'What's he playing at?'

'Well, if you don't know, Jenkins, why would I?'

'And you're sure that's all he said?'

'That's it. Actually, he's so sure I'll be there, he didn't wait for my answer. Maybe he wants to defect, but he needs his handlers to trust him. Maybe this trip was to convince the KGB that he won't abscond.'

'Perhaps. Sir Laurence isn't going to like it.'

Alistair looked at Jenkins. Given what Vlatkov had said about compromising photographs, Alistair thought that the understatement of the century.

CHAPTER TWENTY-TWO

Ivantra

11th April 1966

Frank closed the door to his room and removed his cold weather gear. He'd been away only an hour. From his window on the fourth floor of the Ivantra Hotel, he'd seen Alistair and Sergeant-Major Cox leave. And he'd left soon after, going straight to the river and crossing to the eastern side of the dam wall well below the spillways and from where he'd seen Jenkins secreted on the edge of the easternmost spillway. He'd also run into the trees and seen the cars. Parked well back and hidden from view by the forest, Frank had observed the Soviets arrive. Four had walked with Vlatkov to the edge of the dam on the eastern side, where a few minutes of last instructions had been given to Vlatkov. But none of his handlers had gone with him onto the wall. If the Soviets were suspicious that Vlatkov wanted to defect, he would have been surrounded by men in dark coats or the rendezvous would never have taken place at all. So, was it a clever ruse to recruit Alistair and gain his trust?

Frank wanted one other piece of information before leaving Ivantra. He checked his watch. He believed Jenkins's party would have returned to one of their rooms within the hotel to debrief. This gave Frank approximately twenty minutes to learn what he wanted to know without fear of running into any of them around the hotel reception or bar. Changing into his pyjamas and wrapping a dressing gown around him, Frank left his room and, using the fire stairs, went to the foyer. It was late now; the foyer was empty and the evening dinner guests had retired. Only a few stragglers still sat in the bar. He couldn't hear any chatter coming from the lounges.

'Can I help you, sir?' the night manager said as Frank approached the desk.

'I have a very bad headache and wondered if you had any aspirin?' Frank asked.

'Should I call a doctor, sir?'

'That won't be necessary. Just some aspirin, if you have any.'

'Of course. I'll get you some, sir. Can I bring it to your room?'

'I don't want to put you to that much trouble. I can wait here. Will you be long?'

'Not long, sir. A few minutes. I have to go downstairs to get them. I'll be as quick as I can.'

'I can sit here. Thank you.'

Frank waited while the young man left, disappearing behind the reception area and into the inner confines of the hotel.

Coming around the reception counter, Frank found the guest register and flipped back through the pages to the 6th of October last year, the date he'd met Dieter Stecker in Helsinki. With his ears straining, he read down the list of guests who'd stayed at the hotel the night before. His eye quickly found Per Sangolt. He noted the address Per had given, wondering if it were true. A little further down the same page was another Norwegian name; Jan Johansen. It was a name Frank didn't immediately recognise, but he knew both the first name and the surname to be two of the most common names in Norway. He read the address Jan Johansen had given. With his ears listening for the night manager's return, he flipped the pages until he found the booking for Jenkins's party's occupancy. Closing the register, he left the reception desk and stood in the foyer staring at some paintings on the wall. A few minutes later, the young man came back. Thanking him, Frank took the foil containing two pills and returned to his room.

He decided to leave Ivantra first thing and be away from the hotel well before any of Jenkins's team came down to breakfast. He unfolded the train timetable, noting that the first train to Helsinki departed just after six. From there, he'd go straight to the airport. He packed his suitcase, then, sitting in the chair by the window, lit a cigarette.

While it was late, Frank knew it would be impossible to sleep. He sat inhaling the tobacco and watched the smoke spiral upwards. What he'd witnessed on Ivantrankovski Dam made his blood run cold, but he couldn't deny his son had proven his bravery. He felt oddly proud of the boy he barely knew. It worried him that Vlatkov had chosen Ivantrankovski Dam for the rendezvous. Frank didn't believe it was accidental. Vlatkov was testing them out about Dieter Stecker's undercover activities and his last visit there in particular.

Was it possible a KGB agent had witnessed the meeting between Dieter and Per? He hoped Laurence would have some good news about Per on his return to London.

Frank set his alarm clock for five. He was booked on the mid-morning flight from Helsinki to Oslo, in case anyone was taking too much interest in the passenger manifests for the flights to London.

* * *

Oslo, unusually, was no warmer than Helsinki. Using the telephone in the Airport, Frank called the secure line and spoke to Joan McKillick.

'How can I help you, Mr Quinn?'

'I need a telephone number, Miss McKillick. I have an address but it may not be correct.' He gave her the Oslo address for Per Sangolt he'd seen in the hotel register in Ivantra.

Several minutes passed before she returned.

'I have two numbers for you to try. One matches with the address you gave me.'

Frank scribbled them down. Both had Oslo prefixes. Putting the required number of coins into the public phone, Frank dialled the first number. A recorded message told him that the number had been disconnected. Frank smiled. Old lessons not forgotten. He dialled the second. 'Per, this is Frank Quinn.'

'Frank! This is a surprise!'

'Perhaps not completely, Per.'

'Ah!'

'Could we meet?'

'You're in Oslo?'

'Yes. Just for the next few hours, though.'

'Sure, where?'

'Can you come to the airport café?'

'I can be there in twenty minutes. It will be great to see you, Frank.'

Frank hung up and went to find a seat in the cafeteria. He hadn't seen Per Sangolt in over twenty years and he hoped he'd recognise the man.

As soon as Per walked into the lounge area, Frank smiled. The man hadn't changed at all; still slim and tall, with strong Nordic facial features. The blond hair, however, was now grey. Frank ordered two coffees, and they sat at a table where he could keep his eye on the departure board.

'Tell me about Dieter Stecker, Per?' Frank asked.

'Ah! I should've guessed. Yes, something was troubling him. He used to write to me, you know. Usual stuff; how are you, what are you doing, that sort of thing. Came every month, regular as clockwork. They were always post-marked from a hotel in Finland.'

'How long did he do that?'

'Years. He liked Norway. I think he would've liked to have stayed after the war. He had a bit of a thing for my sister. But he wore a Nazi uniform. Our people wouldn't have accepted him. And my sister would have been ostracized. That was why he did what he did. To prove to us he wasn't like the others. But he would never have been accepted. He knew that. And she would've suffered. Then when the Nazis left Norway, he went too and the rest, you know. Living in

Estonia, of course, means any contact with us will be intercepted or stopped. So he writes to me from Finland.'

'Do you respond, Per?'

'Yes. Always care of The Ivantra Hotel.'

'And in recent months?'

'A small packet arrived about six months ago. He wanted me to keep it safe, then if he wrote asking for it, I was to take it to Finland, personally, to The Ivantra Hotel where we would meet. I knew he went there to inspect the electrical equipment in the dam's operation room. It was a bit of a journey. While it is a pretty place and I'm glad to have seen it after sending letters there all these years, I wasn't exactly pleased about it. But he saved my neck once. And yours. So, of course, I went. Why do you ask about him? Is he in trouble?'

'He's dead, I'm afraid, Per.'

'I'm so sorry to hear that. He said lives depended on it. I didn't realise he meant his. He said I wasn't to show it to anyone, and I never did.' Per looked directly at Frank. 'Did he work for you?'

Frank smiled.

'I should have guessed.'

'Did you know what this packet contained?'

'No! And I didn't want to know. I knew where he lived. Just having the thing was bad enough. I'm ashamed to say I told him not to contact me again after that.'

'Who knew you went to Finland?'

'My family. A few close friends. And Lars. I still see him from time to time when I'm in Oslo. He hasn't changed. Still campaigning for workers' rights. What worries you, Frank?'

'I think your meeting with Dieter may have been witnessed.'

'Dear God. I didn't see anyone I know. I swear to you I only told my wife, a neighbour and Lars. You remember Lars?'

'Of course. What did you tell them?'

'That I was going to Finland to see an old friend from the war years. Such a sad situation. We all could have died in that war. So I guess we got twenty more years out of life. Even so, sometimes I miss those days. It was, how do you say, life on the edge. Do you see the other Englishmen?'

'They're both Scottish, Per. Not sure they'd appreciate being called English.'

Per laughed. 'Feuds! Such a waste of energy! Give them my regards when you next see them.'

'I will. Did anyone travel with you?' Frank asked.

'No. I flew to Helsinki, then took the train to Ivantra. I stayed one night, met Dieter and returned the next day.'

'Do you know anyone by the name of Jan Johansen?'

'Are you kidding! That's two of the most common names in Norway. But no, I don't know anyone with that combination of names.'

Regardless, Frank believed Per had been followed. He glanced at the departure board. His plane for London was due to board in fifteen minutes. 'I should go, Per. Thank you for coming so promptly. Goodbye and good to know you're well.' They shook hands.

Gathering his things, Frank paid the bill and left, the tall Norwegian waving goodbye to him from the cafeteria.

Placing his passport into an inside pocket, he opened his case and found the one for Patrick Scully, the accountant from Manchester, then went directly to the men's lavatory. In a cubicle there he fixed a fake beard to his chin, put on a pair of glasses, flushed the toilet and left, his reversible overcoat now turned inside out and a new scarf around his neck. Outside, he checked the board again and saw his flight was boarding. Walking briskly to the departure gate, he walked out onto the tarmac behind a couple with a baby. In front of him, he saw her: Ingrid Larsen. He slowed his pace and watched. She was standing at the foot of the stairs waiting in the queue to board. She was engrossed in conversation with a man, approximately forty, and also boarding the plane for London. Frank hung back, keeping his eye on the pair. There was no reason a single woman travelling alone shouldn't speak to a man, but Frank thought he gleaned something about their body language, something that said they weren't strangers.

As Frank took his seat, he noted the man sitting further down the aisle. He looked around for Ingrid. She was several rows in front of him. Even at immigration in England, the pair didn't interact again. Nor while collecting their luggage. Standing outside the terminal, Frank saw them standing in the taxi queue. Again, they stood well apart and there was no conversation. In Frank's mind, any man interested enough to chat with a beautiful girl for more than a few seconds would want to continue the encounter, especially as they had not been seated together on the plane. That the man had not tried to speak with her further in either the customs hall, or at the carousel, or, in fact, at the taxi rank made Frank suspicious.

Hailing a cab, he went straight to Curzon Street. Despite it being late, he hoped Laurence would still be in his office.

'Frank! What news?' Laurence asked.

Frank sat down and pulled the fake beard from his chin. 'Is the Director General in?'

'Not this afternoon. Tell me about Vlatkov?'

'He and Alistair met on Ivantrankovski Dam. It was very brief. I don't know what was said, but there was no trouble. But I'll tell you something I thought didn't ring true if Vlatkov wants to defect. There were four cars of Soviets on the eastern side of the dam, but no one went with Vlatkov to the rendezvous.'

'They wouldn't let him do that if they suspected him. Anything else?'

'Yes. The girl, Ingrid Larsen, who went with Jenkins's team as interpreter; I saw her in Oslo. Was that planned?'

'Yes. Although nothing to do with the mission. She requested to see family while transiting through there. Why?'

'There was a man on the plane. Forty-ish. They spoke briefly before boarding. There was something about her manner. I got the impression they knew each other, but he wasn't family. No kiss on the cheek, in fact, no physical contact of any kind. Can you get a passenger list for the flight?'

'Of course. What do you suspect?'

'I always suspect something, Laurence. That's how we are.'

'I'll find out about her and get back to you. What do you make of Vlatkov being alone?'

'Other than the obvious; I don't know yet. We need to hear from Alistair what Vlatkov said without the others present, Laurence. Something just doesn't feel right.'

'Care to elaborate?'

'When we've heard from Alistair what Vlatkov said.'

'You look exhausted, Frank. You looking after yourself? What about moving back with Grace? She'd look after you.'

'No. How is she?'

'Managing. You know what she's like: pragmatic, stubborn. Just like you. Oh, yes, and something else. John McPherson called in again recently, wanting to see you. Comes to London every month, apparently. I got the impression he isn't well. Said he wanted to catch up with a few of the old faces. Has he contacted you at all?'

'No. He was a good radio operator, as I recall. Really knew his stuff.'

'Perhaps he's bored. Remind me why he didn't apply with the others?'

'He wanted to be in Scotland. Besides Laurence, few SOE really fitted in here after the war.'

CHAPTER TWENTY-THREE

London

13th April 1966

Alistair opened the door to No. 39. All he'd told Jenkins was that Vlatkov wanted to meet again next Tuesday, that they were angry something of theirs had been taken and that his father was to attend. He mentioned nothing about Vlatkov's threat to release compromising pictures of Laurence Dalrymple, if his father failed to show up.

Alistair lifted the telephone receiver and dialled the number for Joan McKillick. 'Good morning, Miss McKillick. Could I see Sir Laurence today? It's urgent.'

'Could you be here in an hour?'

'Of course.' Alistair replaced the receiver. Changing his clothes, he left the Knightsbridge building and hailed a cab on Brompton Road. Leaving the taxi in South Audley Street, he walked towards Leconfield House and entered the building through the one-way glass sliding door. Stepping inside, he took the lift to the third floor, grateful that he hadn't passed Jenkins in the corridors.

Joan McKillick beamed a warm smile. She nodded towards the door into Sir Laurence's office and Alistair went straight in.

'Alistair! Welcome home. I hear you did superlatively.'

'Perhaps. But I didn't tell Jenkins all that Vlatkov said.'

'Oh?' Laurence gestured to a chair and Alistair sat down.

'Vlatkov wants another meeting in a week. He said they were angry that father took something of theirs and I'm to bring him with me or Vlatkov says he'll release some personal information about you.'

'About me?'

Alistair fidgeted with a button on his jacket. While he'd always suspected it, he hadn't had any real proof until now. But how had he Soviets known? 'He said he'd let the newspapers know about your...' Alistair paused before looking up, 'sexual preferences.'

Laurence leaned back in his chair. 'Did he make any approaches to you about working for them?'

'No.'

'You're sure about that?'

'My loyalty isn't for sale. I thought I'd proved that.'

'Good. I had to ask.' Laurence paused, then said. 'Have you told anyone else about this personal information concerning me?'

'No.'

'So what's his game?' Laurence said, almost to himself.

'You're expecting me to know?' Alistair said, but he noted his uncle had neither denied nor admitted anything. 'What did we take from them?'

'Pictures of blueprints for a secret device for rendering all our electronic equipment useless.'

'Bloody hell! And father took them? How?'

'Not for you to know.'

'Why would they ask about them? Surely all that does is draw attention to them? They've virtually admitted they exist. Maybe these plans aren't genuine. Maybe they want to discredit father?'

Laurence nodded. 'Thank you for letting me know about this. I'll deal with it. It's my problem after all. You focus on meeting Vlatkov again. We need to know what our Soviet friend wants, not just speculation about it.'

'And father?'

'I'll deal with him too.'

Laurence watched Alistair leave. The door to his office closed. He swivelled his chair and stared at the sky beyond the window. Things were getting complicated. He didn't like that. The rendezvous had been dangerous. And drawing attention to not only the veracity but also the existence of the blueprints was unusual behaviour, even for the Soviets. What was Vlatkov playing at? Laurence reached for the telephone and dialled Frank's number.

'Frank, how sure are you that the Soviets know Stecker gave you the film?'

'They can't be completely sure. They may know Dieter took them. They may assume he secreted them in Finland. They may even know he posted them to Norway. But they can only speculate they were given to me. To come to that conclusion, they'd have to know I went there regularly, which, given that I use a unique identity every time I go, would be difficult for them. What's this about, Laurence?'

Laurence told Frank what Alistair had confided about the conversation with Vlatkov. 'What if there's a leak here?'

Frank didn't respond immediately. 'Then you have a very big problem, Laurence.'

'If you go to this rendezvous, won't that prove you received the blueprints?'

'Not necessarily.' Frank paused. 'However, given what he's threatening to do, I don't think I really have a choice, do you? Consider the consequences, Laurence. Of course, it could be a bluff to make us do something impetuous.'

* * *

Alistair went downstairs. As much as it was the last thing he wanted to do, he knew he should go to the language laboratory for an hour. Having spent months learning the difficult language, the last thing he wanted was to have forgotten it when he most needed it. As he stepped inside the laboratory, he saw Ingrid. 'Well, fancy meeting you here. I thought you spoke all the Scandinavian languages fluently.'

'I do. But I'm learning Italian.'

'Commendable of you, I'm sure. Lunch?' Alistair asked.

'If you like. Where?'

'Shepherd's Market isn't far.'

'You really know how to show a girl a good time!' She looked at him provocatively. 'What about Wilton's?'

Two hours later, Alistair hailed a taxi for Ingrid.

'I'll probably be dismissed for being away so long,' she said.

'Tell them you were doing research.'

'On what? Oysters and caviar?'

'Some of the best is Russian.' Alistair opened the cab door and Ingrid climbed in. 'It's been a pleasure, as always.'

Ingrid winked at him through the window as the cab drove away.

Alistair walked to the Green Park bus stop and checked the timetable. A bus for Knightsbridge was due soon. He had nothing planned for the afternoon, besides; it gave him time to just stare at the people of London. To see the verdant green of the park and spring daffodils from the first floor of a double-decker bus. Alighting from the bus outside Harrods, he walked to the underground car park.

Stepping into the library, he saw Uncle Laurence sitting by the fake windows. He walked up to him.

'Are you waiting to see me?'

'Yes. I want to ask you more about Ivantra. Go over everything again for me. Every little detail. And what exactly Vlatkov said.'

Alistair looked around. 'Your office not secure enough?'

'Here is better.'

The dinner gong went. Several men got up and wandered out. Laurence pointed to the chair opposite; they had the library to themselves.

'Vlatkov knew my name was Quinn, not Spencer. How did he know that? He said they weren't happy that father took something of theirs and they want him to come to the next rendezvous or they'll release some photographs of you to the press.'

Laurence was silent for a few minutes. 'Nothing else?'

Alistair shrugged. 'Isn't that enough? He said he'd see me in a week. So, he's pretty sure I'll be there.'

There was a long pause.

'Tell me what you know about Ingrid Larsen?' Laurence said.

Alistair blinked. The question surprised him. He could tell his uncle that she had a mole on her inner left thigh, but he didn't. 'She works on the Scandinavian desk. Acted recently for us as interpreter in Finland. She likes oysters and caviar. Speaks all the Scandinavian languages and apparently is learning Italian.'

'What makes you say that?' Laurence asked.

'Met her coming out of the language lab earlier today. Why do you ask about her?'

'She was seen in Oslo the day after she left Finland. While she had permission to do this, there is conjecture about a man she was seen talking to.'

'Do we have a photo of this man?'

'No. Our operative was getting on a flight at the time. Too difficult to do unseen.'

'Is she returning to Helsinki with us next week?' Alistair asked, hoping she would be.

Laurence thought for a moment. 'Not sure. This rendezvous is important. Nothing can go wrong.' He looked up at Alistair. 'There's a lot riding on it.'

Alistair nodded. 'You eating here?'

'No. I'll get back.'

Laurence returned to his office. It was late, but he knew Frank would be at his club. He lifted the telephone receiver and dialled the number for The Oxford and Cambridge Club in Pall Mall. 'Frank Quinn, please.'

Five minutes later, he heard Frank's voice.

'What is it, Laurence?'

'I need to see you, Frank. It's urgent.'

'Here?'

'No. Can you come here?'

'If you wish. I'll be there in half an hour.'

Given the hour, it surprised Frank that Joan McKillick was still at her typewriter. 'Still here, Miss McKillick?'

'Reports, Mr Quinn. Just thought I'd get a few done, so tomorrow isn't so hectic.'

Frank smiled, knocked on Laurence's door and stepped inside. 'What's so urgent?'

Laurence told Frank what Alistair had said about Vlatkov knowing Alistair's real name.

'Then I must go, Laurence. No conjecture about it. For Alistair's sake as well as yours.'

'It's a trap, Frank. They've got us by the balls and they know it.' Laurence stood. 'I'm a bloody fool!' Laurence rubbed his multiple chins. 'I chastised Greenslade recently for not keeping his penis in his trousers! I've been so careful. Vetting them before I meet them. But they planted someone to entrap me. It'll be the end of my career, my knighthood, and possibly my freedom if this gets out.'

'Maybe it isn't you they're after, Laurence.'

'Dear God! They get me, you, and Alistair. A total dog's breakfast!'

'And they may force the acting Director General to resign sooner than expected,' Frank added.

'All of us. Gone. What a coup for them! It would take us years to recover and even more to get back any credibility. Especially with the Americans.'

Frank stood. 'Perhaps we can still win this.'

Laurence looked up as though someone had just thrown him a lifeline. 'How?'

'We take Vlatkov. I'm sure the KGB would give us a few photographs of you to get their boy back.'

'You think it can be done?'

Frank nodded. 'It is possible he wants to defect, but he's being careful, hedging his bets. There were four cars with him there last week. Yet, he was allowed to meet Alistair alone. He's convinced them he's trustworthy and can bring them a prize.'

'You.'

'Or Alistair. But yes, ultimately me. It all depends on whether he comes alone again to the rendezvous. I want a few old hands I can trust there too.' Frank paused. 'What of Ingrid Larsen?'

'Leave her for now. She's unimportant.'

Frank stood to leave. 'Did you get the passenger list?'

Laurence sat forward and pulled a sheet of paper from under a stack of files on his desk. 'I didn't see any name there I recognised.' He handed it to Frank.

Frank's eye coursed down the list. His eye settled on one name: Jan Johansen. 'Don't worry, Laurence. We'll get Vlatkov. It'll be alright.'

CHAPTER TWENTY-FOUR

Mayfair

14th April 1966

At five minutes to five, Frank walked into the café opposite the front door to the MI5 building, Leconfield House. Removing his hat, he ordered a pot of tea, then went to sit just off to one side of the front window and against the side wall. It was raining. He put the evening newspaper on the table and waited. At ten past five, Ingrid Larsen stepped through the sliding glass door and walked out onto the street. She paused on the pavement only for a moment to lift her umbrella, then walked to the corner with South Audley Street, where she turned right.

Frank stood and put on his coat and hat. Despite Laurence telling him to leave her, Frank's gut, and the name Jan Johansen on the passenger list, told him she was involved in something and he wanted to know what. Leaving a sixpence on the table for the tea, he left the tea-room. Outside, he raised his umbrella and walked to the intersection with South Audley Street. He could see her walking briskly north. Frank crossed Curzon street and stayed on the left side of South Audley Street, keeping Ingrid Larsen on his right and about twenty yards in front. He hung back, occasionally turning to look at windows, the umbrella concealing his face. Instinct told him where she was going. Entering Grosvenor Square, she walked straight into the United States Embassy.

Frank returned to Curzon Street. He had no intention of hanging around Grosvenor Square where his presence would be picked up on every C.I.A. surveillance camera around the building. He walked through the glass sliding door to the elevators and pressed the button. He'd been away about forty minutes. He went straight to Laurence's office.

'Is he in?' Frank asked the loyal secretary.

'Sorry, Mr Quinn. He left about half an hour ago. I'm about to leave myself. Is there something I can do for you?'

'If it isn't too much trouble, could you get me the file on Ingrid Larsen? Right away, if possible.'

'Of course.' Joan McKillick placed her handbag and gloves on her desk beside her already covered typewriter. Within ten minutes, she'd returned with the file on Ingrid Larsen. She handed it to Frank.

'Would you like to sit inside?' She nodded towards Laurence's office door.

'Thank you. I will.'

She handed him the key to Laurence's office. 'Just switch off the light when you're done, sir. And, if you'd be good enough to make sure the door is locked when you leave. Just hand the key to the guard on duty downstairs as you go.'

'Of course. And thank you again.' Frank opened the door to Laurence's office, then closed it softly behind him. Switching on the light, he sat in an armchair by the window, the file on his lap. Outside, he could see the rain was strengthening, the round drops of water hitting the windowpanes.

Ingrid Larsen's file wasn't thick. Frank believed she was too young to have a questionable history. Although, he thought, Alistair was younger, and despite his evident recent bravery, he was, from all reports, no saint. Frank's gaze returned to the file. He read the contents. She'd been born in Oslo, Norway in 1944 to parents, Lars and Brigitte Larsen. Frank looked up at the window, then again at the file, his mind alert. Ingrid Larsen had come to England in 1962 when she was eighteen years old to work and improve her English. As well as English, she spoke her native tongue of Norwegian plus Danish, Swedish, Finnish, German and Russian. She'd held only two jobs since arriving in Britain; one with the Board of Trade for twelve months, the other with MI5 for four years. He checked her interview and language skills report. The references he only glanced at, knowing that no one submits bad references. One was from a former headmistress of her school, the next a Lutheran minister from Norway and the third from a public servant at the Board of Trade, praising her secretarial abilities. There was no mention of a husband or any family living in Britain. Her file stated she boarded at a house in Pembridge Road, Notting Hill.

Frank looked up at the window again. He didn't like coincidences. Even old ones. Through the rain-soaked windowpane, he could see lights from the buildings opposite were on and a wet night was descending. Studying the few pages the dossier contained, he saw there was no reference to any work with American firms. Her file was unremarkable in every way.

Handing the key to the guard, Frank left the building. The rain was heavier now and rushing people and peak hour buses jammed the roads. Huddling into his overcoat, he strode towards Park Lane and, after several unsuccessful attempts, hailed a cab.

'Pembridge Road, Notting Hill, thanks.'

'Right you are.'

Frank climbed in and the vehicle drove away, merging with other traffic on Park Lane. Bayswater Road was jammed with traffic. He sat in the cab outside Lancaster Gate as the meter ticked by, the traffic crawling until it stopped again outside the Soviet Embassy. 'The tube station will be fine,' he told the driver, frustrated with the delay. He paid his fare, then alighted. Passing Notting Hill Tube Station, he walked along Pembridge Road, keeping an eye on the street numbers, to the intersection with Portobello Road. About two doors along was a corner shop. Lowering his umbrella, he walked in and picked up a newspaper, the four-storey, light-blue painted building opposite in his peripheral vision. Several lights were already glowing in the upper room windows there. He reached into his pocket for some money to buy the paper. From the corner of his eye, he saw the front door to the house opposite open. Three young women emerged; one of whom was Ingrid. Standing on the front steps of their building, they scrambled to raise their umbrellas. He could see them huddling together, chatting, the occasional high-pitched burst of laughter loud enough for him to hear. Ingrid's attention was entirely on her friends. He watched them scurry across the road then run towards Portobello Road, doubtless to find a cheap place to eat. He estimated he had about an hour. But forty minutes would probably be enough to check her room thoroughly. He waited until the chattering group was well down Portobello Road before leaving the corner shop. He pulled his collar up against the rain and crossed the street. Reaching into his pocket for his lock-pick, he ran up the front steps and stood on the doorstep. There were three locks on the front door. Just as he was about to insert the device into the first lock, the door opened and a young man appeared.

'Hello! Do you know if Ingrid Larsen is in?' Frank said, his fingers pushing the lock-pick into his sleeve, his foot slightly propping the front door.

The young man descended two steps, then turned. 'No idea! Try room five.'

'Thanks,' Frank said, surprised the young man was so forthcoming. He wondered about that. The sixties! All rock'n roll and odd clothing. It was a new era and not one he found particularly enticing. If his job hadn't made him wary, the war had made his generation cautious, but not these youngsters with their slicked hair and nonchalant attitudes. He thought of his son and Alistair's reckless decisions; of his liking for motor bikes, American styled clothes and girls. Frank thought all this indolent living would get him into trouble one day, if it hadn't already. And it made him vulnerable. Vulnerable. His mind went straight to Laurence Dalrymple. Such stupidity. And now they were all paying for it. Frank found room five upstairs and quickly picked the single lock.

He closed the door quietly and stood staring into the room, his eye taking in everything. It contained a single bed, a dressing table covered in various pots and jars of face creams and scattered with more bobby pins and hair spray than he'd ever seen. He opened every drawer, carefully checking the contents, then under and at the back of each, but every drawer contained only women's clothing. He checked the wardrobe. Again only clothes. Carefully, he lifted the end of the wardrobe and checked the timber panel at the back for anything stuck there. On the other side of the room, under a window that faced the rear of the building, he saw a small trunk. This contained a coat for the winter months and blankets. He closed the chest and stood in the middle of the room, his eye searching every ledge or panel that could contain a concealed hiding place. On the windowsill, above the trunk and almost completely concealed by a curtain, was a framed picture of a man and a woman with a child of approximately ten years of age. Frank stared at the picture. With them was another man, some years younger than the couple. They were all arm-in-arm and smiling broadly. Frank stared at the faces. The group was a family. The child he could see was Ingrid at about ten years of age. The other, younger man, he recognised immediately.

Taking his miniature camera from his pocket, he snapped a shot of the photograph. Checking he'd left the room exactly as he'd found it, he slipped into the hall, then relocked the door and descended to the street. The man he'd seen Ingrid Larsen talking to on the tarmac at Oslo international airport, although now possibly close to twenty years older, was the young man in the photo. And in that photo he'd been wearing a British Army uniform.

CHAPTER TWENTY-FIVE

Mayfair

15th April 1966

'I'll telephone Max Guzmann. How dare he!' Laurence said. 'And Frank, thank you for trusting your instincts. I'll find out the identity of this man, but not before I have a piece of Max.' Laurence glared at the developed and enlarged photo of the picture from Ingrid Larsen's bedroom in Notting Hill.

Frank stood. 'When is the briefing for the second rendezvous?'

'Tomorrow.'

Frank left Laurence to telephone his counterpart at the US Embassy in Grosvenor Square. Setting Ingrid to spy on MI5 was serious enough, but Frank believed it was more likely that Max Guzmann had been caught in a honey trap. While Max was learning the precious little that Ingrid knew, what interested Frank more was what she had taken from that overgrown sorting box of a building in Grosvenor Square. If it included highly classified information, it would see her imprisoned for espionage and Max on the first flight back to Washington with his career in tatters, if not in prison himself.

Frank closed the door to Laurence's office and nodded to Miss McKillick. Through the closed door, he could already hear Laurence's raised voice on the telephone. Frank took the stairs to the lower floors, his mind on Ingrid and her connection to a man she'd known for twenty years; a man who had once been in the British Army and who now went by the name of Jan Johansen. But until he had a verifiable identity for this man, there was little he could do.

Leaving Leconfield House, Frank walked out into Curzon street, and slipped into Shepherd's Market, walking towards Piccadilly. It was only a short walk, but he enjoyed it. In Piccadilly, people stood in queues for buses while shoppers hurried passed. Crossing Piccadilly at The Ritz, he turned into Arlington Road, then cut through to St James's Street, and walked towards Pall Mall and The Oxford and Cambridge Club. He needed a quiet place to think, and he was closer to his club than his office in Broadway. A thought was taking seed in his mind and it troubled him. He sat alone in his room at the Oxford and Cambridge Club and closed his eyes. He'd never been a superstitious man, but he felt anxious in a way he hadn't felt since the war. He decided he should see his son before tomorrow.

At six o'clock, Frank dialled the number for the building in Knightsbridge. 'Room Thirty-Nine, please.'

'Hello?'

'Alistair. It's your father speaking. Could we meet?'

Alistair drew in a sharp breath; the call unexpected. There was a long pause. 'I suppose so. It would have to be tonight.'

'Yes, I know. Dinner then at my club?'

'The Oxford and Cambridge?'

'Yes. Say seven. I'll reserve a quiet table.'

Alistair hung up. While he'd often rehearsed what he'd say when finally they met, now he just felt confused. He went downstairs and poured himself a double whisky, then returned to his room and dressed. Half an hour later, he took a taxi to Pall Mall.

His father met him in the entrance to his club, at the foot of the stairs.

'Father.'

'Alistair.' Frank indicated the elegant staircase that led to the reception rooms above.

'We can't discuss tomorrow here, but I wanted to see you privately. To see how you are, now you know what I do.'

Alistair paused on the stairs and stared at his father. 'Really? Not sure I understand, though.'

'I know. You would never have understood, and that's the point. It was always possible, if you had known about my life, you would have said something that would compromise me. I don't mean knowingly. Although that was always a possibility, given your rebelliousness. You were always such an impetuous boy. And a sensitive one. While you took some extraordinary risks, even when you were little, I never thought this life would suit you. I didn't want you getting into it. But it appears it found you. Or at least Laurence did.'

'Is that why you beat me so much while I was growing up?'

Frank's expression was one of complete surprise. 'No more than usual, surely.'

'What does that mean?'

'It's how I was raised. I don't subscribe to all this liberalism. Makes the young precocious and disrespectful. Your parents are your parents, not your friends.'

Alistair stared at his father. Within the space of a few minutes, his father had shared more about his opinions than Alistair had ever heard. But regardless, nothing his father said would convince him that Victorian child-rearing practices were beneficial or loving.

They continued up the stairs into the dining room and were taken to a table in a quiet corner. Once having ordered, Frank shifted in his chair and leaned forward. 'Alistair, I just want to be sure you understand that this life can be extremely dangerous and sometimes even boring. But one thing you must know, now that you are involved, is who to trust. Before you speak to anyone, you must find out if they can be trusted. Even people you think are trustworthy may not be. I don't mean they are intentionally going to betray you, although some may. It has been my experience that few people can really hold a confidence, which is why it's so important to keep your own counsel. Moreover, while this life requires some degree of bravado, it also requires quiet courage and an extremely cool head. No emotion, Alistair. *Neither Despise nor Fear*, remember our family motto? Emotion clouds judgement and makes you either act impulsively or hesitate. And both will get you killed. Never let your guard down. Even when you think you're on safe ground. Especially then. Attention to detail. Always watch and listen before you act. But once you do, act decisively. Don't ignore your instinct. Sometimes that will save you when logic doesn't.'

Frank paused. Alistair could see his father's expression had become intense. He was in another world, reliving past missions and possible mistakes. Then, in an instant, as though snapping out of a trance, he changed again when their food arrived and the wine was poured.

Alistair had never heard his father talk as he did this night. He talked about Africa and his father, J. W. Quinn and about the early memories of his childhood there.

By the time his father put him in a taxi around midnight, Alistair felt almost euphoric. He felt grown up, and more importantly for him, accepted by his father. But above even this, he felt included. He leaned back in the taxi. He'd never had a conversation with either of his parents like he'd just experienced. Although only seventeen, he felt in control of his life and he couldn't wait to do this mission with his father.

* * *

'I hear you had dinner with Alistair. How did it go?' Laurence asked.

'Keeping tabs on me, Laurence?'

'Not you. Alistair. He's young, and this mission is important.'

'It'll be alright,' Frank said.

'Did you discuss this morning's briefing?'

'No. But I want you to include Miss Larsen in this second trip.'

'What! I was about to terminate her employment with us.'

'Let's give her enough rope and find out who she's involved with. It'll also be a valuable lesson for Alistair.'

'You're running a huge risk, Frank.'

'I know, but I want some others there too, Laurence. People none of Alistair's team know about.'

'Who?'

'Cox is going, isn't he?'

'Yes. Along with Jenkins, Harper and Thorne.'

'I want John McPherson there too.'

'Anyone else from SOE on your list?'

'Yes. Lars Larsen and Per Sangolt.'

'Bloody hell, Frank. I don't even know if they're still alive.

'They're alive.'

'Larsen? Related to Ingrid?'

'Yes.'

'What are you up to, Frank?'

'Hunting, for now. Get them into Finland, would you Laurence. Separately though.'

'Why do you want a patrol of old men, Frank? They must all be in their fifties by now. Well, at least late forties. They may not be up to it. McPherson looks old and tired. He, they, could be complete liabilities to you.'

'Make sure McPherson has a transmitter in his luggage.'

'Why not take a younger team? I can provide you with any number of fit young men who can be immediately available.'

'Because I trust these men, Laurence. And I trust very few people with the life of my son. As far as Jenkins and his lot are concerned, they are there as a support team. Nothing else. That is all they need to know. I also want a lorry with a Finnish driver in Ivantra township parked outside the Lutheran church at ten o'clock on Tuesday night. It must be ready and fuelled to take us by road to Vaasa on the west coast. We'll send a radio confirmation en route if we have Vlatkov with us. I also want a boat, skippered by some of our people with sailing experience to look like a husband and wife yachting holiday. So a pleasure vessel of some kind, one that's large enough for us all. We'll sail from Vaasa to Hull. Ask Joan to organise passports for us all, including Larsen, Sangolt and Vlatkov.'

'And Alistair?'

'Get one for him, too. If, for some reason, I cannot take Vlatkov, then Alistair returns with Jenkins and the others. I'll stay behind to tidy up and return a few days later. If Vlatkov is with us, then I want Alistair with me.'

'It's high risk, Frank. What about I organise an RAF flight? Or a submarine? The Director General can arrange that.'

'Too obvious, Laurence. And if the Finns or Swedes learned of its presence in the Gulf of Bothnia, there'd be hell to pay. My way is more covert and simpler if we had to disappear into a crowd or the Baltic for a while. And regarding the Director General; get the Finns to agree to no security interference in Ivantra with Vlatkov but no mention to our Director General of anything else. I'd rather keep this between ourselves until it's over.'

'You haven't left me much time to arrange it. And K won't like it!'

'You have tomorrow, Laurence. Surely sufficient time. And about K. I'd prefer K didn't know about this.'

'Why?'

'Just a hunch, but let's just keep this between us for now.'

Frank left the building. He wanted some information and there was only one person who could not only access it without questions being asked but who could access it promptly, even on a Saturday. He strode down through Shepherd's Market into Piccadilly. Returning to his club, he placed the call to the secure line.

'Hello?'

'I need to see you. It's urgent.'

'Where?'

'My old office in Broadway. Can you do that?'

'I'll be there.'

Frank took a taxi to Queen Anne's Gate and entered the now soon-to-be former home of MI6 through the back entrance. Despite SIS's recent acquisition of Century House in Lambeth, he preferred his old office and had done little in the way of preparation to move into the new premises. Packing boxes sat one on top of the other in the outer office. Frank hung his coat and hat on the stand, then reached for his keys.

He unlocked a filing cabinet, then placed an envelope on his desk. Inside was a copy of the blueprint film Stecker had given to him of the Soviet microwave device. Beside it was the crumpled note.

'Frank?'

He looked up. 'Thanks for coming.'

He turned the note so the Head of MI5 could read it.

The Director General sat. 'Where did you get this?'

'It was in the envelope Dieter Stecker gave to me in the ferry terminal last October. A last-minute addition.'

'Dear God! You've been sitting on this for how long?'

'Long enough for me to know that it's genuine.'

'I think C should be brought in on this. It would be wrong of me to keep the Head of MI6 in the dark. You know what sighting these troops means?'

'Yes, I do know. Although I don't think Dieter did. If the meeting between Per Sangolt and Dieter was witnessed, as I now believe it was, then the Soviets may also have seen a military build-up in the area and investigated it. If they learned what they're really about, it would be catastrophic for Western defence. And regarding C, hold off informing him just for now. I'll say it was my idea. If I'm wrong, exposing this could precipitate an international crisis. One that would cause us and C huge embarrassment. For now, the fewer people who know about this the better.'

'I agree. But I cannot keep it from him for long.'

'Understood.' Frank pulled out a copy of the photograph he'd taken in Ingrid's room. 'I need to know the name of this man. As soon as possible. I've also asked Laurence to locate him, but I think it will take his team too long to identify him and I need the information today. If I'm right, this photograph of him with Ingrid and her family was taken outside the NATO headquarters in Kolsås, just outside Oslo. He could still be in the British Army. Could he have learned about the Stay-Behind Armies while stationed there? Is it possible he passed that information to the Soviets? I don't need to tell you what is at stake if the locations of the all the NATO Stay-Behind Armies across Europe became known to the Soviets. Let's assume they knew about the NATO base in Kolsås, or worse, that it housed a Stay-Behind unit and have now become suspicious of a group of soldiers on the Finnish-Soviet border. They may put two and two together and go looking for others. It wouldn't take them long to learn the full extent of this in Europe.'

'As you say, catastrophic. Is that why Miss Larsen has been so cosy with the Americans?'

'Entirely possible.' Frank paused. 'It's just a hunch at this stage, but I sense someone else's involvement and I want to keep my suspicions to just you and me for now.'

'What do you suspect, Frank?'

'If the Soviets have learned about Laurence's homosexuality, they will not hesitate to exploit it. So, for his sake, I wouldn't want those photos of him to be published. But that aside, Laurence places too much faith in young men. Jenkins, Thorne and Harper, even Alistair. None of them have been through what we have.'

'What are you proposing, Frank?'

'A trap.' Frank indicated the chair before his desk.

Half an hour later, the Director General of MI5 stood to leave. 'You're sure about this, Frank?'

'I can't see any other way. The location of those Stay-Behind Armies must remain secret. If the Soviets know where they are, there will be nothing stopping their westward expansion. We'd be sitting ducks for invasion. Western democracy, as we've known it, would be gone forever.'

'I'm willing to stay quiet for a short time, Frank. But if you don't inform C about this soon, I will have to. In the meantime, I'll get this man identified and arrange the boat. I'll leave the information in a sealed envelope with Joan McKillick for you to collect this afternoon before the briefing. Will that be soon enough?'

Frank nodded. 'Thank you.'

The Director General stood and left Frank's office.

The doubt wouldn't leave him. Why would the Soviets want him to attend the second rendezvous unless they were planning something? Was the target himself or Alistair? Or were they just wanting to put a face to a name? Frank hoped so. But with the Soviets, things were never that simple. It was more likely they wanted him. Lifting his head, he looked around his old office. So familiar a space. It held memories of the war; of successful missions and the enemy defeated. But this war, with their former ally, the Soviet Union, was a very different game. Played out behind walls; of operatives meeting in the dark, and dead bodies left in the snow or drowned in the Baltic. Gone forever; no one knew where. But worst of all, no one held accountable. But of one thing about this second rendezvous, Frank was certain; it wasn't about the Soviets getting back the film of their microwave device.

Frank leaned back in his chair. If what he planned to happen was feasible, he needed everything to be in place before they left for Finland. It didn't give him much time.

When Frank arrived at Curzon street for the 5pm briefing, he went straight to Laurence's office. 'I'd be interested to know what Max Guzmann said when you confronted him about Ingrid Larsen?'

'Very sheepish. Classic honey trap. But then, I can't be too judgemental.'

'Does he know what she took?'

'Max was cagey about that. Why would he pay her to inform on us? She knows nothing. Besides which, if he wanted to know what we're doing, he could've just asked. Perhaps he thought he'd get a sanitised version of events. Which would be correct. She will have told them we did a mission to Ivantra recently. Fortunately for us, she wasn't at the rendezvous, so it won't have yielded them anything valuable.'

Frank looked down at the navy blue carpet, his mind alive with possibilities. Guzmann had mentioned nothing about NATO bases to Laurence, but if that was what Ingrid had stolen, Frank guessed Guzmann would be in a state of acute anxiety and keen to keep his indiscretions to himself. Despite being a Saturday, Joan McKillick, who'd been called in to attend the briefing and to hand out the airline tickets and passports, wasn't at her desk on Frank's arrival. He made an excuse about going to the lavatory to see if she'd returned to her desk. 'Anything for me, Miss McKillick?'

'Yes, Mr Quinn. An envelope has arrived,' she smiled.

Frank took the envelope and continued on to the men's lavatory. Once inside the cubicle, he opened the envelope. His eyes scanned the page.

Colin Quentin Urquhart, Lieutenant. Stationed in Kolsås, Norway from 1954 to 1960. Current rank and posting; Captain, Commanding Officer, Achnacarry Commando Training Facility, Scotland.

CHAPTER TWENTY-SIX

London

16th April 1966

When Alistair walked into Jenkins's office a few minutes before five, his father was already there. Jenkins was seated behind his desk scribbling on a desk pad, exuding nervous energy. Alistair nodded to his father, but other than a quick glance, there was no communication between them. A minute later, Thorne and Harper joined them. For one moment, Alistair wondered if Bill and Ben were ever seen apart. He looked at them, at their clean shaven appearance and neat hair. Nothing about them ever changed. Whenever they spoke, which wasn't often, he hadn't detected any accent. He wondered if, like him, they'd been to one of Britain's greater public schools, which with time eradicated regional accents. The door opened and Cox walked in. The last to arrive was Ingrid Larsen. She took the only vacant chair, one by the door. As she crossed her legs, she winked at Alistair.

Jenkins stood. 'Thank you for coming. Before I begin the briefing, I'd like to welcome Mr Frank Quinn of SIS to the team. His knowledge and years of service will be an asset to this mission. As we all know, Vlatkov requested a second meeting. The Soviets want to meet Mr Quinn, but we don't know why. This is highly irregular and places Mr Quinn in extreme danger. Therefore, everyone must be on high alert. Thorne and Harper will take up positions at the western end of the dam wall again. I'll be mobile, and Sergeant-Major Cox will cover both Alistair and Mr Quinn while on the wall. If Vlatkov follows the same routine, he'll approach from the eastern end and meet Alistair in the centre. Have him squarely in your sights, but do not fire unless you hear the command from either myself or Mr Frank Quinn. I trust that is OK with you, sir?'

Frank nodded.

'I'll arrange for everyone to have the same weapons as previously. Sir, I'm happy to arrange your preferred pistol or leave it to you to organise.'

'You needn't worry about me, Jenkins. I've been looking after myself for some time now.'

'Of course, sir.'

'Alistair, you and Cox will fly out on Tuesday morning on the early flight. Thorne, Harper, myself and Miss Larsen will go Monday. The only change will be that this time we are not to meet until we are all in Ivantra at the hotel there. As before, Miss Larsen is only to act as interpreter and to accompany us to the hotel. On no account is she to be exposed to any danger. With Miss Larsen's help, I will arrange the rail tickets when in Helsinki on Monday and leave two tickets for you, Alistair, and Cox with the ticket office in Helsinki Terminal. As you all know how to get to Ivantra, travelling there shouldn't present any problems. The rendezvous is scheduled for Tuesday 19th April at 22.00, so you will need to be in Ivantra no later than mid-afternoon on the 19th. As this mission is, to say the least, unusual, I don't want any heroics. But we must expect the unexpected. It must be considered that Vlatkov either wants to defect or it's for the Soviets to identify Mr Frank Quinn. It is my opinion that if Vlatkov comes alone to this rendezvous, he will either attempt to kill Mr Quinn or defect. If others are present...'

'Jenkins,' Frank Quinn leaned forward.

'Yes, Mr Quinn?'

'If Vlatkov comes with others, we're probably all going to die. But for what it's worth, I think Vlatkov wants to defect. So, let's just see what he wants without too much more speculation.'

'Of course, Mr Quinn. Questions anyone?'

There were none. The meeting with Jenkins concluded. Frank was the first to leave. Alistair followed him out to the corridor, hoping to spend more time with him. But his father evidently had other ideas. Alistair saw him hurry away, taking the stairs to the lower floors. He didn't know where his father was going, but wherever it was, it didn't include his son.

Ingrid was at his elbow. 'Dinner?'

'I thought you'd never ask, Miss Larsen.'

'It'll have to be a quick one, I'm afraid. I have to pack if I'm leaving on Monday.'

'I can be quick,' Alistair said.

Ingrid's smile broadened. 'The pub in Shepherd's Market then?'

'Sure.'

Ingrid slipped her arm through his and they took the lift to the ground floor. 'I do hope Jenkins books the same rooms in Ivantra.'

'My thoughts precisely, Miss Larsen.'

Two hours later, Alistair hailed a cab back on Curzon Street for Ingrid and, a minute later, another for himself.

'Knightsbridge, thanks,' he told the driver. He stared through the window. For the first time in his life, he felt apprehensive. This second rendezvous was high risk and his father would know this. It also had all the hallmarks of an assassination where he and his father would be the prime targets. He wondered why his father had agreed to meet the Russian in such dangerous circumstances. In fact, he wondered why he'd agreed to meet Vlatkov at all. He visualised his father almost running down the stairs at Leconfield House. From his purposeful gait, he'd been eager to get somewhere, but wherever Frank Quinn was going, the man hadn't confided it to anyone. Alistair wondered if his father had even given him a second thought.

Entering through the carpark, Alistair went straight to the library and poured himself a whisky. Two men were seated there. They were a good deal older than himself and he would have little in common with them. He sat in a chair and sipped his drink, his mind on his father's strange behaviour: the cordial chat at his club, his inclusion in the mission, that he'd agreed to meet Vlatkov in highly unusual circumstances, and his rather dismissive behaviour towards him after the briefing. Frank Quinn was as much an enigma to Alistair as he'd ever been, and it left Alistair feeling used in a way he didn't like. He laughed aloud. The two men in the library looked up from their evening papers briefly but said nothing. 'Well, fuck him!' Alistair mumbled under his breath and gulped the remaining whisky whole.

CHAPTER TWENTY-SEVEN

Knightsbridge

19th April 1966

Dorothy was at his door. He could hear her attempting to open it quietly. He'd been awake for hours. Nerves. They always impeded a good night's sleep. He sat up and switched on the light.

'Morning, sir,' she said. 'Sorry to disturb.' She put the breakfast tray on the side table.

'Morning, Dorothy. I wasn't asleep.'

'An early breakfast, so I'm guessing you're leaving us this morning, sir?'

'Yes.'

'Safe journey then,' she said, smiled at him and left the room.

He checked his watch. He had plenty of time. Rising, he poured a cup of tea and took a bite from the corner of some raisin toast. He and Cox were, as last time, the last to leave London. Jenkins had ordered that they be at Heathrow and checked into their flight before nine.

He left Knightsbridge just before seven and well before the morning rush heading into the capital. Sitting in the cab, he thought about the forthcoming mission. It all seemed odd to him. Surely returning secret documents that were no longer secret was a futile act? Both Vlatkov and his father would know this. So why? Was it possible the only reason his father was going was to prevent the release of lurid pictures of his uncle? Despite that having major ramifications for the Service and his uncle in particular, there had to be more to it. Whatever was happening, his father considered the risk of exposing himself to the Soviets was one worth taking. Alistair stared through the window at nothing in particular. None of it made much sense.

As the taxi drew up at the airport, he saw a man standing near the entry doors to the terminal. He wore a grey uniform and appeared to be attempting to control the movement of traffic around the airport building. Alistair visualised the Soviet guards he'd seen on the Finnish-Soviet border. He wondered if he should have mentioned what he'd overheard there. He'd dismissed it as unimportant, and now it was too late to speak with his uncle. Perhaps he should tell his father, but he didn't even know how his father was getting to Heathrow, much less Finland. Doubtless, Uncle Laurence had arranged a service driver. Moreover, he didn't know if his father was on the same flight or had already left like the others. It would have to wait. There was nothing he could do now.

Cox was at the check-in counter. As Alistair reached for his passport and ticket, he saw the Sergeant-Major striding towards the passport control officials. Alistair followed at a distance, finally catching up with the Scot at the boarding gate. Walking across the tarmac, they boarded the Scandinavian Airlines plane together, but there was no conversation between them.

Alistair found his seat. Cox was already seated in the row behind him. Placing his pack in the compartment above his head, Alistair sat down, his long legs protruding out into the narrow aisle. He glanced around at the other passengers. He hadn't seen his father, but he surmised Jenkins's grovelling had probably procured a first-class ticket for him. Buckling his seatbelt, Alistair closed his eyes, as the hostess went through the life jacket wearing procedure.

Alistair liked Helsinki. For a city, it felt cosy. He liked the park that ran down the main thoroughfare. More especially, he liked the colours. People wore bright clothing, children played in the park. The women wore beautiful fur-trimmed coats and hats. It was like a Christmas card, but it was a Christmas scene he'd never experienced as a child. Christmas for him was a day of solitude and stodgy food and, if he were lucky, a present; although how many train sets could one child have?

Walking out of the airport building, he waited in a queue for a taxi. Cox was a little way behind him, but he knew they were to take separate taxis to the railway terminal. Half an hour later, he alighted from the cab and walked across the bustling square towards the railway station. Despite being mid-April, it was still cold in Finland and a biting wind made him button his coat. He walked into the station, glad of some heat. Through the ticket barrier, he saw Ingrid standing on the platform with numerous shopping bags over her arm. It surprised him to see her there. She'd evidently stayed a day longer in Helsinki before taking the afternoon train to Ivantra. Whatever the reason, he was delighted to see her. She was wearing the long leather coat with fur trim and looked magnificent. He beamed as he walked towards her. Without Jenkins or Sergeant-Major Cox hovering around him, he grabbed her around the waist and, drawing her to him, kissed her mouth.

'Why, Mr Quinn, how presumptuous of you!'

'Just playing my part, Miss Larsen.'

Alistair and Ingrid entered the Ivantra hotel together and went straight to the Reception desk. From the numbers on the room keys, Alistair could see that Jenkins had arranged rooms for them on different floors of the Ivantra Hotel this time. Ingrid's was on the second floor while Alistair's was on the top; about as far away from Ingrid's room as could be found. Kill joy! Alistair thought. They rode the lift to the second floor, and both alighted. Alistair carried her suitcase to her room and, kissing her again, left her to settle in. If Jenkins thought allotting their rooms on different floors would stop them, he was in for a surprise.

The group's cover remained unaltered; that of British engineers. They were to stay only one night. Alistair hadn't seen his father since arriving. Neither was he present in Jenkins's room for the final briefing at four o'clock.

'Father not joining us?' Alistair asked Jenkins, taking the chair by the window.

'Mr Quinn had some urgent last-minute business which detained him. He's making his own way, but will be here at the required time. Would you brief your father when he arrives about the dam and its environs?' Jenkins asked. 'No need to reconnoitre the dam again. It'll be the same routine.'

Alistair glanced out of the window. The scene below showed spring's advance. The trees had lost most of their snowy covering and dark green foliage was making it colourful. The river beyond, however, was still not much more than a trickle. But everything seemed clear in the pristine air. Within minutes, Bill and Ben arrived, followed by Cox.

Jenkins was talking again. 'We follow the same procedure as last time. Alistair will meet Vlatkov on the dam wall. Then Mr Quinn will join him and find out what Vlatkov wants. No heroics, nothing unexpected, no sudden unscripted moves. Just a straight-forward rendezvous, then return to the hotel. We meet back here at eleven for a debrief. Got it!'

'And if the Soviets do something unexpected?' Alistair asked.

'You have a weapon with you, Alistair. Anything unusual, use it.'

After the meeting, Alistair wandered down to the foyer and strolled into the bar. His father was sitting in the same booth he'd chosen to drink champagne with Ingrid the week before. He sat beside him.

'How are you?' Frank said.

'Fine. You just arrived? You missed the briefing.'

'Good. Nothing I haven't heard before.'

'There is something you should know.'

Frank looked up. 'Oh?'

'When we were here last time, I reconnoitred the other side of the river, and around the border town of Svetlovorsk.'

'You crossed into Soviet territory?'

'Yes. I went to the border town, to the guard's hut there. I over-heard the border guards chatting. They said they'd gone into Finland and found an underground bunker. Then, I overheard the radio schedule. The guard was specifically asked by whoever was at the other end if he'd seen the soldiers again. The guard said they hadn't. But here's what concerns me. They mentioned Finnish soldiers in plain uniforms. At the time, I didn't think it important, thinking they were talking about Finnish border guards, but on reflection, they specifically called them soldiers, not guards. Do you know anything about this?'

'I don't think it's anything for you to worry about, Alistair. I've always believed Vlatkov wants to defect. He's a clever man. Could be he's told his handlers he can turn you. Or me. It could be how he's contrived to be alone at the rendezvous. So far, it's worked.'

'What are you expecting?'

'I have no idea. But whatever happens, keep your head down. And don't be afraid to use that pistol you carry.'

CHAPTER TWENTY-EIGHT

Ivantra

19th April 1966

They drank Russian vodka, which Alistair thought appropriate given the circumstances, and he told his father about Ivantrankovs-ki Dam. Frank sat listening to Alistair describe a dam he already knew about. He lit a cigarette, his mind on what Alistair had told him about the Soviet border guards. It confirmed to Frank that the Soviets had become suspicious of the unusual troop movements. And with Ingrid syphoning intelligence from Max Guzmann and the involvement of Captain Urquhart, Frank believed the Soviets had put two and two together. All he could hope for was that they didn't know the extent of the NATO Stay-Behind armies. What the Soviets actually did know had become vitally important.

Alistair checked his watch. It was just after six, the rendezvous in four hours. He lay on his bed, staring out the window at the evening sky. The conversation with his father had been perfunctory and his father had made light of the guards' chatter about Finnish soldiers. Alistair stood and wandered over to the window. Staring at his own reflection in the glass, he wondered why he still cared what his father thought.

He drew in a long breath and focused his gaze on the scene below, wondering if he would seek Ingrid. He hadn't seen her all afternoon, but now he knew he needed to focus on what lay ahead. The Soviet side of the river stared back at him. The forest there was thick with fresh growth and rain had recently fallen. Puddles of water lay around the hotel forecourt. A car door closing drew his attention to a group of men arriving at the hotel. One carried hiking gear and others unloaded quantities of luggage. He turned away from the window. Something nagged him. Despite what Jenkins had said, he wanted to see the dam again before the allotted time.

Grabbing his coat, he left his room and went downstairs. Without pausing, he strode through the foyer and out into the cool evening. He hadn't gone fifty yards before he heard footsteps behind him. Placing his hand on the pistol in his pocket, he turned. Cox was behind him, his pace increasing.

'You want something, Sergeant-Major?'

'Same as you, I'm guessing. I don't like surprises.'

Alistair turned, his hands remaining in his pockets. As they approached the dam wall, he could see a man on the path. 'Hold back, Alistair,' Cox said. The man appeared to be looking over the spillways, watching the icy waters. He then walked towards the eastern end of the dam and out of sight. Alistair and Cox approached the western end of the dam wall and waited. The man appeared to have left. Alistair looked around the site for the hiding places Thorne and Harper had used previously. A copse of low bushes was where he guessed Bill and Ben had secreted themselves. But they would not be so well concealed now. The snow that had previously covered the branches was gone, and it would now be easier to see anyone positioned there. Cox stood beside him. The Sergeant-Major had a deep frown on his face.

'Where were you last time?' Alistair asked.

'There,' Cox pointed. In the lengthening Northern twilight, the position was entirely exposed.

'And Jenkins?'

Cox shrugged.

Alistair walked towards the centre of the wall and peered over the left side. Despite the thawing lake, it was still too early for the Finnish authorities to start the nightly routine of releasing the water. He crossed to the right side of the wall. There, the large boulders remained exposed. Alistair looked along the dam, then strolled towards the eastern end. Standing just short of the eastern observation tower, he stared down the road that he knew led to the Soviet guards' house and Svetlovorsk. There was no sign of anyone there. He glanced up at the windows in the eastern tower overlooking the dam wall. Again, no one was evident, but his skin bristled. He felt their presence. Thrusting his hands deep into his pockets, he turned and walked back along the dam. Just as he was approaching the western tower, a tall, thin man wearing workman's clothes and a cap suddenly appeared on the wall. He'd come from the western observation tower and was walking towards him. Alistair gripped the pistol in his pocket. The man spoke to him, but as Alistair didn't understand Finnish, he shrugged. The man waited a second or two, then walked away, heading east, towards the other tower. Alistair shuddered. He felt suddenly vulnerable. Cox was beside him in seconds.

'What did he want?' Cox whispered. 'Did he speak Finnish or Russian?'

'Finnish, I suppose. It wasn't Russian. But I don't know what he said.'

'We should go back.'

'Should we inform Jenkins?'

'About what? That we saw a workman on the dam? Not an altogether surprising occurrence, is it, laddie?'

Alistair nodded. 'Of course. What about hiding places? I think it's more exposed this time. Any suggestions?'

Cox turned around, his eyes scanning the area. 'There are a few.'

'Where?'

Cox pointed to a spot where five trees stood together on the western side. 'If a man stood there, he could, with a telescopic sight, fire a direct hit.' Cox paused. 'Don't worry, Alistair. Jenkins has it all figured out. Besides, Thorne and Harper are good marksmen. They don't miss.'

'Been to Achnacarry, have they?' Alistair said.

'They all have.'

Alistair and Cox walked slowly towards the eastern side, but no one came to stop them. He wondered if the man he'd seen earlier was watching them from the tower. Alistair stopped, a shiver coursing through him. Staring into the distance, and beyond the eastern end of the wall, was a wide open area, with a stand of trees about twenty yards further back. There was one set of footprints in the snow and no tyre tracks. Alistair thought the footprints must belong to the workman he'd seen earlier on the dam wall.

Cox turned and stared over the spillway, the burly man's watchful eyes scanning the area below. From the east, they heard a lorry; the gears shifting. The noise was becoming louder.

'We should get back to the other side of the dam now,' Cox said.

Alistair nodded. They strode back together to the other side, then took the path down beside the river bed to the hotel like two friends out for a brisk walk.

This night, dinner was to be taken in their rooms. Alone. He wasn't hungry. Although, if all went to plan, he would be later. He nibbled at some sausage and mashed potato, but left the cabbage, a vegetable that would forever remind him of school. Just before nine, he checked everything, then closed his door and went to Jenkins's room.

Inside, Alistair cast his gaze around those present. 'Where's Miss Larsen?' he asked as Jenkins closed the door.

'Sent home. Took a bus to the station and is on the last train back to Helsinki.'

Alistair felt the sting of disappointment, but he knew it was for the best. Not only was this rendezvous vital to learn what Vlatkov actually wanted, but his father would be there and Alistair wanted to make a good impression. Although, he'd settle for not looking stupid. A minute later, his father and the rest of the team arrived. Alistair sat on the bed, allowing his father to take the only chair in the room.

'These are the negatives of the microwave device Vlatkov wants back,' Jenkins said, taking the film from his briefcase and handing it to Alistair.

Alistair took the envelope and placed it into his inside coat pocket. He saw his father's eyes dart to the envelope, but he said nothing.

'Remember! No heroics!' Jenkins said. 'And be ready to leave at your allotted time. No lateness. Too much is at stake!'

Alistair thought Jenkins was fussing again. Had his father not been there, he may have said so. But his father's presence had had a curious effect on the group. Everyone, including himself, was sombre, morose even, but trying to appear attentive.

Returning to his room, he waited by the window. At nine-twenty, Alistair saw Jenkins, along with Thorne and Harper, leave by the front door. They all wore unseasonably heavy overcoats, and he knew they carried their weapons concealed beneath the layers of clothing. Minutes later, Alistair heard the knock on his door. Cox stood in the corridor, Frank Quinn beside him. Alistair let them in, closing the door behind them.

'You have the envelope?' Frank asked.

Alistair pulled it from his coat pocket.

'Don't bring it out unless I ask you for it. OK?'

'Fine,' Alistair said.

Unlike both himself and Cox, who wore the heavy warm military styled overcoat, his father had chosen to wear a tweed overcoat and a hat. There was nothing military about his appearance. In fact, Alistair thought he looked more like a country squire or an inspector for the Water and Sewerage Board than a seasoned operative with Britain's Secret Intelligence Service.

They left the hotel at ten to ten by the front entrance. The sun had long since set, and the darkness was all-encompassing. Ahead, Alistair could see the dam, its blazing lights like a beacon glowing in the night. As they approached the narrow path, Cox hung back, and Alistair heard him take up his position on the road. Alistair stood in the dark, his hand gripping the pistol in his pocket. His palms felt sweaty and his pulse rate increased. His eyes were wide and fixed on the eastern end of the wall. His father was beside him now. Alistair waited. Neither man spoke. At the stroke of ten o'clock, his father stepped forward into the blazing light.

CHAPTER TWENTY-NINE

Ivantrankovski Dam
Finnish-Soviet Border
19th April 1966

Alistair stood still and held his breath. His father stood waiting in the powerful light; exposed and vulnerable. Alistair's grip on his pistol tightened. He was about to step forward when his father extended his left arm backwards; a signal for Alistair to remain where he was. Confused, Alistair waited in the darkness at the edge of the searing beam, his eyes wide and focused on his father. His heart was pounding. Then a black figure walked towards the centre of the dam.

Vlatkov stood in the middle and waited. Alistair wasn't sure why his father had changed the plan, but this was not the time to question. His father's concentration would be absolute. Alistair noted that Vlatkov had walked more briskly this time, or so Alistair thought. But something was different. The two men approached each other. Alistair felt the seconds tick by; each one the length of eternity. Whatever was happening, he hoped his father knew what he was doing. Behind him, he heard Cox move. He hoped Bill and Ben, along with Jenkins, had the Russian firmly in their sights or they would all be dead.

Alistair waited, transfixed. In the still air, he heard Vlatkov speak. 'Mr Frank Quinn. Good of you to come. Do you have the film?' Vlatkov asked.

'Did you come alone?' Frank said.

'As you see.'

'No one hiding in the trees behind you?'

'Do you have the film?' Vlatkov repeated, his voice demanding.

Alistair knew Vlatkov hadn't answered his father's question. Surely his father would know there would be at least four KGB men hiding somewhere out there in the darkness.

'Is it your intention to defect?' Frank's voice was just audible.

Vlatkov remained completely still, like a deer caught in the head-lights.

'Is that a yes or a no?' Frank whispered.

Vlatkov's eyes hadn't moved from Frank.

Alistair held his breath.

'Why would I do that, Mr Quinn?' Vlatkov said, his voice equally subdued.

Frank slowly raised his left arm and removed his hat.

With that, a barrage of machine gun fire rang out from the right side of the dam, the noise deafening, the rapid firing filling the still night air with shattering intensity. The brilliant lights above the dam were extinguished in a second, plunging the middle and western end of the dam wall into total darkness. Two seconds later, the eastern observation tower erupted, exploding into the night, sending brickwork and glass flying in all directions. Gun fire coursed rapidly from both sides of the dam wall. People were running. Alistair could hear the Soviets yelling over the mayhem.

'Back! Back!' Jenkins was screaming as more bullets from both ends of the dam fired into the mayhem. Alistair couldn't see where the gunmen were, but the air was thick with strafing bullets. The noise was intense, the loud percussive cracks exploding in the darkness like rapid thunder. Alistair felt himself being pulled down. He fell. Cox had him pinned down, the Scot lying beside him on the ground.

'Stand up when I say. Follow me and keep up!' Cox said into his ear. Two seconds passed. 'Now!'

Alistair stood and ran, following Cox into the darkness, his hand gripping the Browning in his pocket. They ran back towards the western side of the dam and along the road that led from the dam back into Ivantra township. He could hear pounding feet running behind him. With his head up, he ran into the darkness, gulping cold air into his heaving lungs. He could just see Cox running ahead of him. Behind him, he heard more running feet, their heavy footfall pounding on the bitumen road. He had no idea whose. He hoped it was his father and not a KGB death squad. Cox pushed him to one side, then down again, and they waited by the edge of a road. 'Don't speak! Keep down and be ready to move when I say,' Cox said into his ear.

Alistair could still hear Jenkins's frantic shouting. 'Back! Back!' But his voice seemed more distant now. Machine gun fire still cracked the night, the rapid staccato splutter loud and brash in the thin, cold air. In the dark night sky, he could see the orange glow of fire. Then several people ran past him at speed. One was carrying something. He thought there were four or maybe five men, but he didn't know.

'Up!' Cox whispered, and pulled Alistair to his feet. Cox was pushing him on. It was all happening too quickly. His mind was numb. He realised they were not heading towards the hotel. Was Cox betraying him? Was he running into a Soviet trap? Had his father betrayed him?

Slowing his pace, he broke free of Cox's tight grip. 'What's happening?' he demanded.

'Not now. I'll explain it all when we're in the lorry?'

Alistair baulked. 'I'm not taking another step till you tell me what's going on.'

'We're kidnapping Vlatkov. But if you don't shut up and move, I'll shoot ya' myself.'

Off to his right, Alistair saw the lights. Buildings and streets, houses with fences and families. Lights were on in the small wooden homes and Alistair guessed they were in Ivantra village.

'Move!' Cox shouted in his ear.

He ran, recognising his father now in front of him with four others. In silence, they ran on, taking a side street towards a large white building. Alistair saw it was a church. Parked outside was a lorry. As they approached, a man got out. Without waiting, he opened the lorry's rear doors, returned to the driver's cabin, and started the engine.

CHAPTER THIRTY

Ivantra

19th April 1966

Alistair stared at the faces around him; men who sat without speaking. Together with his father and Cox, were his uncle, John McPherson, sitting with his feet straddling a radio transmitter. Beside him was Vlatkov, his hands bound and a gag in his mouth. On his right were two other men Alistair had never met, who his father introduced as Per Sangolt and Lars Larsen. Even in the darkness, Alistair could see Per Sangolt was the man he'd seen on the Ivantrankovski Dam wall, the tall thin workman who wore a cap. Apart from Vlatkov, all men in the lorry knew each other and Alistair realised they were all former SOE.

'Is anyone going to tell me what's going on?' Alistair asked, his chest still heaving from running in the bitter cold.

'Soon,' Frank said, checking his compass.

The lorry rattled on. Smooth tarred roads soon replaced bumpy unsealed surfaces. They were moving at speed; the lorry swaying on the uneven back roads. No one spoke. Alistair looked across at his

Uncle John sitting on the bench seat opposite him. Alistair thought the man looked exhausted, but he seemed to be smiling. John looked up, catching Alistair's eye and beamed. To Alistair, it said so much; it was a smile of true fulfilment, of genuine love and real inclusion, like being a beloved member of a close family. But there was something else in his expression. Alistair cast his gaze along the line of men. All of them wore the same expression; it was familiarity and pride in belonging to an elite and secret sect. Alistair realised they'd done it all before, and given that there were two Norwegians among them, most likely in Norway. His father spoke. 'We've been driving for two hours now. Per will you signal the driver?'

Per Sangolt thumped the rear panel behind the driver and the vehicle slowed, then stopped. Thirty seconds later, the driver opened the door and his father jumped out. Through the open rear door, Alistair could see the brilliant, starry night sky. He thought they were in a forest with conifer trees on both sides of a single lane track. He couldn't see any lights. Alistair stood and was about to jump out when Cox grabbed his arm and pulled him back down onto the bench seat.

'Sit!' Cox ordered in a whisper.

Alistair sat down, feeling rebuked. But while he instantly felt like a child again, he noted that no one else in the lorry had stood up. They all remained exactly where they were.

A second later, he heard the hard cough-like thud of a silenced shot. Cox released his firm grip on Alistair's arm, then jumped down from the lorry and, a minute later, Cox and his father lifted the body of the driver into the vehicle.

Alistair stared at his father. 'Why did you do that?'

'Can't have him talking, Alistair. Besides, no guarantee he was a simple lorry driver.'

Alistair didn't speak. He suddenly felt cold, and he sat back on the bench in the lorry, wondering why his father had deemed it necessary to kill a hapless driver.

'Lars, you drive. We'll change drivers every two hours.'

'Right you are, Frank,' Lars said. Jumping down from the lorry, he disappeared from view. A minute later, Alistair heard the motor start again. Cox and Frank re-boarded the lorry, the body of the dead driver between them at their feet.

No one spoke. Alistair looked around the faces. The driver's death hadn't caused a ripple of comment from any of them. A man had died. A man who doubtless had a family who would expect him to return. Alistair stared at the faces, a frown developing on his brow. Their faces showed no emotion. Emotion. It got you killed. Was he being naïve? Perhaps this driver wasn't an innocent family man. Perhaps his father suspected this driver may have been bribed and would drive them into the Soviet Union. He remembered the packet of money Valerie had given to him and Jenkins's response. A quid or a thousand, if you're on the take, you're expendable. There was no way or time to prove the man's loyalty, especially with all of them in the rear of a lorry with no windows. The truth was, the driver could have driven them anywhere. 'Will the Soviets be looking for us?' Alistair asked.

'Undoubtedly. But they can't follow us. And soon they won't be tracking us, either. We're in Finland not Russia. And it will take time for them to contact any agents they have stationed here. We'll dispose of the body soon and check the vehicle for tracking devices. By heading north first, hopefully we can outwit them. The local police will be all over Ivantrankovski Dam by now. Jenkins and the others may be caught up there for days.'

'Thank goodness, Jenkins sent Ingrid back. At least she isn't caught up in this mess.'

'Not quite true, Alistair. She's sitting in the front of this lorry as we speak.'

'How did she know?'

'She's her father's daughter. I arranged it with Lars from London. When she left the Ivantra hotel, she joined her father in the village,' Frank added.

'So what's it all about?'

'Along with the photographs of the microwave devices that everyone's been talking about, there was a note. A brave man who worked for me had learned of an unusual patrol of military-style troops in the area around the Ivantrankovski Dam. He was concerned who they were. He didn't, however, understand their importance. What you overheard, Alistair, confirmed to me that our Soviet friends know only too well what those troops are all about. Am I right, Vasali?'

Vlatkov's eyes shifted to Frank.

Alistair watched. He didn't fully understand what his father was referring to, but he guessed Vlatkov did.

'Why are they so important?' Alistair asked.

'The soldiers are part of a top secret, NATO backed, Stay-Behind army network. Every NATO country, and even some that aren't, has their own Stay-Behind armies, and each has a cache of weaponry to defend against invasion. There are several throughout Europe, set up after the war in case of Soviet expansion west. This is extremely sensitive information and their discovery and removal would render the West vulnerable to invasion, should the Soviets learn of all the locations.'

Alistair watched his father's eyes as he spoke. They were focused on Vlatkov, who hadn't moved. While it surprised Alistair that his father was talking so freely about such highly secret information, Alistair realised that all those present were trusted men. Everyone, except for Per Sangolt, must have top secret security clearances. The other Norwegians in the group, Ingrid and Lars Larsen, were in the front cabin and unable to hear what his father had said. And Vlatkov was no longer in a position to inform anyone about what he'd just heard.

'Is Vlatkov defecting?' Alistair asked his father.

The Russian's eyes flicked from Alistair to Frank.

'I think that is highly unlikely. Vlatkov was under suspicion from the Soviets because we and the Americans had attempted to turn him to work for us. He was removed and returned to Moscow and required to prove his loyalty to the Soviet Union. So, Vlatkov persuaded his handlers that he could turn you and me. But he also had a trump card. He knew about the Finnish Stay-Behind army.' Frank leaned forward, his eyes so focused on Vlatkov that they seemed to penetrate the man's soul. 'But you haven't played it, have you,

Vasali?' Frank leaned back, a smile spreading over his face. 'And now it's too late.'

Vlatkov stared into the space in front of him. But Alistair could see it in the KGB man's eyes. His father had read him correctly.

'How did he learn about it?' Alistair asked.

'Complicated,' Frank replied.

Alistair turned to face Vlatkov and spoke in Russian. 'Is that true?'

Vlatkov lifted his head and smiled.

'So did you or didn't you want to defect?'

Again, the Russian didn't respond.

'Who do you really work for?' Alistair said to Vlatkov again in Russian.

'Not quite the right question, Alistair,' Frank said, leaning forward and pulling the gag from Vlatkov's mouth. 'Ask him who told him about the location of the Stay-Behind underground base.'

Alistair turned to the Russian, but Vlatkov remained mute. He looked again at his father. 'You mean they didn't just find them? Someone informed the Soviets about them?'

'Yes.'

'One of the Finnish soldiers?'

Frank shook his head. 'No! The Finns have no love for the Russians. It wasn't a Finn.'

'Then who?'

'Not completely sure yet. As I said, it's complicated.'

'What are you planning to do?' Alistair asked, staring at his father.

'Get out of Finland, for now.'

'How?'

'By boat. We'll make a stop soon.'

Twenty minutes later, Per clenched his fist and pounded on the back wall of the lorry. Within a minute, the lorry slowed and stopped. A moment later, the rear doors opened and Lars looked in.

Frank jumped out and looked around. Through the rear doors, Alistair could see a still, dark mass of silvery water in the moonlight. Lars stood to one side of the lake and lit a cigarette.

Frank checked his compass again. 'We'll dispose of the driver's body here. Jock, check his pockets, would you? And Lars, can you give me a hand? John, keep an eye on Vlatkov, and Per, check the lorry for tracking devices, then take over the driving. Send Ingrid back to ride in the rear. From now on, we'll rotate one seat round every two hours.'

'Anything on him, Jock?'

'Clean.'

'Per, anything on the lorry?'

'Nothing, Frank.'

Alistair watched his father. What did his father suspect?

Lifting the body of the deceased driver, Frank and Lars carried him to the lake's edge and, filling his clothes with small stones they found beside the track, carried him out into the lake to where the water was deeper. It took only a minute for the body to sink.

Ingrid jumped down from the cabin and walked to the rear of the lorry. Smiling at Alistair, she sat on the edge of the lorry tray, pulled herself into the space and stood. She went to sit beside him.

Frank checked his compass again. 'Per, for two hours we've been driving north, skirting the lakes. They instructed the driver not to enter any towns and to stay away from all main roads where the local police may, by now, have set up roadblocks. So far, and from what I can tell, he has done as instructed. We'll continue north for a while, then we'll turn west. Lars, you ride in the cabin with Per. We'll rotate again in two hours.'

The engine started and again they drove at some pace through the flat country heading north, north-west towards Kuopio.

There was silence in the lorry for some time. Alistair hung his head. He sensed the warmth from Ingrid's body beside him, but he didn't respond. While he couldn't deny he felt exhilarated at being involved, he felt sick, as though he'd been punched and winded. He'd never seen anyone killed before, and his father had shown no hesitation. The driver had posed a threat and was eliminated. No questions asked. He glanced at his father from time to time. He'd always believed his father didn't know him, but right now, he didn't know his father. Justifiable or not, what he'd witnessed was cold-blooded murder. But what he'd seen was the consummate professional at work, and it was intoxicating.

'Who is betraying us?' Alistair asked.

His father looked up. 'Good question. I'll tell you when I'm certain.'

'But you have your suspicions?'

'I suspect everyone.'

CHAPTER THIRTY-ONE

Central Finland

20th April 1966

Two hours later, Frank thumped on the panel behind the driver. It slowed, then stopped. Per opened the doors to the rear and Frank got out. Cox held his pistol on Vlatkov as McPherson stood, carried the radio transmitter to the edge of the lorry, and jumped down. Alistair was next, followed by Vlatkov, Cox, then Ingrid.

Alistair went to relieve himself behind a tree. From the corner of his eye, he saw John McPherson set up the radio transmitter by the side of the narrow dirt track. His uncle then threw an antennae wire high into the branches of a nearby tree. Connecting the old Morse code key to the transmitter, McPherson tapped out the pre-arranged enciphered message to alert London to their safe exit and that Vlatkov was with them.

'Don't we have anything more sophisticated than that?' Alistair asked, re-joining the group.

'It works, and it's what we're used to,' Larsen said.

'SOE rides again!' Alistair said, his head shaking.

'We may not be young men anymore, Alistair, but we know what we're doing,' McPherson said, lifting the headphones from his ears.

'Is that why you were at Achnacarry?' Alistair asked.

Frank turned around, his eyes flaring. 'What's this?'

McPherson reached for the antennae wires and wound them into a loop, placing them inside the suitcase, then closed the lid on the transmitter. 'Nothing out of the ordinary, Frank. I'd taken some steers to the railway at Fort William and thought I'd drive back via the statue to us all. I saw a patrol on the loch and stopped to watch. That's all.'

'That's true, Frank. I saw him,' Cox said. 'Got the lads away and made sure he didn't see Alistair.'

'But you were talking with Captain Mug...'Alistair stopped himself from saying Mug-Face. 'What is the C.O.'s name?' Alistair turned to Cox.

'Urquhart,' Cox said.

Frank heard the name and spun around. 'What did you discuss with him, John?'

'Nothing of importance, Frank! I introduced myself,' McPherson said. 'Said I'd been in SOE. We chatted a bit.'

'Did he ask you anything?' Frank questioned. 'Think, John, this is important! Did you tell him Alistair was there? Did you say his name, John?' Frank demanded.

'No, Frank! I didn't know Alistair was there. But...,' McPherson paused.

'What?' Frank demanded.

'I just wondered if it had something to do with the burglary at Gracie's.'

'What burglary?' Frank asked.

'She said nothing was taken. Just that they'd ransacked the house. Probably looking for something of yours, she said.'

Frank paused. His mind was processing thoughts and suppositions at lightning speed. 'Photos! That's what they wanted. Photos of us! Change of plan.'

Alistair stared at his father. 'I asked the C.O. at Achnacarry about Uncle John,' he said, tilting his head in McPherson's direction. 'He said he didn't know anyone of that name, but I knew he was lying.'

Frank stared into the surrounding darkness. Urquhart, posing as Jan Johansen, had gone to Ivantra and, with a photograph of Frank's SOE team, had witnessed Dieter Stecker meet with Per Sangolt. Urquhart could identify Sangolt. But who had instructed Urquhart to go there? Frank gripped his pistol. All eyes were on him.

'We should get a message to London to pick up this Urquhart?' Larsen said.

Frank lifted his weapon from his pocket and looked directly at Ingrid. 'When did you take the file of NATO Stay-Behind Army locations from Max Guzmann's office, Miss Larsen?'

'What?' Ingrid said, her intense gaze shifting between Frank and her father.

'Come now, Miss Larsen. You took or photographed the lists from Max's office at Grosvenor Square. And tell me about your relationship with Colin Quentin Urquhart, AKA Jan Johansen; the man in the photograph in your room in Pembridge Road, the man you met in Oslo recently, the man who was billeted with you, Lars, and your family a decade ago.' Frank's gaze shifted from Ingrid to Lars.

Alistair saw Lars make the slightest move. Frank's pistol was raised in a second, his arm outstretched, the hand steady. It was levelled at Ingrid. 'Don't make me use it, Lars.'

Alistair stared from one face to the next, then at Ingrid. He saw the intense, hostile glare in her eyes, the raw emotion. Exactly the situation his father had told him could get you killed. Alistair swallowed hard, his eyes wide. He could see the evidence of uncontrolled emotion playing out in front of him. It made people unpredictable and vulnerable. His father, however, was calmness personified. In that second, Alistair realised, he'd fallen for the oldest trick in the book.

A palpable tension of mistrust sat like an unseen barrier between them, and no one moved.

'Are we walking into a trap, Frank?' McPherson said, his gaze darting around those present.

'Five against three. Or is it four, Per?' Frank said.

'Five,' the Norwegian said, grasping his weapon, his stern eyes focused on Lars Larsen. 'You betrayed us? How could you Lars?'

'I was always a socialist, you knew that, Per.'

'We would have died for you,' Per said.

'That was then!' Lars replied.

Alistair looked at the tall Norwegian standing above them in the back of the lorry.

'So, not working for the Americans, but against them. And us,' Frank said to Ingrid. Per and Lars looked at Frank. The intensity between them paused, but not extinguished.

'I don't know what you're talking about. I don't know any Americans,' Ingrid protested.

'Now, I know that's a lie, because I followed you to Grosvenor Square.'

'We were a team!' McPherson shouted. 'What's happened? Frank? Lars?'

'Don't be naïve, John,' Cox said, his hand gripping his G3K A4 rifle. 'Times have changed. Old alliances aren't valid anymore. And, as I recall, Lars, you always were a card-carrying communist. Looks like the apple hasn't fallen far from the tree.'

Frank shifted his pistol and pointed it at Larsen. 'Who is the London contact?'

Larsen shook his head.

'Urquhart is too low down the scale to pull this off. He'd need inside help,' Cox said, releasing the catch on his weapon. 'We can't take them with us, Frank.'

Larsen gripped his rifle and lunged sideways, letting off a volley of shots as he fell. Sangolt saw the move and, from the rear of the lorry, fired at Larsen. Gunfire ripped the still air in a cacophony of noise for two seconds. Then absolute silence. Larsen and Vlatkov fell into a patch of slush and ice, their bodies still. McPherson lay slumped over the radio transmitter.

Ingrid screamed, then ran to the body of her father. Kneeling beside him, she grasped his pistol, swung round and aimed at Frank.

Alistair raised his Browning and fired.

He stared at her body. He'd reacted; a threat presented, the solution carried out. Training had kicked in and he stared at the consequences of his actions. Ingrid's body lay on the ground, the impact of the shot twisting her small frame sideways, her arm wide, her hand still holding the pistol.

'Check John,' Frank said to Cox.

Frank reached down with his left hand and felt for Vlatkov's carotid pulse. Instantly, Vlatkov's left arm grabbed Frank's wrist, trying to wrestle the pistol from Frank's grip. Frank broke free and held the pistol to Vlatkov's forehead. 'Not a wise move.'

Vlatkov lay back on the ground, clutching his right arm, blood oozing out between thick fingers.

'How bad is he?' Sangolt called from the lorry.

'Flesh wound. He'll live. We'll bind it in the lorry,' Frank said, looking at Cox, feeling for McPherson's carotid pulse. 'John?'

'He's dead,' Cox said, standing.

Alistair couldn't move. He felt faint. He was breathing fast, his eyes riveted to the bodies around him. Men, he'd just been talking to and Ingrid, a woman he'd held in his arms. He could taste her lips, smell her scent. She lay lifeless on the dank ground. He'd killed her. He felt himself shaking.

'Alistair!' Frank called.

Alistair heard his father's voice coming to him through a haze.

'Alistair!'

He looked up at his father and blinked several times. His father was speaking. 'Give Cox a hand to get the bodies into the lorry. Now!

We need to hurry in case anyone has heard the gunfire. And take several deep breaths.'

'We're not going to bury them?' Alistair asked.

'We'll take them with us. No one is ever left behind.'

Alistair and Cox lifted the bodies into the vehicle, starting with McPherson, then Lars, Ingrid, and finally Vlatkov. Per then secured Vlatkov's feet and tied his hands to the metal struts inside the lorry. Cox went to the lorry cabin, returning with a pick and spade. He tossed the spade to Alistair.

'Shovel up the blood, Alistair, and throw it into the lake.'

'What? Why?'

'No trace. Nothing for police dogs or hunters to find.'

Alistair dug into the soft, deep reddish-brown mud on the track. His mouth was dry and his pulse still pounding. What he had done astounded him. It had happened so quickly. But what frightened him more was how easy it had been.

Ten minutes later, Alistair was sitting in the lorry's cabin, his father at the wheel.

'Are you alright?' Frank asked.

'I don't know.'

'If it's any consolation, she would've killed me first, then you. Despite her charms, she was a traitor, Alistair. Urquhart, who was stationed at the NATO headquarters outside Oslo in the fifties, had told Larsen about the secret NATO Stay-behind armies. Ingrid confirmed the extent of the operation by stealing highly sensitive documents from the US Embassy in London and informed her father. Lars passed the information onto the Soviets. Urquhart then travelled to Finland posing as a Norwegian, Jan Johansen, while in Ivantra he witnessed a meeting between my contact and Per Sangolt. The photo taken from your mother's house gave him a face. Urquhart then identified my contact to the KGB and my contact was killed.'

'So what now?' he asked.

'Vaasa.'

'But it's a trap, you said so! And Uncle John even sent out the message that we had Vlatkov and would make the rendezvous.'

'You got a better plan?'

Alistair sat mute.

'Vaasa is on the coast, Alistair. If we're to leave Finland, it's either by air or by sea. Personally, I'd prefer to stay away from Helsinki. So why not Vaasa?'

The lorry rumbled on. 'So the Stay-Behinds are safe? It's over.'

'Perhaps.'

'What do you mean?'

'Why was your mother's house burgled?'

'You said it was for a photograph of your team and so Urquhart could identify Per. Isn't that right?'

'How long has your mother lived in Reading?'

'Not long. She moved there recently. I didn't even know...' Alistair paused. 'So who did?'

'Good question.'

Alistair was quiet for a minute. 'Angela said some men came from mother's work to help clean up. Did you know she had a job?'

'Your mother has always been secretive. Could it be that nothing was taken during the burglary?'

'But the house was ransacked, Angela said.'

'Maybe the burglary was staged just to get these men inside the house. So they could spend hours there looking for something specific while supposedly cleaning up. Suppose they weren't from her work but just said they were. Would Angela know any different, especially if your mother wasn't actually at home at the time?'

'You mean Soviet agents were there? What's in those photos that worry you, father?'

'Despite it being twenty years old, if it's the one I think the Soviets passed to Urquhart, the photograph not only contains a picture of Per, it also is one of the few photographs in existence of the current Director General of MI5.'

'Do you know who the Director General is?'

'Yes.'

'Why did you shoot Vlatkov and not kill him?' Alistair asked.

'Not sure I did.'

'Then who?'

'Larsen, would be my guess. But Larsen would have intended to kill Vlatkov, to stop him from talking and exposing him. But, and I know it's a hunch, I don't think Vlatkov told his Soviet handlers about the Stay-Behinds. I think he was under suspicion. If he couldn't convince you to defect, it was the ultimate get-out-of-gaol-free card. He'll never be able to use it now.'

'Did you intend to kill Vlatkov?'

'I never intend to kill, Alistair. That would make me a psychopath. However, sometimes, hard decisions must be made. For the benefit of the team, the nation and, in this instance, Western democracy. But these decisions are never taken lightly.' Frank glanced across at Alistair. 'You did the right thing, Alistair, and I'm proud of you. It took courage to do what you did.'

'What are you going to do now?'

'What would you do?' His father glanced across at Alistair again. 'Think, Alistair. What would you do?'

He thought for a few seconds. 'You think Vaasa is a trap?'

'Could be.'

'Then before I did anything, I'd want to know who is waiting for us at the dock in Vaasa, and where they got their information. So, I guess I'd park the lorry away from the rendezvous site and try to find out. Did you know about Lars before tonight?'

'I had my suspicions.'

'He was in your patrol, wasn't he? In the SOE, that is.'

'Yes. But Jock was right. Old alliances don't count anymore.'

'Are you expecting trouble in Vaasa?'

'Before I learned of the photograph taken from your mother's place, I'd have said no. But now?' Frank ran his hand over his day-old beard. He paused.

Alistair could see his father was thinking, his mind focused. Several minutes passed in silence as the lorry rumbled on.

'Cox is right about something else,' Frank said finally. 'Urquhart is too removed to have co-ordinated this, Alistair. And I don't believe the Soviets could have connected all the pieces so quickly.

Someone at MI5 is assisting them. Someone in our own Security Services wants us... out of the way. And they came pretty close to achieving it. We'd have walked straight into it. Larsen, both father and daughter, along with Vlatkov, would've killed us all. By sheer luck John mentioned the burglary at your mother's and that he'd stopped by Achnacarry. Then you saying Urquhart denied knowing McPherson made some connections fit together.'

'Are these NATO bases really so important?' Alistair asked.

'About as Top Secret as can be imagined. Larsen risked his daughter to get the information. Max Guzmann will be forced to resign and probably should be convicted of stupidity, if nothing else. The Larsens would've been heroes in the USSR if the KGB knew about the extent of the Stay-Behinds. We must assume they know one exists in Norway and now possibly one in Finland, which will make them suspicious there are more. But all they really know is that some troops were seen around the Finnish-Soviet border. Nothing unusual there. Urquhart's career is finished. He'll spend years in prison for espionage. But something tells me another is yet to be found.' Frank was silent for a few minutes. 'Poor old John. He was a good transmitter. The fingers of an angel, so the Director General used to say.'

'The Director General was in SOE too?' Alistair asked.

'In a manner of speaking, yes. The Soviets may already have a copy of the photograph taken from your mother's house.'

'They can identify him?'

'We must consider it a possibility, yes.'

Alistair dropped his head forward. His mind was on his uncle John. 'I loved him. Uncle John. I loved Scotland because of him.'

'And he you. Nothing will ever change that, Alistair.' Frank paused. 'Once it's dawn, we'll start disposing of the bodies in the lakes. One good thing about this part of Finland is the vast number of the things. Anyone looking will need years. Larsen first, then Ingrid. I'd prefer to bury John at sea, if we can manage it.'

'How did Vlatkov arrange the meeting on the Ivantrankovski Dam with the Finns? There was no one in the western observation tower. At least, I don't think there was.'

'You're right, Alistair. But it's never what you know. Always who.'

'You arranged it?'

'I did.' But Frank was lying. His mind was on who had.

CHAPTER THIRTY-TWO

Central Finland

20th April 1966

Dawn was lighting the horizon with its crimson-yellow glow. It was beautiful and stood in stark contrast to the events of the night. Frank slowed the lorry and stopped, pulling on the handbrake. Alistair jumped out and walked to the rear of the vehicle, then opened the doors. Cox was sitting opposite Vlatkov, wide awake, his weapon still firmly gripped in his hand, his eyes fixed on the Russian.

Sangolt woke as the doors opened and looked out.

Cox stood. 'Thank goodness you stopped. I need a leak. And he probably does too.' Cox jumped down from the lorry while Sangolt untied Vlatkov's feet and pushed him to the rear of the lorry. 'Out!'

Vlatkov squatted on the lorry floor, then swung his legs over the edge and jumped out, falling onto the track. Cox bent over and grabbed the man by the collar, pulling him up. 'Hold the pistol on him, Per,' Cox said and went to relieve himself by a tree.

'I need food and water!' Vlatkov demanded. 'And a doctor!'

'Later. You'll eat when the rest of us do,' Frank said.

Alistair glanced at his father, who appeared unmoved by Vlatkov's pleas. Truth be told, Alistair was a bit in awe of his father. Just as he'd said on the night they'd had dinner together in London, Frank Quinn belied emotion. Quick, analytical, decisive action, and complete ruthlessness when required. Alistair understood that now. He stared at Ingrid's lifeless body. The thought of what he'd done should have made him feel something. He'd acted quickly, without hesitation. It was done in a second. He saw a threat and took action, instinctively, and it had come easily to him. It was a high stakes game where she'd played him like a fool and paid the price for losing. The image of his father sitting in that frayed chair in his study, chain-smoking surfaced in his memory. He glanced up at the man, Frank Quinn. Alistair wondered about his father's years of total indifference towards him. Perhaps it hadn't been driven by disinterest, but the complete reverse. His father did a job that was secret and dangerous. And the responsibility of taking life was the secret burden of an officer of the Secret Intelligence Service. Perhaps that was why his father had been so distant with him his whole life. His father hadn't wanted this life for his son. Alistair saw his father with fresh eyes now.

Cox walked back towards them, re-buttoning his fly. Going straight to the lorry, he opened the rear door and climbed in. Alistair stared at the body of Ingrid Larsen. He'd glimpsed her eyes moments before he'd killed her. What he'd seen was her entrenched fanaticism, and it was overflowing with deadly emotion. He'd fallen for a honey trap and had only his father to thank that he wasn't right now either dead or on his way to the Lubyanka.

Frank was next to drive, with Alistair beside him. Neither spoke as the lorry bumped along the narrow, untarred forest road. In the darkness, Alistair looked through the windscreen at the stars above them. A half-moon flooded its light down on the virgin forest and patches of snow still lay amongst the trees, untouched by human feet. No vehicle had driven this way since the last snow had fallen. Flat, wet land with not a soul or an animal in sight stretched away for miles.

'Do you know where you're going, father?'

Frank nodded. 'Never used this road before, but as long as we are travelling north and slightly west, we'll come to a settlement. Once on the tarred road, there'll be signage to Kuopio.'

'All figured out?'

'Always best.'

A few minutes later, Alistair saw the wide expanse of another lake. The moonlight glistened over the tranquil waters. Frank slowed the vehicle and stopped, pulling on the handbrake.

'We'll put Larsen here,' Frank said and jumped out of the lorry. Alistair went to the rear and opened the doors. Inside, Cox and Sangolt stood. They lifted the body of Lars Larsen from the lorry. Minutes later, they stood around their former comrade on an un-sealed track somewhere in the middle of Finland. 'You were once a friend, Lars. So for those times, I salute you.' With that, Frank and Cox saluted. Sangolt stood to attention. Alistair stepped forward to lift Larsen's body.

'Not this man, thank you, Alistair,' Frank said. 'This is our sad duty.'

Lifting Larsen's weighted corpse, Sangolt and Cox threw their former comrade into the lake, his thin body making the smallest splash.

'And Ingrid?' Cox asked.

'Not here. Just in case one is found.'

Cox nodded, and they climbed back into the lorry.

Half an hour later, Frank pulled the lorry up again and got out, Alistair joined him at the back of the vehicle. 'You can sit this one out, Alistair, if you'd prefer.'

'No. I killed her. I bury her.'

'As you wish.'

Alistair collected the stones and weighted her clothing. Carrying her body, he walked into the lake and lowered her into the icy waters, her blonde hair floating on the surface around her face. Cox and Sangolt looked on, but said nothing. In the silence, Alistair watched the girl sink until the ripples travelled beyond sight. Then he turned and waded back to the land. Without speaking, he climbed into the lorry once more, sitting in the front passenger seat, his lower legs and feet wet and cold. He felt angry; not with Ingrid, but with himself for being so easily fooled, and swore it would never happen again. He stared through the windscreen at the virgin forest. Nothing moved. 'Should we contact London? They probably know about the debacle on Ivantrankovski Dam by now.'

Frank started the engine. 'I thought it went rather well. And we'll contact London when we're closer to Vaasa. That way, Alistair, no one knows if we are alive or dead or, in fact, where we are.'

'But surely the Finnish Police will give them a list of the dead?'

'I don't know if Jenkins, Thorne and Harper were hit. They may be alive. I suspect they are. And no one there knew about John McPherson or the Norwegians. The only ones they won't be able to locate are Vlatkov, Cox, you and me. So they'll assume we've been taken by the Soviets.'

'Did Uncle Laurence and the Director General know about your former SOE team being here?'

Frank nodded.

'Won't the Finns wonder about Vlatkov, if they knew about him being in Finland to meet you?'

'They'll assume the Soviets took him to Svetlovorsk. And with Lars's involvement, the Soviets may have wanted either to take us or kill us on the dam wall. Happily, they didn't get the chance. The local police here may spend some time looking for us, but they'll soon give up.'

'Why? A diplomatic incident on their soil?'

'That's precisely why. Too embarrassing all around and in view of how things played out, the Soviets would only deny it. We'll be out of Finland by tomorrow. Our safety lies now in radio silence and staying mobile.'

'If the Finns know not to look for us, why are we leaving Finland covertly?'

'Because someone on our side wants us dead, Alistair.'

CHAPTER THIRTY-THREE

Central Finland

20th April 1966

The lorry slowed, then turned left. Alistair sat facing Vlatkov, his Browning L9A1 in his hand. He thought the Russian had the resolute face of a condemned man, but he didn't see forlorn hopelessness. His gaze shifted to his father, asleep in the rear of the lorry. Alistair checked his watch. Almost two hours had passed. The lorry lurched to the right and he could tell they'd finally left the unsealed road and were now on a tarred surface. With the vehicle's change of movement, his father sat up. Alistair glanced at him. Even though Frank had had little proper sleep, Alistair could see the clear, determined expression of total concentration.

Frank looked at his watch. 'Hit the rear panel, would you, Alistair?'

The vehicle slowed, then stopped. When Cox opened the door, Alistair could see the morning light, the sunbeams hitting the trees and making the lakes like silvery mirages. Cox and Sangolt came to the rear of the lorry.

Frank jumped down. 'I calculate Kuopio is about five miles away now. I'll take over the driving. I want all of you in the rear and out of sight from now on until we leave Kuopio for the west coast. Jock gag Vlatkov now. While in the town, I'll re-fuel the lorry and buy some food for us all.'

'I thought you didn't speak Finnish?' Alistair asked.

'I have a little. But I know a bit of Swedish. Should be fine.'

Cox and Sangolt climbed in and sat along the sides of the lorry beside Alistair, opposite Vlatkov.

The door closed and a minute later; the engine roared again.

'I'll watch him, if you'd like to sleep,' Cox said.

Cox sat with his rifle pointing at Vlatkov, his eyes fixed on the Russian. Alistair leaned his head back and closed his eyes.

Frank drove into Kuopio. He checked his watch. About half-past eight. Finding a depot on the outskirts of the town, he drove in and filled up the lorry. A lorry drivers' rest stop was at the rear. Locking the vehicle, he strolled into the café and spoke to a middle-aged woman there in Swedish.

'I have to drive to Helsinki this morning,' Frank lied. 'Can I buy some sandwiches and coffee for the trip?'

'Lucky for you, I speak Swedish. Few around here do. You're a little too far east for most Swedish speakers.'

Frank smiled. 'The pay is better with long haul.' He watched the woman scribble the order on a slip of paper. He could see her eyes darting to him. She seemed to be checking him, his clothing and appearance. Perhaps she thought him too well dressed for a lorry driver. Perhaps she'd heard a radio broadcast about events in Ivantra or that the police were looking for foreigners. Frank stepped forward and leaned on the counter. 'I like your hairstyle, if you don't mind me saying. Very modern. And chic. I'll tell my wife. I think that style would suit her. Are you Swedish?'

The woman smiled. 'No. But I come from the west coast.' The subject of why he was so far east appeared to have been forgotten. Frank continued to chat small talk, on the unseasonal weather and the price of bread. Fifteen minutes later, he had five thick sandwiches and two thermoses of hot coffee. 'Are you sure I can't pay you for the thermoses?'

'Just return them when you're through next time,' she beamed.

Frank smiled and, thanking the woman for her kindness, left the café and ambled back to the lorry. Closing the driver's door, he started the engine and drove away from the depot. Skirting the town, he drove west now, the drive to Vaasa at least ten hours. If the woman had suspected him and telephoned the police, he reasoned, he would be stopped before leaving Kuopio's outskirts. With his left hand, he took his pistol from his coat, checked it, and placed it into the driver's door compartment. Checking the side and rearview mirrors frequently for police cars, he drove out of town. Half an hour later, Frank stopped the lorry on a side road and opened the rear doors. He passed the sandwiches and coffee around.

'From here to Vaasa is about ten hours,' Frank told them. 'You can remove the gag now, Jock. We'll continue to drive in shifts of two hours on, two off. And two in the cabin, two in the rear; one to sleep, the other to watch Vlatkov. And be careful, Alistair, when it's your turn. He'll attempt to get you to release his hands. He'll say he can't escape inside the lorry. Which is true, but he could knock you unconscious and escape by jumping out of the moving lorry. He'd be miles from anywhere, of course, but he'd consider that a worthwhile risk to take.'

Alistair looked his father in the eye. 'Don't worry. I won't succumb to his flattery.'

Cox drew the lorry up on a side road. They'd driven all day and Alistair felt the growing need for undisturbed sleep. He blinked multiple times, telling himself that Sangolt, Cox and his father were twice as old as himself. Opposite him, Vlatkov appeared to be asleep. Sangolt also had his eyes closed. Yawning, Alistair waited for the rear doors of the vehicle to be opened.

He heard the handle turn. The door opened a crack, the evening light flooding in. Cox stood beside the doors.

'Alistair, out! You too, Per,' Cox said.

Alistair stood and went to the edge of the lorry and jumped down, Sangolt joining him. Cox closed the door behind them and they joined Frank by the roadside. From inside the lorry, they could hear Vlatkov's protests.

Frank checked his watch. Although now nearly seven o'clock, it was still light, sunset not due for a couple of hours. 'We're on the outskirts of Vaasa now. The rendezvous was scheduled to be at the old Customs House in the port at nine tonight. That's about two and a quarter hours from now. But before we go there, we'll find the fishing boat that's waiting to take us to Shetland.'

'You arranged two boats?' Alistair asked.

'Yes,' Frank paused. 'A spare, just in case.'

'You arranged this too before leaving?' Alistair asked.

Frank nodded. 'Always best to have an alternative escape route, Alistair.'

'Why Shetland?' Alistair asked, thinking the place about as remote as could be imagined.

'Out of the way and British. Can't have Vlatkov seen. The Soviets will be looking for him, so it must be a place where they will find it difficult to stage a rescue. He needs to be gagged from now on. And once on board, I don't want Vlatkov off the ship until we are in a British port.'

Sangolt and Cox climbed back into the lorry, Cox gagging Vlatkov. Alistair sat in the cabin with his father. On the northern side of Vaasa harbour was a sizeable fishing co-operative building. Frank drove in. It consisted of one extensive building, a cold store, and three smaller huts. Frank and Alistair wandered towards one hut and knocked at the door. Within a minute, the door opened and Frank spoke to the men inside in Norwegian. A tall, well-built man walked with them to a large fishing trawler berthed at the wharf a little distance away.

'Nice boat,' Frank said, then took a pipe from his pocket and went about lighting it. Alistair watched his father at work; calm, completely at ease. Within minutes, Frank was shaking the man's hand and walking back towards the lorry.

'We leave in an hour. Jock, you and Per load John's body and make sure Vlatkov is on board and tied down.'

'Frank, this trawler captain? No trouble with him? No awkward questions?'

'He was expecting us, Jock. I always intended to leave Finland this way. He's also cleared it with the Finnish Customs to depart at eight.'

Cox smiled. He turned to Alistair. 'You have a lot to live up to, Alistair, if you're ever going to be as good as your father.'

'Get John's body and Vlatkov onboard now,' Frank said. 'Alistair and I will take the lorry and leave it in the back streets near the Old Customs House.'

Cox went to the rear of the lorry and opened the doors. Together, Cox and Sangolt carried the body of John McPherson on board the trawler. Minutes later, they returned to the lorry. Cox climbed in and stood over Vlatkov. 'We're leaving. If you're clever, and I think you are, you'll come quietly. You know, firsthand, that this isn't a game. If you cause trouble, you die. It's as simple as that. And the Gulf of Bothnia is deep.'

Alistair watched them head towards the trawler.

'We'll take the back roads from here to the old port, Alistair.'

Frank retrieved his pistol from the cabin, then went to the rear of the lorry. He took a grenade from Cox's pack, placed it into his coat pocket, then joined Alistair.

Twenty minutes later, Alistair stood with his father near a group of reddish-brown timber boat-sheds adjacent to a long, solid, rectangular structure painted mustard yellow. In front of it was a long, wide wharf and about twenty yards away, several large sea-worthy boats were tied up to the wharf. Amongst them, Alistair saw an enormous pleasure cruiser, the sort that wealthy Greek entrepreneurs or Hollywood film stars owned. A woman was on deck. A man wearing a white captain's cap was standing near the gangway.

'A bit on the noticeable side, isn't it?' Alistair asked.

'Oh yes!' Frank added, a smile crossing his lips.

Alistair looked at his father. 'You staged this too? Who do you suspect?'

'Let's just find out.'

'It shouldn't be too difficult. There's no cover between the building and the boat,' Alistair said.

'You see those crates and luggage further down, Alistair?' Frank pointed. 'I'll circle the building and toss a grenade into them. You watch who comes out. Then use the back streets to get back to the trawler as fast as possible. As soon as you arrive, get on board and stay below with the others. Wait no more than fifteen minutes for me.'

'Why so little time?'

'Despite the number of islands around this port, there's only one way out of the Gulf of Bothnia and it won't take them long to find the fisherman's boat and entrap us in the gulf.'

Alistair nodded.

Frank left their position at the southern corner and ran around the rear of the building, stopping under windows and peering around doors. The building, even though only one storey in height, was a large place, the windows well above ground level. In the early evening light, Alistair kept his eye focused on the far corner of the structure. Three minutes later, he saw a dark figure at the far end of the building some hundred yards away. Four seconds later, the detonation resounded around the hard surfaces, the shock wave thumping in his chest within seconds. People came running from the building.

Alistair stared at the group. He counted eight men. Some he knew would be officials, some may be fishermen, but a few would be traitors. Among those running, he saw Captain Mug-face; Urquhart. Beside him was Jenkins.

CHAPTER THIRTY-FOUR

Vaasa

Finland

20th April 1966

Alistair waited only a few seconds. He stood, his jaw clenched, his eyes fixed on Jenkins. He felt betrayed and angry. Emotion. No time for that, he thought. He could see Urquhart and Jenkins turning in circles, their eyes searching for Frank Quinn's team. Alistair ran back around the Old Customs House, crossing a wide intersection and disappearing into the streets behind the waterfront. He ran on, as fast as he could, more from who he'd seen waiting at the Old Customs House than from any sense of immediate danger. Although, he knew it wouldn't be long before Jenkins had men out looking for them. It was nearly sunset. The warehouses that lined the back streets were closed for the day. Alistair hurried on, his boots pounding the old cobbles as he ran. He felt such anger at the man's betrayal. Jenkins was one of the first people he'd met at MI5. He recalled Jenkins lecturing him about loyalty and asking if he'd kill his own mother for his country. Hypocrite! Alistair thought. Betraying murderous hypocrite! Alistair wondered about Harper and Thorne; he hadn't seen either of them. Were they traitors too? He couldn't process it all now. Ten minutes later, he saw the trawler. His father was already by the vessel when he arrived.

'Recognise anyone?' Frank asked as Alistair stepped onto the trawler. The Captain cast off the bow and aft ropes, then went to the coach house and switched on the engine. Seconds later, the vessel pulled away from the wharf.

Alistair nodded. 'Urquhart was there with Jenkins. Jenkins, of all people. I'll throttle him when I see him. All that bullshit about loyalty!'

'Put it down to experience, Alistair. Right now, we need to get out of sight.'

The ship started threading its way between the islands and out into the gulf. It was dark now and the lights of Vaasa were twinkling across the water. As they passed the Old Customs House, Alistair could see through a porthole the whole waterfront was congested with police cars, their flashing lights illuminating the wharves. Alistair continued to stare at the quay. He wondered what lies Jenkins would tell them. The man would thread a web of deceit to save his own neck.

Frank stood on the deck, the captain's binoculars in his hand. From inside the cabin, Alistair could see his father's coat flapping in the wind, his hair blowing to one side. A strong wind and rough seas were causing the trawler to roll in the waves. His father stood, his feet astride, his face turned back towards the receding Finnish coast.

Once the ship entered the Baltic, Frank stood beside the Norwegian Captain, a man of about Frank's age. Alistair joined them.

'I understand we're going to Shetland?' the Norwegian said.

Frank nodded.

The fisherman stared at Frank, a slight squint in his deep-set blue eyes. 'Would I be right in guessing you know that stretch of water?'

Frank looked out to sea. 'Perhaps.'

'Rode the Bus, I'm guessing?'

Frank turned to face the captain, but he didn't respond. 'Mind if I use your binoculars again?'

'Be my guest,' the Captain said.

While Alistair hadn't understood the bus comment, he noted his father hadn't admitted any previous connection to special wartime duties, but the fisherman had most likely guessed. His father's wartime activities continued to surprise him. And the memory of his father's accurate and calm assessment of their current situation was a salient reminder of the business Alistair had signed up for. Oddly, in his head, he heard Jenkins saying that what they did was serious and that he'd probably die alone. Jenkins. Alistair gripped the pistol in his pocket. Every time he thought about the man, Alistair seethed.

The captain went to check on some rigging, leaving them alone on the deck for a few minutes. 'Did you suspect Jenkins?' Alistair asked.

'I suspect everyone, Alistair. Until proven wrong. Or right.'

'Cox said Urquhart wasn't high enough up the chain to have orchestrated this. Is Jenkins?'

'Jenkins has a senior role. And a top security clearance. He has access to all records and moves freely around both MI5 and, when the need arises, MI6. He's well placed to devise all manner of things.'

'Will he be arrested?'

'He isn't on British soil currently. So we'll have to wait for him to return.'

'What if he doesn't?'

'Then we'll know he's guilty. But remember, we still have Vlatkov. A good bargaining chip, wouldn't you say?'

Alistair hoped he'd get the chance to confront Jenkins once back in England. That was if Jenkins returned. Perhaps he thought he'd got away with it; that he could continue to work both sides. If he did, he was in for a surprise. Alistair thought of Uncle John, whose body was on board, and Larsen, Ingrid, and the unknown lorry driver whose bodies would never be found. Solitary deaths. Instant and savage. He stared at the horizon. You'll still die alone. Alistair also remembered Jenkins saying that none of it mattered. Was that because Jenkins was passing it all onto the Soviets anyway? Jenkins had also said he'd been to Achnacarry in Scotland. Now it made sense.

CHAPTER THIRTY-FIVE

North Sea

21st April 1966

When the fishing trawler sailed into the North Sea, the sea was calm and a light, southerly breeze filled Alistair's nostrils. While in the Baltic, he had experienced no problems with sea sickness but in the unexpected calm of the North Sea; the trawler yawed and pitched its way through the endless swell that rolled its relentless way east across the North Atlantic uninterrupted from the coasts of North America. He breathed in the salty air, hoping to quell the growing uneasiness in his stomach.

'The Norse gods are with us today,' the Captain said. 'But then, it isn't winter.'

'Where is home?' Frank asked him.

'Bergen. You know it?'

'I've been there.'

Alistair grasped the gunwale trying to stifle a yawn, the prelude, so Sangolt had told him, to sea sickness. The ship pitched again and fell into a trough, creaking timbers and sending salt spray over the bow. Alistair vomited over the side, hoping his father and the others hadn't seen him. He stared at the horizon. As far as Alistair could see, the sea stretched away to the west forever.

'Still wanting to go to Shetland?' the Captain asked, his head indicating Alistair standing by the rail.

'Yes, and he'll get over it,' Frank responded.

The Norwegian stood, his hand on the helm. 'There's something you could do for me. If you don't mind.'

'What would that be?' Frank asked.

'I won't be staying in Lerwick any longer than to refuel and buy provisions. Can't expect pleasant weather in the North Sea to last even in spring.' The gruff Norwegian paused before speaking again. 'I'd be grateful if you'd pay a visit to a memorial in Scalloway for me. Nils Karlsen My older brother. He was in the Norwegian resistance. Died in '41 on the Shetland Bus.'

'It would be my honour,' Frank replied.

Alistair looked at his father chatting to the hardened fisherman. He saw what he thought was an immediate affinity between the two strangers. It lasted only a few seconds, but it spoke of another time. Of hardship and danger. His gaze shifted from the captain to his father. Stern men. Professionals in their field. He was grateful for this time with his father. He also acknowledged that he was developing something for his father he never thought he would; respect.

While the weather held, and while still in the North Sea, they held the burial for John McPherson. Sangolt, a hard and solitary man who, Alistair guessed, had seen much during the war years, had tears in his eyes. Alistair stared at the face of his favourite uncle one last time. Even in death, he loved the man. Tears flowed down his cheeks and over his jaw, then dripped to the deck. Pursing his lips, he sniffed, then stood erect as the body of John McPherson slipped into the sea, the childhood memories of Glenrothie flooding his memory. He glanced at his father, whose face remained stiff and unmoved, but Alistair believed the man was inwardly crushed by the unnecessary death of one of his oldest friends.

No one spoke much for hours after the burial. There was no eulogy. Alistair had stood with three men who'd known John McPherson from the war and had served with him. And now they had been together at his death. Alistair remembered the nameless lads he'd trained with at Achnacarry and understood the close bond of serving men. He only had his childhood memories of Uncle John, but they were innocent memories; of happy times, of hunting together and of school holidays in Scotland. But he surmised that even if John McPherson had died peacefully in his sleep in Scotland and had a funeral held at the local church, nothing of his wartime service would be mentioned. It was all classified; secret for years to come. Alistair looked again at his father's face. He thought in the end, perhaps his uncle would have preferred it this way.

Lerwick, the principal town in Shetland, was smaller than Alistair thought it would be. It nestled, or rather clung, to the shoreline. Its few grey stone buildings huddled around the harbour front while some were built right into the sea. As different as could be imagined from Finland, it exuded privation and hardship for those who called it home.

Frank stepped ashore, then went to the harbour master's office on the waterfront to telephone the local police as he and the Director General had determined. He then placed a second call to the Director General to have Urquhart and Jenkins detained as soon as they arrived back in England.

He dialled the private line and waited.

'Frank! Thank goodness. I was beginning to think the North Sea had swallowed you all up. Who's with you?'

'Alistair. He did well. We have Vlatkov. Larsen is dead, as is his daughter, Ingrid. Also, sadly, John McPherson.'

There was silence for a few seconds. 'Good news about Vlatkov. I'm sorry to hear about John. He was a good man. Did Alistair crumble?'

'No. In fact, it was he who killed Ingrid Larsen. If he hadn't, I'd be dead.'

'Surprising! And Cox and Sangolt?'

'No disloyalty there. Urquhart and Jenkins were at the Old Customs House.'

'Where's the Russian?'

'Here and still on board, but the local Lerwick Police will be here shortly. He's injured, gunshot wound to the arm. He'll be fine. I'll instruct them to keep Vlatkov well locked up until they receive instructions from you.'

'Tell them to keep him under lock and key. Twenty-four hours surveillance. No visitors except the doctor. No moving him out of his cell. And I don't want to hear he's hanged himself either. I'll look after him now. You've done enough for the time being. Just get yourself and Alistair back to London. Tell Cox to return to Achnacarry. He's in charge for the time being. And I'll inform C.'

'No, not yet.'

'Why?'

'Just until we have everyone involved arrested. Have the military police arrest Urquhart once he's back and away from Jenkins. Jenkins, we should bring back to London. I want him where we can keep an eye on him.'

Frank hung up and returned to the quay. Meeting the local Police Inspector at the wharf, Frank went with Vlatkov to the rear of the police van. He wanted to make sure the man was secure and in custody. 'Don't let him out of your sight, Inspector. Twenty-four hour surveillance! The prison doctor can visit but no one else and never unsupervised. This man is extremely dangerous and should be hand-cuffed at all times. On no account is he to be left alone to either escape or take his own life.'

'Understood, sir. I've arranged a suitable cell for him. Until your people come to transfer him to London, he'll be watched day and night. You have my word on it.'

'It may be a while, so watch him closely.'

'Very good.'

Alistair watched Vlatkov being escorted away. He hoped never to see the man again. He waited on the quay beside Cox until his father re-joined them.

Per jumped from the trawler to the wharf. 'I'll leave you here, Frank. The captain has agreed to take me to Bergen. I can get a train home from there.' Per gripped Frank's hand. 'Never thought I'd get the chance to work with you again.' He looked across at Alistair, who stood beside his father. 'This man is a hero. You must be very proud, young Alistair.' The Norwegian turned to Cox. 'Good bye, Jock. Good to see you again.'

Alistair walked with his father and Cox away from the wharf towards the township. Turning left at the Market Cross, they found a hotel and something to eat. After the meal, he walked away, leaving his father and Cox to reminisce about old times. He wanted the solitude. Wrapping his coat around him, he wandered along the narrow road back towards the Market Cross and down to where the boats lay tied up to the wharf. He stared out over the water to the island of Bressay, his mind on the events of the last week.

He was seventeen years old. Had successfully completed Commando training, he could speak Russian, had overheard highly sensitive intelligence while on Soviet soil, had taken part in a raid, and been party to a kidnapping of a Soviet KGB agent. He'd also taken a life. He stared into the waters slapping against the wharf and breathed in the salty air. His hand felt the Browning in his pocket. His fingers loosely wrapped around it, playing with it, the metal cool against his palm. Even though it had been a reflex action, killing Ingrid had been done in an instant. What amazed him most was how easy it had been. He recalled what his father had said about killing; the burden of responsibility and the consequences of guilt. But the truth was, he felt nothing. Hunching into his coat, he turned and walked back along the road, heading for the Queen's Hotel on the seafront, where his father had booked some rooms. On the wind, he caught the aroma of the sea. Despite the cold and the incessant wind, he liked Shetland. There was something hypnotic about it. It wasn't a place for frivolity; it was the domain of the mentally and physically tough and he felt part of it.

Looking up, he saw his father walking towards him.

'Has it helped?' Frank asked.

'What's that?'

'Clearing the head.'

'Maybe.'

'I'm going to the post office to book our passage. We'll leave on the first ferry for Aberdeen tomorrow.'

'Another boat?'

Frank smiled. 'Yes.'

'And Vlatkov?'

'SIS will escort him south. You've done your bit.'

Alistair watched his father walk away. Perhaps his father thought he'd feel guilt or remorse for what he'd done. A half smile spread over his lips. He knew he should be horrified. But he wasn't.

CHAPTER THIRTY-SIX

Britain

22nd April 1966

The crossing had been straight forward. Aberdeen lay before them. Alistair thought the weather was quite pleasant and a warm sun came and went behind thick Scottish clouds. Sharing a taxi, they drove to Aberdeen Railway Station. Cox purchased his ticket for Spean Bridge, Frank and Alistair theirs for London. In the railway forecourt, Frank shook hands with Cox. Alistair noted the firmness of the grip; two men who had little in common but who complemented each other perfectly. Alistair nodded at the stern Scot. 'I won't say it's been a pleasure, Sergeant-Major, but thank you all the same.'

'You did alright... for a toe-rag! You know where I am.'

Alistair laughed. 'Can't bear to be parted from me, Sar-Major?'

'Watch your puny arse. Your father and I may not be there next time to save ya' backside.' Cox picked up his pack and, without waiting for a response, walked towards the platform for Spean Bridge.

Laurence was standing at Euston Station, waiting for them. Alistair walked with his father and uncle across the station forecourt. A service car stood waiting outside.

Alistair got in and closed the car door. He sat in the rear with his father, Uncle Laurence in the front with the driver.

'What's happened to Jenkins?' Alistair asked.

'Nothing, as yet,' Laurence said.

'What?' Alistair asked.

'We're playing this, Alistair, as though you and your father are still missing. And we're playing dumb about the explosion at the Old Customs House in Vaasa. Internal matter for the Finns. Nothing to do with us. We've got Jenkins under a twenty-four-hour surveillance though.'

'Whose stupid idea was this?'

'The Director General's. Not mine, I can assure you. If it'd been up to me, I'd have had the blighter thrown into a dungeon the second he stepped foot back into Britain.'

'So who's watching Jenkins?'

'Thorne.'

'Thorne! But he and Jenkins are thick as thieves.'

'Glad you think so. He works exclusively for the Director General, actually.'

'Where are they?'

'Jenkins arrived back here yesterday. We're keeping him busy with paperwork currently. Jenkins sent Thorne and Harper home as soon as you disappeared with Vlatkov. Urquhart has been quietly removed by the Military Police and is being kept in a Scottish military prison until we have Jenkins where we want him.'

'And where's that?'

'K wants to take him when he's with his Soviet handlers. No defence then. No ambiguity. So it's watch and wait. His phones are being tapped and his every move is watched by Jim Skardon's best watchers. It's just a matter of time. And it won't be long.' Laurence paused. 'When did you suspect Jenkins?'

'All indications were that Jenkins was co-ordinating it all,' Frank said.

'Did Vlatkov have the photographs? The pictures... of me, I mean. Was that genuine?'

'They weren't on him. I don't know what he's done with them. But I don't want Jenkins touched until I can have a word with him.'

'I'm not sure about this, Frank. It's risky. What if Jenkins flies the coup?'

'How can he, with all the surveillance you have on him? We could offer him immunity for the negatives,' Frank added.

'You'd do that?'

'Why not? He can only refuse. Either way, he'll know we are on to him and he'll either run or fold. And we still have Vlatkov. I'm guessing the Soviets would exchange almost anyone to have him back.'

'As it's rather late now, why don't I drop you both off at your clubs and we can talk further about this in the morning?' Laurence said.

'Suits me, Laurence. I'm tired. Alistair, I'd be pleased if you'd have a late supper with me tonight?' Frank asked, turning to face his son.

Alistair looked at his father. That his father now wanted to spend time with him was a novel experience. 'Sure,' he said. Besides, the food at The Oxford and Cambridge was excellent, and he was hungry.

The car turned into Pall Mall and pulled up on the opposite side of the street to Frank's club.

'Thanks for the lift, Laurence. We'll see you tomorrow for a thorough debrief.' Frank closed the door to the car. Alistair got out and joined Frank on the footpath as the car drove away. Crossing the road, they walked towards the entry door to The Oxford and Cambridge Club.

CHAPTER THIRTY-SEVEN

London

22nd April 1966

Frank placed his pack on the floor and went to the window and looked out. He could see the rear lights of the service car some distance down Pall Mall now. Allowing the curtain to fall back over the window, he turned to face his son.

'Father?' Alistair said, now sensing that supper had been an excuse.

'How would you like to stay at the Ritz tonight?'

'What?'

'Alistair. Go and enjoy yourself. You've earned it. I'll pick up the bill if MI5 won't. I owe you my life, Alistair. You did well and I'm proud of you.' His father paused. 'I want you to have something.' Frank pulled a signet ring from his finger. 'I want you to have this. It's fitting you wear it now.'

Alistair stared at the ring in his father's hand. 'Why? It's yours.' He'd never seen his father without it on his little finger.

'It bears the family crest and motto. One to remember; Neither Despise nor Fear.' Frank paused, his face serious, his expression intense.

Alistair felt a shiver course through him.

His father continued to stare at him. 'I'll never see you again, Alistair.'

Alistair blinked several times. He couldn't move and he didn't know what to say. What his father had said stunned him. It made no sense. They'd just done a mission together, they'd faced probable death and lived. 'What are you saying?'

Frank smiled, then grasped Alistair's shoulders as though to hug him, but refrained. 'Stay at the Ritz. Please.' Then in a second, Frank grabbed his pack and, leaving Alistair standing in the foyer, hurried towards the stairs to the upper floors. Alistair stared after his father. Frank hadn't looked back and Alistair noted his father was almost running.

Alistair opened the entry door to The Oxford and Cambridge Club and stepped into the street, the door closing behind him. He stood on the pavement for some time. He felt numb. What was his father doing? He stared at the buildings on the opposite side of the street for no reason. What his father had said made no sense. But he knew enough now about his father to know that if his father wanted him, for whatever reason, to stay at the Ritz, then that's what he'd do. His father's last words to him repeated in his head as he walked away. While he didn't know what his father was planning, he had learned to trust his father's judgement. Frank Quinn was a clever man. He arranged things in advance. He left nothing to chance.

Whatever he was orchestrating, Alistair knew his father didn't want him staying in Knightsbridge.

He walked up St James's Street. He wasn't sure how he felt. And he didn't believe that he'd never see his father again. Alistair drew in a deep breath, then stared at the signet ring still in his hand. He slipped it onto his little finger. Looking at it, he twisted it with the fingers of his other hand, his mind on his father. His behaviour was odd, to say the least, but having the ring made Alistair feel as though he'd received his father's blessing for a job well done. For him, it symbolised acceptance into the family; like he belonged and that the flame had passed from one generation to the next. He felt his family line; he was a part of it. Just as much a part as any of the preceding generations; all integral to each other and equally important. Wearing the ring mattered to him now, and he felt proud. He cut through the side street and along Arlington Street before climbing the steps to the glamorous hotel and booked into a suite on the top floor.

Alistair woke abruptly. The telephone was ringing. He blinked, then sat up quickly and reached for the receiver, his other hand fumbling for his watch. Two o'clock in the morning! Only his father knew where he was and he'd half expected a call.

'Alistair?'

'Yes. Who's this?'

'Jenkins.'

Alistair audibly gasped. 'Where are you, you bastard! Or should I say traitor?'

'I'm no traitor, but we don't have time for this. Your father's life depends on you doing what I ask.'

'Why would I ever trust you?'

'How do you think I knew where to call?'

Alistair swallowed. Throwing back the sheets, he swung his legs over the side of the bed and stood up. While he listened to Jenkins, he glanced at the ring on his little finger, hoping by some magic it would tell him what to do and who to trust.

'Get dressed. Be downstairs and outside in Arlington Street in five minutes. Do you have a weapon?'

'Yes.'

'Bring it.'

The line went dead. Alistair rubbed his face, then reached for his clothes and dressed quickly. Tying his shoelaces, he checked the Browning was loaded and pushed it into his coat pocket. Taking the room key, he closed the door and hurried along the corridor, then took the lift to reception.

'Have a pleasant night, sir,' the hall porter said as he passed.

He could hear music coming from the dining room and a singer was crooning somewhere to the late evening diners. A piano played in the background. Leaving the pink interior, he stepped out onto the street, his hand on the shiny brass rail. Even though dark and late, a few people still walked along Piccadilly. Jenkins stood to one side, waiting.

'Well?' Alistair said. He could hardly look at Jenkins, and he certainly didn't trust him.

'We're to be outside the Royal Academy in ten minutes.'

'What the hell is going on?'

'I don't know.'

'What do you mean, you don't know? You were with Urquhart in Vaasa, waiting to kill us. Why would I trust you or go with you anywhere?'

'I was in Vaasa to collect you. And to watch Urquhart. Who, by the way, has been arrested. So if he's been arrested, and I was your enemy, don't you think I'd be in prison now too? Come on, Alistair, there isn't much time.'

Jenkins walked towards Piccadilly. Alistair stared after him. He heard his father's words about trusting your inner voice. 'You may regret this, Quinn, but what the hell!'

The Ritz doorman looked at him, bemused, doubtless wondering why he was talking to himself. But the well-trained man said nothing. Alistair hurried after Jenkins, who by now was on the other side of Arlington Street and waiting to cross Piccadilly.

* * *

Frank reached for the telephone in his room at The Oxford and Cambridge Club. He dialled the number.

'Hello?' A thick Russian accent.

'This is Frank Quinn of MI6 speaking. I wish to speak with your current most senior KGB officer.'

There was silence at the other end, as Frank knew there would be. He waited while the telephone line clicked and crackled. He could hear the Soviets monitoring and tracing the call. Frank knew they would have him located in a few minutes. The Oxford and Cambridge, while an exclusive club, was a public building, not a Security Services building with secure, untraceable telephone lines.

'Who is this?' another thick-voiced man finally said.

'I am Frank Quinn of MI6. I wish to meet with your most senior KGB officer in thirty minutes. Listen carefully. Be on the number 38 bus to Piccadilly Circus. Sit on the top floor at the front. Bring the photographs and the negatives of Sir Laurence Dalrymple with you. In exchange, I will tell you where you can find Vasali Vlatkov. I'll get on the bus at Green Park and alight at Piccadilly Circus, so you don't have much time.'

Frank hung up. He checked his pistol for ammunition. Reaching for his coat and hat, he placed the pistol in his pocket and descended to the street. He strode up St James's Street to Piccadilly. Crossing the road, he waited a few minutes near the Burlington Arcade entrance before walking west towards the bus stop at Green Park.

Frank stepped forward. He could see the bus approaching, the number 38 in massive white numerals emblazoned on the front. His hand played with the pistol in his pocket. No members of the public stood waiting to board the bus with him. He breathed in the cool night air. He expected his contact would already be onboard and, as they always worked in pairs, there would be two KGB men either on the top floor or sitting on the lower deck, waiting and watching for him to step onto the bus at Green Park. The Number 38 slowed and stopped.

Frank stepped onto the bus, his eye immediately taking in who was sitting downstairs. There were two men sitting in the front. Neither had looked up when he stepped aboard. Both were wearing coats and hats. These men, Frank believed to be the KGB officers. Behind them was a woman wearing a thick coat and with a scarf tied over her hair. Behind her sat two other men, one on the right, the other on the left, a few rows apart. Frank placed his foot on the first step to go upstairs as the bus pulled away from the curb. He climbed the twisting narrow staircase slowly, stepping onto the upper floor. No one was there. He sat on the first seat on the left and waited. He faced the stairs, his pistol drawn. He heard the footsteps. At least two people. He held the pistol steady. One man he'd seen downstairs now stood beside him, the other sat on the opposite side.

'Mister Quinn?'

'You have something for me?'

* * *

The No. 38 bus slowed and stopped outside the Royal Academy. Alistair and Jenkins stepped onboard. Jenkins walked straight along the lower deck and indicated for Alistair to sit at the rear of the bus. Alistair looked around at the other passengers. In front of him was a woman wearing a headscarf. There was no conductor. The only other people on board were two men, one on either side and a few rows in front of him.

* * *

The KGB man opposite Frank pulled an envelope from his coat and passed it to him. Frank reached for the packet with his left hand, flipped open the end, and shook the contents out. Two blank sheets of paper fell to the floor. He glanced at the man sitting opposite him. 'So there were no photographs. All a ruse to put names to faces and for Vlatkov to learn what he could. But you don't know where he is. Neither does your mole in MI5.'

The man standing behind Frank drew his pistol. 'We have other ways of finding out this information.'

'Larsen is dead. Also his daughter. And Urquhart has been arrested. Your mole doesn't know where I've hidden Vlatkov.'

'Then you will tell us, Mr Quinn, or you will die.'

Frank glanced at the eyes of both men. The man directly in front of him posed the greater danger. Gripping his silenced weapon, Frank fired one shot, killing the man opposite instantly. As Frank fired, he fell to the floor, twisting his body, his pistol arm swinging wide and fired again at the man who stood beside him.

CHAPTER THIRTY-EIGHT

London

23rd April 1966

Three shots came from the upper level of the bus. Alistair turned around and stared up the stairs to the upper floor, but no one descended. In that second, the woman stood and ran up the stairs to the upper floor. Less than a minute later, Alistair heard the thud-like cough of a silenced pistol fired once. He stiffened, half rising from his seat, but Jenkins blocked his exit.

'Move, you bastard! Didn't you hear that?' Alistair whispered.

Jenkins nodded. 'We move when we're told to.'

'What?'

As the bus pulled away from the curb outside the Royal Academy, another man, as though eager to catch the bus before it left, stepped aboard and went immediately to the upper floor. The two men sitting on either side of the bus and in front of Alistair stood. He could see it was Bill and Ben. He saw them stand on the rear platform, as though about to alight at the next stop or to block the exit.

'Now,' Jenkins said, standing, and he hurried to the foot of the stairs, standing beside Thorne and Harper.

'As I thought!' Alistair heard a female voice say from the upper floor.

'I had no choice.'

'Everyone has a choice, Laurence.'

Then another cough-like sound. The body of a short, thick-set man fell onto the stairs, tumbling down the narrow twisting stairway, his body wedged between the wall and the stair rail. Alistair could see his face. His uncle, Laurence Dalrymple, lay dead, shot through the chest.

Alistair withdrew his pistol and, before Jenkins could stop him, jumped over the body. He ran up the stairs, then stopped just before reaching the upper deck and peered over the railing. From where he crouched, he couldn't see his father. A man's feet protruded from one of the seats into the aisle. A third man lay sideways, caught between the seats, his eyes fixed wide in death. Alistair climbed one more step. He could see his father now, lying in the aisle. Standing in front of him, several feet away, Alistair saw his mother. She stood resolute, a silenced pistol in her hand. Jenkins was beside him now.

'Jenkins, clean up here. Where are Thorne and Harper?' Grace Quinn said.

'Down stairs, Ma'am.'

'Alistair, come with me,' Grace said. She pocketed the pistol, placed her hand on the rail, and went down the stairs.

Alistair could barely breathe. Jenkins passed him and went to check the dead bodies. Alistair wanted to see his father, but he needed to understand. The bus slowed and stopped. He knew his mother wouldn't wait. He turned quickly, glancing back at the body of his father, his eyes lingering over him for a second. 'Are you sure he's dead?' he whispered to Jenkins.

Jenkins nodded. 'Best you go. Talk with... your mother.'

'Did you know she was the Director General?'

Jenkins nodded. 'But we were all under instructions that you shouldn't.'

'Later!' Alistair ran down the narrow stairs and jumped off the bus. He wanted to quiz Jenkins, but he wanted to speak to his mother more. Glancing along the street in both directions, he saw her striding back along Piccadilly. Hurrying, he caught up with her.

'Not here, Alistair.'

'Where then?'

'Your suite is close by, isn't it?' the grey eyes focused on him.

Alistair bit his lip. So much he didn't know. But clearly, his mother and father had talked the previous evening. Together, mother and son walked into the pink interior of the Ritz and rode the lift to the top floor. Alistair reached for his key.

They stepped inside the suite.

'Expecting us to pick up the bill for this?'

'Yes, Mother,' Alistair said, his jaw set. If it had been Jenkins standing in front of him now, he believed he would've punched him.

His mother wandered over to an armchair by one of the luxuriously draped curtains.

'There's a window behind that curtain, by the way. Unlike other places you're probably familiar with.'

'That's enough impertinence.'

'Oh, I think you deserve it. Was that training course in Scotland your idea?'

'Just remember, Alistair, you started it!' Grace leaned forward. 'You wanted inclusion, well, you got it!'

'And father? What did he want?'

Grace sank back in the chair. 'He went along with it. But only because you were so determined.'

'Well, how did I do, ma'am?'

'There's no need for sarcasm, either.'

'So what else didn't you include your son in?'

Grace stared around the room, as though searching for words. 'Leaks continued long after Philby et al. left. We knew it had to be someone at the top. So, a plan was devised. It should have been easy enough, but it had to look genuine.'

'Genuine! Men died for your plan! Good men. Father and Uncle John, for example. Playing with other people's lives has got good and decent people killed!'

'Don't be naïve, Alistair! You father knew the risks. And as far as John is concerned, he and all the others, especially those in SOE, could've died during the war. They expected it. And most of them did! That they didn't die gave them twenty more years of life they didn't think they'd have. John had a good life.'

'And father?'

'Unfortunate.'

Alistair stared at his mother; the grey eyes, the set jaw and thin lips, there wasn't a shred of emotion on her hard face. He remembered his father and twisted the ring on his little finger; Neither Despise nor Fear. 'My God! So what now, Mother? Am I the next sacrificial lamb in the Security Service's machine?'

'Don't be ridiculous!' She looked up at Alistair. 'Have a drink and calm down. Your father knew what he was doing. It was his decision. In fact, it was his idea. As much as he didn't wish to believe it, we both suspected Laurence and when the situation presented itself, he decided it was time to act.'

'So that makes it OK, does it, Mother! My God! There isn't a scrap of compassion about you, is there?'

'Before you go judging me too harshly, I remind you that you killed that girl without too much thought. You may also like to know that Angela is receiving treatment and is considerably better. At least, I only have Brenda to deal with now. The others were a nightmare. Jocelyn, in particular, had a real liking for knives.'

'I didn't know she had multiple personalities.'

'There's a lot you don't know, Alistair. You're too young to know. And you still wouldn't have, if you'd remained at school.'

'Was it you who got Delprado expelled?'

'He did that all on his own. With your help, of course.'

'Where is he?'

'How would I know! I have enough to do without following teenagers around who aren't mine.'

'So, you acknowledge you have a son?'

'You had fun in Soho, didn't you?'

'Does Valerie work for you?'

'She informs. That's all. By the way, next time you run away, don't give your real name. If you'd stayed there informing us about people like the Krays, you wouldn't have been involved with the Soviets at all.'

'It wasn't my decision to leave there. You orchestrated it. All of it! But you knew what it involved. I didn't.'

'Twaddle! The innocent martyr role doesn't suit you, Alistair. You wanted to be part of it! You signed the Official Secrets Act. You did that willingly!' Grace stood. 'I'll give you some time off. I'm retiring myself soon. Officially, anyway. Get a few hours' sleep, then come to Leconfield House after lunch.'

'And if I don't?'

'I know where you are, Alistair. And I don't mean just tonight. You move, I know about it! Don't forget that! Remember; no divorce!'

Grace Quinn opened the door to the hall and left. Alistair stood in the doorway to his suite and watched his mother walk along the corridor. She never looked back.

He couldn't sleep. He thought of his father. And his mother. He sat in the chair by the window and watched the dawn settle over Green Park and drank his way through a bottle of Jameson's Irish whiskey.

CHAPTER THIRTY-NINE

London

23rd April 1966

Rising late, Alistair ate a full English breakfast in his suite at the Ritz before dressing. While everything in him told him to walk away, he knew he couldn't. Despite what she'd said, he wanted answers. His anger and resentment at last night's events still burned, but he knew he had to stay calm. His father had taught him that. Alistair half smiled. Perhaps his father had learned it from being married to his mother. He thought of Angela, his fragile sister and her multiple personalities. If she was better, he was glad of it. But he worried about her future. Perhaps his mother believed Angela would always be with her. Perhaps they fulfilled a personal need in each other. His mind lingered on the people who'd conceived him. Both ruthless, but in different ways. Both compassionate in their own ways; his mother for Angela and his father for the men he'd served with: John McPherson, Per Sangolt, even Lars Larsen, and for a German named Dieter Stecker, whose actions had started the whole thing. But they didn't live for their son. Alistair twisted the ring. Perhaps his father had shown his love for his son, just not in overt ways. Their son had carved his own life from the decisions he'd made. Alistair smirked. Perhaps that wasn't true. In the background, his mother pulled the strings. Always had, and he wondered if she always would.

Alistair closed the door to the suite and sauntered down to reception. Leaving the Ritz, he crossed Piccadilly. Buses were everywhere, as were people. Shops traded and hotels bustled with guests. Restaurants and cafes served cream teas, while shops of every kind catered for people with expensive tastes. All, it appeared, were oblivious to the events of last night. Four men had died. Two nameless KGB men, one of whom had killed his father. And two of the most important men in Alistair's life; his father and his Uncle Laurence.

Alistair strode away, taking the cut-through to Shepherd's Market, then into Curzon Street. Stepping inside the sliding doors, Alistair made his way to the third floor.

'Good morning, Miss McKillick,' Alistair said.

'Good morning, sir.'

Alistair could see the woman was more subdued than usual, but to anyone who hadn't known about the events of last night, there was no hint of sadness. 'Your mother has left you a note, sir.'

Alistair tore it open. It told him to go to Jenkins's office for a debrief of last night, then come to her office in one hour.

He left and took the stairs.

'Morning, Alistair,' Jenkins said. 'I know you weren't close to your father, but all this must still have come as a shock. It has to us all. Especially the Director General.'

'Not that I saw.'

'She doesn't do emotion.'

Alistair glared at Jenkins. 'I told you once my mother was off-limits to you and it still holds. How did he die?'

'Shot. Lower abdomen. Took out the kidney.'

Alistair looked up. 'Who?'

'Not one of us, if that's what you meant. One of the KGB men. Your father took a real risk, and it almost worked.'

'So there were no photographs of... Uncle Laurence.'

'No.'

'And Vlatkov never wanted to defect?'

'I cannot answer that conclusively, but I think it unlikely.'

Alistair stared at the mesh-covered window. 'Why?'

'Why, what?'

'Why was Uncle Laurence working for the Soviets?'

'It certainly wasn't for money or ego.'

'That leaves ideology and compromising material, doesn't it?'

Jenkins nodded. 'I wouldn't know about ideology. It could be that the Soviets threatened to expose his... homosexual preferences. It would have ended his career. Even if the recommendations of the Wolfenden Report are finally made law, it wouldn't have been in time to save him. He'd have been stripped of his knighthood, all honours, pension and probably incarcerated. Men like Sir Laurence don't survive long in prison.'

'Why didn't he run? The Soviets would have taken him, especially with what he knew.'

'Maybe he wasn't as committed to it as others. Perhaps he just liked his comforts too much.'

'A heavy price to pay to remain a member of an exclusive club.'

There was a knock at Jenkins's door. Bill and Ben walked in. 'Morning, Alistair,' Thorne said. Harper nodded.

Alistair watched them sit down. 'Do you know, I know nothing about you two. You were my first introduction to MI5 and I've never said more than a handful of words to either of you. What about lunch?'

Thorne and Harper glanced at Jenkins.

'Go on!' Jenkins said. 'You two could use some sun on your skin after all that nocturnal surveillance.'

'I have to see my...' Alistair paused, 'the Director General, so I'll meet you in Shepherd's Market. Say about half-past one?'

'Ok. See you there,' Thorne said.

Alistair shook hands with Jenkins. 'I can't say it's been a pleasure.'

'You've said that before. It sounds a bit like you're thinking of leaving us? Remember; no divorce.'

'I haven't forgotten. I've been given some time off. So you'll just have to manage without me for a while.'

'I said you were a cocky little bastard.'

'Always was, always will be, I suppose.'

Alistair left the fifth floor and took the stairs to the third. He knocked lightly on Miss McKillick's door. 'She in?'

'Go straight in, sir. She's expecting you.'

'Alistair,' Grace said, indicating the chair in front of her desk. 'Do you have any questions?'

'Truly, Mother?' He was about to say that his whole life was one gigantic question, but he stopped himself. He could see she was waiting for him to respond. 'No, Mother. No questions.'

'Good. As I said last night, I think you should take some time off.' She leaned forward and picked up an opened letter. 'I've had some correspondence from John McPherson's solicitor. You've inherited Glenrothie. Spend a month there sorting out what you want to do with the place, then report back.'

She looked up at him and their eyes met. Grey, distant. She could have been talking to the postman, not her son.

'I've also arranged for you to attend the flight attendant school at Heathrow and it starts in July.'

'Why?'

'Because I require it! You must have a job, Alistair, one that suits our business. And a long haul flight attendant works well.'

'How long?'

His mother frowned. 'Until I say otherwise.' Grace leaned forward and grasped another envelope. 'All the details are written here,' she said and handed him the sealed envelope.

Alistair took it.

'Any questions now?'

Alistair shook his head. 'You seem to have it all worked out. When will father's funeral be?'

'There won't be one. We never admit to the world when we've lost one of our own.'

'The burial then?'

He saw his mother stiffen. 'I don't enjoy having to repeat myself, Alistair. Was there anything else?'

A palpable silence filled the space between them.

'No, nothing else. I'll come and see you once I'm back from Scotland.'

'Good. Close the door on your way out.'

Alistair stood. 'Good bye, Mother.'

He walked down the stairs. He'd thought he didn't understand his father, but he had learned more about him in these last months than he'd ever known. Now, it appeared, it was his mother who was the complete blank to him. He shook his head in disbelief. Parents! he thought. Did they intentionally fuck up their children's lives? Checking his watch, he made his way to the pub in Shepherd's Market. Thorne and Harper were already there when he walked in.

An hour and a half later, he walked towards Piccadilly, then crossed into Green Park. As he walked, he stared up at the sky; it was blue, and he felt the gentle warmth of the English sun on his skin. On the Mall, he hailed a taxi. 'Soho, thanks,' he said, climbing into the rear. He leaned his head against the back of the seat. He didn't really know why he'd said it. But then, so many of the decisions in his life had been made on the spur of the moment. So much had happened, and he wasn't yet eighteen. Spring was almost over and the lovely warmth of summer would soon transform London's parks and streets. With it came the colourful hanging baskets and window boxes and the long twilights he loved so much about life in England. And cricket. Even Achnacarry would be warm, at least warm for Scotland.

The taxi pulled into Old Compton Road, then turned left into Greek Street. 'Pull up here, please.'

The taxi stopped. From his seat in the rear of the vehicle, Alistair stared at the plaque on the wall. The Club. He gazed at the one-way glass in the windows that faced the street. Valerie, he felt sure, would be in the front room getting things ready for another busy night. It would be so easy to knock on the door. Fred would let him in and he could be with her again. He thought of her fragrance, of the bed they'd shared for almost two blissful months. He stared at the door. But suddenly it felt like treading on the past, as though the genie in the bottle had been let out and he was making decisions for himself now. He wasn't the naïve boy Valerie had picked up in the bar anymore. He twisted the signet ring on his finger and thought about his father. He'd spent most of his life hating the man and now he was dead, all Alistair wanted to do was talk to him. His father's words that night repeated in his head. *I'll never see you again* and he felt a cold icy finger course through him. His father had known he'd most likely die. And although his Uncle Laurence hadn't pulled the trigger, he was responsible for the death of Frank Quinn. Neither Despise nor Fear.

Alistair slid open the glass window to the driver. 'Sorry. I've changed my mind. Can you take me to Knightsbridge instead?'

The driver pushed the window back and re-engaged the meter. Alistair heard him mutter something, but it no longer mattered.

He stared at the tray. Dorothy had brought it to him; a breakfast of boiled eggs, toast cut into fingers and tea. Cracking the top of an egg, he paused, then let the spoon fall onto the saucer and gazed around the room; his room, No. 39. Nothing about the establishment in Knightsbridge was different. Every day the same; the same furnishings, the same food, the same chairs, the same revolving door of nameless men coming and going. Who were these people? Where did they go? Where did they come from? Did they have families? Did anyone either know or care?

For the first time in his life, he felt lonely. Was he just a pawn in the games of important people, people who'd included his father and a man he'd once called uncle; Sir Laurence Dalrymple? He remembered Jenkins's words that day... none of it matters, anyway. Why had Jenkins said that? Perhaps Jenkins had become disillusioned about life in the Security Service. No divorce. It applied to Jenkins as much as it did him. Alistair felt the bone crunching intensity of the isolation of the covert world where nothing was either personal or permanent except the Official Secrets Act.

And, his mother.

He stood up and pushed his tray of uneaten breakfast away. Hurriedly dressing, he left Knightsbridge and took a cab to Euston Station. He thought about his future; was it as pre-ordained as that of his classmates at Whittington Hill? But they would not be a long-haul flight attendant travelling all over the world. He stared at the buildings as the taxi drove past Marble Arch, his mind on his recent past. Perhaps time away would help. His mind went back to his favourite uncle, John McPherson, and the last time he'd seen the man. Alistair swallowed, feeling the lump in his throat. He'd loved him and now he, too, was dead. Perhaps he'd sell Glenrothie. It would never be the same for him. He forced his mind to concentrate on the practicalities of life. And death. Once he'd dealt with the past, he could embrace the future. He beamed at the thought of travelling the globe in aeroplanes. He had no idea what it all entailed, but he felt the excitement of the unknown. He always had.

ACKNOWLEDGMENTS

My sincere thanks to my wonderful editor Janet Laurence and to my amazing friend AnneMarie Brear for all their help and encouragement.

ABOUT AUTHOR

V M Knox

Following her secondary education V M Knox trained as a primary teacher then as a nurse, specialising in burns care. While working in the health industry, she studied singing at the New South Wales Conservatorium of Music and worked in a semi-professional capacity as an opera singer for over twenty years.

Coming into writing later in life has meant that her varied life experiences, coupled with a love of history have had a strong influence on her writing. She is a #1 Bestseller on Amazon and has been awarded Publisher's Weekly Starred Review Author status. She is married with two children and four grandchildren and now lives in the Southern Highlands of New South Wales.

Website: https://vmknoxauthor.com/

Also By V M Knox

In Spite of All Terror

In Spite of All Terror is the first in a series of WWII crime / espionage thrillers. Set in September 1940, when Britain stood alone against an imminent Nazi invasion, Reverend Clement Wisdom and other men from the restricted occupations, join the covert Auxiliary Units. Based in East Sussex, these ordinary men by day must become saboteurs and assassins by night. Following the murders of several of Clement's team, he becomes embroiled in the murky world of espionage where things are never what they seem.

If Necessary Alone

If Necessary Alone is the second thriller in this World War II series. Clement Wisdom, now a Major in Special Duties Branch, Secret Intelligence Service, is sent to remote Caithness to investigate illicit encrypted radio transmissions. As soon as he arrives there, an out-station wireless operator is found brutally murdered and Clement becomes entangled in a web of death and silence. Alone, and in the bitter Scottish winter, Clement must stay one step ahead of a killer if he is to remain alive.

Where Death and Danger Go

Where Death and Danger Go is set in the dark days of 1941. Britain fights on alone. Invasion and fear hang in the air. On a winter's night, a German spy parachutes into Cambridgeshire as another man is murdered nearby. Is he another enemy spy or has he been sent to his death? Either way, a killer lurks. Major Clement Wisdom of the SIS is sent to investigate and discovers a web of conspiracy where kidnap, murder and revenge threaten his life and the safety of the nation.

West Wind Clear

By late 1941, the Pacific is a very different place and Japan threatens the security of the region. As Clement is preparing to return to Britain from Australia, he is seconded to lead a small guerrilla force to Singapore, where he is to rescue an important man who is carrying a vital secret. After the apparent suicide of one of his team, Clement becomes suspicious that an enemy spy is among them; one who will kill to safeguard his identity.

On Stage provides real-world insight into both the hospitality industry and life through the eyes of a savvy veteran. Scott Neff walks you through a journey of lessons learned in a straightforward and intriguing format, sharing important information regarding interaction with management, staff, and customers.

—Toby Harris
Co-owner, 451 Spirits

A fully immersive dive into hospitality shenanigans.

—On the Fly Consulting

Through his involvement in Safe Ride or with events hosted at his pub, Scott is extremely conscientious in being the best partner he can be. His involvement is genuine and pure, and I love approaching him with an idea. After brainstorming, we often come up with ideas that evolve into something even greater than the original.

—Kim Niswander
CEO, the Parker Lee Foundation

Scott takes you on a roller coaster ride with many real-life scenarios that hospitality professionals will find themselves experiencing. ON Stage views our hospitality industry as a performance. After all, we constantly have an audience. This book assists to ensure that restaurant and food service operators understand that their performance matters every day. I highly recommend ON Stage for anyone who desires or is already in hospitality management.

—Mark Kelnhofer CFBE, CTA, MBA
President and CEO, Return on Ingredients LLC
Lecturer, The Ohio State University,
Hospitality Management Program
Adjunct Lecturer, Georgetown University,
Global Leadership Program

I've known Scott for 20 years and have never met a more professional food service executive. His take on restaurant performance is a must-read for anyone entering management or looking to gain experience in short order.

—Tom Barnes
Chief Strategist, Mediathink
Author *Future Present*

When I became a limited partner of Publican's, I was not investing in a bar and restaurant, but I was investing in Scott and his management team. While other restaurants have floundered in 2021, our enterprise not only survived the pandemic, but we are thriving. This book is full of insights that are most valuable for people considering a career in hospitality management. However, the lessons Scott shares are useful for anyone who leads an organization or is responsible for managing people.

—Jeff Quayle, Limited Partner,
Publican's United

ON STAGE

LESSONS LEARNED FROM REAL LIFE ADVENTURES AND MISHAPS IN THE HOSPITALITY INDUSTRY

ON STAGE

LESSONS LEARNED FROM REAL LIFE ADVENTURES AND MISHAPS IN THE HOSPITALITY INDUSTRY

SCOTT NEFF

Published by Author Academy Elite
PO Box 43, Powell, OH 43065
www.AuthorAcademyElite.com

Identifiers:
LCCN: 2021920318
ISBN: 978-1-64746-934-4(paperback)
ISBN: 978-1-64746-935-1(hardback)
ISBN: 978-1-64746-936-8(ebook)

Available in paperback, hardback, e-book, and audiobook

All Scripture quotations, unless otherwise indicated, are taken from the Holy Bible, New International Version®, NIV®. Copyright © 1973, 1978, 1984 by Biblica, Inc.™ Used by permission of Zondervan. All rights reserved worldwide.

Any Internet addresses (websites, blogs, etc.) and telephone numbers printed in this book are offered as a resource. They are not intended in any way to be or imply an endorsement by Author Academy Elite, nor does Author Academy Elite vouch for the content of these sites and numbers for the life of this book.

Some names and identifying details have been changed to protect the privacy of individuals.

DEDICATION

ON Stage is dedicated to my father, Leo Neff. Thanks for all the life-lessons, Dad. You are my hero.

CONTENTS

SECTION TWO
THE ROLE OF A LIFETIME

SECTION THREE
SORRY, THE SHOW IS CLOSED, FOLKS

Section Four
Encore

FOREWORD

I, Tom Levenick, have had an opportunity to be *On Stage* in my life, playing for the Ohio State Buckeyes in front of 100,000 people on Saturdays during autumn each year. While that stage was challenging and nerve-racking, it pales compared to the stage on which hundreds of thousands of hospitality workers appear each day, not just Saturdays. Just like sports, the hospitality industry is all about people thrust onto a stage where they are evaluated and critiqued for their every move. Similar to my football experiences, hospitality workers enjoy the thrill of victory and the agony of defeat, filled with joy, laughter, and celebration, as well as unwanted embarrassment, criticism, and failure.

As a fellow author and executive in the beverage industry, *On Stage* is a wonderful look at the hospitality industry from behind the scenes. Whether you are a newspaper food critic, a restaurant industry veteran, a frequent diner on OpenTable®, or a *foodie* who never misses the introduction of a new menu, you will love *On Stage*!

Scott Neff does a wonderful job of ensuring this book is for everyone who enjoys a great night out for dinner, lunch, breakfast, happy hour, or even pizza delivery. He is a master at storytelling; you will laugh, smile, and may cry at times. Get ready for an entertaining adventure *On Stage* and learn about what makes the hospitality industry a joyful experience to millions of people every day.

—**Tom Levenick**
Author of *Buckeyes for Life*
Bachelor of Arts—Journalism—
The Ohio State University
Vice President of National Accounts—
Coors™ Brewing Company
Senior Vice President of Sales—Labatt, USA
Ohio State Football—1978–82

SECTION ONE

CASTING CALL

*The cast of characters in the hospitality industry
are a diverse and interesting group. High school
and college students, entry-level employees, and
seasoned staff vie for the parts ON Stage.*

TYLER

Tyler bought into the Brown Derby™ restaurant in Dayton, Ohio, about a year after the restaurant had opened. He was a GM of another unit in Cleveland before coming to Dayton. He was an intense, peculiar, and erratic character, and I was immediately intrigued by him. Tyler always looked the part of the owner/operator because he dressed sharply with extra starch in his shirts and wore expensive ties. To all, he appeared to be *the* leader of the restaurant. If you weren't sure of something, he had the answer. I think he truly believed that he needed to act out a role in the restaurant setting.

It seemed Tyler wanted someone to notice him. Often, he carried an intimidating look, watching and waiting for somebody to make a mistake. If you made that blunder, he made you pay with an immediate dressing down. When angry, he turned deeply red in the nose and cheeks. I think some of my co-workers purposely tried to provoke Tyler into a rage. They reveled in that intense look and wanted to see his over-the-top actions. Not me. I was a young line cook and had not planned on making a career in the industry at that point in my life. I was happy to perform my job functions but did not call too much attention to myself. Of course, that would all change later!

I saw many positive attributes in Tyler. His ownership mentality was real. He cared about the business more than a manager might and seemed an expert and a savvy veteran. At the same time, I thought what I was learning from Tyler was a list of what *not* to do. I was a student at Miami University at that point and had not seen too many of his comments, actions, or directives in my *Personnel Psychology* textbook. Job satisfaction for the employees was never going to be a priority for Tyler. His personal needs—to be heard and understood—were far greater than his ability to establish strong morale and create a close-knit staff. It was undoubtedly a transformational and unique balance for me to observe and think about.

Tyler's wife worked at the previous restaurant where they had been employed. It was the first time I had seen that in the business. Tyler was the first MAE (married an employee) I had come across. He would certainly not be the last. Over the years, I found it to be commonplace. Tyler was likely 20 years older than his young, beautiful wife. Interesting to me at the time, but not so unusual in my later travels.

Tyler mostly liked working with me. He knew I was trustworthy, detail-oriented, and committed. My last three years of college included cooking, washing dishes, and waiting tables for Tyler at the Brown Derby.

LESSON LEARNED

The customers loved to say that they knew Tyler. That was one of the first times I realized that an owner who worked in the business could be a bit of a rock star. He was ON Stage every day.

Tyler knew it too. His business was not particularly successful or profitable, and he still acted like a rock star. I remember thinking that he would really be an arrogant guy if the place had been incredibly successful. But that was not the case.

Some of the regular customers saw the writing on the wall long before many of us worked there. Charlie—picture Norm in *Cheers*—was a well-established bar regular. He would swing his arm back, and then in an upward motion, he'd tell us: "This is right where aisle four is going to be in the bowling alley that replaces this joint." *I believe the property to now be a post office.*

In many ways, Tyler was one of my mentors. I was drawn to him and never wanted to let him down. At the time, celebrity chefs were rarely in the news. I only remember a few from the time, and they were nowhere near as visible as today. Restauranteurs seemed to be king. I liked the idea that I might be able to be a rock star someday. I didn't long for the *Sex, Drugs, and Rock and Roll* lifestyle, but I wanted to impress people with my performance *ON Stage.*

Lesson Learned

The exceptional staff, managers, and owners who create a show, cultivate an atmosphere where others feel connected and entertained—and make themselves part of the story—see success at remarkable levels.

JOE AND RICK W

J oe was the opening GM of Brown Derby, and Rick was the opening regional manager. Joe mainly was a kitchen-type guy, primarily tasked with getting production from the back-of-house (BOH) crew to the front crew. When he hired me, he was very aloof and quick about it. He told me when to be at the restaurant for training and gave me no other options. And since I was going to make $5.00 per hour when I only made $4.00 per hour at my former job, there were no questions from me!

He did a good bit of the training himself. All the male BOH staff learned not to call the service staff names and be courteous to them. He told us that the restaurant would not be hiring many male servers and that the girls would cry if we were tough on them, and he did not want to see any tears. It wasn't long before this time that George Carlin had come out with *7 Words You Can't Say on TV.*[1] I'm confident that Joe must have listened to George Carlin often. Contrary to what he taught us, *he* often muttered something every time one of the *girls* pissed him off. Typically, it would be something like this "Get the f*** over here, sweetheart," and "Let's run

---

[1] SemanticWarrior. "George Carlin - 7 Words You Can't Say on TV." YouTube. YouTube, February 13, 2014. https://www.youtube.com/watch?v=kyBH5oNQOS0.

this food!" to them. When he thought none of them were listening—but okay if the guys were—he typically muttered something like: "lazy piece of s***."

After working for about six months at Brown Derby, I told Joe I wanted to learn to be a food server in addition to being a cook. Joe was taken aback and said, "How are you going to be a waiter? You aren't even a f*gg*t." I can't say I was shocked, but I don't remember what I said to him. That was a reflection of the world, according to Joe. By the way, he didn't seem to be too worried when the *girls* cried. It seemed abusive then, and undoubtedly that behavior wouldn't fly in today's world—but I don't remember anybody calling him out back then. I did like that Joe gave me one of my favorite nicknames—*Rushbutton*. When Joe wanted something fast, he would say, "Hit the Rush Button," Scotty. Eventually, he told all the other guys that my name was *Rush* and *Rushbutton*.

Rick was in the restaurant a good bit when we opened but not much after that. It was clear that he was Joe's boss, and whatever Rick said went, as far as I could see. He was a big man, probably six feet tall and 300+ pounds. But Rick didn't seem to let that make him any slower. He seemed to glide that mass all over the place-*ON Stage*; that impressed me. With that said, almost everybody respected him. He worked more in Cincinnati and was the regional manager a few years later when I transferred to that unit as a new manager. Shortly afterward, I went to Rick to complain that the GM of the Cincy restaurant was being hard on me; he said, "Scotty, you are lucky that he does not make you eat out beside the dumpster; you're the f***ing new guy." About 15 years later, Rick became one of *my* managers when I was a GM. He took over that restaurant from me as I left the company.

LESSON LEARNED

That is a great example of how people in the biz get to cross back into each other's lives. I hadn't talked with Rick in over ten years before he came to me for a reference. When I worked with him again, I was respectful. After all, I did not know when I would need a reference from Rick. This was LinkedIn® before I even heard the term social media. The connections made in the hospitality business are vital. I found out that my connections typically opened the door to more opportunities than my resume did.

PETE, JUDE, AND RICK E

Brown Derby was a great experience for me. I had made several things from scratch in my previous job, but we mostly cooked steaks, burgers, and barbecue there. Brown Derby was truly a player in the segment that would become a huge part of the American middle-class landscape—Casual Dining—though I did not know the term at the time. TGI Fridays™ were already around, and so was Red Lobster™. They were popular places that served as special occasions for some and a frequent habit for others. This was before there were thousands of these units surrounding every shopping area in the country.

At Brown Derby, I learned how to peel and devein shrimp, cook lobster and other seafood, and a good deal more. Pete, the old navy cook I started working with when the restaurant opened, was a crusty old veteran by the time I met him. He called me *college boy* in a strangely jealous way. I got the feeling that he wished he were younger and *had a different job*. He worked intensely but seemed to always smell like cigarettes. Even after he washed his hands, he seemed to ooze the stale smoke smell. Pete taught me the basics of how to make soup. It seemed like he would often use the same ingredients and cut them roughly to give large chunks of the protein and veggies in the recipes. Everybody loved them. When Pete left the job, it seemed like nobody could make the soup as well. Customers even knew it. I learned the value of an old, smoky-smelling navy cook let go for something silly—being late for work too often.

Jude and Rick were around that kitchen for a long time. They were the lifeblood of the place, and it really would have suffered without them. The two looked great carrying a stock pot of hot stew into the walk-in for cooling. I'll always remember that view. Jude was about five-feet-two and had a Yosemite Sam mustache, and Rick was about six-six and 170 pounds. Both had the big baseball cap on with our restaurant logo on it whenever they worked, and it dramatically changed their appearance. They looked the part of a BOH career crew.

Rick loved cars and spent a good portion of his money on his rides. They were a sense of pride for Rick, and everyone saw him give a big grin when somebody admired his prized possessions. Jude loved to flirt with the servers. As far as I know, it rarely helped him close the deal. I saw some of the cutest girls smile when he would try to play his game. I knew what *that* smile meant: *no way, Jude!*

Both Rick and Jude became my friends, and I enjoyed seeing them every day. Eventually, Rick became kitchen supervisor, which was undoubtedly the right choice. Jude and Rick were the first guys I had known in the business who were truly lifer-type line cooks. They had several things in common: typically, they were smokers, drinkers, and partiers. They were also some of the toughest—mentally and physically—employees I have ever met. They worked in extreme heat, stood on their feet all day, and returned the next shift. Rick and Jude were a rare breed that I saw as some of the most authentic and proud people around.

LESSON LEARNED

I found that the esprit de corps shared in the business is a real connection—a sweating, bleeding, opinionated, and cursing connection that became as much a reason to go to work as almost any of the others. I felt like this connection gave the hospitality industry a huge benefit over other businesses. Not all stages are in public view.

CHRIS D

Chris was a food server the first summer that Brown Derby was open, on break from her marketing studies at Miami University. She was witty, flirty, and made new friends easily, including the kitchen guys. She even seemed to flirt back with Jude! Chris provided additional incentive and reason for me to transfer to school at Miami and take a bit of time out of the business. Several of my relatives had gone to Miami University, and it was on my shortlist to transfer there. Chris helped me find my way to one of the best decisions in my life and career.

She made me think of the hospitality business as a stopover on the way to the real world. But, at some point, I stopped thinking that I was working in the biz until I *got a real job*. Over the years, I found out that I liked to be *ON Stage*, and the hospitality industry gave me a great opportunity to do this. *Miami Merger* was the term that many used for students at Miami University who went on to marry. Chris and I were both a Miami Merger and MAE (married an employee).

Chris is one of the smartest people I have ever met. She went on to be a very successful marketer and executive and always seems to be able to put a uniquely special light onto things she is involved in. She is a perfect consultant to have in so many ways.

LESSON LEARNED

With Chris, I found that I could blend in with people of all types. She was close to many who were incredibly smart and creative. I feel like some of this rubbed off on me! Of the folks who were her best friends, many were LGBTQ. A number of these folks became my friends. I needed this eye-opening experience both personally and professionally. Many of the staff in the hospitality business are LGBTQ and perform well ON Stage. A different lifestyle was more openly accepted in hospitality long before other entities embraced it. Thanks for this lesson, Chris.

DOUG

Doug was a manager in the Cincy restaurant when I trained and worked there. A couple of years later, I got to work with Doug again in Indy. This timing was unique; it was during my promotion to my first GM position in the industry. The month before taking over my first unit, they instructed me to go to Columbus, then Indy to work in units while the GM was on vacation. When I got to Indy, Doug was there to greet me. He was a big, athletic guy. His thick mustache was very typical for guys in our business. In many ways, he was a Tom Selleck lookalike.

Doug told me several different things about the Indy unit that I would need to know. I would be in charge, the boss—boy, that felt *good*. Two of the other managers had been there for some time, so being the acting GM was a special accomplishment for me. Within a few hours of arrival, a customer asked me if the company had sent me to shut down the restaurant. I assured him that was not the case—I was there to help while Doug was on vacation. The customer made it clear that he thought I was lying. I did not know it at that time, but he was right. He knew more than I did. I had not been in the loop of the decisions that others were privy to.

Sure enough, the regional manager visited the restaurant and let the whole staff know that we would be closing the unit the following week. *That good feeling about being the boss left right then.*

Almost immediately, the real craziness began. I found that the GM had likely been padding his inventory. There were probably thousands of dollars' value held on the books that were not in the unit. The employees started openly stealing things. I caught a dishwasher taking a full keg of beer out on his shoulders! Yep, he was a big man! The nautical artifacts throughout the unit were increasingly missing daily. On the last day we were open, the restaurant's bar was packed for hours. Many locals knew it was our last day of operation and came in to have their last cocktails in the downstairs lounge. I thought that we were probably going to do a couple of thousand dollars in bar sales. In those days, most of the beers and drinks were $2 to $4. We had to have served 1,000 drinks for the shift. I was busy inventorying items and trying to get all the employees paid as they were wrapping up their final duties. Just as we were closing things down, I thought I would take a report to see how much we had done in bar sales. Wow, I could not believe my eyes. The sales were under $300. The only solution was that the bartenders had given away almost everything that went across the bar. I was fuming . . . and embarrassed. *The boss was naïve!* I thought I was so smart and found that the value of streetwise experience was more important than a high score in accounting—especially that day.

LESSON LEARNED

Though trained in college personnel management classes and working years in the business already, I had not seen this coming. That sort of thing never happened to me again. "Trust but verify" became part of my working lexicon. **Thanks, Ronald Reagan.** *Street sense and real-life experiences go a long way to keeping the show going ON Stage.*

DAVE B

D ave was a cook with me at Brown Derby. He was a hard worker and good friend but a bit different than some of the lifer cooks in this restaurant. Dave was too smart to work in this particular job for very long. He was constantly pushing his wire-rimmed glasses back up his nose when they slid down. In the heat of the kitchen, he got pretty good at doing this without even thinking about it. He had a unique sense of humor and had a funny little snorting snicker. I didn't always recognize everything that he saw as humorous, but it did not matter. His behavior was reflective of a great spirit in a genuinely good guy.

He was in love with the outdoors—camping and the like. Dave was the guy who had the Jeep® C-J 5. The air ripping through the poorly sealed canvas on the thing as we zipped down the road always made me check my seatbelt. Dave always let out a unique chuckle whenever he saw the look on my face as I saw the road rushing by. He almost always wore jeans and a flannel shirt, which made him small-town Ohio through and through. I often wore the same thing those days.

Dave was good friends with Chris and me for a couple of years. I was the best man at his wedding and know with confidence that he is undoubtedly doing well at whatever he chooses to do.

LESSON LEARNED

Dave was easy to like. He was one of the first people I found made the business an acceptable choice while looking for a career. I looked forward to seeing him every day. He ended up being the kind of person I was drawn to over the years. His was real, unassuming, and a good person. I would have been proud to see my children act like him.

MICHAEL T

I knew Mike was a sharp young regional manager with Brown Derby. When we had a sales meeting early in my tenure as a GM, Mike played cards with a group of us. I only had enough money that the deal came to me once. It was a savvy group, and Mike had done very well to be a part of it.

Mike was a big guy and seemed larger than life to me at the time. He was a sinewy, strong man who I would have always wanted to have on my side in the *ON Stage* daily skirmishes.

As a GM of my restaurant in Mansfield, Ohio, I had finally felt like I had become a *rock star*. My office was huge and even had a sofa in it. I never had an office that big again and certainly never had a sofa in an office again. The unit was on a corner of a couple of rural highways. On the opposite corner was a drive-in theater—by the mid-80s, those were a rarity. The restaurant had a couple of banquet rooms that would fit 400 people. It was a great experience to manage a big place like this. It fed my ego for sure.

Less than a year into my tenure in the restaurant, Mike showed up. I was not sure why he was in Mansfield. I already had a boss, and Mike had other units, none of which included mine. Mike told me that he was buying the unit. As a result, he would not need me but planned to operate it with his brother, Billy. But he told me not to worry because they were making a spot for me in another unit and held true to their word. Mike and Billy still have ownership in that restaurant. By the time I had heard this, they had run the place for about 30 years!

LESSON LEARNED

Even in a business with extreme staff turnover at every level, people like these brothers seemed to be around. Often, you would hear about people who came with the building. This is typically a salute of extreme respect. Their story is like many of the most successful people in our industry.

PAUL

Paul was the regional manager for Brown Derby for a couple of the units where I worked as a manager. He was as well-dressed as any of the management I had ever worked with and certainly looked the part of an executive. Those suits were not meant to get dirty. I rarely noticed Paul impacting anything. He mainly just talked to people rather than motivating or managing them. Paul, at one time, was Tyler's boss, and the sage operating partner rarely seemed to respond to the regional manager. He often acted as if he was not there.

When I took over the unit as GM a few years later, Paul was my direct supervisor. He seemed to be very professional in most of our interactions. At the same time, he was dating one of the managers who reported to me. He had wanted her promoted to manager, and shortly thereafter, it was evident they were dating. She often would tell him things that were going on inside our management team, and it quickly became an untenable situation. I gave Paul my notice when I had a couple of jobs lined up. With several solid lessons learned, I was leaving the first GM job I had held.

LESSON LEARNED

This was one of the first times in my career that I discovered an inappropriate relationship that greatly affected a team. There was resentment all around—and the regional manager put himself into a position where he no longer commanded respect due to his own actions. This is exactly the reason most companies prohibit such relationships in the employee manual.

DARRYL

Darryl is one of the few people in this book I did not meet in the industry. He was my roommate during my first and second years of college.

I started at Miami University in January of 1981. My dad helped me move my things in. I had been in a few dorm rooms the prior semester as I took trips to Oxford to see Chris. The rooms were all small and *cozy*.

When I walked into my room, I looked around quickly. It looked more like a shack made of beer cartons than a room. It smelled like sweat and stale beer. The new roommate was Darryl. He was in a dingy-looking and faded tee, Levi's®, and Converse® tennis shoes. This character was very skinny and sporting a red afro. At that time, I figured he might have been Bill Walton's shorter cousin.

I was not the type to shy away from any person just because they were different from me. My experiences already prepared me for this kind of thing. With that said, I was not expecting this from a Miami University student. Most of the guys and gals I had met on campus were sharp dressers and likely the best of the best. Once we left the room, I shared my reservations with my dad. He always had a good read on people and assured me that Darryl seemed to be a good guy. I was pretty sure Dad was trying to make me more comfortable in the new surroundings.

I was at the Midwest Ivy. People thought and acted as if they were at Harvard, Yale, or Penn. They weren't. They were, however, some intelligent strivers with a serious sense of conservative style. President Benjamin Harrison and Speaker of the House, Paul Ryan, have shared some of the same buildings—and some of the same attitudes. Darryl did not easily fit into these surroundings, and I was embarrassed *this* was the guy I ended up with. *Horrible luck.* I wanted to impress and have friends who were like I wanted to be. People who wanted to be *ON Stage*.

Within a couple of weeks, I realized Darryl was trying to be friends. He played the Beatles and Cream songs on his turntable, sometimes before I was out of bed! He owned a pet rat named Sam, not for a couple of weeks but for a long time. *ON Stage*, he was Jim Morrison in an air band and awesome at it. "People Are Strange," indeed! He was unique in the conservative world of Miami University.

Darryl was a journalism major and placed on academic probation when I met him. The challenges in the classroom were not because Darryl disregarded his studies. Quite the contrary. He wanted to graduate as much as anybody else I met at Miami University. It took him one extra semester, but he did it. He accomplished something incredibly difficult due to his hard work, plain and simple. Many people who may have had more *given* talent have not come close to this accomplishment; Darryl showed that he was up to the challenge.

LESSON LEARNED

My dad had always told me that half of success was showing up! Darryl proved this at Miami University through his determination that they wouldn't deny him. And he wasn't!

Shortly after Darryl graduated from Miami University, he had been unable to secure a job in his field. There were not a lot of journalism jobs available at the time. He knew he had to do something else with his time. So he took a job as a cashier in a convenience store but got fired after selling beer to an underage guy during a sting. Somehow, this was not a big shock for me, but I felt horrible for Darryl.

Eventually, I was able to hire him as a barback to work at Brown Derby. He had no bartending experience at all. At the same time, he had the raw gifts required. He was quick, hard-working, and all the staff seemed intrigued by his quirkiness. That style was a strength for him in the business that rewarded uniqueness. He showed skill that would have made Tom Cruise feel ashamed of his *Cocktail* tricks behind the bar. Darryl started all this long before that movie was ever made, by the way. TGI Fridays had intrigued many at the time, and Darryl was not the only one doing tricks with bottles, glasses, and cocktail tins. I have yet to see any bartender better at this very visible part of the business.

About two months into Darryl's employment with Brown Derby, management at our HQ decided our bar staff would take lie detector tests. Though there was never a plan to use the information—it was a tool to let management know how much revenue was being taken by the staff—the bartenders were not aware of that. It was a legal environment where lie detector tests were already in question, but this was not common knowledge to our staff, or me, at the time. The employees had an opportunity to *tell the truth when they showed deception*; almost all of them did. By admitting the truth, most were fired for theft in the workplace, including Karen, a bartender who had been an original at the restaurant since its opening four years prior. All of us had completely trusted Karen. She admitted to giving away an average of two drinks/day without management approval, which amounted to approximately

2,000 drinks in the time she had worked for us. I felt bad for Karen, but 2,000 drinks—wow!

LESSON LEARNED

At this point, I learned that many bartenders were part of a culture that required them to give away at least some drinks. It was just part of the deal. If you want to keep the best ones honest, give them the ability to give away some drinks with your approval. Better to know this amount than guess. Anybody who thinks they can completely control staff is mistaken—get past that now, get them on your team, and you will be paid back in many ways.

Darryl immediately became a bartender—admissions of theft led to numerous terminations. He had plenty of scheduled hours as we attempted to put a bar staff into place. His hand-eye coordination and ability to learn quickly helped him become one of the fastest bartenders I have ever witnessed. Darryl knew it.

Darryl was my best friend by this point. He was also an employee who reported directly to me. I had never really been in a similar situation with responsibility like this one. In many ways, I failed the test of leadership with Darryl. No matter what he did, I often let him get by with it. On New Year's Eve, the bar was extremely busy. Darryl was instrumental in our success that night, just like he typically would be. But a little after midnight, I looked around the place and could not locate him! When I found him, he was hiding in the walk-in beer cooler, just chilling and God knows what else. My comment? "Oh, Darryl!" Then, I left him. He never stopped laughing at me about that.

Lesson Learned

Though I knew it, the fact sunk in for me that day. Managers who are friends with their subordinates are likely to be ineffective in working together. The boss is rarely able to fulfill his duties as well as he would without an obscured vision of right and wrong.

To this day, I have met few people I would consider having a passion for their job as strong as Darryl's. Though we were friends before working together, I would say that our time shared *ON Stage* solidified our life-long friendship and sense of brotherhood. To this day, I would still wish to spend every bit of time with Darryl that I could, but I don't want to be responsible for his actions!

DAWN

After leaving the Brown Derby, I took three jobs, still trying to confirm if my vocation should be in the hospitality industry. The first of the three jobs was as a waiter at Chuck Muer's Charley's Crab™. It was a great experience in many ways and was a fine-dining restaurant, something I had not experienced to that point. I even got to wait on Gene Simmons at the restaurant. He was great and larger than life—a real rock star.

Chuck Muer was a unique restauranteur; I admired how he renovated historic buildings and created experiential dining environments. After my time of employment with his company, he mysteriously disappeared in the Bermuda Triangle. *Tragic—and big news at the time.*

The second job was as a sauté cook at TGI Fridays. Fridays was the highest volume casual dining chain in the country. The staff, including the BOH, was cocky. After a little time, I fit in well. The kitchen crew used profanity routinely. Even though I had been the GM in three units prior to Fridays, I was still a bit in awe of these guys. They would put out a ton of food and do it with an uncanny finesse. For the amount of food revenue we were producing then, it was almost effortless perfection. The expediter on the cook's line was *clearly* in charge. Nobody questioned him. He said things like: "Ordering another f***ing nachos," "Picking up on those POT STICKERS!" and "Are you *idiots* listening to me?" While working brunch as a sauté cook at Fridays, I learned about "NYO omelets." NYO stood for name-your-own. Yep—anything you wanted in an omelet. What could go wrong? In those days, the checks were hand-written by the servers when they had special instructions. I can't even imagine trying to do something like this today.

My favorite of the three jobs made me realize what I most wanted in my future. I was a bartender in the Kingspoint Pub™. Most of the months I worked at the pub were during football season on Saturdays and Sundays. I loved the way the pub felt with sports and the interaction that all shared. I also worked Tuesday nights. I had been going to this bar for several years. It was close to the Brown Derby and the hangout place for restaurant employees. I relished the place as a customer and felt like it was one of the most comfortable places to *connect* with people from all walks of life.

Dawn was the regular night bartender at the pub. She had a great mischievous laugh and used that, along with her sexy nature, to make great money. I admit she was one of the people I most wanted to see when I walked into the bar—warm, welcoming, and just the right amount of cute. She flaunted what she had, and it worked for her.

Dawn was off on Monday and Tuesday nights. The bartender who worked Monday night also worked several of the day shifts. The bar owner, Jerry, was often at the end of the bar, having several cans of Miller Lite and talking to his friends. Dawn was easily the *rock star*, though. She would often pull up her shirt a bit, pull her pants down just a little, and moon several patrons. Dawn knew she was *ON Stage* and would show the *crack of Dawn* at least once per shift. Some guys stayed for an extra hour to make sure they did not miss the show.

I had some frequent regulars and a good deal of folks who came to see me. At the same time, Dawn easily had twice as many customers come to see her in the pub when she worked.

One time, Jerry, the owner, said to me, "The customers who come to see you must drink more than the ones who come to see Dawn." I told him I wished that were the case, but it seemed impossible. He told me, "That has to be the case because you always do more in sales on Tuesday than Dawn does on Wednesday or Thursday." For just a second, I thought I was in Indy with a sales report in my hand. I don't know if Jerry ever figured it out, but he always seemed to be able to make enough money to either look the other way or just not care about the truth.

LESSON LEARNED

I solidified in my mind that the employees appearing to be the best at bringing in the money may be the best at bringing in money for themselves. At the same time, sometimes it works for both—if there is an agreement with the owner. I never knew if that was the case at the Kingspoint.

JOHN M

I met John when I applied for a cook's job at the Olive Garden® in Dayton. John was the GM who talked to me at a second interview, which I almost skipped. My first interview was with the KM, and he wanted to hire me but needed John's approval.

John looked the part of a GM in that era, the mid-80s. There were very few female GMs in those days. He was rotund and yet incredibly animated and energetic. John had a thick mustache typical of men in our business at the time. His use of polyester in his wardrobe was not what I had expected for the type of leaders I had planned on working with, but his clothing choices were typical of a lifelong restaurant manager. He could have easily been physically intimidating if he wanted to be but never even came close to crossing the line with me. Still, he used this technique of professional intimidation as well as any in the business. At the time, I felt like he was a bit over-the-top with his intensity. With John, it sure seemed that little anybody did was good enough. I still flashback to some of John's lines almost 30 years after my first experiences with him. Think of the coach who won the game but still agonized about the mistakes made and felt he needed to clean those up. Anyone who knows my style years later will recognize some of these traits in me for sure!

This restaurant opening was three weeks after they hired me; I was excited about being part of an opening. Before my interview, I had never heard of the Olive Garden and had yet to track the industry. The company was a division of General Mills™, a company with deep pockets. There was a good chance I would have lots of advancement opportunities. I found that they planned to open 40 units that year and only had 50 in the chain at that point. I liked my chances to move up quickly.

John told me he did not think I should be a cook but should be interviewing for management. I agreed, and within a week or so, had the job. I started as manager-in-training the week that the unit opened—a great time to get the best training and see things done properly. The restaurant opening was incredibly smooth. John was a strong GM with a very firm hand. Not all the staff and managers liked him, but he commanded respect. I had found a mentor in the business, and though I didn't want to be just like him, I sure liked his command presence *ON Stage*.

About four weeks into my training, things seemed to be going very well. I really liked the job, the team, and the company. I was challenged but felt I could earn a good living while not having to work 70–80 hours per week as I did with Brown Derby. Then, it happened. One night, I stayed up late with Owen, my former manager who had consumed too much alcohol and was seriously considering suicide. He had just broken up with a woman and had fallen hard. I kept Owen safe, got him home, and got myself into bed about 4:00 a.m. When my alarm went off at 7:00 a.m., I did not hear it and overslept more than two hours. I arrived at work about 10:00 a.m. for my 8:00 a.m. shift. John was the opening manager, and though I apologized to him, he barely spoke to me. He knew little of me and had every right to cut me loose. I had been working for this company for such a short time; they had no reason to know how much value I might provide them someday. I told John I would stay several extra hours that day to close the kitchen; I did because I felt awful, as if I had possibly made too big of a mistake. But I hadn't. John was very stern with me regarding this blunder but did not hold it against me. It was a valuable lesson for me in many ways.

LESSON LEARNED

I realized that a good leader could be tough and challenging without making a subordinate's mistake into a deal-breaker. I always appreciated it and used this as part of the foundation on which I built teams. Thanks, John.

After being on the opening team of two other units as the KM, I received a promotion to GM for an Olive Garden unit in Cincinnati. By this time, John had been promoted to RM and became my boss. He was still tough but fair and became a no-nonsense RM complementing my young, inexperienced GM. I began to appreciate John's traits and tried to share them with my teams. I called it *the cool p***** style—not to everyone—but I kept reminding myself what John would do every time I came up against tough decisions. Be tough—but have a heart and show it. I wanted people to say, he is "pissed off" rather than he is an "a**hole." I wanted to achieve John's status as a leader that challenged people to be better every day.

After several transfers, I was able to work with John again. It had been more than four years, but I had seen John every year at conferences. He had to be the most conservative person I knew within the company. He went to bed early after a beer or two when other guys were getting hammered and making bad decisions. John always warned not to get caught with our pants down. He did it the right way.

John was able to get me immediately back into a GM spot in Columbus after I left our sister company, China Coast™. I took over another very busy unit and worked there for a couple more years before I felt ready for a multi-unit spot. Though

I interviewed for a regional position a couple of times, the Olive Garden never offered me a spot. I had been a GM for over seven years and felt my career may be slipping by too quickly. When the opportunity to take a multi-unit position with another company came along, I took it. It was a critical mistake and took me years to recover. I was disappointed when not offered a promotion, but that was the wrong reason to leave the job. I could have requested more feedback and made sure to put myself into further contention in the future.

I worked with John again five years later. He was the RM for another company and helped to recruit me to that spot. The company was struggling operationally, but I appreciated working with John again. Easily, he was one of the best in the business.

LESSON LEARNED

Not everybody liked John, but he was one of my mentors for several reasons. He was competent and efficient, straight up and honest with everybody, and took responsibility for things that happened, regardless of how they reflected on him. He was the true leader of every group he was responsible for. Respect was very important to John, and this was essential for me to emulate.

BOB

Bob was a Regional Manager for Olive Garden when I started with the company. He was a massive guy and talked to me about a management position from the very beginning. It was unprecedented for a casual dining concept like this to grow exponentially, but boy, how it did. When I met Bob in 1987, I could not help but notice a great big ring on his huge hand. I asked him about the ring, and he told me it was from his Super Bowl IV win with the Kansas City Chiefs. When I asked him what position he played, he told me: *left out*. All I could say was: "Put me in, coach," and he laughed a big laugh and hired me. I was appreciative Bob put his trust in me. This larger-than-life man was always good to me. People always spoke well of him in the years to follow.

LESSON LEARNED

Bob passed away only a few years after this. He was a big guy, and that always worried me about the stresses of the business. It could easily contribute to your demise if you did not have a solid work-life balance and an ability to keep the body and mind in shape. He was one of the first I remember suffering in the business, and he was not the last.

NASSER

asser was one of my managers when I was a GM for Brown Derby in the mid-1980s. He was a Lebanese immigrant and one of the hardest workers I have ever known. Apparently, his family was wealthy in Lebanon, but unfortunately, they lost that wealth in the civil war in his country; he and some of his family moved to Ohio shortly after those life-changing events. They took jobs as dishwashers and bussers and quickly moved up in the ranks of the business. Nasser worked very hard for me. He was one of the first immigrants I had worked closely with. Let me make my opinion on such issues *very clear* here. Our industry and our nation *need* immigrants. Nasser was a prime example of why.

My friends and I frequented a fun nightclub and decided it was time to take Nasser to the club to help him assimilate to the area around us. The club was called 1470 West and was huge and heaving with business some nights. Nasser attended the club on a unique night that I will never forget.

When we arrived at the club, at least 250 people were there partying. Of the patrons, at least 50 were cross-dressing men. The view was entertaining and hard to miss. Yep. It was drag night. Nasser couldn't help his reactions. He stared, his mouth agape. I warned him a couple of times to stop—it was embarrassing—for him and me! The place was alive with energy. You could feel the base to the blaring music. I heard Nasser say a couple of things to the folks we came with and then, he turned to me and said something I could not fully understand. Once he slowed down the pace of his speech, it was clear what he was saying. "A small bomb take care of entire place." *Of course, Nasser would never have acted on this, but it was clearly alarming.*

LESSON LEARNED

With Nasser, I learned several things that would stick with me for years:

1) *Hard work truly is rewarded in our industry. Show up, work your butt off, and you will get promoted if you have the intellectual capacity to do the work.*

2) *International employees who immigrate often make for a more unique and hard-working staff.*

3) *You can't always assimilate people in weeks, and sometimes in years!*

TRACY

Tracy was a manager-in-training with Olive Garden just a few weeks after I started. He was an attractive guy, a sharp dresser, and operated with a much more refined style than mine. Over the years, we were able to work together several times. When I relocated, he took over my spot with Olive Garden. It was his first GM job. Years later, he was HR director for Thomas and King Inc., a large Applebee's™ franchisee. He convinced me to work for Rio Bravo Cantina™, a Tex-Mex brand Applebee's franchisees were growing. It turned out to be a wrong decision to take this position, but Tracy was well connected in the business, and all his interactions worked to his benefit.

Tracy became an independent recruiter, and I have used him to recruit managers for me in several markets. He is a unique guy and possibly the subject of a future book detailing the balance required for every successful hospitality professional.

LESSON LEARNED

Tracy is a perfect example of how employees in our industry have been able to stay in touch with each other and use the collaboration resources. Before social media, this was common—the old-fashioned way to make connections. I still can tell you that having personal connections with the right people gains you a lot of opportunities—it has been repeated throughout the story of my career and many others.

Fado Forged Group

March 30, 2021

Dear Scott,

Early in 2021, several of us came together for a virtual meet-up in lieu of being able to gather in person due to the COVID pandemic. This group has continuously stayed in touch over the years through texting, emails and the occasional get together in person. On this night, what was scheduled for an hour, turned into six hours of reminiscing. Our spouses and children popped in and out of the video call, we updated each other on our lives, told stories, laughed hard, cried a little, ate and drank.

This group of friends was forged because of you. Your leadership of our beloved Fadó Irish Pub and the community you created has been woven into the fabric of who we've each become. Each of us has gone on to successful careers, started businesses, built family foundations – much of this is due to our time at Fado. More than just a "bar job," our time at the Pub shaped our personalities, our work ethic, our grit, our senses of humor and our need to soak up all life experiences, to live in each moment a little deeper. There was no shortage of nostalgia on this night, we kept coming back to how many of us met our spouses through Fadó and how lucky we are to have these lifelong friendships.

We each have felt the strain of this unprecedented pandemic year. We know how especially hard it has been on the bar restaurant business, the industry each of us holds especially dear. As you continue to lead during these trying times, please know that you are greatly appreciated. While this is certainly not all of the friendships formed through the many years of Fadó, for us, for our group, we hope you enjoy this small token of our immense appreciation to you as a visual reminder of what we affectionately call our "fadó families."

Sláinte,

The Cochranes – Sarah, Bill, Vivian (age 12)
The Henrys – Katie, Justin, Tyler (age 12) and Teagan (age 6)
The Townsends – Brad, Amanda, Evan (age 5) and Emmett (age 3)
Chelsea Mahaffey and Meira (age 3)
The Durbins – Courtney, Tyler, Owen (age 4) and Isaac (age 6 months)
The Ecks – Amanda, Jon, Edie (age 18) and AJ (age 4)
The Davises – Marcia, Paul, Charlie (age 7) and Clyde (age 5)
Danielle and Grant Hundley
The Zolendziewskis – Lindsay, Mark, Landon (age 12), Paxton (age 3) and Nolan (age 1)

Brad Townsend Family

Lindsay Zolendziewski family

Courtney Durbin family

Katie Henry family

Danielle Hundley family

Marcia Davis family

Sarah Cochrane family

Amanda Eck family

Chelsea Mahaffey family

SECTION
TWO

THE ROLE OF A
LIFETIME

To become a savvy veteran in the business,
learn the lessons and play your role well.

TIM

When I met Tim, I was the general manager of fadó Irish Pub™ in Columbus. Hired as a server, he seemed to be very bright and energetic but less likely to have been rewarded earlier in my career; he was a bit eccentric in his appearance and demeanor. I had thought that his co-workers might ignore or abuse him, but I was dead wrong. His uniqueness made him into a leader in the pub . . . of opinion, performance, and quirkiness. As it turns out, he was a natural *ON Stage*.

On Tim's first shift out of training, I was the manager on duty. After a few hours of some substantial volume, he came up to me and said, "Hey, can I be cut now?" I politely told him that I was fine with that. He could be cut immediately but needed to make sure he never came back to work at my pub ever again! The fact that a new server would ask to be cut on his first day was foreign to me. It was indicative of the guy and his lack of concern questioning me.

Tim was unique in his style and had a different way of looking at things, which led to plenty of disagreements, arguments, and heated challenges to my authority. He rarely backed down, which was normally good for Tim, for me, and for the pub. It was often beneficial to have open challenges to the norm. I did not always like it but found Tim's tremendous value over time.

The first termination:

The competition wooed Tim shortly after becoming a manager with us. He chose to give notice to move to Cincinnati to work, which made him a concern. At the time, they were a national competitor and could easily put him into a poor position as a new manager for them. I cut his training short and let him head off to his new venture with a real desire to see him do well.

Rehire:

Tim moved back to Columbus some years later. He picked up some server shifts and worked with us for a few more months until he had a disagreement about his schedule with one of the unit managers. Termination number two was in order.

Rehire again:

A few years later, Tim was hanging around the pub, and we talked about his interest in having another attempt at management with us. It was not unusual to bring team members or managers back, even after termination. I was happy to give Tim a chance to be successful again with us.

He quickly took charge and had *clearly* matured in his time away. Of course, that also emboldened Tim in his time in the pub. He often questioned things I said. Sometimes, he did this to my face. I was happy to get differing opinions, and his expertise in computer operations was necessary. He set up a function on the computer to automatically print some of the daily reports, including an opening checklist all managers in the company were required to perform. At the same time, he hated to follow the rules on many things. Tim actively avoided completing the paperwork. He also failed to keep me in the loop of many decisions. I wanted him empowered to make coherent plans but also needed to be aware of his actions and often, I was not. The technical expertise was a great benefit to all. Yet some of the other activities negatively affected the team.

Tim was proud of telling folks: "I have been fired three times." That was after we argued about several things in the pub. It got heated, and I shouted at him about a couple of things. He quickly told me, "Shut the f*** up." I told him to get out of my pub and give me his keys. He asked if I was firing him, and I told him, "No, but you need to talk to me about this before you work again." He returned the next day. This interaction is one of the worst I have had with any subordinate in all my years in the business. It would have been easy to cut him loose, but I understood his value, which was a bit more than the detrimental effect that he brought for a long period of time. We both learned important lessons in these interactions. Working with Tim actually helped me grow as a manager and leader.

Tim's downfall was his inability to tell the full truth; I never knew if I was getting a completely accurate story. He often appeared to believe his BS. He told vendors, staff, and customers things that often agitated the situation. *He lived for this!* He loved to stir the pot. When confronted on such things, Tim would not be entirely honest about the details.

A few things are deal-breakers in a job that requires a high level of integrity. The result was Tim's last termination.

LESSON LEARNED

Some of the most talented people on your team should be terminated if they can't be fully truthful in all they do. Mistakes are common ON Stage, but any intentional misdirection to cover for errors is a lapse in integrity that crushes the sense of esprit de corps needed to maintain a successful team.

GEORGE

George was a young regional VP with Olive Garden when I opened a unit as a KM in Sterling Heights, Michigan, months before my promotion to GM. He quickly took a liking to me and genuinely seemed to care about my future. He also seemed to exhibit his no-nonsense, cocky style as a young executive from Boston. George was sure to be successful, and I liked that he took me seriously as a young manager within his region.

George joined our opening management team for a special dinner, and I discovered the tradition of drinking saké and Sapporo™ while eating Sushi before openings. I thought it was just an interesting night out when we had the same experience with the Cincinnati opening six months prior.

It was very memorable and bonding for our group and a good way to get to know the team. George knew it.

The opening went well, but I felt I was sharper and stronger than the GM assigned to this new restaurant. While I liked the GM, I did not always support his immature behavior with the staff—a clear error on my part—I should have known better. The staff used my mistake to drive a bit of a wedge into the management team. I had given them the ammunition to do this. Even as a young guy with a solid future, I wasn't experienced enough to see this happening. George didn't miss it.

On the day of my promotion to GM in this dynamic company, George gave me a serious reprimand. He told me he was promoting me because I was a hard worker and knew I would be a great GM, but he also told me that not supporting my boss completely in the eyes of subordinates would hold me back in my career.

Lesson Learned

George taught me that you always publicly support your boss down the line to employees. Any doubts you have need to go upward on the line of command. I made mistakes and needed to learn from them. Thanks for this lesson, George.

When I left my position as a GM with Olive Garden the first time, I transferred to our sister company—a Chinese concept called China Coast. George had left his regional VP job with Olive Garden to be the Director of Operations for China Coast. Of course, I saw this as an opportunity and took it. I was hired into a GM position without even talking to anybody else about this job in an alternative concept.

After giving Olive Garden a six-week notice and making sure to help transition my restaurant, I trained at a location in Indianapolis. That day, I met the China Coast regional manager, who let me know George had left China Coast. I was uncomfortable, as I had not even interviewed with her! Regardless, I still felt confident but shouldn't have been. The upper management prioritized financials over the customer experience. By this point, I knew executing operationally had to be the priority. This repeatedly happens in the restaurant business. If you have stock in a company whose primary business is driven by accountants rather than by operators delivering on a vision, take your money elsewhere!

When recruited to a position with John Harvard's Brewhouse™, George was the Director of Operations for the company. He was sharp and able to make a lot of solid decisions quickly. He left shortly after I opened a new unit in Cleveland as the GM. It was the third time I had worked for George—and the time he was responsible for me was less than two years!

LESSON LEARNED

In my time with Harvard's, I realized that I most liked working for a unique place that truly could be passionate about their food and beverage and genuine, connected service. It was also a great place to use my solid corporate experience while impacting the growth of a company.

IAIN

I met Iain at the Chicago fadó while he was in training for a management position with us. Iain was potbellied, dawdling, bespeckled, and approaching 55 years old. Remember Geppetto in the Pinocchio story? Iain was Geppetto personified. He was anything *but* smooth. At the same time, I instantly liked the guy. He was genuinely interested in what I was doing and seemed to want to learn more about whole house operations. He relocated and knew he might have to do this a couple of times to become a GM.

LESSON LEARNED

I have found that the manager most likely to get promoted is the one who will move to take a spot. Many of the best get passed by if they take their name out of the running when asked to relocate as part of the promotional opportunity.

PAT

I met Pat when I opened the pub in Columbus. He owned an Irish Pub in the area and came in to check us out. At the time, there were lots of rumors going around that Guinness® owned us. While untrue, the story had some legs in the pub community.

Pat came into the pub shortly after we opened, and I had no idea who he was. Some of my staff knew him, though. He was a unique character in his coon-skinned cap. I have never seen anybody else in Columbus in a coon-skinned cap. Clearly, Pat was a local celebrity. Intrigued and drawn to him, over time he became one of my favorite people to have a pint with—he was a great storyteller *ON Stage* and a genuine leader of the community.

I have frequented Pat's pub several times. It was clearly the home of those with Irish heritage—the Shamrock Club membership, Daughters of Erin™, and more made it their home. It was interesting to me to see the attraction those with the last names and heritage of traditional Ireland had at Pat's place. There was a real connection and pride that continues to swell, even in a country of immigrants. There are Greek festivals, Little Italy's, and Chinatowns throughout America. There is nothing like St. Patrick's Day, though. It is a real holiday with religious roots in which people take off work and drink all day. Most are celebrating their Irish heritage or that of friends, relatives, and co-workers.

LESSON LEARNED

People love to feel connected and around others who share similar views and experiences with them. The restaurants, bars, and other hospitality entities that best use connection as part of their business plans win much more often than those that don't. Pat is a winner.

Pat's position as co-founder of SAFERIDE™ is one of many accolades that he has made for himself. He has put countless hours into this community-based activity that helps save lives every year. He is also the best *ON Stage,* as many in the Irish community will tell you. It is his favorite spot at every Dublin Irish Festival. There is much more to the Pat Byrne story. I assume Pat's book will come out soon and will leave the rest of the telling of his story in his capable hands.

BRAD

B rad became a server with fadó in Columbus. Several of our best servers were guys at the time, and many of these men made the business their career.

Brad hit the ground running and was a real asset to the pub. It was clear at the time that Brad did not plan on staying in *the biz* his whole career. He had some real aspirations for his life, and none of them involved food or beverage. Brad had an infectious, nervous energy, and everybody teased him about this—in a good way. Few match his love of the Ohio State Buckeyes. I am pretty sure the worst days of Brad's life were related to Ohio State football losses. The first game he attended in the OSU Horseshoe was with me—a great memory for both of us.

Brad worked with us for several years. He got a graduate degree in Environmental Policy and really believed in what he wanted—to clean up the world and make it a better place.

LESSON LEARNED

With Brad's help, I began a recycling and environmentally friendly policy at this pub. I found a good part of the staff greatly appreciated that our business took the lead on doing things like recycling, even though it was not mandated by governmental policy. We were forward-thinking when many of the owners and managers in our business struggled to get through the minimum requirements. To this day, this pub still recycles, and there is no local government mandate requiring this.

I have stayed in touch with Brad and his wife, Amanda, over the years. They are great parents with a real focus on making the world better.

LESSON LEARNED

Brad is a perfect example of a staff member who has used the hospitality business as his source of financial support for years while reaching his overall goals outside of the business. He never demeaned those of us who decided to stay ON Stage. He made all those around him better than they would have been without his influence.

One of my favorite stories involves Brad. He played guitar and sang in a band. The energetic band played at one of the large outdoor festivals we held. Brad loved being a part of this band and was a humble guy, even when he was on a different stage.

One Sunday night, Rob Thomas came into the pub with his business manager, and Brad met him. Brad's band played some Matchbox Twenty songs, and Brad was a big fan of Thomas. The two of them hit it off, and Rob Thomas asked Brad to come to Detroit for a concert the next night.

Thomas wanted Brad to do a duet with him in Detroit. I wish I had been there to see their version of "Hang." Now *that* is living like a rock star.

I always liked the unique sounds of Rob Thomas and Matchbox Twenty. Now I can't listen to their music without thinking of Brad, the pub, and how impressive that was of Rob Thomas to make Brad's life a little better. Also, this is the kind of thing that happens when good people get together, *ON Stage*.

KIERAN

Kieran was a manager with fadó in Chicago when I started my training. Many respected him, and I saw a lot of him in the three weeks I trained in the pub. He seemed to maintain a unique balance between competence and commitment to the job. When I received a promotion to regional manager, Kieran received an offer to take the Columbus pub GM spot I was about to vacate, but he would not move from Chicago. A couple of years later, responsibility for the Chicago pub landed in my lap. Kieran had left the company to become a GM for another group. When I took on the new responsibility, we needed to find the GM for this important pub.

My instincts told me Kieran was the best candidate for the fadó GM job, and I pursued him. I was right. After he started, we formed a very successful team for years. He was the next natural selection for RM responsibilities. He took that promotion and became one of the best multi-unit operators in the business.

Kieran has an undeniable smile. His passion for the business is infectious. He made me better at my job by being so strong at what he did.

Lesson Learned

Great employees often get great bosses. Their ability to be successful is accentuated. I never wanted to let Kieran down.

A year or so after Kieran came back as the GM, we had GM/HQ conference in New Orleans. While educational, it was mostly fun and a reward for the teams. It was a bit scary that this group was in New Orleans. Many had a reputation for being big drinkers, and the city had a reputation to match!

It was Kieran's first GM conference. He was a great addition to the meetings in many ways, and his leadership was on full display. I was proud of him. On the trip, Kieran wanted to sleep in on *activity day* during the last full day of the conference. He thought it was optional—it wasn't. It was the day after he had been out late enjoying the bars and clubs of *The Big Easy*.

I got Kieran onto the bus to get us to our activity. The bus traveled over a long bridge over the waters surrounding New Orleans. The click, click, click of the seams on the bridge bounced us all. Kieran could barely make it without getting sick from the night before. He was not alone—many on the bus were in the same shape! When we finally made it to the activity, he was understandably relieved. We got off the bus to pick up our paintball gear—in the misty, steamy, jungle-like area outside New Orleans.

Naturally, the first strike Kieran absorbed was right below the belt. I could not help laughing. That was one of the worst mistakes I made that day, but not the only one. I absorbed bruises to my body and my ego for the next several hours. This body struggled to hide behind those narrow trees! *Ow, ow, ow!*

Lesson Learned

It is essential that you embrace authenticity in whatever you do. Kieran helped with the authenticity of an Irish pub, having grown up in Limerick and working at the Shannon

airport. Irish heritage helped Kieran with fadó, but I would have taken him with me to sell shoes! He was as good as it gets in the overall management of people. Firm and fair, but certainly guided by a great heart.

Kieran is in senior management with fadó. His leadership in several markets has tremendously helped retain solid management teams. He is comfortable in making tough decisions. I have met an untold number of great operators over the years. Kieran is the best of the best.

IAN

Ian started with fadó as a general manager in our pub in Las Vegas. His experience in whole house operations was very important, but his command presence made him popular with us. His team looked up to him because they felt he cared about the business as much as anyone and still had their best interests in mind. He was extremely comfortable *ON Stage*.

He is one of the oldest operators I have ever worked with. With that said, he put in more work than many of the managers I have known over the years. He liked to be a publican, showing off that he was the man in charge of the place. People rarely questioned Ian. He was charismatic and played the part well.

Ian had a playfulness that endeared him to many. He got by with saying and doing things most of us could not. His Scottish accent and demeanor worked in tandem to disarm people and made them remember him admirably.

He was one of the most effective managers in the business without trying to do too much. As a savvy vet, he was able to rally a team. His timing was impeccable. As it turned out, he became the man at the helm of the business that achieved the highest jump in sales and profits I have ever seen. In hindsight, it was clear that a good bit of this achievement was probable regardless of who the GM was, but Ian was often in the right place at the right time.

IAN

Lesson Learned

Take the opportunities to put yourself into the proper position to be successful. It takes more than good luck, but it does get easier to get solid results when you are in the right place at the right time. In my career, I found out that I made my own luck often.

CONAL

I met Conal when I started training with fadó in Chicago. He was the bar manager reporting to me when we opened in Columbus. A few years later, he was a hard-working partner in our business in Stamford, CT. We became close in these years, which happened for several reasons, but really, it was a fault in my leadership skills and a weakness I would have to address. I had been through the same thing in the past and learned some valuable lessons. The bonds I shared with Conal led to a friendship, and it clouded my judgment with him as a subordinate. I was responsible for him, yet I still allowed this to happen.

Conal took a GM/partnership position with other investors outside our group. This group had expected that Conal had strengths in several areas of operation to make him a great GM out of the gate in a new concept. They were wrong. Among other concerns, Conal really did not have a solid handle on BOH operations.

LESSON LEARNED

Conal is one of my very favorite people I have met in the business. His strength as a publican ON Stage carried him to more success than many who use only management techniques to build their business. At the same time, it is essential to build well-rounded teams that balance the full requirements of the business. Very few people have all the required skills to be highly successful. That is why so many publications exist on teamwork and building skillsets!

TIM K

Tim was young, energetic, and the life of the party when he started in the Philly pub. He wanted everyone to respect his achievements, which was difficult due to his limited experience. It took him a bit of time to catch up with his own hype.

He was a good-looking guy obsessed with having a great image. Usually, this served him well. He always wanted to look sharp and play the part. The team seemed to like him. He knew he needed to work hard to fit in with a seasoned team.

Tim was able to use his strong desire to be successful in improving his chances. He pretty much willed himself to higher positions (AGM, then GM). He seemed comfortable in each earned position and made himself into a young GM entrusted to our newest location, the high-profile, Miami, Florida, pub. The pub did substantial volume for several years, and Tim managed the unit for an extended time and under the weight of many of the additional challenges Miami provides.

His ability to blend his intelligence and his image kept people believing in his abilities. When he finally caught up to the hoped-for image, it finally paid off in actual performance.

LESSON LEARNED

Tim was probably the best example I can think of for "Fake it 'til you make it" in our business. He often said how much he had done that he became knowledgeable and gained solid results for years. Confidence is one of the best attributes ON Stage.

STEVE

S teve was one of our customers and worked part-time at
the cigar shop next door. He was popular with the staff,
a sharp guy, smart, driven, and a Miami University grad.
After leaving his full-time job elsewhere, Steve became the
manager of the cigar shop. He put together real relationships
with those in the area and was one of the most recognizable
guys in the area. Steve spent a considerable amount of time
with us as a partner in events and as a customer. His love for
the Chicago Bears and Chicago Cubs led to many conversations
over the years. When I think of the Chicago Cubs winning
the World Series in 2016, the first thing that comes to mind
is Steve's genuine joy and exuberance.

An older man, Vince Canzani, started to work with Steve
at the cigar shop. Vince was an incredible photographer, and,
like Steve, our staff got to know him. He was charismatic and
could have been anybody's uncle, and everyone quickly came
to enjoy Vince's company. He sat on our patio and worked
on his laptop. Some evenings, he sat with us for hours. Most
of the time, he drank Diet Coke™. We did not have a lot of
regulars not drink alcohol when they visited with us, but
Vince was one of them.

One night, Vince left the pub close to closing time. He did this often, but this night was different. It was the last time we saw him.

Vince was driving only a few miles from his home and met with a high-speed, wrong-way driver. Though Vince was never famous, he hit the news when he became the victim of vehicular homicide. The wrong-way driver survived and was openly remorseful. His name was Matthew Cordle, and he went on YouTube™ and made the *I killed a man* confession. In it, he said he had too much to drink and had cost the life of another. This gave Cordle shocking publicity—the local media and some of the national media picked it up. He has had millions of views on YouTube. While Cordle was in prison for manslaughter, his sisters started a charitable organization to try to bring awareness within the bars their brother had left that fateful night. I thought that this was great thinking to bring some sort of good out of a tragedy.

Vince's passing hit Steve hard. He became an advocate for responsible actions within a short time and soon became an active partner with Central Ohio Safe Ride. With Steve's assistance, we have been able to provide ride sharing and cab voucher use for thousands of people leaving bars, restaurants, and events.

Lesson Learned

Steve was instrumental in creating a very symbiotic relationship twice. People love to smoke nice cigars and sip on beverages at the same time, and if you drink too much, you need a safe ride home. Be responsible for those around you. Sometimes they need you more than you think.

FRANKIE

Frankie played soccer around the world for several teams. When I met him, he played for the Columbus Crew and the US National team. Another Columbus Crew player who frequented the pub had introduced us. We showed a lot of footie matches on satellite with feeds nobody else had, which gave us a solid leg-up when professional soccer players tried to watch their friends and countrymen play matches. Around this time, I met Brian McBride and John Harkes—a couple of players on the Columbus Crew at times and well-known from the US National team. Both were great representatives for their teams. Chad Marshall and Danny O'Rourke were friends of the pub, and homegrown talent, Wil Trapp, was always great to have around.

Frankie won the MLS Cup for the Columbus Crew in 2008, and our pub had gone along for the ride. We were packed for the final match in California, and the local network affiliate opened the evening news that day from the pub with hundreds of celebrants cheering a professional sports championship in Columbus.

Frankie and the team brought in the MLS cup a couple of days later. He and the boys were happy to share drinking out of *the cup* with our staff. It was a great time and memorable for many. My favorite Columbus Crew player of all time is

Duncan Oughton—a friend of many in Columbus. The drink named after him, *the Oughton8,* is still popular years after its creation!

Frankie is a brand ambassador for the Columbus Crew SC—and a great one, at that. Having him come into the pub for many matches, including those we partnered with the Columbus Crew and US Soccer, is legendary.

Frankie has great stories and is someone people want to have a beverage with and be around. His regional popularity in the market is right up there with any Ohio State product.

LESSON LEARNED

Frankie shows that passion for a brand and an authentic enthusiasm for work propel you to succeed even long after your ON Stage playing days are over.

ROB

Rob was a young Irish student who gained the ability to work in the USA as part of the J1 Visa program. I liked the program because it introduced real Irish characters and traditions into staff who needed this influx of craic or good times with an Irish twist. Rob seemed like his training was effective and should have helped him to become a server with us. But portions of the training did not take. Though a smart young man, he reacted very methodically. Though we knew this, we slowly tried to give him more responsibility. Soon, he waited tables with light supervision—*big mistake.* One day, I had a livid customer approach the bar in disbelief that Rob was waiting tables. I apologized and made the experience for the customer right. I pulled Rob from the floor to coach him on service technique. Rob told me, "Scott, I am really an engineer, not a server." I told him I agreed, and he never served again. I still gave him some jobs at the pub for the rest of his visa, but I didn't put him into any position that could harm the business. By the way, I really liked Rob—great to have a pint with!

LESSON LEARNED

Any staff member who lets you know they cannot do the job you hired them for should be taken out of that job. Our industry proudly provides entry-level spots for many. Many of these staff members leave the business and use it as a vehicle to work their way to college degrees and more. That typically serves our industry well. At the same time, those same employees must perform our basic tasks to remain on the team. Being ON Stage is not for everybody. Sometimes, it is better to exit stage left and do what you are good at.

CHRIS P

Chris was a server at the local comedy club when I met him. He often came into the pub, and staff knew him. He became a member of our team for several years while studying to get his nursing degree. Chris became a staple on the schedule before leaving us. His co-workers respected him, and the customers liked him.

Chris knew how to keep calm, even when ridiculously busy. I think he felt nothing was worth getting all worked up. After getting to know him well, I appreciated working every shift with him.

An incredible story with Chris happened shortly after hearing that a guy in Cleveland had kept three young girls as prisoners for years. His name was Ariel Castro. It seemed there was no way something like this could happen in America. It was disturbing on several levels, but it was even more incredible when Chris told me he had been dating Ariel Castro's son, Anthony. You never know what some people have gone through; I am sure this was severely shocking to Chris.

Chris is still a friend of the pub and very successful in his new career.

LESSON LEARNED

The day Chris told me his story was the last time I felt sheltered from some of the worst of society. It is amazing how many times that front-page news—good and bad—intertwine with the hospitality industry.

THE MAITRE' D AT PETER LUGER IN NYC

Along with three of my good friends, we visited New York the night before our beloved OSU Buckeyes played football against Rutgers. It was a great trip and my first time to view Ground Zero and the World Trade Center Memorial site. The spirit of that area still touches me.

Months in advance, my friend, Allan, made reservations for the four of us on a Friday night at Peter Luger's Steak House™. I had heard a little about the restaurant but really did not know its storied history.

We checked in with the maitre' d when we arrived about 15 minutes before our reservation. As we waited, I observed a couple groups check on the wait time for a table. I thanked Allan for his planning when they learned those groups would not get a table *at all* that night.

When the maitre' d called our party, he realized we were all Ohio State fans. He looked above and past his wire-rimmed glasses and said something about being a Penn State fan. I briefly worried we were going to lose our spot—he seemed annoyed that these Buckeyes were in his midst. It was easy to see that he was probably empowered to do whatever he wanted.

But he was extremely accommodating and made our visit *better* by giving us a hard time. Memories of that evening include a fantastic prime porterhouse, formal service, and a beautiful setting. But more than anything I recollect the most important asset to Peter Luger was the guy that shone *ON Stage*.

LESSON LEARNED

The magic of the restaurant was that we felt like we were part of the place that night. Even in an expensive suit and tie, this guy made us feel that Peter Luger was real, authentic, and wanted to look after four Buckeyes. My buddy got kudos for his choice, and I think many restauranteurs would be delighted for their customers to have this experience.

Author and Darryl

Frankie, staff, the MLS Trophy

Publicans Operating Partners Jason and Monty

Author and father in Key West

Author and Tom Levenick

Kieran and Shannon

SECTION THREE

SORRY, THE SHOW IS CLOSED, FOLKS

*Managing and surviving the coronavirus
while operating bars and restaurants*

KEEPING UP WITH THE NEWS

I typically listen to the news and feel more world-aware than the average American. Even as I saw horrible news from China, then Europe, I did not consider the potential outcome on our country, communities, industry, company, restaurants, and the people they employ and serve.

As aware and involved as I thought I was, the first weekend in March of 2020 really shook me. That weekend, the Arnold Schwarzenegger Classic™ was scheduled in Columbus. The Arnold was certainly one of the largest drivers of revenue in the central Ohio economy. At that point, I had to take the virus seriously but still underestimated the impact it would create. The governor of Ohio, Mike DeWine, had significantly downsized the event and canceled most of its components. He did this *before* any confirmed cases of the virus in Ohio. DeWine had many detractors declare this was an overreach of his authority. In the brief aftermath, he absorbed the wrath of both the right and the left. I am sure it was not easy.

DeWine is a Republican governor of a prominent state, diverging from President Trump's position at the time. He let the science guide his judgment and, at least publicly, let the politics roll right off his back. DeWine appeared to be a great role model for leadership at this unprecedented time. Popularity was not going to happen in the midst of this crisis, so the governor took a beating every day on social media. I am sure I would not have been nearly as strong in the face of the storm. I borrowed strength from him. It sure seemed that the work I needed to do was easy compared to his job. At one point, I had dreamed that I would be a politician, but fortunately, DeWine was the one on the real hot seat. We were both *ON Stage*, but the lights were brighter on his.

Of course, the virus became a political hot potato. At a time when we needed to be united in our fight against a common enemy, wearing a mask or not wearing one would soon be a political statement.

Arnold smoked a cigar and had a whiskey on the patio of the Columbus pub that Sunday afternoon. One week later, we closed for business.

TERMINATING THE TEAM

With all the hours of stressful work and countless lessons before that, nothing prepared me for terminating 70 employees. Two were financial partners. Four had worked with me for almost 20 years. Scores had worked with me for more than ten years. I knew spouses, children, parents—and more. I had no idea how many were going to survive the uncertainty ahead of us. I felt responsible and could not let them down.

In the immediate weeks after the closings, we identified some team members who would not immediately return to work. That part was obvious. For others, it was tougher to decide on their return, but I felt it was essential to be as honest as we could. Our staff deserved to know what I knew, when possible. It was important for the continuation of the business, but it was essential for the survival of many of the people I knew so well.

We had some staff undeserving of returning to the team, especially with the new world ahead of us. For many, this timing was very beneficial. They were unemployed, and it was time to find the next steps in their lives. At the same time, it was essential for the business to strengthen its position to navigate the struggles ahead.

As the units opened, I found many of the crew we had hoped to return were unable to. For several weeks, I communicated with them, but we had not yet been able to provide a place to return and provide for their families safely. There simply was not enough business yet!

Lesson Learned

You must sometimes do things that make you uncomfortable. Get used to it, or you will not be able to rise through the ranks and take on greater responsibility.

CLEANING UP, CIRCLING THE WAGONS, SAVING WHAT YOU CAN

The first week after closing was surreal. We had a couple of teams to communicate with but did not know what to tell them. The timing was very open-ended. We knew we needed to leave the units in good condition to reposition everything again. We also needed to do a solid job to secure the product for food safety or to make sure our valuable wine and spirits inventory remained available to sell when we returned. The valuable liquor inventory was out of sight and under lock and key. It was important to save assets to help us do revenue based on this product. The inventory was one of our most valuable commodities.

We needed to get in touch with several vendors to make sure they knew we would be back and would not be able to pay them for some time. We were fortunate to return any of the beverage inventory we had purchased in the last 30 days. Of course, this was a unique position, and I had no real procedure to get this done. It required an urgency for vendors to accurately pick up and credit several thousands of dollars in inventory. Some of these partners in the business were great and understanding. Others were irritated. It required repeated communication. Fortunately, some vendors shared our losses. Most of them had deeper pockets and reserves than we did. There were many stories about pouring out draft beer because it would not be sold—in my units or stadiums and arenas around the country. Lots of misery to go around!

We spent the money to make certain our draft systems could weather the storm with health concerns and draft quality at stake. I did not even know there was a procedure for this kind of thing without consulting with our line-cleaning vendor.

It was clear along the way that certain things may not survive the extended time away from the business. It was not as clear when we locked the doors that fateful Sunday. For instance, I can't remember a time when orange juice went out of date. It was easy to look around and give away the lettuce, eggs, and milk. It was tougher to know that orange juice was going to expire in three months.

LESSON LEARNED

I say it often and more in 2020—adjust, adapt, overcome. After all, you are ON Stage, and things happen. People are watching you.

DO GOOD

I had always believed in *doing well by doing good*. Parts of this were very easy when we had to shutter the operations. The initial news was to close for at least four weeks, but we expected it'd likely be closer to eight weeks. As it turned out, the eight weeks would have been the best-case scenario. I had reached out to another local restaurant executive with Cameron Mitchell Restaurants™ (CMR) to get his perspective on estimates for time closed. He thought three months, maybe more. That was good planning on their part and likely saved them lots of money.

We called a local food pantry after closing one of our units. They were happy to pick up much of the food to donate. The food pantry was very appreciative of our contribution, and it felt good. We were able to get the food directly to a couple of prior employees—Marcia and Paul Davis. Marcia and Paul spent the next several weeks making and delivering food to many in the community with limited mobility during this challenging time. They made an entirely different menu every day—a special feat no matter who you are—novice or professional. Think Jose Andres and World Central Kitchen, Inc.™ on a local scale. I consider them to be heroic.

One of the days the Davis family delivered food, we also provided them with our beer—a collaboration with Endeavor

Brewing™ in Columbus. The beer was called YNWA ESB. YNWA story is a great one for us. It means *You'll Never Walk Alone* and is synonymous with European soccer and first responders in Europe during the pandemic. ESB means *Extra Special Bitter.* We had put it on tap two weeks before closing. Our publicans partnership financially supported this group. They were doing good work, and we were glad to be a small part of it.

One of our restaurants donated the perishable food to a church connected with our chef, Madison Cullman. Again, this seemed to be an easy decision to help a community in need. It was a win-win that seemed fitting for the day.

We also served lunch to the largest county sheriff's office in Ohio. Through Safe Ride, I had a strong connection with this group. I had some expert help in preparing this food, but personally made the pasta e fagioli soup! One of the things I had missed in the time away from serving customers was project management. We had several officers able to share some good food, and I felt great about it. At the time we served these officers, it seemed like a very easy decision. They had a tough job. We were mostly idled from our work and had an expertise making food and taking on outside tasks. I am proud of this decision on our part. It felt good to help others when we had a chance.

June of 2020 was an interesting time in our business. Staff employed by some of our competitors staged walkouts from their jobs because their restaurants offered discounts to police officers. Another African American man had died at the hands of a white police officer in what turned out to be a murderous act. This reopened some old wounds. The staff of our competitors felt frustrated that their employer was supporting people they had considered to be racist, which made sense to me in some ways. At the same time, it certainly seemed like a real disconnect between the staff and their employer. It appeared

that ownership missed an opportunity for a real breakthrough in a genuine way.

We also heard that a popular taco spot had declined to make a large to-go order for a group of police officers working during the protests. They denied business as I was begging to get some customers to order from us! It was, indeed, an unprecedented time. Their story played out on the stage of local TV news and stuck with me. They were *ON Stage* and missed the right cue cards with their brand.

As my staff returned a few weeks later, I took the opportunity to directly communicate with them by requesting feedback for the kinds of things we were doing. Interestingly, my staff realized these were stories of people individually making bad decisions. We were determined to no longer have base policies but instead take care of the community's best members. Many of those are police officers.

Through Safe Ride, we also had a contact with Ohio Health and served a floor of medical professionals at Riverside Hospital the week before opening the first restaurant. We did all these things while most of the team was away from work. The managers volunteered to cook, package, and deliver these items. Recent management layoffs had no noticeable effect on their actions. They liked to feel connected and needed, as if they were doing good deeds for the community.

LESSON LEARNED

It felt good to see our company's leaders want to help the community. I am sure they also felt the appreciation of many they served. We wanted to do more but were under severe budgetary constraints. Live to donate another day became my directive to my teams. We would be able to do a lot more with some money coming in again soon!

KEEPING THE STAFF ENGAGED

We worked with local and national vendors to put together Zoom™ and team training events. Staff engagement was important, and consistently certain people stayed involved with these events. Those with little interest in these sessions concerned me. There was a real possibility some would face fundamental changes with lingering negative impacts. It worried me that it would stay with them for the important months in front of us.

DIAGEO

Our Ohio contact, Bill, was one of the most engaging. We really liked him because he was true to his word, fully appreciated our commitment to quality with his products, and genuinely connected with our managers, staff, and customers. He was more than happy to put together some entertainment notes and organize some events for us. More than 30 people could be involved. Friday at 3:00 p.m. made sense for the first five weeks of the stay-at-home orders. Some of the staff and regular customers received deliveries of Guinness during this time. My partner, Ian Montgomery, and I funded this to pull it off. Few of the vendors had a budget, but this did not hold us back. This kept some loyal staff and regulars a bit more connected when they would not have been. It was one more little thing to make everybody feel a bit more *normal* at a challenging time.

Shockingly to me, nobody above Bill's level appeared to see the value in the engagement we hoped for. They did not even spend the time to place a phone call or send an email. Bill was great, nonetheless. He lost his job right as we were going back to work. I have lots of respect for him. Of course, it was a time when everybody was trying to figure out the best way forward, and Diageo decided to take a conservative approach.

LESSON LEARNED

I firmly believe that vendors who assist you in supporting your staff know they are doing the best thing they can to build loyalty in the ranks. This loyalty is rewarded with sales for the brand.

WILLIAM GRANT— TULLAMORE DEW, MILAGRO TEQUILA, BALVENIE SCOTCH, HENDRICKS GIN

Our contact with William Grant—Wendy—is one of the best vendors I have ever encountered. She represents her brands well, does what she says she will do, and is extremely competent in hitting the demanded detail at this management level. Her easy-going demeanor worked especially well in this unknown time.

Of course, Zoom and other such platforms offered a new way to connect. We used Zoom for many of these communications.

Tullamore DEW Irish Whiskey™ was the brand we used for our first staff engagement call. Brand ambassadors, Gillian and Ro, were what you would expect. They were young Irish women with a story *ON Stage*. Ro even played her guitar and sang a tune for us. It sure felt good to share an adult beverage with people and listen to Irish music. That was something I had really missed while in quarantine! It was very unusual at the time, but it was something to take our minds off the world's uncertainties.

Hendricks Gin™ is a brand that has a cool mystique around it and mixes incredibly well. I never really liked gin, but it became part of the mixology I directed when I tried Hendricks. Mattias, the brand ambassador, was compelling and made us feel there were more things we could do with the brand. For several years now, customers have sought more of an experience while engaging with premium brands such as ours. They want to be *in the know* and want to share in a story. Mattias made such stories memorable. Wendy made time to attend all these Zoom events, and she was great on this one. It was so clear that she cared about her brands and made sure they were highly visible to our teams. I know they became more top-of-mind with Wendy's input.

The Balvenie Scotch™ ambassador, Neil, was very interested in putting a professional spin on the humor and upbeat approach to his job. He basically told me that my hope to bring back the Rusty Nail cocktail was old news. That hurt. It also made me like him.

Neil was able to pull off a virtual whiskey and chef's dinner with us for fadó. He allowed us to put together the strengths of our two brands and be engaging with both. Our chef, Jason, was intrigued by Neil and enjoyed the challenge of pulling off something we had never done before.

Milagro Tequila™ was a brand with incredible quality at a reasonable price. The reposado was one of my favorites. There are so many people that have a love or hate relationship with tequila—I love it. Add a little fresh citrus, and you don't need much more mixed in. Jaime, the Milagro ambassador, was able to warmly connect with our team—the fact that I was drinking tequila at the time may have had a little to do with my impressions on this Zoom event!

Ro with Tully DEW, Mattias with Hendricks, and Jaime with Milagro are on YouTube making recipes we helped create with them. This was fun for all and something we shared with countless customers. Thanks for all the work you did to make all these connections for our teams, Wendy. We could have done little without you!

TAUB COMPANIES-
GUNPOWDER GIN

These guys have a product few consumers really know. The quality is there, the story is good, and they were all about keeping the staff involved. Gunpowder™ is an Irish brand, and it made sense for us to leverage their expertise. Their young brand ambassador was magnetic and likable. We appreciated that he performed an evening Zoom event for us live from Ireland. With a 6:00 p.m. EST start, that meant he was doing this event with us at 11:00 p.m. in Ireland!

BENZIGER WINES

I was invited to be on a Zoom event with several executive-level hospitality managers with Chris and Jamie Benziger. Jamie is a second-generation winemaker; the Imagery Estate™ brands she directs are award-winning and gaining in popularity. Her passion for what she does is infectious. Though Jamie came across as very humble, she knew she was in an enviable position with the mystique that surrounds her industry.

Chris Benziger was great on the call. We were fortunate enough to have him take the lead on a Zoom event specifically for our team. Chris went above and beyond the call of duty with his enthusiasm for his brand. He really hit home on how important it was to balance the environmental impact with the quality of the grapes. This was something I had heard before from others associated with wines from California. At the same time, I had given this little thought. Chris changed that. He made it clear that the required balance with the land is not optional—it is essential for the long-term quality a winemaker seeks. Having a glass of wine with him virtually created the need to add to my bucket list. Now, I need to go to see Benziger Family Winery©!

Chris got our group some great prizes for three of our employees. One of these bottles was from his personal collection. It had a great story and went to one of the most deserving of our staff.

Chris had a great line on the call that went something like this, "I want this one to look like a $30 bottle, taste like a $20 bottle, but only cost you ten bucks." It was clever, and I liked it. It was something I could use to add one more story. If I got the line wrong, Chris, I apologize!

OTHER VENDORS
OF ASSISTANCE

Our friends at St. Killian's™ and Heidelberg Distributing™ also stepped up to assist us. Keeping up the morale and engagement of our teams was essential. These guys had always been interested in doing more than only selling us things. They seem to genuinely care about the team and wish the best for them. Thanks, Miles and Stephan. We appreciate you.

LESSON LEARNED

Your vendor relationships can really add value for you. It is essential to work toward win-win outcomes, and then they will present themselves to you frequently.

APPLYING FOR GOVERNMENTAL HELP—THE PPP AND MORE

The assistance for small businesses was in the news. It seemed as if everybody who knew I ran a small business asked if we could take advantage of this loan. Essentially, if you could spend the money according to the strict guidelines, portions of the loan were forgivable, and therefore, a grant that did not have to be paid back.

Basically, the PPP would make sure many previously laid-off employees had a place to return to work. It also allowed businesses to spend a substantial portion of the approved funds on utilities, rent, and similar expenses. Many of these costs were not eliminated even if the business could not operate due to government mandate.

The majority partners that operated our units would be able to take advantage of PPP. This partner had employees, and I was one of them. If we did not have this money available to us, we would have struggled to survive during closure and the immediate months that followed. I was rarely in support of the federal government propping up private industry—this time was different.

How to best take advantage of these governmental programs could be their own publications. I will leave that to those experts.

There were other programs to support our survival. The state of Ohio made funds available to us—we were grateful. Kudos to the Ohio Restaurant Association™ for their tireless efforts toward these ends. John Barker, Tod Bowen, and their teams are true leaders and deserve special recognition for their support.

Our Board of Directors included two gents with solid financial backgrounds; they gave good advice to our publican's united partnership that helped us navigate the times. We are thankful for them.

LESSON LEARNED

Surround yourself with financial experts. You do not have to be an accountant and understand all the nuances of the markets and investments if you have the right people around you to help guide your decisions. If you are an operator, you may need different skills from your partners. The chances are the better you are ON Stage, the less time you spend dealing with accruals and balance sheets.

SURVIVING FINANCIALLY

In order to pay for the immediate losses to our business for the first three months of 2020, I had to go to every one of my financial partners and ask for ten percent of their original investment. It was not to get any more value but *to survive*. Most came up with funds, believing in what we were doing. In a way, this was blind faith in our ability to be good stewards of their money, and I was pleasantly surprised. We wanted to do all we could to reward this strong vote of confidence. I had to borrow the money to cover my portion.

In the months to come, we needed to operate the businesses differently. Every cost we could save or reduce was considered. Of course, we wanted to minimize the impact on customers and staff. At the same time, everything was urgent.

Some of the things we did included: Clean the toilets and mop the floors frequently to save on janitorial costs. Clean the windows, and do without some of the frills. Complete as many of the repairs locally when possible. The labor cost had to be better, so wash some dishes! Of course, this was a challenging time to make this happen. *Do what you must in order to make it to the other side.*

LESSON LEARNED

Your parents likely told you to save money for a rainy day. Your parents were right.

THE LANDLORD HELP
IS ESSENTIAL

Almost every restaurant was closed for a governmental mandate. I'm sure few had provisions in their leases to allow them to forgo rent if forced to shut down by the government. Within a few days, most lease deals were reviewed by restaurant and hospitality business owners. By April 1, landlords checked their mail and found little money from the hospitality enterprises.

Of course, we were still allowed to provide to-go food sales. That worked fine if you were a pizza shop or served Chinese food. Suppose your core business relied on events, sports, beverage business, and connecting with your customers. In that case, it was going to be very tough to generate enough sales to justify operating this way. When interviewed on national news, Cameron Mitchell had a great analogy when asked if the take-out business would help him make it through the governmental shutdowns. Basically, he said that take-out sales would be able to do a little business, but this would be like putting a tourniquet onto a severe wound. There would be catastrophic long-term results.

Restaurants rarely have enough reserve to close for months. Paying rent during the closure time was difficult for many of them. The landlords had many tenants affected by the virus in one way or another. The restaurants with a majority of their revenue in food and beverage sales on-premises were affected the most. Of course, the same was true for other hospitality industry tenants such as cinemas and hotels.

Landlords surely wanted to make sure tenants knew they had a lease with specific language. Tenants needed to follow the lease or were in violation. Of course, this was true. At some point, though, they all needed to look at the entire situation differently. *The pressure was on everybody.* The amazing thing to me was how clear the math was! Each landlord and tenant would have to give some. Nobody wanted to blink. I knew people were heavily involved in the leasing and in a worse position than even the restauranteurs. Every day was another day of bad news. Big retailers were hurt. Small retailers were hurt. Cinemas, planned events, and hotels were all likely trying to renew a lease—not the one they had signed in better times. The future was not looking good, but the *now* was even worse. I am sure many planned their retirements in March, April, and May of 2020.

Many of these leasing personnel needed the hospitality industry to be open for business. They needed to show their investors and financial institutions that business was returning to normal.

LESSON LEARNED

When everything in your world looks tough, know that somebody else is putting even more personal strength into their day just to survive. Be empathetic to others, even when they may appear to be your adversary. "Seek first to understand, then be understood."[2]

---

[2] Covey, Stephen R. *The 7 Habits of Highly Effective People.* Simon & Schuster UK Ltd., 2020.

SECTION FOUR

Encore

The show goes on, but not for everybody. Brief predictions for the future. The importance of staff retention and promotion from within.

THE NEW WORLD FOR
OUR INDUSTRY

We don't have a crystal ball, but the pundits will give their take on what comes next. Some trends seem to be obvious, but others are yet to be seen. Of course, it is almost essential for operators to take a different approach to the next phases of our business. The old model did not work very well for most of the industry. It was already tough to make money. The business was highly competitive for everything. The best talent was relatively expensive for the value they added to the mix. Food and beverage input costs continue to jump, with companies scrambling to raise prices while improving their value proposition.

Our businesses are heavily regulated. The hospitality industry has regular visits by the health department, the fire department, and liquor control. The required permits and licenses only get more expensive and difficult to navigate every year and differ from one locale to another. Those costs are likely to get even higher as local and state governments try to regain their financial solvency.

Some predictions:

1) Input costs will rise, possibly more rapidly than seen in years. It will be tougher to get what you ordered for lots of reasons. The more complicated your offerings, the more likely you will be unable to fulfill all your inventory. Simplify.

2) Labor costs will rise for quality BOH staff and management. Great FOH staff are incredibly valuable.

3) Compliance with all regulations will cost more.

4) Social distancing will have a knock-on effect to design, when possible. Customers are less likely to want to sit right next to others while dining.

5) We need to change our business model with all this in mind.

6) To-go and delivery were already on the rise with Grub Hub™, DoorDash™, and UberEats™ prior to 2020. After markets fully open again, to-go will be more specialized, and consolidation will occur in the delivery services. Home meal prep continues to grow. Some brands will not need delivery services at all when things turn around for them. The more experiential your brand, the less likely you want somebody else to deliver it.

7) Coming up with unique ways to do events while still operating within regulations does not end. Zoom and Microsoft Teams™ are viable alternatives to face-to-face meetings and will continue in many ways.

8) Competitors will drop in the coming months as they run out of money.

9) Second-generation spaces will be available to those who have their complete business plans ready to go and financing in place.

10) Current staff and management retention takes on a bigger focus. You will discover that it is harder to find new team members, making each of your current staff exponentially more valuable. Of course, you need more detail on this prediction. *That* story is being written while you read this one! In the meantime, you better make sure to do the following:

A. Communicate your expectations clearly and honestly.

B. Listen closely to what your co-workers are telling you.

C. Again, using Steven Covey's, *The 7 Habits of Highly Successful People*, respond to their concerns and give them a reason for your actions. Think Win-Win.

D. Tell them how they can take on more responsibility.

E. For the best performers or the ones with the greatest potential, give them additional duties and responsibilities, and reward them for it. This includes community involvement!

F. Have integrity in all you do. People around you know it and will follow your lead.

G. Establish goals and benefits for the entire team. If the group is successful, the business should reward the whole team, including the BOH staff.

H. Fire the people who are detrimental to the team. The sooner you cut them loose, the better off you will be. This appears to be counterintuitive—it is not. It is *addition by subtraction*. You receive more credibility by the remaining staff. They will stay longer and trust you to make the required tough decisions.

I. The alternative is that you should give those employees who support the team several chances to be successful! Many mistakes are forgivable. *The 7 Habits of Highly Successful People* tells us if the balance of their bank account with you is positive, it is easier to forgive. Thank you, Steven Covey. Every time they do something valuable for the team, they make a deposit. And each time there is a mistake, they take out a withdrawal. If there is still positive value in the account, they should remain on the team. If the account is overdrawn, see H above!

J. Malcolm Gladwell's, *The Tipping Point,* tells us that little things make a big difference![3] Take care of the little things. Examples include granting requests off from work whenever possible.

K. Danny Meyer's, *Setting the Table* says to have tough conversations with heart.[4] Recognize a job well done.

L. Kary Oberbrunner's, *The Deeper Path*, tells us that so many people *numb* pain rather than confront it.[5] Assist by sending people in the right direc-

---

[3] Summaries, Must Read. *The Tipping Point - Malcolm Gladwell*. Primento Publishing, 2011.

[4] Meyer, Danny. *Setting the Table: The Transforming Power of Hospitality in Business*. New York: Harper, 2008.

[5] Oberbrunner, Kary. *The Deeper Path: A Simple Method for Finding Clarity, Mastering Life, and Doing Your Purpose Every Day*. Powell, OH: Author

tion to get help rather than giving up on them. Alcoholism and drug abuse are rampant in our business. Survival *ON Stage* is significantly easier when you uncover and eradicate self-limiting beliefs and actions.

M. Jon Taffer's, *Don't Bullsh*t Yourself,* tells us to kick excuses to the curb.[6] According to Taffer, the excuses include fear, knowledge, time, circumstance, ego, and scarcity. All are used in varying degrees at different levels in the hospitality business. They often are the reasons why people give you the excuse why they *can't.* Eliminate excuses. Teach all to take personal responsibility, and you will have a winning team.

N. Wright Thompson's, *Pappyland,* tells us that you remember some people because of their voice, the way they walk, or other things.[7] A smile is one of them. Thompson's book is a stellar example of the things that matter to so many. Tradition, family, and nostalgia are among them. Oh, and whiskey. The staff you retain with memorable smiles or the uncanny knack of frequently making others laugh or smile are typically the best *ON Stage.*

O. Cameron Mitchell's, *Yes is the Answer. What is the Question?* tells us to know and understand that some of the most successful people in the future are going to be "troubled teens," and you have a

---

Academy Elite, 2018.

[6] Taffer, Jon. *Don't Bullsh*t Yourself!: Crush the Excuses That Are Holding You Back.* New York, NY: Portfolio/Penguin, 2018.

[7] Thompson, Wright. *Pappyland: A Story of Family, Fine Bourbon, and the Things That Last.* Waterville, ME: Thorndike Press, a part of Gale, a Cengage Company, 2021.

chance to help them with their "epiphany."[8] The epiphany is that this business is for them. They may thank you in many ways. Mitchell built a restaurant empire based on strong training and associate retention.

LESSON LEARNED

Adaptation and making considerable changes with the right timing will be the only way to thrive ON Stage. Many will fight change. Don't get caught up in the reasons why not to do something. Make an educated calculation, dig deep, and get it done. Put people first—not just in corporate philosophy but in all that you do.

---

[8] Mitchell, M. Cameron. *Yes Is the Answer. What Is the Question?: How Faith in People and a Culture of Hospitality Built a Modern American Restaurant Company.* Oakton, Virgina: Ideapress Publishing, 2018.

GLOSSARY OF TERMS AND ABBREVIATIONS

GM—General Manager

KM—Kitchen Manager

RM—Regional Manager

HQ—company headquarters, front office

FOH—Front of House employee, such as servers, bartenders, hosts

BOH—Back of House employee, such as cooks and dishwashers

Regulars—regular customers

MAE—married an employee

ACKNOWLEDGMENTS

I have been impacted by many who helped me to achieve success on several levels. Many of you know who you are, and some of the stories you have been a part of are *legendary*.

My mother and father shaped my early life and instilled ethics within me that I have shared with others through the years. Dad told me that I was likely *a little too nice* to be a businessman. Many who have known me through the years would beg to differ!

Chris, Christy, and Kathleen, thanks for the patience and affection even when I got home hours after I told you I would. Chris, even though I hang out with authors now, you are still the best writer I have ever met!

My sons, Justin and Christian, have both been involved in the operations over the years. Christian has decided that this is a *role of a lifetime*. I am proud of them, and they are my favorite employees *ever*!

Thanks to Tom Levenick, who steered me to Author Academy Elite. You are one of the few I have met with more stories than I do! I am proud to call you a friend—a true *Buckeye for Life*! Felicity Fox, I am so glad you were assigned to help me as a liaison. I needed the help, but also enjoyed your infectious love for writing. My grandkids will get your book, *Where the Holidays Go*, for Christmas.

My mentors in my early years were instrumental in my development. Thanks to Jim Nemeth from Brown Derby and

John Mareks with General Mills. Two women who reported to me over the years were incredible operators and made me better—Joan in Champaign and Libby in St Louis. Your hard work and dedication to your staff were obvious to all.

Restaurant executives, Brad Blum, Ron Magruder, and George Carey, were all extremely successful at high levels and committed to those who worked for them. I wanted to share their leadership traits. The Olive Garden only had four policies when I started!—*Hot food hot, cold food cold, get the money to the bank, and keep the restrooms clean.*

For more than twenty years, I have worked with Jamie Hurst, Sarah Cochrane, Dani Magnani, and Greg Williams. I have great respect for these co-workers and have been able to share some of the most memorable parts of their lives with them. I am honored. There are so many more I know well, and I appreciate that I could have been a small part of your career progression.

My Safe Ride partners have helped in the community and surely saved lives! Steve Crain, Ed Gaughan, and Pat Byrne, thanks so much for your commitment to this valuable service.

Publican's United board members, Jeff Quayle and Eric Bae, have been steady guides of our hospitality management company. Others in the group have been incredibly supportive and trusting, even in the turbulent times we have weathered. Financial operating partners, Ian Montgomery and Jason Mrugacz, have skillsets unmatched by many in the business. I lean on you every day, and you just keep impressing me with the amount of work you can take on. You are the future.

Fadó pubs have employed some of the best in the industry. A firm belief in developing and promoting from within has served the company well. John Stevenson, thanks for talking me into taking the leap to join the group. You are one of the people I point to as a unique voice in a business always in need of a fresh approach. Kieran Aherne is a legend to many, moving up through the ranks to become one of the best operators

I have ever met. Thanks for all the support over the years, Cindy Coplen. I am always glad to have you in my corner! James Moore, you are one of the hardest working people I have met and part of so many of my favorite stories! YNWA. Eric Peterson, you have been handed some of the toughest decisions ever to be thrown at top operators, and you still are a natural *ON Stage*. Thanks for all that you do for me. John Picirillo, thanks for always showing me the way forward. Your early adoption of so many new tactics and techniques has kept us in the game. Without your guidance, we could have easily been mired in the past. Kieran McGill, thanks for the trust and the guidance you have provided for me. I am proud to tell others I am your partner. I still look forward to the stories that remain for us to write together *ON Stage*.

ABOUT THE AUTHOR

Scott Neff was born in Dayton, Ohio, and is proud of his Buckeye upbringing. His parents were teachers and artists, and Neff often borrowed strongly from these skillsets passed down to him from his mom and dad.

In high school, Neff got his first restaurant job with Jed's Steak and Ribs™, in Beavercreek, OH. He stayed at Jed's for two years while learning to love the business, though he may not have known it yet. Though a great place to start in the business, the interaction and esprit de corps at Brown Derby restaurants helped to mold Neff into the accountable operator he would become.

After graduation from Miami University in 1983, Neff became a full-time manager in a restaurant. It would become a career choice over time while he took a journey with several twists and turns.

Over the years, Neff has worked with some of the largest hospitality companies in the US. He also has been instrumental in concept development within several groups, large and small.

His progression over the years has taken him from dishwasher to regional management. He now owns and operates two partnerships with heavy involvement in the community and restaurant operations.

In this book, Neff offers you lessons he learned along his journey and how his adventures have led him to have a role in some of the stories he tells.